The
Peasant
Queen

An Esther Retelling

The Peasant Queen

An Esther Retelling

ASHTON E. DOROW

This is a work of fiction. All characters and events portrayed in this novel are either fictitious or used fictitiously.

THE PEASANT QUEEN

Copyright © 2020, Ashton E. Dorow

Life & Lit Press
www.LifeandLitblog.com
@Life.and.Lit

Cover and interior by Roseanna White Designs
Cover images from Shutterstock.com

ISBN: 978-0-578-77128-1

To my middle school English teacher, Mr. Rankins.
His teaching transformed my writing
and turned my mild love of reading into an obsession.
None of this would have been possible without him.

Prologue

The Kingdom of Acuniel

Western Europe, the 13th Century

Arabella

I RACED DOWN A GRASS-COVERED HILL OUTSIDE of Caelrith, my skirts tangling around my legs. The capital city stretched out behind me in the morning sunlight, and the sound of my best friend Gloriana's laughter floated on the wind. "He is coming!" she screeched.

My strides increased in strength and I grinned, relishing the feel of the wind's fingers through my hair. I, a girl of ten years, loved nothing more than running through the knee-high grasses of the countryside surrounding my beloved home. How freeing it was to be outside of the confining city walls, running wild in the open space, the sights and smells of nature all around.

Gloriana caught up to me, her face flushed, a thrilled grin stretching her lips wide.

"I shall catch you!" Frederic, our pursuer and most faithful companion, was but fifteen feet behind us now and swiftly gaining. Despite being two years our senior, he never objected to a game of chase any time the opportunity arose.

I shouted with glee. *He shan't catch us. We can outrun—*

Suddenly, a loud neigh brought my eyes from the swaying grass disappearing beneath my feet. Gloriana screamed and stumbled to a halt, her small hands flying to her mouth. I stopped just as an enormous horse reared in front of me, nearly crushing me beneath its great hooves. A scream escaped my own mouth as I leapt back in fright.

Frederic bounded up behind us, bumping into me after his sudden stop.

A boy looked down at me from atop the towering stallion, his piercing blue eyes pinning me in place. I stared up at him, my own eyes wide in awe and fear.

Another rider reined in beside him, and, with sudden horror, I realized who I stood before.

King Roland of Acuniel rode astride the other horse, and the boy who had almost killed me was his son... the Crown Prince Rowan.

I hastened into a clumsy curtsy.

"Pardon us, Your Majesties." Frederic bobbed his own awkward bow.

The king seemed like a regal giant, towering over us atop his massive, copper-colored steed, his royal crown glinting in the overcast sunlight. "'Tis well, children." He gave a long-suffering nod of his head. "Forgive us for startling you."

I could only stand and stare up at the young prince. His gaze travelled over each of us, but kept coming back to me. He watched me, studied me with serious eyes; but in his mouth I glimpsed a lightness, the bud of a smile that was surely breathtaking when allowed to bloom.

My heart beat a pitter-patter rhythm. *Certainly, he is the most handsome boy in all of Acuniel...*

"Thank you, Your Majesty. You are most gracious." Frederic spoke for us all, dipping another quick bow.

King Roland nodded again and wheeled his horse around. "Come along, Rowan. Your mother is expecting us."

The young prince pulled his eyes away from mine and turned his horse about, following his father back towards the capital city.

Gloriana slowly regained herself and turned to me, saying something. I nodded, but hardly knew why I did so. I had not heard a single word my friend said, for the handsomeness of the young prince still occupied my mind. He was so... *enchanting* that I could think of nothing else. Never before had I seen a boy like him, and I felt sure I never would again.

That day was the start of much in my life.

It was the start of my girlhood infatuation with Rowan—which would meet an untimely end. And, though I had no clue at the time, it was the start of a journey—one that I never could have envisioned in a million years.

Chapter 1

Ten years later…

"ARABELLA!" I TURNED AROUND TO SEE GLORI-
ana hurrying towards me, squeezing awkwardly between two
young men before stumbling down the street. "Wait for me!" I
stopped and waited for the red-faced girl to catch up. When she
reached me, she smoothed back her blonde hair, panting hard.
"Must you walk so fast?" She glanced around at the busy market, making eye contact with the snickering fellows she had just
squeezed past. "People are staring at me as though I lost my mind."
     I laughed but received nothing save a glower from my friend.
I sobered and cleared my throat. "Forgive me. I shall try to walk
slower next time."
     We continued at a slower pace, arms entwined like little girls,
the early June sun beating down on our necks as the sounds of the
market buzzed in our ears—people buying and selling, the shouting out of prices to passersby, customers arguing over those prices.
     Our little kingdom of Acuniel was experiencing a recent boost
in its economy. A blessed change from recent times.
     Ten years had passed since that fateful day when the king and
his son nearly trampled us. And much had changed… So much.
     Two years after that day, the king and his wife were murdered
after a visit to Trilaria, the neighboring kingdom to our north.
Days later, Rowan became king. The tragedy shook our kingdom,
from the wealthiest of noble, to the poorest of peasant. All had
loved and revered King Roland and Queen Matilda, and their

death—which most believed Trilaria was responsible for—angered them to the point that they welcomed the war the new king launched mere hours after his coronation.

At first, the war was fought with vigor and zeal, but soon, Rowan and his cause lost favor in the sight of the people. The new king frequently kept himself locked within his palace, removed from and disinterested in his subjects. When not in residence there, he lived on the front lines, leading his troops to battle. He had poured our kingdom's resources—both monetary and human—into the war, draining us all dry. Taxes were steep, the economy had plummeted, and nearly every family in the kingdom had lost at least one loved one in the king's precious war.

After eight years of endless fighting, death and destruction, poverty and starvation, most citizens of the kingdom had had enough. Though very few were so bold as to openly state their feelings, many hearts had hardened against the king.

Just as mine had…

"I hear King Rowan is returning soon from his latest trip to the Trilarian border." Gloriana's offhanded comment pulled my attention away from the marketplace and my thoughts.

I stiffened, jaw clenching, as was always the case when someone mentioned Trilaria.

When I was two, my family moved from Trilaria to Acuniel. From the moment I heard of Trilaria's alleged guilt, I hated to believe that such a thing could be possible. All these years later, my heart still refused to turn against the place of my birth.

"Arabella?" Gloriana's tone said this was not the first time she'd spoken my name.

"Oh… yes?"

She rolled her eyes. "I was saying that the king is returning soon. What do you think of it?"

"You know I care little about the king and his war." I flicked a hand in the air. "In fact, we'd probably be better off if he never returned."

Gloriana eyed two palace guards standing watch at the edge of the market. "You had better not let any of the king's men overhear you. You will be put in the stocks—or worse!"

I waved a hand at her again. "I care not a—" I tripped on a loose stone and went flailing forward. Before I could regain my footing, someone caught me around the waist and twirled me about to face them. "Frederic!"

He grinned down at me, holding me firmly against his chest. "Hello, Arabella." The now very handsome and grown up Frederic quirked a brow at me. "Watch your step."

His family, too, had come from Trilaria. Except they moved to Acuniel when he was a boy of eight years. I envied Frederic. He could remember the town he'd lived in, the people he'd known. Always interested in my birthplace, I longed to know more, but only had the stories I heard as a child. Now, hardly anyone spoke of the place for fear of inciting the king's wrath.

Frederic still held me close, smiling into my eyes. "Umm… Fred, you may let me go now."

"Oh, forgive me." He released me and stepped back. "You look beautiful today, Arabella."

"Thank you."

He stepped closer again and smoothed a piece of hair from my face, bending his head down to look at me. There was a flirtatious glint in his eye I did not like. Frederic bent his head further, his lips aiming for my cheek. I blushed and turned my head. "Fred… I have told you before…"

He stepped back and frowned. "I know, Arabella. Yet I cannot understand why you refuse me so."

I took his hand and smiled. "Oh, Fred," I sighed, "I know that. And *you* know what I have said. I do not wish to marry yet. And I value your friendship too much. Mayhap one day, but… not today."

He begrudgingly nodded his understanding of the familiar conversation. Poor Frederic had been head-over-heels for me since we were children. At times I thought mayhap I could feel the same, but something always held me back. I could not quite see myself as his wife.

I grabbed Gloriana, who had been watching from behind with a bold smirk, and dragged her down the street, away from Fred. "I cannot understand why you will not give that man a chance. He has been in love with you forever, and he is *so* handsome." A giddy smile colored the girl's voice. "Why can you not find it in yourself to care for him?"

I sighed. "I do like Frederic, I do; I am very fond of him."

"Well, what else do you need?"

Frustrated, I looked to the heavens for help. "He is a good

fellow and will make a good husband for some maiden one day, but not me. I do not have feelings for him. And I fear I may never."

My friend shook her blonde head. Why could she not understand that I wanted more out of a relationship than what Fred could offer? Something more than mere *fondness*.

I looked to the sky to gauge the time of day and realized with a start that it was almost noon. I would be late for my visit with my uncle, especially once I went home to retrieve the food I had prepared for him.

"I have to go." I released Gloriana's arm and made to leave.

"Where are you going?" she asked, upset at me leaving her alone in the teeming market. I began pushing through the crowd. "Arabella!"

"I forgot I am to go visit my uncle at the palace!" I cast a look over my shoulder, but by then Gloriana was lost in the sea of people.

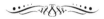

The guards let me in the without trouble. Uncle Matthew—my guardian since my parents' unexpected deaths six years ago—worked as a scribe in the Chancery. His skilled fingers, along with those of many other scribes, penned every proclamation, royal act, letter, and more that helped keep the kingdom running. I came to the palace to visit or bring him food at least once a week.

I'd just rounded a corner in one of the hallways—well familiar with the way to the Chancery—when I saw him.

Two men supported King Rowan on either side, his face contorted in pain. I recognized him right off, even after all these years. Despite my frequent visits to the palace, I had not actually seen him up close since his coronation, almost a decade ago. I had still fancied myself in love with him then, hopelessly infatuated by his good looks. Now, those girlish fancies were long gone, but he was still as handsome, or perhaps even more so than he had been that day.

They were headed straight towards me. I panicked and hurried forward, hoping to be able to walk quickly past. King Rowan met my eyes as I approached, and held them for a long, scrutinizing moment, just as he had that day atop his horse.

How had I not felt the icy chill of his gaze all those years ago? I looked down and stopped to curtsy low, letting them move past me. My cheeks burned with heat. How ridiculous I must look standing in the king's hallway, a shabbily dressed peasant girl with a basket of food in her hands, and clearly not one of the hired serving maidens. In fact, I was surprised King Rowan did not shout at me and ask why I was wandering around his palace. Perhaps whatever made his face contort that way kept him from doing so?

Whatever the case, I cared not; I was only grateful.

The king and his men gone, I fled down the hall.

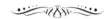

Rowan

The knights carried Rowan into his chamber and sat him in a lounge chair. During his last skirmish with the Trilarians, he had taken an arrow to the arm. He'd been lucky the shooter's aim was bad. A few inches over and the deadly projectile would have pierced his heart.

A physician had already tended the wound, but during the ride home, the sutures ripped open. Now, blood oozed through the reopened hole in his flesh, making him feverish and weak from loss of blood.

All of his royal advisors and government officials came bustling in a moment later. His manservant, Reginald, hurried forward with a bowl of cold water and some clean cloths, and began dabbing at his forehead. Rowan tried to wave the man away, annoyed, but Reginald ignored him, continuing to fuss over him as another servant came and forced King Rowan out of his shirt. He winced, fighting back a growl. He felt suffocated with everyone buzzing around him, but he forced himself to remain calm.

"My king, you cannot keep doing this," said one of his advisors—a gray-haired man named Lord Favian, who had served his father before him.

"Doing what, Lord Favian?" Rowan shifted in his seat to allow the royal physician, who had just come in, to begin re-sewing his wound.

Favian sat on a stool beside Rowan. "Fighting these battles! If you keep venturing out to the front lines, wanting to fight this war yourself, one of these days it shall get you killed! Today has only made me and the others more certain of it."

The older man clasped his hands together and looked down, sighing, as if contemplating his next words. "My king… Rowan, son." He was the only one of his subordinates that had the liberty to use his Christian name. The only person at all, for that matter, now that his parents were gone. "You must secure an heir before you get yourself killed. You *must* marry."

The physician pulled the cat-gut suture tight at that moment, and Rowan yelled, not so much from the pain, but from what Lord Favian had just said. "What? I will not! Not now."

"You must think about the kingdom, what would happen if you died and left no heir behind? No queen to take over, no child? There would be chaos!"

"Cassius is next in line. He is the highest-ranking member in my court since he is my closest advisor. If something were to happen to me, the crown falls to him. Simple as that."

Lord Favian gave Cassius a sidelong glance. "Pardon me, Your Majesty—and you, Lord Cassius—but I believe 'tis still best for the kingdom that we ensure there is a blood descendant to take the throne." Lord Favian took Rowan's hand and stared earnestly at him. "It is what your father would have wanted. I know."

Rowan scowled and jerked his hand away. Favian *knew* what sharp pain those words caused. "I think 'tis *my* choice. What if I care not about what happens to the kingdom?" His voice was a bark, harsh and underlined by the pain searing his arm. And his heart.

"But Your Majesty—"

"If the king says he does not wish to marry, then should it not be his decision?" Lord Cassius spoke up.

Rowan threw up his good arm. "Thank you! At least *someone* is on my side."

"Why should you care so much, Lord Cassius?" Favian narrowed his eyes at the other advisor. "Are you over eager to attain the crown?"

The dark featured man stood by the fireplace, resting his arm atop the mantle. "I only wish to honor my king's wishes."

"And *I* only wish to keep my king and country from destruction." Lord Favian looked back at Rowan still lying back in the lounge chair while Reginald dabbed at his head with a wet cloth. "King Rowan, I beseech thee. At least consider what I have said. My fellow nobles have already said they agree." He looked to the other men present, and they all nodded fervently. "'Tis not only I, but all of us who believe you should marry. All the nobles, from here to the farthest border." Favian gave Cassius another lingering glance. The man met his gaze then looked to the king.

"I see as these others do, my lord," the man said at length, still leaning on the mantel, "that it would be… best if you did find a wife."

Rowan skewered Cassius with a look, perturbed that he had ceased to be at his defense. He still did not like it. But… he always listened to Cassius. The man had served him well in his reign as king, as he had served his father before him.

Rowan heaved out a heavy breath of defeat. "I…" he gave each of the men present a hard look, "I will agree to your proposition."

Chapter 2

Arabella

"WHAT DO YOU SUPPOSE THAT IS?" GLORIANA craned her neck in the direction of a crowd gathered in the town square.

"What about the baker's shop? Your mother will be expecting us soon."

"The bread can wait."

I stifled a groan, allowing myself to be dragged along behind her. As we neared, my annoyance faded to curiosity when I noted the excited faces of some in the crowd. Gloriana and I pushed through the wall of bodies until we could see what drew their focus.

A man had just finished nailing a piece of parchment—the same expensive, high-quality kind I had seen in the Chancery with my uncle—to a post, the king's seal firmly stamped to the bottom right corner.

The man, dressed in the royal colors of gold and red, stood straight and tall and began reciting the document.

My grandfather, the son of a successful merchant back in Trilaria, had been a well-educated man. As a child, he had taught me to read; so now, even as the man cried out the paper's message, my eyes ran over the document, growing wider with each word.

Hear ye, all citizens of the Kingdom of Acuniel.
    His Majesty, King Rowan, wishes to announce his search for a bride. All young maidens are eligible. Representatives shall be dispatched to each province to choose six of the very fairest maidens as candidates. The king shall treat all maidens as the most prestigious of palace guests and lavish them with the finest luxuries in the kingdom.
    After two weeks of preparation, the King himself shall choose the finalists. Each finalist shall have the honor of a private outing with the King, and then His Royal Majesty, King Rowan of Acuniel, shall choose his bride!

My heart thudded dully. *Surely, one could choose not to go.* Then I read the last line of the proclamation…

    Refusal to comply with this decree is considered an act of treason against the crown and all of Acuniel, punishable by death.

A sinking feeling settled in my stomach. The last thing I wanted was to spend time with, let alone *marry* King Rowan—no matter how handsome he was or how much I once liked him.

But really, how could it happen to me? There were dozens upon dozens of fair maidens in Caelrith alone. Hundreds! What were the odds of me being chosen?

Oh God, please spare me from this.

"Is this not the most exciting news, Arabella?" Gloriana exclaimed, tugging on my arm as the man finished reciting the proclamation and turned to leave.

I remained mute.

"Can you think of anything more thrilling? Pampered like a princess, then chosen as queen!" Gloriana clasped her hands together and grinned, her blue-green eyes sparkling with excitement.

The girl had always been too naïve for her own good. How could any maiden in her right mind, with a true love for her country, be willing to marry a king who cared nothing for the needs of his own people, who constantly bled them dry to feed his own bloodlust and hatred?

"Are you not excited, too, Arabella?"

"Not at all."

"What?" Gloriana gaped at me. "Would you not want to be queen and have all the luxuries of living in the palace? You could have everything!"

"But do you not care about all he has done? Your own brother was killed because of King Rowan's war!" Just three years ago, Gloriana's brother, David, fought in the king's army in one of the largest battles between Acuniel and Trilaria. He was run through with an enemy sword and left to bleed out in a muddy creek bed, alone. He had been conscripted into the army without his consent, and his death nearly destroyed Gloriana's mother.

A shadow crossed the girl's face. "I—I suppose it does matter some… But *to be queen*, Arabella. Surely the king cannot be that bad. Perhaps you judge him too harshly."

She is impossible! I swallowed a cry of frustration and turned around. "I need to go now, Gloriana."

"But why? We have yet to buy the bread for Mother."

"I really would rather go home. Your mother will not mind if I do not return with you."

Gloriana scowled as I started away from her. "Very well then."

Once I was out of view of the people gathered in the town square, I broke into a run, my gray-blue skirts flying as I weaved in and out of alleyways.

I reached my uncle's house, panting hard, flipping back stray pieces of my dark hair. "Uncle Matthew? Uncle Matthew!" Was he home from the palace yet?

"I am right here, child. Cease your shouting." Uncle Matthew emerged from his room in the back of our cottage, his brows knit closely together. He was a stout man, barely taller than I was, with a dark beard and graying hair. He was serious in nature, but kind, with a heart of gold. Matthew of Caelrith adored me, loved me as his own daughter. And I loved him like a father.

"Now what is the matter with you?" He tucked his chin and looked at me from under dark, bushy brows.

"I have seen the proclamation, Uncle." I knew that he had already known about the proclamation. He worked in the Chancery, after all. No doubt his own hands had penned many copies of the document. "Why did you not tell me?"

He nodded and smiled lightly, taking a seat in a chair around our small kitchen table. "Because I knew you would react this way."

"How could this happen, Uncle? I cannot imagine anything more dreadful!"

"Oh, calm down, Arabella. They shall choose six maidens from each province. Six from each of ten provinces. There is every likelihood that you shall not be chosen."

I sat in the chair across from him and put my elbow on the table, resting my head in my hand. "But what if I am?" Tears pricked at my eyes. Silly and over-dramatic mayhap, but I cared not. "I do not want to go. I do not want to leave you."

"I think you are reacting a bit prematurely, my dear. You may not even be chosen as a candidate." Then his kind smile that I so dearly loved returned, and he winked at me. "Though I cannot imagine why they would *not* choose you. I honestly believe you are the most beautiful woman in all of Caelrith, if not all of Acuniel!"

I closed my eyes and groaned. "Ugh, you are no aid at all, uncle."

He laughed heartily, the sound rumbling from deep within his chest. "I know, sweetheart." He patted my cheek. "But 'tis the truth. To me anyway."

I sighed and leaned into his hand. "If I am chosen, what am I to do? If the king were to discover…"

Shortly after the start of the war, so intense was the king's hatred that he passed a law decreeing that any and all Trilarians found within Acuniel's borders would be arrested and put to death. Mayhap his decree would have leniency toward someone who had spent more of their life in his kingdom than in that of his enemy. But it was not something I wished to find out.

"I know." His brows furrowed and he patted my cheek again. "You shall continue as you always have—conceal your lineage at all costs." Uncle Matthew pulled his hand away from my face. "The king is extremely intolerant when it comes to that." He lowered his head and looked sorrowful. "The poor man is a slave to his hatred and desire for revenge. I pray God heals him one of these days."

Ire stirred in my chest. "How can you sympathize with him? That—that *monster?*"

"Arabella! Watch your mouth." Uncle Matthew swatted my hand that rested on the table, then pointed an ink-stained finger at my face. "You may be twenty years old, but you are never too old for a good spanking. He may not be the best king in the world, and I know how you feel about him, but he is still our king and you will respect him."

My pride smarted as Uncle Matthew went on. "I know you are angry—and with good reason. 'Tis no small thing to lose your parents, especially in the way you lost them."

I looked down at my lap, sorrow replacing my anger at the mention of my parents. And all the memories that came with it.

"But not even King Rowan is outside God's saving grace. 'Tis not wrong to hope that he may find his way back to the Lord, set aside these things that are destroying him and his kingdom. And you should be hoping the same thing, rather than condemning him."

Indeed, the king had been raised a devout Christian; the former king and queen were good people, serving God and teaching their son to do the same. But it seemed when his parents died, so did his love for God.

"I know you are right…" I set my teeth and exhaled roughly. "Though it does not change that I would loathe marrying him."

The following morning, I strolled through the streets of town, basket dangling from my arm and my uncle's coin jingling in my pocket. Uncle Matthew had tasked me before he left for the day with going to the market to buy bread and a choice cut of beef—the expensive meat being a special treat for us. His effort to cheer me, I supposed.

I went to the bakery first and bought a loaf of fresh-baked bread that smelled so delicious it made my stomach growl. It was so tempting. I couldn't resist and pinched a small chunk off the end to nibble on as I headed a few streets over to the butcher's shop.

The city was alive this warm summer morning, largely due to the proclamation the day before. Already I'd seen several mothers and their daughters buying flashing baubles and fabric for new gowns—if they were fortunate enough to be able to afford the frivolity. Each one hoped to attract the eye of Lord Hugh, the current Lord of the Treasury and the nobleman chosen to pick the Caelrith candidates.

I spotted another mother and daughter fussing over a collection of fabric laid across a table at a merchant's stall. The mother held a sapphire blue silk up to the girl. "The king shall surely notice you in this." She clucked her tongue. "It shall take nearly all our savings to purchase it, but 'twill be well worth it once you are queen."

I rolled my eyes.

A shadow fell across my path. It was a man, tall and gangly and dressed in fine clothes, with a greasy black beard that curled around an unsettling grin. A sparkling gold tooth broke the pattern of his yellowed teeth. "Good day, fair maiden."

"Good day," I said simply, coldly. His beady eyes seemed to stare beneath the layers of my gown. I held my basket against my stomach, a barrier, however small, between me and this man. "Excuse me, but I must pass. Goodbye." I moved to go around him.

He caught my arm and sneered. "Wait, my dear. We have only just met."

I looked him up and down, giving him a look that said, *"Who do you think you are?"* as he gripped my upper arm. Clearly, he understood my nonverbal question, for he then said, "Allow me to introduce myself. Lord Hugh, at your service, my lady."

I gasped before I could stop myself.

He let me go, a self-satisfied gleam in his eyes, and began to circle me like a vulture. "You are not pleased to see me? Are you not as these," he motioned to the mother and daughter diagonally to our left, who now twittered excitedly at the sight of him, "simply dying for the opportunity to be queen?" I did not answer, only looked back at Lord Hugh defiantly as he continued his circling. I had never met the nobleman before—obviously—and had heard little about him. But soon, I formed a *very* strong opinion of him: nasty, licentious. Frightening.

"Nice, yes… very nice." Lord Hugh came around my backside and ran a lock of my hair between his fingers.

My boldness returned and I jerked away. "Pardon me, my lord, but I really must leave." But he only caught my arm again, his sinister smile never leaving his pale face. At first, I wondered why no one took notice of him harassing me right in the middle of the street; but then I remembered. He was a nobleman, and no one here would dare confront him for accosting an innocent maiden. "Please, my lord, I—let me go. My—my uncle is expecting me." It was a lie, but surely God would understand.

"As you wish, my lady. But I shall see you again."

I swallowed.

Lord Hugh lifted my hand and kissed it, his wet lips pressing into my skin. Then he turned and left, sauntering away while I rubbed my hand on my skirt and tried not to lose my breakfast.

Two days later—the day of the choosing of the candidates—finding myself unable to sleep, I rose much earlier than normal. After already three hours of being awake, it was just now a suitable time to fix the morning meal.

I stirred porridge over the fire, and swallowed past a lump of anxiety in my throat. My stomach had been unsettled all morning. I was a tangle of jittery nerves, unable to focus on anything.

What if they come for me? What if I have to go to the palace? What if—

The porridge bubbled over, scalding my hand. "Ouch!" I moaned and reached for a cloth, which I used to quickly pull the pot off the fire. Unfortunately, in my haste, the boiling porridge sloshed out onto my bare foot. I clattered the pot onto the nearest surface, muffling a scream of frustration and desperately trying not to burst into tears. Or break something.

I cradled my burnt hand to my stomach and stooped to wipe my smarting foot with my other hand, muttering angrily to myself all the while.

"What is all the commotion about?" Uncle Matthew stopped halfway across the room and laughed. "Not having good morning, I see?"

"Not at all." I stood up, blowing fruitlessly on my stinging hand.

Uncle Matthew came forward to wrap his arms around me,

hugging me tight. Exactly what I needed. A loving embrace from the man who'd taken care of me throughout most of my adolescent years. He had become my second father, and I, the daughter he never had.

He put his hands on the sides of my face, his smile a comfort to my anxious heart. "All will be well, Arabella. Be at ease." I nodded and laid my head on his shoulder for several moments, trying to collect myself.

What a mess I was! How could I possibly get through the morning feeling so unsettled and irritable? *God, help me…*

I finally lifted my head, feeling more at peace.

Uncle Matthew and I sat down to steaming bowls of porridge and began to eat. I had barely taken three bites when, *Bang, Bang, Bang!* Someone knocked, or rather pounded, on our door. We stopped mid-bite and looked at one another. A weight descended in my stomach and pinned me to my chair. I put my spoon back in my bowl, appetite gone

"I'll get it." Uncle Matthew walked to the door and opened it. I knew who it was even before I turned to look.

Lord Hugh stood on our stoop, that nasty sneer curling his lips, revealing his pointed gold tooth. I stood, unable to break his chilling gaze, my legs heavy as lead.

A short, fat man dressed in the royal colors of crimson and gold pulled out a scroll and began reading. "Lord Hugh doth hereby proclaim, under the authority of the Crown, that ye, Arabella of Caelrith, are to be escorted to the palace as a potential bride of His Majesty, King Rowan of Acuniel. Failure to comply shall result in charges of treason, for which the penalty is death."

The air left my lungs. *Why, God? I asked You to spare me from this!*

I wanted to cry. I wanted to scream. I wanted to run.

But two large men dressed in royal surcoats approached and took me by the arms.

"Wait! Please!" I wrenched free and ran into Uncle Matthew's arms. All the peace I had felt mere moments ago faded away, leaving nothing but dread.

I hugged him tight, burying my face in his shoulder, letting my tears fall. "I cannot do this. I cannot go."

He pulled back and looked me in the eye, holding my face

in his hands. Uncle Matthew wiped a tear from my eye. "But you must. Keep your chin up, my dear. All will be well. I promise."

But you told me that before. And now look what has happened.

"Dry your eyes, sweetheart. I shall always be nearby; you know that. And who knows? You may be back in but two weeks."

I nodded resignedly before he handed me off to the two burly men. They held my arms much tighter than necessary, so tight I knew I would have bruises come morning. Did they think I would suddenly sprout wings and fly away? "You're hurting me!" I squirmed in their arms, trying to loosen their grip. They did not reply, only pulled me through the door so gruffly that I tripped and almost fell.

The men lifted me off my feet to place me in the back of a wagon filled with five other girls: the miller's daughter, Ellyn, whom I'd met a few times; three girls I'd never met; and Agatha, the preening daughter of the wealthiest merchant in the city. Two of the ones I didn't know wept silently, while Agatha and the miller's daughter glowed with excitement. The fifth girl, seated next to me, looked stricken, her pretty eyes wide with fear.

As we pulled away, I stared at Uncle Matthew and the home I had called my own for the past six years, watching it fade from view along with all my hopes. What would happen to me now?

Chapter 3

WHEN WE ENTERED THE PALACE, THE GIRLS *oo-hed* and *awed*. None of them had ever even entered the palace gates. Well-acquainted with the hallowed halls of the king's residence, I hung back quietly as the others gawked—though there were things I myself began to gawk at as we ventured further into the palace than even I had ever been.

Caelrith Palace was a true masterpiece; a giant fortress with massive columns, towering ceilings, colorful ten—and sometimes even twenty—foot long tapestries hanging from the walls.

Lord Hugh and his two giant minions led us through the palace and deposited us in a wing consisting solely of bedchambers. As we stood in the hall, a group of maidservants met us. One matronly woman with a large nose, sharp eyes, and prominent bosom stepped forward, her hands clasped at her waist. Her gaze was stern, intimidating. "I am Miss Merriweather, the king's head housekeeper. I shall oversee your transformation into sophisticated young ladies suitable for court and the title of queen." She motioned toward the rooms surrounding us. "You shall share rooms in groups of three and will be assigned a maid who is to take care of you and see to your every need for the duration of your stay."

"You." Her thick finger found me. "And you two," she added, pointing to Ellyn and the girl who'd looked so frightened in the wagon. "You three will be with Mavis." A woman stepped forward with a small smile, her eyes crinkling at the corners as she did so. I was thankful her demeanor seemed kind and welcoming. Perhaps she would make this stay a bit more bearable.

The maid motioned for us to follow as Miss Merriweather assigned rooms and maidservants to the other girls. She took us inside a simply but tastefully furnished bedchamber. A large, carved bed sat against the wall to the left of the door, and another smaller bed sat on the opposite side, clearly an addition to the room for this particular occasion. An exquisite tapestry adorned the wall above the larger of the beds, and a dressing table with a costly glass mirror sat in one corner while a table and three chairs sat in another. Straight ahead was a small fireplace to heat the space.

"Again, my name is Mavis." The middle-aged woman bobbed a small curtsy. "I will be seeing to your hair, dressing and undressing, and anything else you might need." She clasped her small work-worn hands together at her waist and smiled. "And what are your names?"

I spoke up first. "My name is Arabella of Caelrith."

Ellyn nodded. "Ellyn of Caelrith, daughter of Harold the miller. Pleased to meet you, Miss Mavis."

"Farah," the other girl said so softly it was almost a whisper. Her pretty face bore the look of an animal going to slaughter.

"What lovely names. I hope you shall have a pleasant time here. The king has a great many plans for the next few weeks. You shall be treated like royalty!"

Ellyn, and even Farah—who seemed about as eager to be there as I was—brightened at the words. But not I. Everything about royal life grated against my inner being. I wanted—well I was not sure what I wanted. All I knew was that everything that came with being queen, not the least of which was having the king for a husband, would not be my life's fulfillment.

"I will let you three get settled and then I will be back to see to your baths." Mavis curtsied to us, which still seemed strange to me, and slipped out the door.

Ellyn turned in a delighted circle, her movements stirring the lavender scent from the dried blooms scattered amongst the rushes coating the floor. "Have you ever seen anything so beautiful?" She clasped her hands together by her face with a grin. "Just think of what the queen's chambers must look like." She gave an impish wink. "And the king's."

"Ellyn!"

"Oh, come off it. Do you not want to be queen?"

"Not at all."

She gaped at me. "Surely you jest."

"Not at all."

Ellyn turned to the timid Farah shrinking in the background. "Do *you* want to be queen?"

Farah tucked a piece of her chestnut brown hair behind her ear and glanced up shyly through thick black lashes. "I—I suppose it would be pleasurable. Living such a life of privilege, I mean." Whether the girl's answer was truthful, or a result of peer pressure, I was unsure.

We chose our beds, Farah and I taking the larger, four-poster bed, and Ellyn, the smaller bed. She said she would prefer her own space. Soon our maid returned with other servants trailing close behind, bearing massive tubs. They left again and returned with steaming pitchers of water.

Mavis assisted us with undressing—another foreign experience—before we climbed into the tubs of hot water. The steaming liquid felt wonderful against my skin. The warmth of it, and the quiet of the room as Mavis washed each of our hair, allowed my mind to slow and absorb reality. I closed my eyes and relaxed against the wood, trying in vain to mentally transport myself back home, to a different time.

The image of my mother arose in my mind, squeezing my heart. Her kind, loving face filled my memory. I pictured her as she was in the last month before I lost her. Her face pale… sick… cold…

Then my father appeared. His happy smile warmed my heart. Then that good feeling vanished when I remembered how I had lost him.

'Tis all King Rowan's fault. Him and his stupid, incessant war.

Was it not enough that he had cost me my family? Now he must also steal me away from my home and force me to live in his palace, to dress up and parade for him so he could study me like an animal in a menagerie and decide if I was worthy to be his bride. Whom did he think he was to pluck a maiden from the populace to wed without her consent?

This madness *was* his idea, yes? Who else's could it be?

"What are you thinking about to make your brow furrow so?" Ellyn's curious tone made my eyes pop open.

"Hm? Oh, nothing." I slipped down in the tub, about to submerge myself in the water. "Nothing at all." Then I sank down into the water's comforting depths.

Throughout the rest of the day, the other candidates arrived, some not until late in the evening. When it was time for the evening meal, Ellyn, Farah, and I gathered in the Banquet Hall. Giant tapestries hung on the walls depicting religious scenes, sconces with flaming candles on the wall between them. More candles covered the food-laden tables, and a mammoth iron chandelier hung above. Maidens from all over the kingdom milled about the room, some mingling, some silently assessing the competition, and others, like Farah, hanging back in distress.

A blonde-haired young woman with pale green eyes and a mouse-like nose flitted across the room. She was incredibly slender and large busted, but her face was rather plain, with cold, pinched features. She turned her nose up as she observed those in the room. Somehow, her gaze came to rest on me and stayed there. Whether or not she realized I noticed I was unsure, but she made no effort to hide her assessment of me. She was sizing me up like a lion readying to attack its prey.

I suppose she must think I am competition. Well, no fear!

We seated ourselves around the two tables for the evening meal. I chose a spot beside a girl I did not know. "Pardon me." Someone tapped my shoulder. I turned around to see a girl politely smiling down at me. "Would you be so kind as to change seats? I wished to sit beside my cousin."

"Oh, yes of course. Pardon me." I rose and looked for another place. Ellyn and Farah were just taking their seats across from the girl who had been staring at me.

Ellyn waved me over. "Come sit here with us, Arabella."

This ought to be interesting.

I walked to the seat she indicated, next to Farah. The staring woman now swept my form with her gaze so quickly most would have missed it. But I did not.

Anger rose up in my chest. Then the words my parents—and

uncle, too—had so often spoken came to me. *Kill them with kindness.*

I smiled politely.

"This is Lady Katherine of Azmar." The thrill Ellyn felt at meeting and dining with one of the nobility colored her voice. She practically oozed admiration for the woman, who still kept her gaze focused solely on me. "Her father is Lord James, Duke of Azmar."

A few of the nobles had unattached daughters, so naturally they had chosen their own as candidates. Clearly, Lady Katherine was one of these.

I gave another polite smile and nodded in deference to her station. "'Tis a pleasure to meet you, my lady. I am Arabella of Caelrith."

A slight sneer curled her thin lips. "Good evening."

This killing her with kindness plan was going to be harder than expected.

We served our trenchers from the platters of food before us and began eating. The food was delicious, some of the best I had ever eaten, and, as much as I despised myself for it, I overindulged in its goodness.

"Arabella, is it? How is it for you to be in such a grand place? Surely you have *never* seen anything so fine?" Lady Katherine asked as I was in the middle of chewing.

I quickly swallowed the turkey in my mouth, and my ire along with it. "Actually, I have been here many times. My uncle works in the Chancery. But yes, 'tis very fine."

Her mouth twitched. I was not the poor, uncultured peasant she thought me to be. "Oh, how nice." Her voice was soft, airy. "Tell me, are you thrilled at the possibility of being chosen as the king's bride?" She leaned forward and grinned.

"I am unsure." It was not exactly a lie, was it? If Lady Katherine was so worried about me becoming queen, what would it hurt to keep her mind fretting a while longer?

Lady Katherine said nothing more, merely continued picking at the minuscule pile of food on her trencher.

Soon, the door opened, and an older man entered, followed by King Rowan. He strode in, his face set in hard lines, his right arm nestled tightly to his stomach in a sling.

I almost choked on my food.

Squeals from a few of the girls echoed off the high ceiling. Others managed to bridle their excitement, but their fervent whispers amongst themselves gave them away. King Rowan surveyed us with disinterest, a slight frown creasing his handsome forehead. Was his standard of beauty so high that he found none of us attractive? Or was he always this dour?

Several girls batted their lashes as he walked around the room. Nearly everyone sat up straighter, a visible wave of bodies stretching to hold themselves in perfect posture. I tried not to roll my eyes. Or laugh.

Their efforts awarded them nothing but a deeper frown from King Rowan.

I resumed eating and concentrated on avoiding his eye. Just as the king and the older man were exiting at the opposite end of the room from where they entered, I chanced a glance up while lifting a bite of food to my mouth—and made eye contact with King Rowan.

His blue eyes stared at me for several moments, bringing heat to my cheeks. Did he recognize me from the other day in the hallway?

King Rowan frowned again and swiftly left the room.

I put the food in my mouth, making myself chew, suddenly acutely uncomfortable. All eyes came to rest on me, the one girl the king *actually* looked at.

And the darkest look of all came from just across the table.

Rowan

Rowan and Lord Favian exited the Banquet Hall, the heavy wooden door thudding shut behind them. That girl… She stared at him so strangely with her dark eyes, looking all at once shocked, embarrassed, and disgusted. She was different from the others. The other candidates had smiled, batted their lashes, endeavored to show off. This girl—who felt so familiar, yet he could not place her—seemed to be the only one not eager to throw herself at him, the only one who ignored him.

He rubbed a hand through his hair. It would be a lie to say he was in any way happy with this situation. He did not want a wife. There were many beautiful girls in that room with whom other men would find pleasure. But Rowan? The idea had yet to appeal to him.

"You look distraught, son."

Rowan looked to Lord Favian, whose wrinkled brow furrowed in concern. "'Tis nothing, Favian."

"Ah, I have known you too long to believe that. Tell me what troubles you?"

Rowan pushed out a rough breath. "You should know what. 'Twas your idea."

Favian looked at the floor and nodded. "This is about marrying."

"Such does not appeal to me. Not yet. A wife… A family…"

"But mayhap 'tis what you need, Rowan. What God wants for you?"

Rowan pursed his lips. Ever since his parents' death, he'd cared little about God. He attended services on special occasions, as a nod to his parents' faith and to tradition, but he felt no personal connection. Not anymore.

Now other things took precedence in his life.

Favian put a hand on Rowan's shoulder and leaned forward to look him in the eye. "Listen, lad… You may not care so much about God anymore, but I do. If you will allow Him, He shall direct your path. He knows what He is doing."

Rowan considered those words. His heart still hardened against it all. No matter what Favian said, he was not sure about marrying *any* of the maidens in the Banquet Hall.

Not even the one with the beautiful dark eyes.

Chapter 4

Arabella

MAVIS WOKE US BRIGHT AND EARLY, WHICH WAS the only part of our new routine that resembled our normal lives. She dressed Ellyn, Farah, and me in simple linen gowns and brushed our hair until it shone, then plaited it with careful twists. I was comforted by the simple attire, but it did leave me wondering. Did they not want to dress us in gowns more fit for the king's court? Could it be that the king would get to know our true selves, rather than altered, showy versions of whom we really were?

All of my questions were answered the moment our maid led us into a large room *full* of trunks. The girls squealed with delight as the maids flipped open the trunk lids to reveal the brilliant colors of dozens of gowns and the glistening metal of jewelry.

"Choose whatever you like. It shall be yours to keep when you leave," Miss Merriweather announced.

The maidens rushed forward in a wave of laughter and squeals, nearly trampling one another in their eagerness. Ellyn grabbed Farah and pulled her forward, leaving me at the back of the crowd.

I loved pretty things as much as any girl; I enjoyed feeling beautiful. But this was such excess. Was it wise for the palace to spend so much on clothing and jewelry when the kingdom was suffering?

I suppose one could see this as a sort of charity. These girls would be able to feed their families for a year or more with even just a few these items.

I walked to one of the lesser crowded trunks and began sifting through its contents. *Just enjoy this, Arabella.*

The gowns really were exquisite. I had never even touched anything as lovely. I pulled out gown after gown until I found one I liked. It was light blue, with long, flowing sleeves, a fitted bodice with little buttons going up the back, and a full skirt. Intricate beadwork edged the rounded neckline, cuffs, and hem. *Perfect.* I smiled to myself, holding the gown up.

"Oh, is that not lovely?" I turned around to see Lady Katherine standing behind me, four garishly colored gowns draped over her arm. "So nice and… *simple*—just like you."

"Thank you, Lady Katherine."

She pinched her lips and sauntered off.

I suppressed a wry smile and moved to another trunk. Necklaces, bracelets, rings, and more spilled from its depths. Spotting nothing of interest, I went to another trunk, the one through which Ellyn and Farah were busy digging. Already Ellyn had several pieces piled in her lap. I sat down beside her and began searching as well. I did not care for jewelry, but mayhap I could find a brooch, or something for my hair?

I soon found a delicate golden circlet inlayed with sparkling diamonds. I looked it over, contemplating the jeweled headpiece. *What could it hurt to have a little fun? After all, I shan't be here long. And this could feed Uncle Matthew and I for a year, two, mayhap more.* I sat the circlet atop my head. "How does it look?"

Ellyn and Farah gaped.

"Oh, does it look that bad?" I reached a hand to take it off.

"Oh nay, nay!" Ellyn exclaimed. "You look stunning. You must keep it."

I smiled and took the circlet off. Then Ellyn noticed the dress lying across my lap. "Your dress; 'tis exquisite. But is that all you chose?"

"Yes."

Her eyes widened. "You need more than one! There are so many to choose from and we are to be here for *two whole weeks.* You will need more dresses, especially for when we spend time with the king."

She stood to her feet and reached down to me. "You simply must have more, Arabella." I took her hand and let her pull me up as I clutched the gown and circlet in one arm. Her big, blue eyes sparkled. "I shall make you look like a queen!"

For the next week, I felt as though I were wasting away my days. I was used to rising at dawn and cooking, working around the house, going to market. But here, in the palace, our days were spent bathing regularly in steaming water infused with flower petals, scented oils and soaps, eating rich food, and lounging with the other girls. I felt useless, but I had to admit I did enjoy it. A little. Mostly because of the food.

Of course, not all was fun and games. Every day, Miss Merriweather schooled us in different aspects of being royalty. Etiquette, the responsibility of a queen, et cetera. Lady Katherine and the other noblewomen among us rolled their eyes and ignored half of what the dour woman said in her lectures. Apparently they thought they already knew everything.

One afternoon, as a gentle breeze blew across the land, the candidates relaxed in the garden at the open center of the palace. It was a quaint inner courtyard filled with shrubs, bushes, and fragrant blooms. I reclined against a stone bench, closing my eyes and enjoying the cool air on my face—such a relief from the hot summer sun. Musicians played a lilting tune a short distance away, adding to the serenity and cheeriness of the setting.

A commotion coming from the other girls caused my eyes to open. King Rowan walked towards us, two men trailing behind. One was the man who had accompanied him when he'd entered the Banquet Hall that first night. The other I had never seen before. This man had dark, curly hair that grew far down over his ears, a pointed chin covered by a neatly trimmed black beard, and dark eyes, deep and intense. He met my gaze and held it for a long moment.

I looked away from him and instead watched King Rowan as he came to sit in a chair ten or fifteen feet to my right, nestling his wounded arm, still held in a sling, against his abdomen. The musicians halted their song, everyone stopping to stare at the king. He lifted one lordly hand. "Carry on."

The musicians slowly resumed their playing. Every maiden sat up straighter, fixing their skirts and subtly smoothing their hair; one even stuck her ankle out from under her skirt in an effort to catch the young king's eye. He did notice, looking at it for a few seconds before turning his head away. *Was that an eye roll I detected?*

I fought down a smile and looked at a rose bush to my left.

"Arabella! Come. Dance with me!" Ellyn pulled at my hands.

"What? Nay. We would appear foolish." I glanced to the king who eyed us with an inscrutable expression.

"Nay, we would not. 'Twould be fun." She pulled me to my feet. "Live a little."

I threw another quick glance towards King Rowan, who still watched us, forefinger touching his lips, and then to Lady Katherine, whose smug smile contorted her features. "Alright, if you insist." Who cared what the king and Lady Katherine thought about me anyway?

We put our arms around each other's waist and clasped hands. Then we skipped around the garden, turning in circles to the musician's lively song. I smiled at Lady Katherine as we passed. She and her coterie of other noblewomen frowned, making me realize that we still had the attention of the king. That had been Ellyn's goal, no doubt.

The group of haughty women rose and took a turn about the garden, shooting arrowed glances at us all the while.

Other girls joined in on our antics, twirling across the grass and laughing while the musicians thrived on the excitement and played all the more vigorously.

Suddenly, I tripped on something—a rock?—and went tumbling, Ellyn going down with me. Startled cries came from the others as we landed with a thud in a flurry of skirts and flailing limbs. The music screeched to a halt. Ellyn rolled off me, falling to her back, gasping in outrage.

I looked up.

Katherine smiled smugly down at me just a few paces away while her little group twittered behind their hands.

I knew she was the one who tripped us. I scowled darkly and she looked away as if nothing had happened. Did she not stop to think that the king would notice her treatment of us and disapprove? Who would want a queen like that?

Well... I thought, as Ellyn and I struggled to rise to our feet, brushing the grass from our gowns and picking a leaf or two from our hair. I glanced to where the king sat with a smirk on his lips. *King Rowan actually might.*

"Oh, oh, who am I?" Ellyn rose to her knees atop the bed Farah and I shared, clasping her hands beneath her bosom, sucking in her lips, and looking down her nose at Farah and me. "You must *not* slurp your soup or the king shall have your head!"

"Miss Merriweather!" Farah exclaimed as she and I fell back on the bed, laughing hysterically.

When we recovered, I added, "There is nothing "merry" about the woman, I am afraid."

"Yes! Miss "Stormyweather" is more like it."

We all burst out laughing again. Then we heard a noise from down the hall, and we covered our mouths, fearing it was Miss "Stormyweather" herself. After a few moments of silence, we decided all was safe and sat upright again, still muffling our laughter.

"And what about *Lady* Katherine of Azmar?" Farah whispered.

"Yes, I do think she despises you, Arabella." Ellyn frowned. "I thought she was nice when I first met her, but after she tripped us today in the garden! *Ugh!* And right in front of the king!"

"I think she fears I will rob her of her "rightful" place as queen."

"Did you see her face when we drew the attention of King Rowan today?" Ellyn laughed devilishly. "She was furious!"

"She is just jealous because she's so plain and you are such a beauty," Farah said.

I rolled my eyes. "Both of you are far more beautiful than I. The king would be a fool indeed not to fall in love with either of you."

"Do you really think so?" Ellyn glowed. Farah, on the other hand, still looked skittish of the idea.

"Yes, of course I do." I climbed under the thick covers, suddenly noticing how heavy my eyes were. "Now, let us go to bed before Miss "Stormyweather" discovers we are still awake."

With a sigh, Ellyn moved to her own bed, Farah climbing in next to me. Ellyn blew out the candle by her bed, and I blew out the one beside my own, plunging the room into darkness save for the tiny bit of moonlight coming from the small window high up on the wall.

I snuggled under the covers, trying to find a comfortable position. All I could think about was Lady Katherine and her rude treatment. She hardly intimidated me. Her humiliating us in front of the king today did not matter. But I could not help but feel sorry for her. Why? I disliked her and her attitude, but should I not have compassion towards her, treat her as kindly as possible? After all, nothing goads someone who hates you more than being kind and showing that they cannot affect you. Perhaps she would change. Or was that merely wishful thinking?

I knew God was trying to tell me these things… though part of me did not want to hear them. I sighed as Ellyn started to snore across the room, then whispered a prayer for the Lord to grant me a compassionate and gracious heart.

Chapter 5

THE FOLLOWING WEEK BROUGHT THE DAY I HAD
been both longing for and dreading since entering the palace—the
day the king would choose the six maidens from whom he would
select his bride.

I dared not feel certain that I would go home this day. By now,
I knew anything was possible.

After breaking our fast in our own quarters, Mavis pulled out
the gowns we would wear for the ball later that night. I decided to
wear the blue gown I'd chosen for myself a fortnight ago, and the
diamond studded circlet.

Once our baths were prepared, I slipped down inside the water and rested against the tub. I breathed in the steam, its warmth
clearing my nose and my head. My muscles relaxed, and for a moment, I forgot all the stress and worry that I felt. I sighed, feeling
utterly contented. But I knew it would not last long.

After our baths, Mavis divided her time between each of
us, lacing us into our gowns and arranging our hair however her
trained eye saw fit. I sat before her at the dressing table as she
unfastened my hair from its braid. She placed her hands on my
shoulders and leaned down to whisper by my ear, a smile in her
voice. "I will make you extra pretty tonight, hm? I believe you
could very well win our young king's heart."

I turned to look at her. "Why do you say that?"

The woman's mouth stretched even wider. "Because you are
beautiful, for one, but more than that, you have a good spirit, a

kind heart. Something our king could benefit from, if you ask me."
She patted my shoulder and set to work on my hair, separating it into sections for her to weave into small braids that she would incorporate with the rest of my hair into a beautiful coiffure.

"But… what if I do not wish to be queen?" I met her eyes in the mirror.

"Not wish to be queen?" Mavis repeated in a whisper, her voice oozing astonishment.

"I do not want all of this." I motioned about the room. "'Tis grand, even fun, yes, but 'tis not me. Marrying the king… I fear I could not tolerate it."

Mavis frowned, fisting her hands on her ample hips. "I know the king may not be the greatest ruler in the world, but we could do much, *much* worse. He and his court have bestowed this opportunity upon you, and I suggest you embrace it, child, and be grateful."

I turned back around, feeling as though someone had slapped me across the face as Mavis continued fixing my hair. Was she right? Should I be embracing the situation rather than keeping it at arm's length? Enjoy it while it lasted? Was I truly overlooking a great opportunity lying at my feet?

The opportunity to do what, though? What *good* could come from being in the king's palace?

"If it makes you feel any better, dear, I will tell you something you really were not supposed to learn yet." She leaned in close again. "The king and his counselor, Lord Favian, arranged for all of your families to come to the ball tonight."

My heart lifted. Yes! Perfect! I would see dear Uncle Matthew again. Though he worked in the palace, I had never had the opportunity to see him in the past weeks.

Seeing my uncle was exactly what I needed. He was wise. Surely, he could offer guidance.

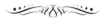

Rowan

Rowan rubbed his lower lip with his thumb, resting his elbow atop the armrest of his throne. He quietly observed the maidens milling about the Great Hall. Each was beautiful, he supposed, in their own way.

His blue eyes roved over the crowd, examining each one. Tonight, he would choose six of them to go on outings with—which he was dreading—and from them, would later choose his bride—which he was dreading far more.

One girl with strawberry blonde hair and a comely face stood near one of the food tables, absently scanning the room. Another with black hair stood conversing with a young man. At first, Rowan thought it to be her brother or another relative, but then the girl batted her eyelashes, leaned much too close, and touched his arm. She was flirting with him. No good. Though Rowan did not desire a wife to begin with, if he had to marry, he wanted a wife that would be true to him. And this maiden likely would not be such a one.

He moved on, spotting Lady Katherine, her mousy nose tilted up as she watched the other candidates around her. Her father had chosen her because she was his daughter, naturally, but also because he hoped to pressure Rowan into choosing her as queen. Many had long speculated that Rowan would wed the Duke of Azmar's daughter, for he was one of his wealthiest, most powerful nobles. Rowan had never shown an interest in this, however. Lady Katherine's attitude did not appeal to him. He'd seen her attempt to humiliate two of the other girls one day in the garden. He used the word *attempt* because it seemed the act did not embarrass the girls, or at least one of them, at all.

He felt obligated, though, to select her as a finalist; and would, if only to save Lord James, the Duke of Azmar from having a conniption. He simply wouldn't choose her to wed. If he had wanted that, he would have married her straight off without going along with this whole candidate business Favian had devised.

Now he looked to his right, where two girls stood conversing. The girls who had been dancing that day in the garden, the ones Lady Katherine had tripped. He'd delighted in their silliness, their girlish antics; such a change from the stiffness of the nobility with whom he routinely dealt. One of the girls had blonde hair and merry blue eyes, and, as he'd noticed from his few encounters with the candidates, an innocent, girlish demeanor.

The other, he noticed when in the garden the other day, was the dark eyed one from the Banquet Hall. The only one that seemed completely unaffected by him. She did not preen and blush when he entered the room. Did she want to be queen even the slightest little bit?

Her eyes flitted across the room, then came to rest on him. They quickly looked away.

Those eyes... The girl and her lovely eyes seemed so familiar, as though he'd seen her before, before the time he'd noticed her in the Banquet Hall. He was sure of it. Rowan racked his brain for when it could have been.

Yes! The day he'd returned home from Trilaria, she had been walking down the corridor and met his gaze. Why had she been there in the first place?

Rowan adjusted his position, still feeling slight discomfort in his shoulder. At least he didn't have to wear the sling anymore.

Lord James—or as Rowan often referred to him, Azmar—came to his side. "You see my dear Katherine?" The stout man pointed to his daughter across the room. "She is the picture of grace and beauty, is she not?" Pride emanated from the man's voice.

Rowan rubbed his hand across the stubble already growing along his jaw. "Oh, yes, Azmar. Quite."

He leaned in close to Rowan's ear. "You shall choose her, yes?"

A simmer of anger started in Rowan's blood. "We shall see, Azmar. Perhaps I will choose your daughter, but I am the king, and I can choose whom I wish."

Lord James stepped back, his fleshy face matching the crimson color of his clothing. Slowly, he spun on his heel and left to resume his seat.

Rowan continued perusing the crowd, growing less and less enthusiastic about his approaching task. Lord Hugh sauntered to Rowan's side. He stood behind the throne, resting his arm on its back. "There are a great many beauties here tonight, my king."

"Indeed."

Hugh looked around the room then bent down to point at one in particular. Rowan followed the man's finger and found at the end of it the girl with the dark eyes.

"That one there." Rowan sensed, more than saw Hugh smile dangerously in the girl's direction. "She is an uncommon beauty. I intend to make her my wife after all of this, just to let you know, sire." The man smoothed his black beard. "The longer I think of it, the more perfect the idea seems. Yes… she shall do very nicely for my wife. She has spirit, that one; I saw it in her eyes when I met her. A spirit that can be tamed… and I shall enjoy it." Lord Hugh chuckled low in his throat.

Rowan clenched his jaw. This man had just made a grave mistake by revealing his intentions. He could read Lord Hugh's thoughts, and it was clear they were less than honorable.

He did not wish to see this girl—or any of them—harmed by the likes of Lord Hugh. He knew what this man was like, and he was not about to allow him to force that young maiden into marriage. That was one thing he couldn't tolerate: the kind of treatment Lord Hugh and men like him bestowed upon women. *Gross. Revolting—*

"And what is this maiden's name?" Rowan asked, tamping back his anger.

"Arabella of Caelrith, my lord."

Arabella… Rowan rubbed his jaw again as he watched her turn to an older man, her diamond studded headpiece sparkling in the candlelight. *Well, Arabella of Caelrith. You just earned a place among my six finalists.*

Arabella

I turned to run into the arms of my uncle. He chuckled and squeezed me tight. "My sweet Arabella. How I've missed you so." His familiar, warm smell instantly soothed me, made me feel home again.

"I have missed you, too, Uncle Matthew. So much!" I buried my face in his shoulder and tried not to cry out of sheer joy to see him.

I lifted my face, shaking my head. "Oh, Uncle. I feel wretched. Mavis said I should be grateful for such an opportunity, that I could do… something. I know not what. But what if I do not want that?" I searched his eyes, even as he searched my own in bewilderment. "I knew that you could offer me guidance."

"Who is Mavis?"

I barely resisted rolling my eyes. "She is my maid, Uncle."

He looked at me with those fatherly eyes of his. "All I can tell you is to pray, seek the Lord's direction for how you should approach this opportunity—if you even have an opportunity." He patted my shoulders. "All of this may very well end at any moment. Then you shall have nothing to fret over any longer." He touched my cheek and smiled softly.

"But I—"

"Quiet now." He motioned toward the dais. "The king is rising."

Reluctantly, I turned and looked to the king who stood atop the raised dais, his royal robes falling onto the stairs at his feet. "My loyal subjects, for the past two weeks, the finest maidens of our kingdom have gathered here under my careful watch. Now has come the night where I shall choose six of these women as potential brides." He surveyed the crowd, pausing to catch his breath. King Rowan looked happy enough, I supposed, but something in his eyes seemed to reveal a reluctance similar to my own. Mayhap he did not want this as much as I thought.

"I have seen every maiden gathered here and have now chosen those elite six." He looked to the opposite end of the room from me. "Mary of Ellswick… Joan of Baines…. Meredith of Klinton." Three beaming girls walked towards the king, ascending the steps and stopping to stand a few feet in front of His Majesty after bobbing curtsies.

King Rowan glanced to his left, at someone behind him, before straightening his stance. "Lady Katherine of Azmar." Katherine walked towards the dais, a satisfied smirk twisting her thin lips.

Then King Rowan looked my direction, not directly at me, but near me. I froze. "Ellyn of Caelrith."

Ellyn gasped before she could stop herself, her delicate hand belatedly flying to her mouth. She blushed crimson, collected herself, and floated towards the king, curtsying low before taking her place beside the others.

Then his eyes searched the crowd for a moment. "And lastly…" His eyes moved back in my direction. And landed on me. Staring me in the face. "Arabella of Caelrith."

Dread swept over me and I turned to my uncle. I shook my head at him, as if the gesture could do any good. He only prodded me forward. "Go, Arabella. Pray, as I said. Follow God's will. Listen to Him. He shall lead you in the right direction."

God would lead me? Did my uncle even know what he was saying? At the moment, I sincerely doubted it.

I looked up at King Rowan as I ascended the stairs and made a quick curtsy. He watched me intently. Not lecherously, like Lord Hugh, but not kindly either. Just… watching me. Studying me. Almost completely devoid of emotion. *Almost.* The only emotion in his face I could not read, could not name. What could he possibly be feeling?

I turned to face the crowd as their cheers thundered across the hall. The handclaps and voices echoed in my ears. The cheery faces blurred before my eyes, and I found myself speechless.

Where was my life going?

Chapter 6

"ARABELLA. A WORD, IF YOU WILL?" I TURNED TO see Lady Katherine approaching, her emerald green skirts whispering over the floor. We had just been dismissed from our latest etiquette lesson with Miss Merriweather. I paused outside the doorway of the room we used for our lessons and waited for the noblewoman to reach me.

When she did, she snagged my elbow and pulled me to the side. "Listen here, you *peasant*." She spat out the word as if it were poison. "I know what game you play, and if you expect to win, I advise you to think again."

"Pardon me?" I leaned away, startled by her vehemence.

"You know of what I speak. It was long expected that the king and I would wed, so I know not why the king allowed you people to enter his palace in the first place. 'Tis absolutely preposterous!" A vein pulsed in the woman's forehead. "If anyone is going to marry him, it shall be me."

"My lady, I am afraid you are mistaken. I have no desire to *steal* the crown from you, if that is what you are suggesting."

"You lie!" The words were a hiss, reminiscent of a snake. "You are a devious little wench. I have seen the king look at you on a number of occasions. What have you done to attract such attention?"

I snorted. Miss Merriweather would have scolded me had she heard the unladylike noise. "Nothing. I have never even spoken with him."

She shoved my arm away, fury building in her face. "Fine. Keep your lies. But I shall win his attention, I can promise you that. And you will return to the hovel from whence you came."

Lady Katherine turned in a whirl of green skirts and stalked down the hall. For her sake, I prayed her time spent with the king would go well.

Rowan

Rowan adjusted the heavy cape hanging from his shoulders, the weight of the velvet cloth making him uncomfortable as he waited for Lady Katherine to join him for supper. Already he tired of these visits with the candidates, though it was only his third. It was why he'd only planned to dine with Katherine rather than go for a ride or picnic as he had done with the women before her.

Those outings, with Mary of Ellswick and Meredith of Klinton, had been tolerable. Even though both had stared at him with big doe eyes and taken every opportunity to brush against him. This third rendezvous, however, was going to be a pain. Rowan could think of few things worse than spending an hour or more with Lady Katherine of Azmar.

Just then, the door to the Banquet Hall opened and the lady herself strode in, her long skirt flowing behind her. She wore a lavish violet gown with a low-cut neckline, chosen for obvious reasons. Katherine smiled and curtsied low when she reached him. "My king."

He flicked a hand, gesturing for her to rise. Rowan indicated that she come to her seat at the table. "Thank you, sire, for inviting me. I am honored that you would have me dine with you in such an... *intimate* setting." She picked up her skirts and sat down. Her dark lashes fluttered as Rowan took his seat at the head of the table, to her right. "And may I say—"

"Is it not a bit presumptuous to assume you have leave to speak, my lady? If I address you, you may answer."

She looked down, her eyes blinking in surprise. An uncharacteristic blush bloomed in her cheeks. "Of course, Your Majesty."

Rowan began eating, then Katherine did the same. "What do you think of the quarters I have provided for you and the others?"

"Oh, splendid, sire."

"And what of the other maidens? What say you of them?"

She waved one of her long-fingered hands, her lips puckering in disdain. "Oh, they are practically children, all climbing over one another to be your bride. 'Tis quite pathetic." She glanced up at him, looking for permission to continue.

"Is that so?"

"Yes. One in particular seems quite obsessed with you, my king."

"And who might this young woman be?" He took a bite of his roasted chicken, her statement arousing his interest.

Katherine feigned thoughtfulness, her finger against her lips. "I believe her name is Arabella of Caelrith, sire."

"Is that so?" Rowan rested his elbow on the arm of his chair and put a finger to his cheek. That was an outright lie. The others may be obsessed with him, but Arabella, of all people, was not. Though he had yet to meet her, he was certain of that fact.

"Yes, she is most conniving. Mayhap you shall see for yourself soon."

"Mayhap."

The rest of the meal passed quietly, for the most part, with only snippets of conversation from time to time. After they finished their meal, Katherine spoke up again, her eyes meeting his with boldness.

"What are you looking for in a wife?"

Rowan looked up in surprise, forgetting his instructions for her not to speak unless spoken to first. He opened his mouth, but no reply formed.

"'Tis a simple question, my king, if you will permit me to say so." She gave a small laugh.

"Very well." He frowned at the forward question. "I suppose I am looking for someone who is…" Rowan thought for a moment. What *did* he want in a wife, if he had to have one?

"Kind," he decided. "Smart. Competent. Honest…" *Which you, m'lady, are not*, he added in his head. "And true to me and me alone."

Katherine rose and knelt beside his chair. She boldly rested her hands atop his arm and stared up at him through dark lashes.

Rowan looked down at her in incredulity. "Do you not think *I* am those things? I could be a wonderful wife."

Rowan opened his mouth to give her a sharp reprimand for her forwardness, but Katherine rose and put a hand to his cheek. She leaned forward and kissed him lustily on the lips.

Rowan had to admit his flesh enjoyed it. He'd never kissed anyone before, and the resulting sensation it caused was pleasurable. But he knew this was wrong. She was *so* far out of line.

He broke away. "You are out of bounds, Lady Katherine! You presume far too much to believe you may kiss me!" He stood, scraping his chair across the floor. She stumbled backward in shock. "I am your king. You are my subject, and shall behave as such, nobility or not!" He jabbed his finger at the door. "Leave my presence this instant! Before I have you thrown out and sent back to your father."

Katherine blinked and hurried to the door, stumbling on her dress as she went. She fled the Hall, just as Lord Favian stepped in.

The older man's brows were raised in question, but Rowan offered no answer. He was too upset, rubbing his mouth with his fingers, trying to erase the feeling of her lips on his.

This was the final straw. No longer would he suffer the pressures of his nobles. He would make his own decision, no matter who liked it.

Arabella

I silently counted the minutes, wringing my hands and waiting for someone to knock on my door and lead me to the king.

"Stop fidgeting, Arabella. You are making me nervous," Ellyn complained from her perch on the bed.

"Forgive me. I am nervous, as well." I smoothed my hands over my red silk gown. The fitted bodice did little to aid my anxious breathing, and the flowing sleeves got in my way when I tried to do anything. Such a bothersome garment.

"Here, let me adjust this." Ellyn rose from the bed and came to reposition my diamond circlet resting atop my modestly arranged hair. "You look beautiful, Arabella. Though I do not see why you had to choose such a simple ensemble."

I ignored her comment and looked to the small window high in our wall. Darkness covered the earth outside, the moon bathing the ground in its silvery glow. What could King Rowan have planned for us at this late hour? Even supper had already passed.

God, help me through this. If I can just endure this night, then it shall all be over. On the morrow, when the king announces his bride… I shall go home.

A knock sounded on the door. I opened it to find the older man I had seen with King Rowan several times. He smiled warmly. "Come this way, my dear. The king awaits your arrival."

I accepted the arm he offered and we started down the torchlit corridor. "Your name is Arabella, yes? From here in our own fair city of Caelrith, I hear?"

"Yes, my lord."

"A beautiful name. Fit for a queen."

I faltered in my next step and the man tightened his grip on my arm to steady me. "'Tis normal to be nervous, my dear." He patted my hand. "There is nothing to fear from Rowan."

This man had to be very close to the king for him to use his Christian name. That meant what he said had to be true. Right?

My heart slowed its rapid pace a bit.

"Forgive me. I just realized I have not introduced myself. How rude of me." He stopped and took my hand, holding it in one of his large, warm ones. "My name is Lord Favian."

I gave a quick curtsy. "'Tis a pleasure to make your acquaintance, my lord."

Lord Favian took my arm again and we resumed walking.

"And here we are." We stopped in front of a set of double doors, and Lord Favian gently prodded me forward. I walked to the doors and put my hand against the smooth wood, feeling like an animal going to the slaughter. "The king awaits, my dear."

I looked back at him.

He smiled kindly, almost fatherly, and motioned for me to enter. Something about the man put me at ease.

I drew a deep breath and opened the door.

King Rowan turned to face me when I entered, his mouth set in a grim line, his eyes surveying me in one quick swipe. I came forward and curtseyed low to the ground, my skirts widening into a circle around me. I glanced up at his stony face as he motioned for me to rise.

We stood in the Great Hall. I had only been here once, for the ball a week ago. At the north end of the cavernous room, majestic with its rounded ceiling and colorful tapestries hanging from the walls, stone steps led up to the king's throne. Two smaller thrones flanked his on either side.

"Walk with me." He swept his hand toward a door on the opposite end of the room. I nodded, slipping my fingers into the crook of the one he offered. An overwhelming feeling of awkwardness consumed me as we exited the dark room. I was keenly aware of the hard strength radiating from the arm entwined with mine. It made me squirm.

"Forgive me." He yawned. "I grow tired of these rendezvous. That is why I elected for us to only take a walk about the palace." King Rowan looked to me, a question raising one of his dark brows. "Does that please you?"

"Yes, sire. A walk suits me fine."

"Arabella, is it?"

"Yes, my lord. Of Caelrith."

"Right."

"My uncle is one of your scribes—Matthew of Caelrith."

"Is that so? How interesting," he said, though he sounded the opposite.

I could scarcely believe I was conversing with King Rowan. This was the same boy I had seen crowned at such a young age, the boy I had longed for with youthful fantasies. Yet here he was, a boy no longer, now a *man* I did not long for at all.

He turned his serious gaze on me. "And your parents?"

My parents... Their faces popped into my mind's eye. "They passed away some time ago." Grief welled up in my heart. "My uncle is my only family."

"You have my deepest condolences." He turned to face forward again.

Anger boiled in my chest. His condolences? He had no idea how he had affected me—and not for the better. His carelessness and selfishness had caused me to lose everything. And all he offered was his half-hearted condolences?

"Are you enjoying your stay here?"

"Yes, my king," I lied, pulling back my frustration.

We came to a walkway near the front of the palace, high above the courtyard, where large, open arches looked out over the cobblestoned yard beneath. The moon and stars cast their light over the world below, making the torches appear faint compared to their brightness. "'Tis a beautiful view." One could see much of Caelrith beyond the palace's defensive wall.

"Yes." His deep voice was a low rumble in the night air. "One of my favorites, in fact."

Silence reigned for several moments before he turned to me again, his hands clasped behind his back while he stood before one arch and I before another. "You are not like the others," he said matter-of-factly. "The other girls went to great lengths to please me. But you," he looked at me as if I were the strangest creature he'd ever seen, "you make no fuss; you do not attempt to seduce me with your charms. In fact," he cocked his head, "I have the suspicion that you do not even like me very much."

I sucked in a breath and did not reply, looking anywhere but at his face. A blush crept into my cheeks.

"What do you think of me?" He waved a hand up and down himself. "Do you think me… handsome? Charming? Intelligent, mayhap?" His eyes glinted with humor.

"If my king will permit me to say so, you are handsome, I suppose—"

His brow shot up. "*Suppose?*"

"And I am sure you have your charms. But I must confess," I shook my head, "the idea of marriage does not appeal to me."

"Love outside of marriage then?" He narrowed his eyes at me. "You prefer to stay… unbound to one man?"

"Nay!" I quickly defended, my head jerking up in surprise. "'Tis not that at all!"

"Forgive me for insulting you, but I must know these things. Mayhap 'tis only marriage to *me* that does not appeal to you, then? Or is it marriage and love in general?"

I kept quiet. I could not very well shout, *Yes, Your Highness, marrying you is the last thing I ever want to do!* He would probably have my head before one could say, *"Long live the king."*

"You never said anything about my intelligence," King Rowan noted with a lift of his brow. "Do you not think me smart? Competent?"

I clasped my hands before me and boldly met his eye. "In all due respect, Your Majesty, I do not wish to insult you with my true opinion."

He scoffed and turned to look out the arched window. "You have a quick… *impertinent* tongue. Were you anyone else, I would mete out punishment for such words forthwith." He turned to look at me again. "Coming from you, however, I somehow find them more amusing than insulting."

I felt pleased by his amusement with me, in spite of myself.

The king turned to me then and reached out his hand. I placed mine in his and he kissed it softly but meaninglessly, clearly devoid of emotion. I curtseyed and he stepped away. "Until the morrow, Arabella. Lord Favian will show you back to your quarters." He motioned behind me, bringing my attention to the older lord who seemed to have appeared out of nowhere.

I went to Lord Favian's waiting arm and dipped my head. "Until the morrow, Your Majesty." And just like that, our evening together was over as quickly as it had begun. Was my company so unbearable that he could not deign to spend longer than thirty minutes with me?

I knew not whether to be relieved or insulted.

As Lord Favian ushered me to my quarters, I mentally breathed a sigh. Regardless of his reasons for cutting our evening short, it was all over now. This unfortunate turn of events was done, finished. I was sure of it. After all, the king could hardly think he wanted to marry me after *that* conversation.

I felt free as I stepped into my room, closed the door, and leaned against its wooden frame. I closed my eyes and sighed.

All. Over.

Chapter 7

THE BUZZ OF EXCITEMENT HOVERED OVER THE Banquet Hall. For the day had finally come that their king would choose a queen.

Today, every citizen of Caelrith, and I assumed, all the other people of Acuniel, celebrated the choosing of King Rowan's bride. I was celebrating, but not in the same way as the others. Inside, I rejoiced over the knowledge that I would be going home this day. Soon I would leave this place and be sleeping in my own bed again.

I looked to where Lady Katherine sat, diagonally across from me at our banquet table. Ever since she had supped with the king, she had behaved differently. Oh, she was still snobbish, to be sure; but she had slacked, keeping to herself far more and scarcely saying a word.

She glanced up at me, her eyes hardening before looking back to her trencher.

I turned to Ellyn when she addressed me.

"Hm?"

"You never told me about your evening with the king." Her blue eyes sparkled with curiosity.

"He took me for a walk about the palace."

Her pink lips fell open. "That is all?"

I laughed. "Yes, that is all."

"I would have thought King Rowan would plan something better than that. Something other than a *walk*." She said the word as if the king and I had done nothing but sit and stare at a wall together.

I ignored her and looked to the king's table atop the dais. Lord Favian, whom I met the night before, sat at King Rowan's left. The man with the dark, tanned features, whom I'd seen with the king in the garden, sat at the king's right hand. He looked around the room with assessing eyes, studying each person.

He turned his head and those eyes met mine. I quickly looked away. Had he felt me watching him?

I tried to eat, but my appetite was slim. I felt too restless. Too eager to be *home*.

Out the corner of my eye, I looked back at the king's table, but not at the mysterious lord. This time I looked at King Rowan. He fiddled with his food, contemplation creasing his forehead. I wondered if he already knew whom he would marry, or if he was still mulling over the decision even now.

When the meal ended, we moved into the adjoining Great Hall, where musicians played a lilting melody. When the last guest had entered the Hall, four men blew three sharp blasts on golden trumpets draped with the Acunielian flag.

King Rowan took to the dais, his royal advisors and other officials lined up behind him. Last night, the king's head had been bare, but this day he wore his golden crown. He stared at the audience gathered before him, his mouth set in that customary grim line. Did he ever smile?

"As you all know," he began, "I have found myself in search of a wife. My advisors and I have agreed that now is the time when I must marry and secure an heir to Acuniel's throne."

I took a deep breath. *All the more reason for me* not *to marry him.*

"I have had the privilege of getting to know six of the finest maidens in Acuniel." Somehow, I felt this speech was something previously arranged by one of his advisors. Lord Favian, no doubt. It sounded like something the kind, polite man would say. "And now I have chosen my bride. The maiden I shall marry is…"

Here it comes. Here it comes.

Then his eyes came to rest on me and I caught my breath.

"Arabella of Caelrith."

My heart sunk into my toes as cheers and applause filled the room. Ellyn grabbed my arm and squealed, thrilled beyond measure for me even though she had wanted her own name to be called. All air vanished from my lungs. I felt faint. How could this be? I had paid him so little attention. I had not made an effort to *win* him as Katherine had accused. I had even hinted that I did not think him intelligent!

Yet he chose *me*.

Ellyn prodded me from behind. Other hands found me and carried my unwilling body forward. I did not know whose hands they were, and I did not look to see. All I could do was stare ahead at my now future husband. King Rowan.

Where was he six years ago when I still thought he hung the moon? Mayhap I would have been more willing then.

I reached the foot of the stairs leading to where the king stood. There was neither compassion nor love in his gaze, only a seriousness that made my heart palpitate—not in a good way.

I curtsied low to ground. My legs shook so violently that I almost toppled sideways.

The king descended the steps, took my hands, and led me to stand before his throne. Then he glanced to Lord Favian. I did not look, but I was sure the man was urging the young king on. King Rowan lowered himself to one knee. I struggled not to pull my hands away as a panicked feeling swept over me.

"Will you marry me, Arabella?"

I hesitated, though I knew it was not a real question. There was no option of no or even maybe. There was only one way I could answer.

"Yes…"

The lord who had caught me watching him stepped forward and handed the king a ring. It was a beautiful thing, a thin band of gold with a large ruby set in it. King Rowan placed it on my finger. If he was trying to be gentle, it did not show. He scraped my knuckle in the process of cramming the snug band onto my finger.

Placing my arm atop his, he led me out of the palace and up onto a wooden platform erected just outside the palace gates. The people's cheers were deafening, their happiness palpable. But I did not return their smiles. I stared at them, stone cold. Numb.

I spotted Frederic standing directly in front of the platform. He met my eyes, my own shock mirrored in his face. His eyes turned dark, his body tensing as if he wanted to rip me from the king's grasp. Fred despised him as much as I did—mayhap worse. And my friend had not yet given up hope that one day I would change my mind and return his affection for me. This would crush him.

Why, God? The crowd's noise overwhelmed me, making my ears ring. *I thought You were going to bring me out of this place, spare me from this fate.* I glanced over at King Rowan, who stood beside me, still holding my arm. His handsome face was as serious as ever and he watched his people with even less enthusiasm than I did, if such a thing were possible.

What do You think You are doing, Lord? Or are You even doing *anything?* Anger boiled in my chest. *Are You sitting idly by while my life is torn asunder? Is this a result of Your guidance? Or Your neglect?*

I dug my nails into my palm, hoping that maybe, just maybe, it was all nothing but a nightmare. Then I felt the pain and knew immediately that I was foolish for even thinking such a thing.

It may be a nightmare, but it was real. It was all too real.

That night, I stared at the ceiling above my bed—for the last time in that room, I noted. The next night... well, I did not want to think about where I would be.

I shuddered and rolled over.

In the morning, I would marry the king. I would promise to love and to cherish him until death do us part. Bound to him for the rest of my life. I had not been aiming to marry soon, despite the fact that I was nearly out of the supposed "prime" age for marriage, but I had known that when I did, I wanted it to be for love. Now I would be shackled to a man whom I did not love at all. Forced to bear his children, to live at his side forever.

Panic was setting in, mad hysteria. Hot tears rolled down my face. Uncontrollable sobs escaped my tight throat. Suddenly, I could not breathe, and before long, I sounded like I was dying. I *felt* like I was dying, not just physically, but emotionally, spiritually, in every way possible.

How could this be happening? It was not supposed to be this way. It was unfair! Everything I had ever known, everything and everyone I loved, everything I had ever wanted was being *ripped* away from me.

And worse… if the king discovered who I was, where I was really from, I would die for sure. I doubted even the queen was exempted from his law.

That was when a mad idea formed in my brain.

Mayhap I could find a way out of this place. Mayhap I could sneak out, tonight, before the wedding on the morrow. "I could not go home of course, they would find me there," I whispered as if someone could overhear me, rolling onto my back again. "But I could steal across the border and cross into Trilaria." Sadness welled in my heart. "Though I would not be able to tell Uncle Matthew good-bye…"

No, I could not do that. But I could escape to the farthest reaches of Acuniel and send word for my uncle to join me.

I threw the covers back and climbed out of bed. I pulled off my nightgown and put on the simplest gown I had, tugging it down and then putting on matching slippers. I had no cape with which to hide my face, but I would have to make do. I slipped out of my room, the candle from my dressing table in hand.

I needed more supplies than what I had, but I was not thinking clearly. I was practically delusional, holding onto a far-fetched notion that I could somehow slip out of the fortified, heavily guarded palace. But of course, anything is possible—evidenced by the very situation that drove me to such madness.

I stole down the corridor, now the only one occupying this wing of rooms. It was eerie being alone in that section of the palace where so many girls once stayed. Now they were all gone… except for me, the one maiden out of sixty that the king desired to marry.

Why did he wish to marry me?

I tiptoed down the stairs, searching for a safe, clear entrance to the defensive wall. Mayhap there was an inconspicuous servant's entrance I could exit by.

I wandered until my frantic searching made me lose track of my placement within the palace. Was I in the back of the palace, the side? How could I retrace my steps?

Suddenly, I stepped on the edge of my gown and fell forward, dropping my candle and throwing my hand out in an effort to catch myself. My hand snagged on a sconce bearing a flaming torch, keeping me from slamming into the stone floor. The sconce gave way beneath my weight. I stifled a screech as a portion of the wall shuddered and slid open to reveal a big, black hole.

My heart leapt. A secret passage!

"I wonder where it goes." A mixture of spine-tingling trepidation and stomach twisting excitement ran through me. "Surely, it must lead out of here."

I stared into the forbidding black depths of the passage. Could I really escape?

Footsteps scuffed behind me. "My lady?"

I gasped and jumped around to face the voice, my hand flying to my throat.

It was that lord with the dark, assessing eyes. I gulped. "What are you doing?" His voice was smooth, low, with an almost sultry quality.

"Oh—oh, you scared me," I stuttered, "uh… Lord?"

"Cassius."

"Yes, Lord Cassius, I was just… taking a walk. I could not sleep. Thinking about the wedding," I added with a shrug and a weak sounding chuckle.

He motioned to the open passage at my back. "I see you found the secret passageway."

"Yes, I did. By accident."

He nodded. He could see right through me; I was sure of it.

Never moving his eyes from my face, Lord Cassius reached and pushed the sconce back into its original position. The wall closed with a loud *scrape* and a *thud*. No wonder he'd found me. The sound had to echo all the way down the corridor.

"You should be getting back to your chamber, my lady." He offered me his arm. "A bride must have her rest."

I hesitated, glancing down at his arm. The man made me nervous, but I could hardly refuse his escort. I slipped my arm through his and let him lead me back the way I came.

How ridiculous I had been to think I could actually escape with no trouble. Yes, I found the secret passage, but who knew where that led. And even if it did lead outside the city walls, there was no way I could make it anywhere far on foot, with no food or water or money. *What a fool you are, Arabella.*

Lord Cassius brought me to my door and stopped to kiss my hand. "Good night, my lady. Sleep well." Then he opened my door, waited for me to enter, and left, shutting me back inside my prison.

I leaned against the door, feeling my hope dissipate into thin air, resignation settling over me. There was no way I could leave. I was trapped. In the morning, I would marry the king… and that would be it.

My fate was sealed.

Chapter 8

Rowan

ROWAN STUDIED HIS REFLECTION IN THE LONG mirror while Reginald busied himself around him, adjusting his wedding clothes.

Anxiety and frustration formed knots of stress in his back. Why had he allowed his advisors to pressure him into this arrangement? Even if he *was* marrying the intriguing Arabella of Caelrith...

She interested him in many ways, he had to admit, but he'd chosen her more so to protect her from Lord Hugh, rather than because of any affection he felt for her. If he had no romantic interest in any of the women, he could at least choose the one whom he would be keeping from a worse fate. Perhaps fondness would grow between them in time. But love? No. Love was something of which Rowan was sure he was incapable.

And he didn't *want* to love anyway. Other things mattered far more. There was no time or space in his heart for sentimentality.

Reginald came forward to place Rowan's crown atop his head. For many kings, the weight of the crown symbolized the responsibility that rested upon them, the needs of their people. However, for Rowan it was much different.

The weight of his crown reminded Rowan of his father.

The king before him, who had worn this very crown.

Whom his enemies to the north had senselessly murdered.

It reminded him of his life's mission, the only thing he wanted in the world: to avenge the death of the last two people he had ever loved.

Arabella

My attendants dressed me like a doll atop a stool, bustling about me with twittering voices and girlish giggles. When they finished, I stepped forward to look into a mirror. "Oh, my lady, you are simply a vision!" one exclaimed.

I pasted on a smile, but deep inside, I was screaming. The traditional bridal blue gown, symbolizing purity, had yards and yards of silk fabric, yet I still felt naked. I did not belong here, wearing these sorts of clothes, living this sort of life. But there was no way out. I had to grin and bear it, and hope that somehow, someway, God would help me through it—though I was still angry with Him.

Mavis stepped forward to place a thin gold circlet atop my hair that fell loose over my shoulders in the traditional bridal way. Then she handed me a bouquet of daisies and herbs—symbols of innocence and fertility.

I looked down at the beautiful, fragrant bouquet and felt grief well within my heart. I was getting married, and my mother was missing it.

I wish you were here, Mother.

My darling Arabella. My mother's voice spoke in my mind, reminding me of a long-ago conversation. Our last conversation. *You mustn't cry, my dear. All shall be well.*

But it shan't, Mother. Not if you are... My voice had faded as the realization that she was leaving me hit me square in the face.

I know... But remember that God is always with you. As I shall always be... My mother had placed her thin, cold hand over my heart. *In here, my dear. I shall always be in your heart.*

You will see father again.

Her sad yet hopeful smile still burned so clearly in my memory, even after six years. *Yes, dear... He shall be waiting for me.*

"M'lady?" I looked up, my reverie shattering. Mavis' kind face met my eyes. "'Tis time."

My attendants carried my train and led me to the courtyard, where knights dressed in mail and red and gold surcoats waited to escort me. My dutiful guardians marched at my side as we made our way through the crowded streets of Caelrith. The people clamored for a view of their future queen, one of their own people, a commoner.

I wondered for a moment how so many people, who regularly vocalized their dislike for the king, could suddenly be so enthusiastic about him choosing a bride from amongst their own daughters. What parent wanted their daughter forced into marriage with a man like him?

A familiar face caught my eye. Frederic. He met my gaze, his eyes colder than I had ever seen them. If only I could go to my old friend and bid him farewell. Surely, I would never see him again.

Suddenly, Fred's continued offer of marriage seemed very appealing. *I should have accepted while I had the chance.*

Soon we approached the Caelrith Cathedral. Its doors stood open wide, and before the entrance waited the elderly priest and King Rowan, my groom, in all his stern-faced glory.

I stopped beside the king, facing the man of God, and the crowd fell silent. The gentle breeze blew the hair from my face as the priest began. "Dearly beloved, we are gathered together here in the sight of God to join together this man and this woman in holy matrimony; which is an honorable estate, instituted of God, and into which holy estate these two persons present come now to be joined. Therefore, if any man can shew any just cause, why they may not lawfully be joined together, by God's Law, or the Laws of the Realm; let him now speak, or else hereafter forever hold his peace."

If anyone objects? I object! But I was too afraid to speak aloud. What could my outburst do? Despite what the law said or whatever the priest thought morally acceptable, the ceremony would continue because Rowan was the king, and no one would question him.

Silence reigned.

Then the priest addressed the king and I. "I require and charge you both, as ye will answer at the dreadful day of judgment when the secrets of all hearts shall be disclosed, that if either of you know any impediment why ye may not be lawfully joined together in matrimony, that ye confess it. For ye be well assured, that so many as be coupled otherwise than God's Word doth allow, are not joined together by God; neither is their matrimony lawful."

King Rowan glanced at me then clenched his jaw. "There is no impediment."

I looked down at the flowers in my hands and fiddled with their stems.

"Very well. My King, wilt thou have this woman to be thy wedded wife, to live together after God's ordinance in the holy estate of matrimony?" The rest of the priest's words faded from my ears until the king's voice snapped me to attention.

"I will."

Then the priest turned to me and repeated the same litany of questions. My answer lodged in my throat, and for a long moment, I could not bring myself to speak. I felt all eyes on me, including those of my groom, waiting for the answer I had no choice but to give. "I will."

The priest turned and bid us to follow him into the church. Soft, potent rose petals crushed beneath our feet as we walked down the aisle. Incense and gentle murmurings from the nobles seated inside weighted the air. Time seemed to slow. Every step stretched into an eternity, filled with dread over my fate.

Finally, we stopped before the altar.

"Please join right hands."

The king obeyed, taking the shaking hand I offered him and securing it tightly in his. His hands were large and strong, rough from years of combat. My small one was lost within his.

I trembled inside. Any moment now, this man would be my husband, and I would be completely at his mercy. Suddenly, I was not only angry, I was afraid. Was he a violent man? Would he be as cruel to his wife as I had heard he was with his enemies? Would he strike me if I did not do exactly as he wished? Would he force himself on me?

I felt the heat of his gaze as I stared at the place where my hand disappeared inside his. My legs grew weak and I refused to meet his eyes.

"My King, please repeat after me. I, King Rowan of Acuniel..."

The king obeyed, repeating his vows. "I, King Rowan of Acuniel, take thee, Arabella of Caelrith..." Once he finished, I dared to meet his gaze. He stared at me still, emotions I could not define passing over his blue eyes.

"M'lady?"

I looked at the priest. He waited for me, shifting from foot to foot.

I gave him a little nod and he proceeded, asking me to repeat after him. When I came to, "Until death do us part," the full weight of that statement hit like a rock in the pit of my stomach.

Until death do us part. I barely knew this man, yet I was pledging to love, honor, cherish and *obey* him forever. *Forever.* I was giving over my past, my present, and my future to a man I did not love. I was pledging all of me to him. Giving him my everything.

My everything.

That was such a weighty statement—which scared me to the point of tears. I tried desperately to hold them back, not even noticing when King Rowan let go of me to retrieve the rings. Without me hearing him, the priest spoke. "With this ring I thee wed," King Rowan repeated. The next second, his large fingers slipped a golden ring on the fourth finger of my left hand, beside my ruby betrothal ring.

The priest instructed me to do the same. With a shaky voice, I said, "With this ring… I thee wed," and slowly placed the golden band on my king's finger, my heart pounding painfully in my ears.

"Now, let us pray."

King Rowan and I knelt before the altar. I clasped my hands together and bowed my head as the priest said a lengthy prayer in Latin. I tried to pray, but I could not. My mind was far too scattered.

Instead, I looked at my new husband through the veil of my hair, wondering what life held for me in the coming days. His head was bowed, his eyes closed in respect, but his lips did not move in prayer. His mouth was set in a firm line, his brows drawn down over closed lids.

Abruptly, his eyes opened, and he was staring at me. My heart jumped and I blinked, hurriedly looking down at my clasped hands again. Thoughts of prayer finally able to form, I squeezed my eyes shut. "God—I know not why I even bother to pray," I mouthed quietly, my heart pricking with bitterness. "I do not understand this! Please… tell me why. Show me what Your purpose is. I do not see how You can work it for good. Are You even listening to me anymore?"

The priest finished his prayer with a resonating singsong, "*Aaameeenn,*" echoed by the congregation. We rose, the king again taking my right hand.

"I now pronounce you man and wife. What God hath joined together, let no man put asunder." The crowd stood and clapped, the applause echoing even from those gathered outside the church. "Your Majesty, you may now greet your bride with a kiss."

A jolt of panic surged through me. The king shook his head at the priest. "Nay, Father, I believe we shall forgo that part. There is time for that later."

The old man shook his head vigorously and chuckled. "Nay, sire, if I may say. 'Tis tradition." He smiled and waved one hand at us in a hastening gesture.

I averted my eyes from both the king and the priest, heat rising in my cheeks.

Then, before I even realized it was coming, King Rowan took hold of my upper arms and kissed me. My heart jumped painfully into my throat.

Only once in my life had I been kissed—by Frederic when we were children. Then it had been an innocent, playful kiss, more of a peck really. This, on the other hand, was a hard, manly kiss, much different from that first one. But it was devoid of passion or tenderness. It was gruff and angry. Very much like Rowan himself.

He kissed me quickly, though it seemed an eternity, and released me, taking a step away. His eyes were dark and stormy as he stared at my face, his lips wet from kissing me.

I wanted to melt into the floor and disappear.

Did he look that way because he was angry? Frustrated? Or was he feeling something else entirely?

"It is my pleasure to present to you," the elderly priest futilely shouted over the din of people, which had only grown louder once the king kissed me, "His Majesty, King Rowan of Acuniel, and his beautiful bride and future queen, Arabella."

King Rowan took one of my clammy hands and led me back down the aisle. Escorted by the six knights, we walked through the throng of well-wishers. The journey back to the palace seemed far shorter than the one to the cathedral had been. When we reached it, we entered the courtyard and made our way to the top of the castle wall, above the front gates. From there we could see the pulsing crowd of people cheering, "Long live our future queen, Arabella!"

"Let the troubadours sing of her beauty!"

"May the King and Queen have many children!"

My cheeks flushed hot. But that was nothing compared to when a new chant arose, starting with one person and quickly spreading through the crowd. "Kiss! Kiss! Kiss!"

Not again!

The king shook his head and raised a hand, but the people would not cease. "Kiss! Kiss! Kiss!"

Rowan turned to me, his usual scowl deepening. Reluctantly, he took hold of my arms. I put my hands up to touch his chest in an effort to push him away, but my arms had not the strength to exert any force. I gulped when I felt the well-shaped muscles of his chest through his clothing.

I looked into his eyes, trying to plead with him not to do this again, but he remained unmoved or at least oblivious to my silent pleas. He leaned in and I squeezed my lips together, bracing myself for another kiss. His lips pressed against my tight, unyielding ones and lingered for only one second before retreating. It was much quicker than our first kiss, but the crowd went wild, loving the show.

My heart hammered in my chest, my ears, my toes. If I felt so shaken by a small kiss, how was I to bear what else was to come this day?

The feasting and celebration lasted most of the day, until nearly sunset. I knew the tradition of the wedding guests escorting the bride and groom to their chamber, but I still was not prepared for the horror of dozens of guests escorting the king and me upstairs. After practically shoving us inside and offering a few well-wishes, they shut us in for the night.

Rowan and I stood several feet apart, both of us staring at the door.

My stomach heaved. Surely, he could hear the threatening

churn of my insides, along with the pounding of my heart. What would he do? I was so afraid of him I could scarcely breathe.

Slowly, my legs shaking so violently that I know not how I even remained standing, I turned to face King Rowan, waiting for him to move, to speak... anything.

Chapter 9

ROWAN TURNED TO FACE ME, HIS BLUE EYES blank. He lifted his finger and pointed behind me. "Go."

At first, I feared I had not heard him correctly. "Wh—what?"

He took a step toward me and I clutched my hands to my chest, drawing away from him.

"Go!"

"B—but I…?"

He flung his arm out in a sweeping gesture across the bedchamber. "Do you *want* to stay here?"

"N—nay… Nay!" I stumbled back as he moved towards me again.

"Then go to your own chambers." He again pointed behind me. "Through there." I stumbled backward again, edging towards the door in a state of shock. "Go! Before I change my mind."

I turned and ran then, flinging open the door and not even stopping to admire the sitting room between his room and mine. I entered my chamber, hastily shut the door, and flung myself on the bed, tears already rolling down my face. I heard his door slam, the sound echoing off the walls of the room between us.

I curled up in a ball, not bothering to shed my heavy, uncomfortable wedding dress. I cried big, fat, hot tears that burned my cheeks. I sobbed and cried in relief, in fear, in self-pity, frustration, anger. I know not how long it lasted; all I remember is that eventually, at some point in the night, I fell into a much needed, deep, dreamless sleep.

Sunlight, bright and intruding, stung my eyelids, forcing them open them just as Mavis entered, humming to herself. She startled aback at seeing me, clutching the bundle of fabric she carried to her bountiful bosom. "Oh, m'lady! W—what are you doing here? And still in your wedding dress! Why—"

"I do not believe 'tis any concern of yours." I cringed at the harshness in my voice.

The woman ducked her head in embarrassment. "Of course, m'lady. 'Tis no business of mine at all."

Mavis laid the bundle of fabric across the bed. It turned out to be more than mere fabric. It was a beautiful, golden gown covered in the most intricate embroidery I had every seen. I sat up, pushing my hair out of my face and reaching to touch the gown. "'Tis a masterpiece."

"Aye, that it is, m'lady."

I peeled off the mussed and wrinkled wedding dress, donned a fresh chemise, and sat at the dressing table so Mavis could brush my hair. She moved an ivory comb through my tangles, methodically and quietly working, while I watched the door that led to the sitting room joining the king's chamber and mine.

What is he doing? I wondered absently. Did he still sleep? Or was he also preparing for my coronation?

Mavis pulled hard at a stubborn knot. "Ouch!"

"Pardon me, m'lady."

Silence reigned for a moment, save for the sound of the comb sliding through my hair, then Mavis spoke up. "You do not care much for the king…do you?" It was more a statement than a question.

I shook my head, slowly. "Nay, I am afraid I do not."

"Well," she patted my shoulder, "I am sure love shall grow in time. Even a man like the king would be foolish not to see what a treasure you are."

I shook my head again. I did not want love to grow, no matter what she said.

I again stood before the elderly priest, dressed in the stiff gold gown, the bodice so tight I could barely draw a full breath. A long red train hung from my shoulders and trailed over the steps behind me.

Rowan stood to one side of the priest. Rich, ornate robes draped his powerful form, a train identical to my own cascading from his shoulders to pool around him. His royal crown sat atop his head, gleaming in the light that streamed from the stained-glass windows. He watched me, no doubt remembering last night as clearly as I was at that moment.

The priest took my hand and led me to a throne before turning to address the crowd. "We gather here today, in the sight of God, to crown a new monarch; one who shall reign beside our king as his queen. If anyone has any objections to this woman being our sovereign queen, please speak now."

Silence.

"Then let us pray." He began a liturgy in Latin and dabbed oil with his thumb upon my forehead.

When he finished, he turned to receive a pillow bearing a ball and scepter. I took them from him, feeling the weight of them, the weight of a kingdom, in my hands. The cool metal warmed beneath my sweaty fingers.

"Do you, Arabella of Caelrith, beloved bride of our king, vow to support your husband as he rules our land?"

"I do."

"Do you solemnly vow to uphold the ideals and laws of the Kingdom of Acuniel to the best of your ability?"

"I do."

"Do you vow to protect and serve your people to the best of your ability, working in their interest for the good of the kingdom and the crown?"

"I do." I could not help but feel King Rowan had broken every one of these same vows he'd made all those years ago.

"Do you vow to be a kind and just ruler, seeking God in all your ways?"

"I do."

"And do you vow to protect Acuniel and its people from its enemies, no matter what the cost?"

"I do."

He received the crown from an altar boy. "Then by the power vested in me by God and country, I crown thee, Arabella, Queen of Acuniel."

I could scarcely believe my ears. I was queen of a kingdom, *my* kingdom. Of all Acuniel. Many little girls dream of being princesses, and I had done the same—especially when I fancied Rowan—but never in a million years did I believe I would actually become royalty. And not just a princess, but a queen!

Bile rose in my throat. It was far too much to absorb. My head swam and I feared I would faint.

The crown settled on my head, snapping me out of my daze. "All rise in honor of Her Majesty the Queen!"

I rose, still holding the ball and scepter, and prayed the heavy crown would not topple off my head and roll into the crowd.

The entire assembly stood, but they did not stay that way. Every single person in the room bowed to one knee.

I glanced to my left.

The old priest bowed.

I glanced to my right.

All of the king's men knelt. Favian and Cassius. Even King Rowan himself bowed at the waist.

I felt woozy again. And very hot, like the sun was a few feet in front of me, beating down upon my face. I'd never received such recognition and respect.

The priest removed the ball and scepter from my hands as everyone regained their feet. Then someone took my arm, setting it atop theirs. I looked. Rowan. He led me out of the church amid claps and cheers and shouts of, "Long live the queen! Long live Queen Arabella!"

Through the streets we went, flowers cascading through the air. Children ran along the edge of the path, little girls squealing with delight when I looked their way, no doubt dreaming of being royalty themselves. I smiled—genuinely, for once. It was hard not to enjoy their admiration. And for the tiniest moment, being queen did not seem so terrible.

That was not to last.

The next morning, I awoke still exhausted from the long night of feasting and dancing. The full weight of my circumstances settled back onto my shoulders like a heavy burden. I felt lost and alone.

Why could I not be an ordinary person living an ordinary life, just as I always had. What made *me* so special?

I allowed Mavis to assist in my dressing, then hurried down the stairs to the Chancery.

Uncle Matthew was coming down the hallway as I approached, a rolled parchment tucked under his arm.

"Thank God I found you, Uncle." I fell into his arms.

He let out an *oomph* as I hit against his chest. His chuckle rumbled against my ear. "Good morning, Your Majesty."

I jerked back as if stung. "Nay, do not call me that. Please. I am your niece, your flesh and blood."

Uncle Matthew cupped my cheek. "Of course, my dear. I was only teasing."

"Forgive me." I looked up at my uncle's face, again relieved that he would always be so close. "I am at a loss for what to do, Uncle. I cannot be married to the king. He is a beast of a man."

"He cannot be all that bad."

"Nay, Uncle, he is as I say."

My uncle enveloped me in his arms. "All shall work itself out in time. You shall see."

I frowned over my uncle's shoulder, unconvinced. "Nay, I fear I shall *not* see."

I felt him shake his head. "Trust in the Lord, my dear." He sounded completely confident in those words. I wanted to gain strength from them, feel that same confidence, but could not.

Trust in the Lord? Trust had done nothing for me so far. I'd trusted in God to deliver me from this place, and where was I now?

Still here...

With a crown on my head.

Chapter 10

I PUSHED BACK MY CHAIR AND MADE TO RISE from the dining table, intent on retiring immediately, when a voice halted me. "M'lady."

I looked to my left. King Rowan stood beside his chair, one hand behind his back. "Walk with me?"

It was not so much a question as it was an order. I nodded, keeping my eyes to my half-empty trencher. My appetite had been low the last few days. "Of course, my king."

My arm slipped through the crook of his as he led me out of the room. We walked in awkward silence for so long I felt I would burst. Something needed to be said, but what?

My mind circled back to one question that had hounded me these first few days of our marriage: Why me? Clearly Rowan held no romantic feelings for me. He had not made a move to pursue any sort of intimacy between us—yet. If he was so uninterested in me, why had he chosen me as his bride?

The question was driving me mad. And I had to know the answer.

I managed to clear the knot in my throat and force out, "My king…"

"Yes?"

"You see, I was wondering… That is… I was wondering why you chose me. Of all the women at your disposal, why did you wish to marry me?"

He stopped and released my arm to face me. "I beg your pardon?" His jaw clenched tight, and for a moment, I feared I had made a terrible mistake.

"'Tis just," I looked down, taking a step away, "'tis clear you do not think of me in a romantic way. Could you not have found affection in another?"

"Are you suggesting I made a mistake in choosing you?"

"Nay." My hands grew clammy. I kept my eyes on the tips of my slippers peeking from beneath the generous folds of my skirt. "I only inquire, my lord."

The heat of his gaze was like an iron fresh from the coals. It burned over the top of my head and down my spine. For a moment, he said nothing, then, "I chose you because your manner intrigued me." I lifted my face and he angled away from me. "The other maidens," he paused to shake his head, "their demeanors did not please me." One blue eye found my brown ones. "You behaved differently, which I admired, and I found that to be a quality well suited for a queen."

He abruptly turned to face me fully. "You are correct in that I do not harbor a romantic interest in you. But… after all, most marriages are that way, so it should not come as a surprise."

I nodded.

"In time, I am sure we shall develop a…*fondness* for one another. And children must come, eventually. 'Twas the whole reason for this arrangement to begin with, after all."

"Of course."

We stayed silent for several moments before I found the courage to speak up again. I hated myself for what I could not keep from asking. "You said you chose me for my demeanor. Do you find my looks lacking then?" I dared the faintest glimmer of a smirk, my question so similar to the one he'd posed to me on our last stroll.

His blue eyes traveled over me, slowly, from head to toe. I squirmed. "Your beauty is pleasing," he let out a heavy breath, "though you are a bit too skinny."

My mouth fell open. "Too skinny?"

A small smile edged his lips. "Have I offended you?"

"You are not so perfect yourself, sire, if you do not mind me saying so." I squinted my eyes at him, crossing my arms. Miss Merriweather would have been appalled. "I do believe your nose is a bit crooked." My, I was feeling daring.

One of his large hands touched his nose. "Pardon?"

"Forgive me." I drew back, afraid I had gone too far.

He shook his head and scoffed. "The others would have lauded my looks, but you choose to point out my flaws. You do not like me very much, do you, Arabella of Caelrith?"

"I try not to be so transparent, sire."

He surprised me with another scoff and a shake of his head rather than a stormy reprimand. Heat flooded my face. Had I really just admitted, right to his face, that I disliked him?

"In truth, one of the main deciding factors in my choosing you was Lord Hugh. He told me that he intended to marry you after the contest."

"He said *what?*"

"'Twas a bad move on his part, for I know what sort of man Lord Hugh is, and I shan't allow any innocent maiden to be bound in marriage to the likes of him, if I can help it." He eyed me. "You did not wish to marry him, did you?"

"Oh Heavens, nay! I certainly did not."

He nodded and stayed silent.

"What sort of man is he, really? I mean, he did seem lecherous, but your expression speaks of more."

The king crossed his arms over his wide chest. "Lord Hugh is a brutal man. If he does not get what he wants, he turns violent." He furrowed his brow, sorrow in his eyes. "His wife… She committed suicide ten years ago."

My blood went cold. Had marriage to Lord Hugh really been so horrible that his poor wife felt death would be better than life?

"I see." For once I was grateful to be where I was: with him. He'd chosen me in order to protect me. To say I was shocked would be an understatement.

So the man is not completely heartless.

"Now," he lowered his arms and offered a bow, "I bid you goodnight. Do you wish me to escort you to your quarters?"

"Nay," I quickly cut in. "I shall walk on my own."

"As you wish." Without another word, Rowan turned and strode away, his footfalls echoing down the corridor.

"All rise in honor of King Rowan and Queen Arabella." I entered the Great Hall on the king's arm, dressed in my gold gown, my hair fixed in an elaborately braided style that had taken Mavis an hour to complete. The assembled nobles rose to their feet and bowed low.

My heartbeat skipped into a double-time rhythm. This was King Rowan's first time presenting me to the court as his queen. I knew the nobles would criticize my every move. I was a commoner in their midst, and they were no doubt bitter over the fact the king did not chose one of their daughters for his bride.

We moved to the dais. I stood before my throne—it was so hard to believe I actually had a *throne* now. With a gesture of his hand, King Rowan took his seat, and I and the rest followed suit.

Lord Cassius, whom I discovered was even higher ranking in the king's court than Lord Favian, rose with a scroll in hand. He welcomed everyone before reading off the first item of business.

I shifted in my seat, trying to listen to Lord Cassius speak about tax reports but all too aware of the dozens of eyes watching me. I scanned the crowd and spotted Lady Katherine sitting near her father, Lord James of Azmar. She angled her nose into the air, her eyes piercing me with disdain.

I had ruined her plans to become queen. Would she now be out for revenge? But what harm could she do me now as queen?

I crossed and uncrossed my ankles beneath the folds of my skirt, fiddling with my sweaty hands in my lap. Being before the court, open to ridicule and scorn with such new responsibility on my shoulders... It was overwhelming.

I eased in a deep breath, willing my raging heartbeat to calm. I had hoped my unrest would go unnoticed, but I was not so fortunate. King Rowan reached out to touch my hand.

Immediately, I pulled away. I could feel the open disgust showing on my face, my insides recoiling at his touch.

Suddenly, it hit me like an avalanche—the pure hatred burning within my heart.

How long had that all-consuming emotion been there?

He sat back, returning his attention to Cassius.

All these years, I had told myself that I did not hate the king, merely disliked him. But, really, I *had* hated him, so much, for so long. He'd been the reason my parents died, and every time I thought of how they were taken from me, how they died a mere two months apart, something boiled inside me. Even then, as I looked at him sitting there listening to his closest advisor speak to the court, my heart pricked and burned with bitterness. And hatred.

I hated him, *loathed* him, with everything in me.

Tears stung my eyes and my breath, already constricted by my gown, grew short.

I was not supposed to hate anyone—I knew that. But somehow, I had allowed it to grow within me for years. I had fallen prey to the same thing that so consumed the king, the very thing that cost me my parents and caused the country such strife.

The thing I hated him for being... I had become myself.

I bit my lip and tried to hold myself together, but the burden was too strong. Before a full minute passed, I was about to burst. I turned to whisper to my husband just as he was about to add something to the discussion. "May I be excused? Just for a moment."

King Rowan looked at me, jaw clenching. "Yes. You may be excused—for a moment."

I rose and walked calmly to the nearest door, clutching my hands in my thick skirts. Ignoring the prying eyes and curious whispers, I slipped out the door and leaned against the wall. Then I let the tears flow. They rolled down my face, hot trails on my skin. Slowly, I slid down the wall and huddled in a heap of golden fabric. Sobs left me in ragged breaths, even as I tried to stifle them with a hand.

I thought back to the day my mother and I learned of my father's death, then of the night when I told my mother goodbye and watched her slip from this life before my very eyes. They would be so ashamed.

"God forgive me," I got out between sobs. "Forgive me for hating him." I shook my head and smoothed back loose wisps of hair. "I still know not whether You are listening, but...." I still knew I needed His forgiveness.

"Forgive me. Help me to look at him without bias, help me to find the good in him somewhere. Help me to forgive." I knew then that Uncle Matthew had been right. I needed to pray that the king would find his way back to God and have a change of heart.

Was that the good I could do here? To help him find his way back?

"Help me, Lord, to understand. Help me to see Your purpose here. There is a purpose in everything that happens to us, good and bad, is there not? And please, help him find his way back."

Chapter II

Rowan

ROWAN SWUNG HIS SWORD IN AN ARC OVER HIS head, clanging it against that of the man he was sparring with. He pressed forward until his blade was a mere hair's breadth from his opponent's neck.

"Mercy!"

Rowan pulled his sword away and the knight dropped his weapon, putting his hands to his knees. His chest heaved as he worked to catch his breath.

Rowan wiped sweat from his forehead with the back of his hand. He ran his fingers through his damp hair, looking up into the cloudy sky. "My king." Rowan turned to the knight who addressed him. He was pointing to the walkway overlooking the courtyard. "Your lady watches."

Rowan followed the man's finger to one of the stone arches. There, his bride of almost three weeks stood in a deep blue gown, one hand resting against the pillar to her right. Her dark brown eyes flitted across the courtyard and came to rest on him. What was she doing up there?

They usually saw little of each other throughout the day. She kept to herself, doing… whatever—he really was unsure of what she did to occupy her time—and he was constantly busy with his kingly duties. They saw each other at meals, ran into one another whilst heading to their own chambers, but other than that, they virtually lived separate lives.

He looked away, sheathed his sword, and moved to drink water from a ladle a page offered him.

Rowan had made no move to pursue any sort of relationship with her. He had not kissed her since the wedding, had not even touched her in anything other than an innocent way.

She was his wife in name only.

And it would stay that way, for as long as he wished. This was one area of the situation he *could* control: how long it took him to produce the heir his advisors so desired.

"Bring the horses!" Rowan handed the ladle back to the page. "Mount up, men! Let us ride before these clouds release their fury." A squire brought his horse forward and Rowan took hold of the saddle horn, swung up into the seat in a sweeping arc, and then adjusted his reins.

"My king." Arabella was suddenly at his side, staring up at him from the side of his horse.

"Yes, my queen?" Rowan tried to keep his irritation at her interruption from reflecting in his tone.

"Do you ride to battle?"

"Nay. We ride to the training grounds outside the city."

"Oh." Her face lit up. The wind brushed one wayward curl across her cheek.

Rowan gritted his teeth. She may not have been asking to come along in her words, but her face, her eyes, spoke of her hope that she might escape his palace even for a short while. He sighed. "Would you care to come along and watch?"

"I would enjoy that very much, sire." Then her face fell. "But I am afraid I know not how to ride."

"Then mayhap today would not be the best time. But I shall see that you learn to ride soon."

She nodded and took a step back, that curl brushing across her cheek again in an endearing way. "Of course."

Favian stepped forward, having just exited the palace in time to overhear the conversation. "Sire, could she not ride with someone? I would gladly mount up and allow her to ride behind me."

"Nay, Favian. Today is not a good day."

His advisor arrowed a meaningful look his way. "But sire, can you not see that the girl is in desperate need of a change of scenery? She has not left the palace grounds in over a month."

Rowan skewered the man with a glare. He was the king, he

could just say no. But he knew Favian would never let him hear the end of it if he did.

"Really, Lord Favian, 'tis well with me." Arabella put up a reassuring hand. "I understand. I am fine st—"

"Put her up here with me."

Arabella stilled. Her beautiful, dark eyes met his in shock.

"I shall see that you learn to ride. But today you ride with me."

Rowan waved to one of the young knights. The man hurried forward, his cheeks blushing as he smiled shyly at the queen. He tentatively put his hands around Arabella's waist and lifted her to sit in front of Rowan, who put an arm around her to pull her up the remaining inches. Her legs hung to one side of his horse, her slippered feet and one shapely ankle peeking out from beneath her skirt.

Rowan removed his arm and quickly looked away, ashamed of himself for noticing. She adjusted her skirt, leaning away from him, tension evident in her every move. "Be at ease, m'lady."

She gave a tentative smile, still not looking at him. "Yes, of course." Hesitantly, she relaxed against his chest. He felt instantly warmer. *Too* warm. The sweet scent of lavender wafted up to fill his nostrils.

Rowan cleared his throat, reached for his reins again, and turned his horse about. Arabella startled and lurched to the left, nearly falling from the gelding's back. In one swift movement, Rowan caught her with his right arm and pulled her back up. "Forgive me. It seems I shall have to hold onto you as we ride."

She nodded and settled back again. He could feel her stomach expand and contract with each breath.

I shall have a stern conversation with Favian about this.

He kept his grip loose and tentative at first as they moved through Caelrith to the city gate; but once they began cantering down the hill to the training grounds and the terrain grew rougher, Rowan had to tighten his hold.

And much to his annoyance… he liked it.

Arabella

I sat on a boulder, the hot summer sun peeking through the gathering clouds and warming me until sweat trickled down my back. But I cared not. I was only happy to be out of the palace, seeing something other than walls. Finally, able to breathe.

If I was sweating this badly, I could only imagine the state of the knights running through a mock battle in the field before me. They were dressed in heavy chainmail and breastplates, wielding large, hefty steel weapons.

It was no wonder King Rowan was so strong.

My eyes found him on the "battlefield". He was fighting a knight equal in height, but lesser in build, leaner and quicker. That did not hinder Rowan at all, though. At present, he had the advantage over his opponent.

Even from my great distance, I could see the determined, fearsome look on the king's face. If he was this intense in practice, there was no fathoming his ferociousness on the actual battlefield.

It struck fear in my heart, once again.

My husband was a hard man. I had seen a bit of his temper show through on our wedding night when he demanded I leave his presence. If I were to anger him greatly one day, what would happen? If I were to push him over the edge, push him to the point where he could not bridle his frustration—would he lock me in the dungeon? Would he strike me?

I shuddered to think of seeing that same ferocious glare that he wore in battle directed towards me. That strong arm swinging down to hit me.

God, please let that never happen.

In the days since realizing the hatred I harbored towards the king, I had endeavored to let go of it—no matter how much it pained me to admit my wrong. I was making much headway in the effort; however, I still struggled with accepting my life's sudden change of course. Many days I would wake expecting to be back in my uncle's cottage, hearing his merry whistling as he prepared for the day. Instead, I woke to see a servant removing my chamber pot from the corner. What a lovely thing to wake up to…

And nights were no better. There had been many times in the past three weeks that I had cried myself to sleep, burying my face in a pillow lest Rowan overhear me. The last thing I needed was him coming to investigate.

How in the world had I, a simple peasant girl, suddenly become queen? One day, I was sweeping the floors of the cottage my uncle and I shared. The next, I was sleeping on a down-filled mattress and being served breakfast in bed, if I so desired.

There were moments when I felt at ease in my new surroundings, as if I were getting used to them. Then there would come moments where that too familiar feeling of fear and panic would rear its ugly head, and I felt certain this must be some sort of terrible dream.

I was waiting to wake up, but that moment would never come.

The "battle" ended, and the king's captain—I had yet to learn his name—said something to the knights gathered into formation. Did all this planning and practicing mean the king was preparing to return to the battlefront?

The men dispersed to their mounts tied to trees on the right side of the field. King Rowan approached and motioned for me to follow. His brow, furrowed as it always seemed to be, dripped in sweat. His brown hair stuck to his forehead, and a bit of dirt streaked one cheek.

I had to admit that, though dirty, he looked rather handsome in his chainmail and chest armor.

Thunder rumbled and a bolt of lightning ran its jagged course through the sky. The king turned to me. "Ordinarily I would insist practice continue despite the rain, for real battle does not halt for the weather. But with you along, 'tis best if we head back before the storm hits."

He swung up into the saddle. If only he would have me ride with someone else. I was reluctant to be so close to him again. The feeling of his chest pressed close to my spine, his arm tight around my waist...

Nay. Definitely not.

Then he waved me forward. "Take my hand."

I did as he said. It happened so fast I was not sure how he did it, but one moment I was standing on the ground, and the next, I was in the saddle, seated behind him.

"Oh."

"You had better hold on." He tugged at the reins as his horse shied from another loud roll of thunder. Awkwardly, I wrapped my arms about his midriff, clasping my hands together across his abdomen.

I could not wait to learn how to ride on my own.

He shouted to the men. A moment later, the horse leapt forward. I gasped and tightened my hold around King Rowan's waist as we galloped towards the palace, reaching it just before the heavens opened up.

Chapter 12

A FEW DAYS LATER, I SAT IN MY ROOM, STARING out the open window. A warm summer wind blew into the room and onto my face. It gently toyed with my hair, pushing it back behind my shoulder and then forward, over it again. I reached up to brush a piece out of my eye.

I knew not what to do, but I knew that I needed to do *something*. Otherwise, I would give into my overwhelming sense of homesickness and go utterly mad.

Perhaps an excursion through the palace would provide the needed distraction. *I wonder if Rowan would mind me having a look around.*

I rose and reluctantly braided my hair. The king and any others in the palace would be sure to ridicule me if I were to leave it flowing about my shoulders. The queen was always supposed to have her hair up, like a proper married woman.

With my hair now braided and put into a rather haphazardly pinned bun, I slipped out of my room. A chambermaid walked down the hall towards me, humming softly to herself, a pitcher of water hugged tightly in her arms. She startled when she saw me and dropped a quick curtsy, almost upsetting the pitcher in her arms. Water splashed onto her sleeve. "Oh, Your Majesty! A thousand pardons, my queen."

It was still hard for me to grow accustomed to people addressing me as thus. I had always been simply *Arabella*. Now the only person who used my given name—besides Uncle Matthew—was the king, and even he called me by a title most of the time.

"Think nothing of it."

"I was just bringing this water to your room so you may wash before supper." She lifted the pitcher, then noticed her damp sleeve and blushed. "Do you require anything, my queen?"

"Nay, I was just going for a stroll. Carry on." I reassured her with a gentle smile.

The girl nodded and stepped to the side, allowing me to pass.

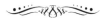

I wandered for some time, circling through decades-old staircases, weaving through dimly lit corridors, and cautiously opening doors for a peek at what lay beyond. Occasionally, I ventured in, but most often I looked inside, shut the door, and moved on.

So far, I had yet to run into anyone, and I hoped it would stay that way. Unless it was a servant. One of them I could mayhap encounter without too much embarrassment.

A shiver traced down my spine to remember that Lord Hugh still sojourned with us here in the palace. I had managed to avoid him well, rarely even conversing with him at meals. But were he to catch me alone... I wondered if he would still bother me, in light of the fact that I was married to the king. Would my new status deter his advances? Or would it not matter to him?

Again, I shivered, but forced such terrible thoughts from my mind and pressed on.

My hand came to rest on the handle of another door. Though near the Chancery, I was unsure of what this room held. Cautiously, I peeked inside. The room was filled with almost ceiling-high shelves stacked with book after book. *This has to be where they keep all of the royal documents.* Most of the rooms I'd seen had not been anything special, but this one... this one I had to see.

The question of, "What can I do here?" had been niggling at the back of my mind for days. Mavis had said that I could do much good as queen, but what exactly *was* that good?

Seeing this room, a thought came to my mind, a possible goal, a purpose that would provide an answer to my questions.

Even as the war against Trilaria waged and everyone else became convinced of their guilt, I had refused to believe what others took for fact. I was unable to believe that the country and the king I had heard so much good about from my family could be responsible for such an atrocity. Even now, I did not want to believe it, though I had no information to support my theory.

I knew very little about the tragedy, to be honest; the details were rather hazy in everyone's minds, in fact. So, whether Trilaria was guilty or not, I was curious. Even if it was only wishful thinking on my part that the Trilarians could be innocent, what could it hurt to know more?

And this room, being the holding place of the kingdom's history, could hold the information I sought.

I looked over my shoulder, right, then left, checking to see if anyone approached. Then I stuck my head further into the room, making sure no scribes lingered among the shelves of documents. Empty. I entered, staying as quiet as a possible, as if the papers would suddenly spring to life and come together in the form of King Rowan, shouting at me for my trespassing.

I stared in awe of the room. So many books! There was tome after tome of writings recording, as I knew from Uncle Matthew, all of the palace's daily events.

If that is true, then there must be something written about the king and queen's murder. I surveyed the room. *But where?*

I picked up one of the dusty volumes from the shelf I stood before and quickly flipped through it. The pages I scanned spoke of a party held two years ago, the sudden death of one noble that same year and the succession of his son after him, and various ordinary events.

I needed to go further back in time. At present, I was towards the right end of the room, at the front. I reasoned that the order of the dates corresponded with the rows of shelves, going from left to right, and front to back. If that was the case, then I needed to go further back and to the left. I only hoped that these records went back far enough, that the older records were not kept somewhere else.

Careful to put them back exactly as I found them, I replaced the book and walked a few rows over. I pulled out a volume from the middle of one shelf. It was darker back here, but there was just enough light for me to make out the date. *Yes!* The first page's record was from eight years ago. But months before the death of the king and queen, which occurred in December of that year.

Flipping further through the book, I found it—the account of the day of King Roland and Queen Matilda's murder.

My heart hammering in my chest, I hurried back to the center of the room and deposited the heavy book onto the desk. I smoothed my hand over the page, noting the tear stains marring the otherwise perfect script.

Being the niece of a scribe, I knew that scribes strove for perfection in all their work. If they misspelled a word, made the wrong stroke, or dribbled ink on the page, they would scrap the work entirely and begin again, even if they were on the last word.

It broke my heart to see that the scribe who penned this wept as he wrote, smudging some of his elaborate writing. I was glad the scribe had been allowed to keep his work, for I felt the tear stains, the imperfections, made his work even more beautiful. It showed the depth of the people's love for their king and queen, and their angst over their passing.

Feeling sorrowful myself, I began to read:

> *While sojourning with the Lord of Dallin after their visit to the Kingdom of Trilaria, His Majesty, King Roland of Acuniel, and Her Majesty, Queen Matilda, were assassinated by disguised assailants. They were soon identified as Trilarian soldiers. The Crown Prince Rowan—*

"What do you think you are doing?"

I gasped and looked up.

Lord Cassius stood on the other side of the desk.

"M-m'lord," I stammered, nearly scared out of my wits, "you frightened me."

He did not respond for a moment. Again, I got the impression that his eyes could see straight through me.

Slowly, never moving his eyes from my face, he leaned forward and smoothed back the parchment with his right hand. Only then did he look down. His eyes quickly took in the words before returning to look me in the eye. Then he snapped the book closed.

"You should not be in here, my queen. These are precious, important documents. Not only are the daily records stored in this room and those adjoining it, but also the laws of the land and many other important pages. They must be handled with the utmost care."

"I understand."

"Then I suggest you leave." His voice was low and smooth. "Now."

I nodded, quickly, and sidled around him to all but run from the room.

And immediately came face-to-chest with King Rowan.

My heart stopped beating then raced a hundred times as fast when I realized whom I had run into. The king caught my shoulders in his large hands and set me back from him. His face was a mask of barely controlled fury.

"What are you doing?"

"I-I was just," I stammered, trying to catch my breath and calm my raging heartbeat.

He looked from me to the doorway I had just exited, then back to me. "Were you in the Hall of Records?"

"Yes," I admitted, feeling like a child awaiting a scolding.

His expression hardened more still; not exactly the same ferocious glare he'd worn when fighting a few days ago, but just as terrifying. "You are not to be in there! 'Tis no business of yours. You could start a fire and destroy everything. And many of the records in there are not for your eyes but are private information."

"But why ca—"

"Nay!" He jabbed a finger at me. "I am the king! *You* listen to *me!*" He towered over me, fury knotting his brow. "*I* say that you are forbidden to be in there, queen or not. You may be my wife, but that does not give you leave to do whatever you please."

I nodded furiously, tears hot in my eyes, so angry that I could have slapped him across his kingly face. "Alright, *Your Majesty!*"

With one glance over my shoulder, I knew that Cassius stood in the doorway watching the whole scene. I turned back to face Rowan, gave him a withering glare, then swept past him, tearing down the corridor without giving even so much as a thought to Miss Merriweather's lessons on decorum.

I stood on the allure—the walkway atop the palace wall—for what seemed an age. Angry tears streamed down my face and stray wisps of my hair sticking to my wet skin. Several passing guards gave me curious and worried looks; one even stopped to ask if I was well, but I brushed him off, saying that I needed time alone. He had reluctantly backed away and moved on.

From this vantage point, one could just make out the top of my uncle's house.

My home.

No matter how long I lived here in the king's palace, that little house would always be my home.

I missed it so much. I missed my uncle so much. Even though I saw him regularly, 'twas not on the everyday basis I had grown accustomed to the last six years.

I reached up to wipe tears from my eyes and cheeks, first with my hand, then, when that proved futile, with my long, billowing sleeve. I thought back to the document I had been reading before Lord Cassius showed up. I had not been able to finish reading it, which perturbed me. I still wished to know so much about that fateful day.

The more I thought about it, the more I questioned if perhaps—even if I could not help the king himself—I could look into the king and queen's deaths and finalize in my mind whether or not Trilaria was really responsible.

If I were to do that, I needed to know more of what happened that night. King Rowan, I knew, held the key to all that I wished to know, but I doubted I would get anything out of him any time soon. After the incident over the Hall of Records—information would have to be found elsewhere.

Even if my girlhood belief that my homeland was incapable of such a senseless act turned out to be nothing more than wishful fantasy, perhaps I could at least convince the king to end the war. Had he not done enough to avenge his parents already?

I closed my eyes in frustration. *Is that my purpose here? To put an end to this constant fighting? The death and destruction that has hurt so many?*

I rubbed my forehead with my hand, tired of thinking, tired of trying to unravel my own destiny.

"My queen?"

I stifled a groan and turned around, expecting to find one of the nosy guards again. Instead, I came face to face with Lord Favian.

"Hello, m'lord."

"Hello, Your Majesty. I heard you were up here…"

I grimaced. *Wonderful. It seems the entire palace is aware of my weeping.*

"I wanted to come see how you fared, and escort you to supper, if that is your wish." The man's expression was not judging or contemptuous, only kind and father-like.

"Thank you, Lord Favian. I would much appreciate that." I offered a soft smile. "But I fear I must freshen myself before we sup." I grimaced and rubbed a hand over my windswept hair, having taken the loose bun down long ago, deciding I cared not what people thought of me.

"Yes, that would be best," he said gently, with a hint of teasing. "But first," the older gentleman stepped forward to stand beside me, resting his hand atop one notched tooth of the stone parapets, "tell me, what troubles you so?"

I sniffed and shook my head, not wanting to share all of my tumultuous emotions with him just yet. "I am homesick, I suppose."

He nodded, turning to look out at the city with me. I knew he did not believe for one moment that homesickness was my only distress. But, to his credit, he did not press me further. "Where did you live before this?"

I extended my arm and pointed to the roof of my uncle's house, just barely visible. "There. That is where my uncle and I lived." I smiled to myself, remembering the smell of my old bed, how I enjoyed cooking for my uncle and I, sitting by the fire with him at night while he read one of the few precious books we owned, and I did the mending.

Lord Favian nodded, saying nothing for a second, two, three. Then, "I know you must prepare for supper, but there is something I wish to show you." He offered me his arm and I took it with no hesitation.

Lord Favian led me down the allure, towards the entrance to the tallest tower of the palace. We climbed the stairs for what seemed like an eternity until we reached the highest keep of that tallest tower.

Inside the small room was a built-in stone bench, and above it, a small, arched window. I moved towards it, wondering what could be so special about this particular place. But once I looked out, I knew immediately why he'd brought me here.

The view was incredible. One could see past the city walls, to the rolling hills beyond. The entire city of Caelrith stretched beneath us. And in perfect view was my Uncle Matthew's house.

"This tower has the best view in the palace." He stayed near the door, allowing me my space.

"I see that," I replied, my voice breaking. I cleared my throat in embarrassment and gave him a small smile over my shoulder. "You have my deepest gratitude, Lord Favian. This is the greatest gift I have ever received."

Chapter 13

Rowan

ROWAN LINGERED IN THE BANQUET HALL LATE that night, sitting in his chair, sipping watered wine. He contemplated pouring himself some non-diluted drink. Perhaps then he could erase the thoughts swirling in his head.

He took another swig and pushed the cup far away from him, resisting the temptation to muddle his brain until he couldn't think at all.

Two things tormented his mind, Arabella being one of them.

He was at a loss for what to do with her. One moment, he would find himself admiring her exquisite beauty and charming personality, so unlike his own. The next, he wanted nothing to do with her, wished he had never allowed his nobles to pressure him into marrying. She made him so... *frustrated*. He knew not why. He just knew that she did. Like earlier, when she rammed straight into him, his heart had thudded painfully in his chest then boiled in anger with her for poking her nose where she did not belong.

Cassius had informed him of what exactly his queen had been reading in the Hall of Records.

The writings from the day his parents died.

That was the other thing that tormented his mind.

His parents. Namely his father.

Why did Arabella have to dredge all of that up again? Why was she reading such a document? What business of it was hers?

His father's face kept appearing in his mind's eye. Rowan looked so much like his father. The brown hair, the blue eyes, the strong jaw. The only thing he had not inherited was his father's patience.

He had always been so patient with Rowan, no matter what.

"Now son, you must remember, when you are king, you are not the people's dictator or taskmaster. You are to be more of a father to them. Love them, guide them the best you can, have their best interests in mind, as I do for you," his father had said while walking with him along the perimeter of the garden.

"But father, they are just lowly peasants. I am their master. Should they not do anything I say?"

Rowan's father had sighed and patted his shoulder. *"Son, if you are fair and just with your subjects, they will have no problem serving you. They will loyally serve you in turn for your loyal serving."*

"A king must serve his people?"

"Yes, son. Very much so."

The memory brought pain to Rowan's heart, and he pushed it aside.

His father made many such speeches to him over the years. And Rowan had always wanted to be just like him, to do everything just as he'd taught him. Somehow, along the way, in his quest for revenge, he had lost sight of that desire.

But what did it matter? He was not even sure his father had been right about many of the things he said.

Rowan groaned and rubbed his forehead with his fingers, attempting to ease the tension in his brain. These tormenting thoughts of Arabella, of his father, of his kingship—they were driving him mad. He felt angry, lost. Bitter. All he could think to do was to take it out on something.

He rose, downed the last lingering bit of liquid in his cup, then hurled the metal vessel across the room. The cup clattered against the wall and fell to the ground with a resounding *clang*.

Rowan collapsed back into his chair, holding his head in his hands. "Why, God?" he ground out angrily for the millionth time in the past eight years. "Why did you do this to me? *Why* did you let them die?"

The door to the Banquet Hall opened, making Rowan sit bolt upright. It was Lord Favian.

"What do you want, Favian?" he growled, relaxing his posture again.

"Well, hello to you as well." The older man took a seat next to

Rowan and leaned forward, hands atop his knees. "You upset her greatly, my king."

Rowan, resting his elbow on the arm of his chair, rubbed his hand over his face. "So?" He scoffed with a shrug. "She was nosing into places she did not belong. Those records are none of her concern."

"But why?"

Rowan scowled at the man in disbelief. "Because. I just do not want her in there."

Favian eyed him for a long moment, clearly finding his reasoning lacking. "You could have at least been more careful in your response."

Rowan refused to meet his advisor's eye. Who cared if he was being childish?

"You frightened her—you *do* frighten her," Favian continued. "She wept atop the wall—as I am sure you have heard by now—for a long while. And you saw how she behaved towards you at supper. She drew away if you even came within inches of her."

"*What* could give her cause to be frightened of *me*?" Rowan tossed his hand in the air.

Favian's responding look said, *"Must you even ask that question?"*

Rowan rolled his eyes. "So I may have been a bit harsh on her. Mayhap I *am* harsh with her."

Favian shook his head and sat back. "You would do good to be kinder to her, Rowan. You must understand her present state. She has been taken from her home, brought here, made to marry you—"

"She did not have to marry me."

Favian gave him another knowing look. "You and I both know there was never an option for her."

Rowan grumbled, growing progressively more perturbed by this lecture.

"As I was saying, she now finds herself in these strange new surroundings, without family, without friends, married to *you*," Favian emphasized again, gesturing at him with his hands. Rowan responded with an offended glare. "She feels lost. She is still adjusting to this new life."

Rowan folded his hands over his stomach, leaning back in his chair to stare up at the rounded ceiling of the Hall.

Lord Favian sighed heavily. "All I am saying is 'twould do you good to have some compassion towards the girl. Try to understand how she feels and choose your actions accordingly. 'Tis no small thing to suddenly become ruler of a nation."

The meaning of the man's words was not lost on him. He knew Favian referred to his own sudden crowning. And because of that, Rowan had to admit that he *could* relate with Arabella in some small measure.

Rowan sighed, sat forward, and rested his elbows on his knees. "You are an unmitigated nuisance, Favian. Are you aware of that?" He was half-teasing, half-sincere.

His father's longtime friend and advisor, now Rowan's as well, looked down as he chuckled and smiled. That smile lingered for a moment before his face fell serious again. "She is incredibly homesick."

Back with the subject of Arabella, Rowan thought with some annoyance. The man was nothing if not persistent.

"I showed her the tower. She can see her house from there."

Rowan's head shot up. "Well, I thank you, Favian, for giving away my private spot to her. Now I cannot go there to think and be alone for fear of running into my wife." Belatedly, Rowan realized how absurd his words sounded.

"You sound like a child pouting over having to share his toy." Favian's disapproving frown made him feel uncharacteristically ashamed. "'Twould do you good to spend more time with her. She is your *wife*, after all."

Enough of this. Rowan rose and headed for the door. "You seem to be an expert on what is good for me this night. *I* think 'twould be good for *you* to mind your own business."

Arabella

The horse beneath me neighed and shied to the right. I pulled in the reins as I was taught, bringing the horse's head up, keeping him in place.

"Good, m'lady, very good," the knight who was teaching me to ride said. "Now take him about the courtyard."

I nudged the animal with my heel, and we started around the courtyard at a slow trot. My horse's hooves clicked on the cobblestones as we made a wide circle—well, he was not *my* horse. The chestnut brown animal belonged to the knight teaching me. I hoped King Rowan would provide me with a horse of my own so I might ride whenever I wished, without robbing a knight of his mount.

"Now try going faster," the young knight called. He was about my age, give or take a year, with sandy hair and a bright disposition that I already knew I liked very much.

I kicked the horse harder and we quickened our pace. I leaned into the saddle and gradually worked up to a canter. It was the first time I had ridden this fast, let alone without the knight guiding me.

"*Woohoo!*" The knight raised his fists in triumph.

I grinned, feeling equally as proud of myself. Bringing the horse towards the knight, I pulled in the reigns and circled him, breathing hard.

"Excellent, my queen," he grinned up at me. "It seems you are quite the natural."

"'Tis because of your wonderful teaching," I said as he helped me down from the saddle. "Forgive me, your name... You said it was Gavin, yes?" I felt terrible that I could not remember for sure.

He grinned and nodded, sweeping into a low bow. "Yes, my lady. Sir Gavin, at your service."

I curtseyed, smiling. "A fine name, Sir Gavin."

The knight's eyes wandered to a point beyond where I stood. "Pardon, Your Majesty, but it seems someone wishes to speak with you."

I turned to look.

Rowan stood across the courtyard, watching us, his expression straight and serious—of course—but surprisingly placid.

I turned back around and began rubbing the horse's nose to distract myself. It had been two days since the incident outside the Hall of Records. Thus far, I'd managed to avoid him save for at meals, and even then, we did not converse. But now, it seemed my luck had run out.

I sensed his approach behind me while Sir Gavin backed away

respectfully, giving us space, but thankfully leaving me with the horse. I needed something for support in order to face the king again.

My heart beat faster once I knew Rowan had stopped directly behind me. Out the corner of my eye, I saw his hand reach forward to rub the horse's velvety nose.

"Hello."

"Hello. Do you wish to speak with me?" *Or shall you yell at me again?*

"It has been brought to my attention that I put you in great distress the other day. 'Twas not my intention to…" he paused for a moment, seeming to contemplate his next words, "cause you such… emotional stress."

My cheeks colored pink. *Wonderful.* The last thing I needed was yet another person knowing of my embarrassing tears.

"Forgive me."

Immediately, I turned to face him. "What did you say?"

Rowan furrowed his brows. "Must I say it again?"

I knew this goaded him. He clearly hated admitting he was in the wrong. But what mattered was that he *was* admitting it, which both shocked and impressed me.

"Nay." I stepped back, allowing the horse's head to fall between us. We stood rather close, I'd noticed after I turned around, and it made me uncomfortable. "You merely surprised me."

He cocked his head and looked over that of the horse as the animal tossed its mane. "Will you not accept my apology then? Do you not believe that I could sincerely feel contrition for my actions?"

"Nay…" I said carefully. "I shall forgive you freely." Then a thought came to me. "After all, 'tis what God would do."

"*God?* You seek to do as He would do?" The question sounded almost mocking.

"Of course. I try to, anyway. You do not?" I already knew the answer to my question, but still wished to hear how he would respond.

"Not so much anymore, I suppose. My parents raised me differently, but since their death—" He looked away, his Adam's apple bobbing as he swallowed. "I know not whether He is even there at times."

I studied him, feeling compassion towards him for once as I

saw the emotions—the pain, confusion, bitterness—all pass across his blue eyes as they scanned the palace walls, looking for a distraction from the uncomfortable conversation. I could relate to him, in a way. I had struggled with much the same feelings as he. In fact, I struggled with them still.

Nothing in my life made sense at the moment, but most things that happen in life do not. You can only learn to get through it, even if you lack understanding.

I knew that was what I had to do—find my way through, make the most of where I'd been placed, and quit protesting so much. And pray that someday I *would* understand.

I hoped that Rowan would do the same, learn to let go of the past, the pain, the hurt, the anger, and step into a new life. Because it was not benefitting anyone.

"But He *is* there, Rowan," I whispered. It was the first time I had ever addressed him by his Christian name. It slipped out before I even knew, but I did not regret it. Because when I spoke his name, something changed in his eyes. He looked at me, surprised, and his eyes softened for the first time since I had known him.

And they were startlingly beautiful.

"A horse," he said, breaking his gaze away from mine and moving to pat the animal's neck. "Sir Gavin's horse is a fine animal. We shall find you one even finer, on the morrow, if that is your wish. My supplier is always willing to assist me, even on the day of rest."

"But what about church?"

"What about it?"

"I was hoping… well, I thought mayhap we could attend services in Caelrith on the morrow." So far, I had only attended service in the palace chapel, where the short, rotund, and very kind Father Josef ministered. Rowan had accompanied me a few times, but not every week. I missed attending church at the Caelrith Cathedral, and hoped to go there again, and that Rowan would come as well. He certainly needed it, and rubbing elbows with his people could not hurt either.

He thought for a moment before answering. "I suppose we may go, then afterwards go purchase the horse."

I grinned at him from over the animal's soft, brown head. "Perfect."

I fiddled with the end of my long sleeve, sitting beside Rowan on the front row of the church. Every eye watched us, I knew, for the king rarely ventured out into the public like this.

I tried not to appear too uncomfortable with my once fellow citizens staring at me, but instead focused on what the minister was saying. The same elderly man who married us began quoting a passage of scripture: "Trust in the Lord with all thine heart; and lean not unto thine own understanding. In all thy ways acknowledge him, and he shall direct thy paths."

I thought about that a moment as he continued. That particular passage spoke straight to my heart. *Lean not unto thine own understanding… He shall direct thy path…*

I had to let God take control. He'd placed me here for a reason, whether that reason was clearing Trilaria's name, helping the king back to Him, or something else entirely. Instead of trying to figure out why, I simply needed to trust Him, lean not on my own feeble understanding, and let Him have His will. He would help me find my way in this new life. He would protect and comfort me, keep my heart and soul from being destroyed in the loneliness.

But truly, was I so alone?

I glanced at Rowan to my right, his warm arm pressed against mine. I was still uncertain about him, but there were others. Lord Favian, for instance, was very kind to me. Surely, he was a friend. And Mavis, she was friendly to me.

However, neither of them could compare to my friends of old: Gloriana and Frederic. We had grown up with one another, shared a bond that ran deep and strong. Would I ever see them again?

As soon as the service ended, the king and I rose. I subtly adjusted my crown as I stood—this one of several I now owned. It was not like the showy ceremonial one I had been crowned with; rather it was a smaller, more delicate piece, solid gold crafted into a leafy design. Crowns still felt so odd atop my head. I refused to wear one every day, only on special occasions and in public, like this.

Rowan took my arm and began leading me out of the church, the few knights who had accompanied us following at either side.

A familiar face caught my eye. Gloriana waved to me from a short distance away, her pretty face beaming in excitement.

"Oh, please, sire." I tugged on his arm to slow him. "May I go see my friend?"

"We must be departing, Arabella."

"Yes, but please. 'Twould only take a minute." My eyes pleaded with him, and I guess it was enough for he sighed and relented.

"Very well. But be quick about it."

I pulled away from him, pushed past the guards, and rushed into my friend's arms. "Oh, how I've missed you!"

"And I you." Gloriana squeezed me tight before pulling back to look at me in my lavender gown embroidered with gold thread, and the delicate crown that held a gauzy veil covering my hair. "You look dazzling!"

I laughed and replied my thanks.

Gloriana peered over my shoulder, biting her lip, her eyes alive with intrigue. "How is he? Is he wonderful, like I thought? Or is he as boorish as you assumed?" I knew exactly who *he* was.

Rowan.

I glanced back. He stood in the middle of the small circle of knights, watching us, his expression reeking impatience.

"Actually…"

"Is he a glorious kisser?" Gloriana cut in, her grin wide and mischievous.

"Nay. I mean—I wouldn't know."

My friend gaped at me. "Why?"

I glanced over her shoulder and saw Frederic across the room. He offered me a pleasant smile, though his eyes portrayed his displeasure.

"Really, Gloriana, I must go." I looked over my shoulder. Rowan still watched us, but the lines of impatience deepened in his forehead. "The king is waiting for me." I did not wish to hear any more talk of Rowan and I, and neither did I wish to upset him again so soon. I turned back to give my friend fierce embrace. "I hope we can see each other again soon." She hugged me back, then I broke away and returned to Rowan's side.

Rowan

Arabella chose an excellent animal, one Rowan himself would have been proud to ride. It was a white and gray mare named Gemmula, Latin for "little jewel".

Now she trotted beside him atop her new horse as they made their way back to the palace. He could not help but notice what a vision she was in that lavender gown, with her crown perched smartly atop her head, and her gauzy veil floating in the breeze, teasing him with glimpses of her creamy neck. Not to mention, her position upon the mare's back was a very attractive one, her feet and ankles peeking from beneath her skirts.

Rowan looked straight ahead and steered his thoughts a different direction. He cleared his throat, preparing to say something to break the silence when Arabella did it for him. "Oh!"

The guards, two at the front, two at the back, pulled up short. "Does something alarm you, Your Majesty?" one asked over his shoulder, the other man beside him scanning the deserted streets for danger.

"Nay. 'Tis only them." She pointed to an alleyway, between a pair of small two-story, half-timber buildings, where two filthy children huddled. Before he could stop her, Arabella slipped from the saddle and hurried over to them.

"What do think you are doing? Do you know these ruffians?"

The children's eyes grew wide, and they backed away just before Arabella reached them. "Shh, you frightened them," she hissed at him over her shoulder.

She reached out her hand, crouching down, beckoning them closer. After a few seconds, the children stepped forward again, where Rowan could see them. They were filthy, head to toe, and dressed in threadbare rags. The younger one, a little boy, had strips of dirty cloth wrapped about his small feet, while the older one, a girl, was barefoot.

Arabella spoke softly to them. He was unable to hear what she said, but he saw that she smiled as she spoke. Whatever it was, it made the children smile as well. Then Arabella reached into the pocket of her gown. The sunlight glinted off the gold coin she then handed to the children. Their little eyes stared at it in awe before looking up at Arabella in wonder. They said something to her as she stood straight again, then hugged her tight about the legs and scurried off.

Arabella watched them depart before returning to her horse, where one of the guards assisted her back into the sidesaddle. "Why did you give those children money?"

She looked at him as if he were a lunatic. "Because they are starving." She hesitated, her eyes full of meaning. "Their father died a year and a half ago, with you… fighting in Trilaria."

"What about their mother? Is she not around to care for them?"

"With no man to take care of her, she lost her home and had no way to care for them." Arabella looked down, her face falling in sorrow. "They know not where she is now."

The children's mother had deserted them? Left them alone in the streets to fend for themselves? Rowan felt a moment of grief over the fact that their father had died fighting for his cause. He never gave a thought to the consequences of his warring.

But what did it matter? If the men were willing to fight, then they entered the fray knowing the potential consequences, the dear price they more than likely would have to pay.

However… many of them men who fought for him over the years, the last few especially, hadn't entered willingly.

"I gather you do not agree with my fighting?"

Arabella's expression told him he was correct in his assumption.

"Would you not have me defend the kingdom from its enemies? Mete out the consequences for the killing of my parents?"

"There is a difference—a fine line between fighting to protect, and fighting for revenge. Fighting to help others and fighting for one's own means. A *very fine* line… I only hope you know which side you are on."

He looked away from her, fury rising in his chest. Who was she to question his motives? She could not know the pain and trauma caused him. She could not understand what drove him! She was not there when his world turned upside-down!

Was this not a worthy cause? Was it not worth it, no matter who or how many got hurt in the process?

"I just wonder," she said softly, cautiously, "if mayhap the war has done all it can. Is it really doing *any* good anymore? Is it worth all the loss? You cannot understand how—"

"Nay. *You* cannot understand." He glared at her, anger flashing in his eyes. "You should mind your own business, Arabella."

Chapter 14

ROWAN FLIPPED THROUGH THE STACK OF MAPS
and papers, finding the one documenting his most recent attack
on Trilaria. Ever since Arabella questioned his motives for continuing his war, it was all he could think of.

He scanned through the detailed accounts stored in the Hall
of Records, not knowing what good it was doing to read them, or
what exactly he was hoping to accomplish. He supposed he was
searching for a reason, a valid purpose for continuing his war with
Trilaria, other than the fact that he wished to avenge his parents.
Searching for a way to put his mind, and the questions it was
bringing to him, to rest.

Cassius stepped into the room and approached the desk where
Rowan sat. He idly ran one finger along the desk's wooden edge.
"Busy at work, my king?"

"Mhm…"

Cassius moved to pick up a map showing the shared borders
of Trilaria and Acuniel. He studied it in silence for a long moment.
"Are you planning another battle, perhaps one to end this feud
once and for all? We could launch our greatest attack of all. You
could stay at or near the front lines, leading the army yourself, as I
know you prefer. It may do you good, since it seems you are… less
than happy here with your new bride."

Rowan thought about it for a moment. "Nay, Cassius. Not
now."

"But sire—"

"I said, nay!" Rowan slammed the map he held back onto the

desk. "We shall worry about that in the future. But right now, I shall do as we planned before—settle in to *married* life," he emphasized, giving the man a pointed look. "You and Favian were the ones who forced me into it, after all."

He was none too enthused about "settling in" to anything, but neither was he ready for more fighting just yet. No matter how much his head told him not to let Arabella's words deter him from his mission.

"Send word for the troops to withdraw and stay to our side of the border until further notice." Rowan returned his attention to his maps and papers. He could feel his advisor's incredulous stare boring into his lowered head. After a weighted moment, Cassius stepped back and bowed, one hand clasped to his abdomen, his other arm swept out to the side. "As you wish, Your Majesty."

Then the man turned and left the room.

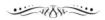

Arabella

I turned a corner on my way to the garden and found my uncle hurrying down the corridor towards me. "Uncle Matthew! How good it is to see you." I met him halfway and started to give him a hug.

"No time for that." He brushed me off, his expression serious, worried. It scared me. What could be so wrong that my uncle would refuse my hug?

"Is something amiss, Uncle?"

"I am afraid there is." He cast a furtive look up and down the corridor. "We cannot speak of it here, though. Come." Uncle Matthew took my arm and we slipped into the nearest room. It was a bedchamber, thankfully deserted. He shut the door tight.

"What is it, uncle? What is wrong? You are frightening me."

"Arabella, 'tis the king."

My stomach dropped. "What has he done?"

My uncle waved his hand. "Nay, nay. He has not done anything. Rather, someone is planning to do something *to him*."

Alarm flared in my chest. "What?"

"I overheard the king's royal cupbearer speaking with one of the servants that assists him in serving wine at the king's table. They spoke of a plan to assassinate the king."

I took a half step back, one hand coming to my throat. No matter what my previous opinion of him had been, I did not wish to see Rowan murdered.

"You must warn him of this, put a stop to this plan before it is too late." My uncle clutched my arms in earnest.

"Why me, Uncle? You are the one who uncovered this plot. Can *you* not go to the king?"

"I fear he would not believe me; I am merely a lowly scribe. But you are his queen, his wife. Surely your word must hold more merit."

I tried to catch my breath and think. *Would* he believe me? I was not as close to him as people assumed. We were the most *unmarried* married couple I had ever heard of. Would he listen to me any more than he would listen to my uncle?

"Are you sure of what you heard?"

"I am positive. They spoke very clearly of it."

I turned away, dread filling every fiber of my being. "I must tell the king right away."

Two hours later, at supper, I sat to the right of the king. He had been busy with meetings all afternoon, his attendants informing me that he was not to be disturbed. Even before we entered the banquet hall on each other's arm, he was preoccupied, not giving me a moment to speak. I wrung my hands in my skirt. I *had* to say something, but how? When?

I watched every move the cupbearer and other servants made. Would the cupbearer or his accomplice act this night? On the morrow? In a week?

As I tried my best to force food down my constricted throat, another thought popped into my head.

What if they want me dead, too?

I gulped down the piece of chicken in my mouth, the food suddenly making me feel ill. My appetite vanished.

Rowan flicked out his hand, catching my attention. The cup-bearer came forward with the king's wine atop a silver tray. After the king was served, then the servants would serve the rest of us. As was custom, the cupbearer raised the goblet to his own lips. Testing for poison.

Poison.

The king's drink! Alarm bells rang in my head.

I studied the cupbearer, watched as he placed the rim to his lips, tipped the cup upward. His throat bobbed as if swallowing, but the action looked strangely affected.

Rowan took the silver cup from the man, starting to bring the rim to his lips. Something was not right.

"Nay!" I rose from my seat in such a hurry that I almost toppled my chair. "Halt!" Every eye swiveled in my direction.

Rowan froze, the cup resting against his lips, though he had yet to take a sip. He narrowed his eyes. "Arabella, what is the meaning of this?"

"The cup! 'Tis poisoned."

The entire table gasped collectively. Rowan pulled the drink away from his lips. "Have you gone mad, woman? My cupbearer is supposed to *keep* me from being poisoned. He tasted the wine first."

I pinned the cupbearer with my gaze. "He did not take a sip. He pretended to. There is poison in that cup."

Alarm flashed across the cupbearer's eyes before they hardened into stone. "I resent that accusation! Why should *I* poison the king?"

"I know not. But I beg you, my king, please believe me. There is poison in that cup. I am certain of it." I lifted a silent prayer that my gut instinct was indeed correct, and that I had not just made a scene in front of the king's officials for nothing.

Rowan lifted the drink and sniffed it. His eyes met mine, doubt written there. "I will trust you on this. But I must investigate the matter further. Guards! Arrest this man and throw him in the dungeon."

The cupbearer turned and ran for the door, all but sealing his guilt with that action alone. Two guards intercepted him, gripping him by his arms and dragging him away. The man tugged and fought against them. "I shall not go down for this alone! Do you here me? I will not!" he bellowed, just as the Hall door slammed in his face.

The meal clearly over, everyone rose and awkwardly departed, whispering quietly amongst themselves. Favian approached Rowan and asked if he wished him to stay, but Rowan quickly replied no and Favian reluctantly left as well.

Rowan collapsed into his seat again, supporting his head in his hand and staring at the discarded cup. After a second or two's hesitation, I stepped back from the table and also headed for the door.

"Arabella." Rowan's low voice stopped me in my tracks. "Please. Stay."

Slowly, I turned around, surprised he wanted my company. I returned to the table and resumed my seat at his right.

He said nothing, only sat there staring, so I did not press him. I gave him space, allowing him to take in the events of the last few minutes.

"You saved my life," he finally said matter-of-factly. "I know your opinion of me has not always been the best—that much has been apparent. But yet," he turned his serious blue eyes on me, "you warned me of a threat against my life, even though my death would mean your freedom from a loveless marriage."

"I could not allow you to be killed, no matter what I feel. 'Twould not be right. 'Twould be as if I murdered you myself."

He stayed thoughtful for a moment, the room again falling into silence. Eventually he spoke up, "I thank you, my lady, for uncovering this plot and putting a stop to it."

"Actually," I quickly put in, "I cannot take credit for the deed. 'Twas my uncle who uncovered the plot. He overheard the cupbearer and another servant speak of it and came to me straightaway."

His brows raised. "Your uncle, the scribe? I shall have to reward him then." He rubbed a hand over his mouth. "I cannot believe that one of my own subjects would wish to kill me. And you said there was another?"

"Yes, though my uncle and I know not his name. Mayhap the cupbearer shall divulge it. After all, he did proclaim that he would not go down for this deed alone."

"Yes… let us hope." Rowan sat back in his chair for so long that I grew anxious. I could not stand to sit alone with him that way for much longer, not with this heavy silence hanging over us, the aftershock of death so nearly cheated.

Finally, I made to stand. "May I be excused now, sire? I am afraid this day... its events have taxed me."

He lifted his chin out of his palm. "Hm?" It seemed to take him a moment to comprehend what I said. "Oh, yes, of course. Go. Rest." His mouth went into that signature grim line of his. "I am afraid this day has sorely taxed us both."

The next morning, I slept in later than usual. Not waiting to summon my maids, I dressed myself in a hurry, threw my hair into a quick arrangement, and pinned on a short veil, the filmy piece effectively covering my less than perfect hairstyle.

Once presentable, I slipped out of my room and headed for the dungeon.

When thinking about last night's incident before falling asleep, I contemplated what the cupbearer stood to gain by murdering the king. Hatred was motive enough, to be sure. But did the cupbearer really wish to throw the kingdom into even worse chaos with the unexpected loss of their king? With no son yet born from our union, who could possibly be next in line to ascend the throne?

If I questioned the cupbearer about his and the other servant's involvement in the attempted poisoning—if that servant had been found—perhaps I could learn why they attempted such a scheme in the first place.

When I reached the door leading to the dark stairwell that spiraled down into the depths of the palace dungeon, I paused. Who knew what I would encounter in the dark, dank place? Were there other prisoners down there? Would I see the cupbearer or someone else being gruesomely tortured? I had heard tales of some of the devices used to punish criminals and extract information from those captured. I did not wish to see them period, let alone in action. But something about the entire matter left me strangely unsettled. Something was still terribly wrong. And I had to know what.

I entered the stairwell lit by flickering torches every ten feet.

The temperature dropped as I descended, sending a shiver up my spine, despite the late summer heat above ground.

I emerged into a dark chamber, barely illuminated by torchlight. To my right, a row of filthy cells stretched long and disappeared into the darkness ahead. A few feet to my left was a table and chair, where there sat a large, fat man dressed in black. He snored softly, his head lolled forward on his chest. Just past the man was a dark doorway, perhaps leading to the dreaded torture devices.

Something scurried past, its hair brushing against the tops of my feet. I screamed and jumped back, snatching my skirts to the side.

The jailer snorted and sat up. It took a moment for him to recognize me. "Your Majesty!" He jumped to his feet, his chair clattering against the wall. He smoothed back his unkempt black hair. "What are you doing down here? The king would be mighty cross were he to learn you were in the dungeon."

"Forgive me for startling you." I found my wits again, my hand against my chest. "I came to see the prisoner."

"The cupbearer?" The man scratched his scruffy chin.

"Yes. Please, may I speak to him?"

"Oh, have you not heard, my queen?" He peered through the darkness at me, shaking his head. "He and the other fella that was in on it were executed at dawn."

"*Executed?*" I staggered back a step. My heart sank like lead. I had not thought they would put him to death so soon. Why so suddenly, and with no trial?

"Yes, my queen." The man stepped forward, noticing my distress. "The cupbearer confessed everything, including the name of his accomplice, and at dawn they were both hanged." The jailer scoffed a laugh. "You know, at first, they told me someone put them up to sneaking the poison into the king's wine. But when Lord Cassius and the captain of the guard came down for more questioning, they changed their story. I suppose they hoped to shift the blame to avoid the noose, but thought better of it."

I put a hand to my forehead. *Or perhaps they had been telling the truth.* What if someone *had* put them up to the task of murdering the king? That idea made more sense—someone with something more to gain from the king's death using the men as scapegoats.

Bile rose in my throat.

"Are you well, my queen? Forgive me if I shocked you."

He pulled the chair out from behind his desk so I could sit down. "Nay, 'tis not your fault. I just hoped to speak with the cup-bearer before…"

The jailer put a hand on the back of the chair and leaned down to look at my face in concern. "May I ask what about, m'lady? Mayhap I can assist you."

"Nothing." I shook my head, brushing off the question. There was no way he could give me the answers I sought. The only ones who could do that were dead. "'Twas nothing."

Chapter 15

I COULD NOT SLEEP THAT NIGHT. IMAGES OF THE cupbearer kept flashing through my mind, keeping me tossing and turning into the wee hours.

They had not given either man a trial. Even if they did admit to the crime, did they not deserve that much?

And what of their change in story—first saying someone recruited them to commit the crime, then retracting the claim? Had that really been an attempt to shift some of the blame off their shoulders? Or had they been telling the truth?

My stomach quaked at the idea that a potential killer still lurked somewhere.

I threw back the covers, in too much distress to sleep, and donned my sleeveless tapestry robe over my long-sleeved nightgown, intending to go the tower. It had become a favorite place of mine.

But when I opened my door and entered the sitting room, an unexpected sight met my eyes.

Rowan sat in one of the chairs facing the fire, dressed in a long, loose shirt over a pair of dark leggings. He turned to look at me when I entered, his eyes mirroring my own surprise.

"Oh." I jumped back into my doorway, pulling my robe tighter about my chest. He had never seen me not fully dressed, just as I had never seen *him* in this undone state. It sent heat into my face and set my heart into an awkward gallop. "Pardon me, my king." I kept my eyes anywhere but on him.

"Nay, you may stay. Do not leave on my account."

Hesitantly, I lifted my eyes to look him. "Please... sit." He gestured to the empty chair at his left.

Slowly, expecting him to change his mind, I went to the chair he indicated, settling into its soft cushions. I pulled my long hair over my shoulder, suddenly wishing I'd had Mavis braid it before I went to bed. "It seems we both suffer from lack of sleep," Rowan said to me, the tips of his fingers resting against his full lips. "'Tis difficult to rest after someone tries to kill you." His mouth quirked in a grim half-smile.

"Yes. I understand what you mean, sire. Though I was not the one in jeopardy, the incident still troubles me."

"How so?" His brows knit together, and he cocked his head. "You truly feared for me?"

I looked down, my heart beating faster at both his inquiry and steady gaze. "I suppose I did." I could not yet tell him the full extent of my worry, the dark possibilities plaguing my mind.

"*Suppose?*" he teased, referring to our previous conversation when I had said I *supposed* he was handsome.

I laughed lightly. "Yes, sire."

He nestled against the back of his chair, his hands folded over his abdomen as he stared into the fire. He really did look handsome sitting there with the fire's warm light illuminating parts of his face and casting others into shadow. His long legs stretched out before him, his bare feet crossed at the ankles. I noticed that one could still make out the shape of his muscles as the loose fabric lay across his chest. *How strong is he really?*

I bit my lip and looked away, angry with myself for noticing, not to mention *contemplating* the extent of his strength. Inwardly, I berated myself for not using the door that led directly into the hallway as my exit point.

I chanced a glance at him again, wondering how much longer this uncomfortable silence would go on, and was chagrinned to find that he was staring at *me*. "What?" My cheeks flushed hot.

"I can tell you are contemplating something."

I stiffened, and I am sure my eyes went wide as the moon.

"Your mind always seems to be turning. And I cannot help but wonder what goes on in that head of yours." He studied me as if he could not fathom my being. "You freely voice your opinion of me like no one else and question my beliefs. Few people in my life can get away with that."

He turned in his chair to face me more fully. "Is it that you wish to scold me again, as you did the other day?" His expression... I could not read it. It was cross, yet not at the same time, somewhat bewildered or perhaps even amused. "Is that why you sit there looking as though you are about to burst?"

That was not the case at all, but I could not very well tell him that I sat there thinking of his muscles. *Heaven forbid!*

"Forgive me, my king, if I upset you. 'Tis not my intention. I guess I am merely an opinionated and curious person."

He settled back into his seat again, stretching with a little groan that did strange things to my stomach. "Well then, my good Queen Arabella, may I appease your curiosity? What question do you bring to me this night?"

I sat there for a moment, thinking. Here was a perfect opportunity to ask a question I had been wanting the answer to for a long time. But did I dare ask it? I was not eager to arouse his wrath again.

I would have to tread with the utmost care.

"Well... I have wondered," I dared to look up and into his eyes, turned dark by the firelight, "what exactly happened the night your parents died?" I braced myself for his reaction. To my amazement, he only widened his eyes in surprise before looking back to the fire. His face fell into one of sorrow and wretched torment, and I was almost sorry for bringing up something that caused him such pain.

"I was there, that night. I saw it all—or almost all of it." He breathed deep and released the breath in a huff. "We had just traveled to Trilaria on a diplomatic visit. My father and King Wesley had a dispute before we left, over something that I cannot even recall now, but nothing that should have warranted what happened.

"Our party was staying with the Lord of Dallin, just within the border. After supper that night, I went to my parents' chamber to speak with my father about something. When I opened the door, they were going out the window."

"They?"

"The Trilarians," he said, with such finality in his voice that there was no way I could question him. "They were just escaping like phantoms in the night, out the window, dressed in long black robes with masks that covered their faces. Each of them had silver pendants bearing the Trilarian crest. I had heard tales of these men—the king's specially trained assassins." His face was hard, angry, but his eyes shone with unshed tears. "I shouted at them and one stopped and turned to look at me. He lunged at me and we fought. He cut me deep, right here." Without looking at me, as if it were an involuntary movement, he lowered the neck of his shirt to reveal a long, vicious scar. I shifted in my seat, uncomfortable with that glimpse at his muscled chest.

"I dealt him an equally bad blow, cutting him on his arm and chest. That was when he gave up, shoved me to the ground, and disappeared out the window."

He pushed out a heavy breath, swallowing several times, clearing his throat, obviously trying to gain control of his emotions. I watched him, searched his face. It was as if he were no longer this hard and powerful king, but a heartbroken, vulnerable boy.

Rowan caught me studying him and cleared his throat, rubbing a hand over his face. "That is when I noticed… that is when I noticed my parents. My father," he stretched out his arm, indicating the area near the hearth, "he was laid out on the ground. My mother across the bed on her back, staring up at the ceiling." His expression was vehement, his voice growing in intensity as he spoke, though it trembled under the weight of his emotions. "Both their throats were slit. The blood… was everywhere."

I shivered at his detailed, gruesome description of the scene. His voice broke and he covered his eyes with his hand. When he pulled it away, his eyes were dark and angry, hard and vicious. "They did not deserve that, Arabella. They deserved to live out their lives, grow old together, and die in the peace of their own home." He tore his gaze away from mine, no doubt hating himself for baring his pain to me in such a way.

Without even thinking about it, I rose and knelt beside him, touching his arm. "Forgive me. I should not have asked you to speak of it. 'Twas wrong of me." Tears stung my own eyes. One slipped down my cheek, in anguish for him. I understood the pain of losing one's family. It was a feeling no one should ever have to feel but do far too often.

Finally, Rowan met my gaze, angry tears boiling in his eyes. Somehow, he kept them in check, and not a one slipped down his face. I envied his control. I, for one, had never been very skilled at controlling my emotions, especially when it came to tears.

"Congratulations, my queen." His voice was shaky, yet hard as steel.

"For what?"

"You have done what no man has been able to do. You have managed to strip down your king's defenses and peer into his innermost heart." Rowan stared hard at me, and I at him. He seemed to be warring inside, between feeling either extreme anger and resentment towards me, or extreme gratitude.

"Go." He pushed my hand away from his arm. "Go, now."

His mask of granite was back in place, all traces of vulnerability hidden once more. I stood and returned to my room without a moment's protest.

This time, as I sat in my chair beside my open window, I did not cry for myself like so many times before. I cried for Rowan the tears he would not allow himself to shed. Because of the pain and resentment caused by of his parents' murder. Because he needed help, he needed God to heal the wounds of the past and free him of the hatred, as He had freed me.

And I cried because the evidence compiled against Trilaria was insurmountable, and even I could see why Rowan and others had concluded that they, and they alone, were guilty. But somehow, deep inside, my intuition told me that there was more to it than just a senseless act of violence. Just as I felt the attempt on Rowan's life was not as simple as it appeared...

As each day passed, that feeling inside grew stronger, refusing to let go. If no one else wanted to know the truth, I did. And I would have to be the one to find it.

Chapter 16

MAVIS SIDLED INTO MY ROOM BACKWARDS, CARrying a tray laden with food for me to break my fast. "Just sit it over there, Mavis, and I shall eat momentarily." I gestured to the small table near the window as I finished buttoning up my gown. Today, I had opted for a simple dress that was rather plain compared to most of my gowns. It was almost like those I used to wear, but of much better fabric and quality, of course.

Mavis always insisted on her or one of the other maids assisting me in dressing, but I still preferred to dress myself, when I could get away with it. It felt strange to have someone else put my clothes on for me.

I did not mind their insistence on arranging my hair, however. They could accomplish much more elaborate styles than I ever could.

My hair still needed fixing this morning. The dark tresses fell in chaotic waves over my shoulders and down my back. My stomach grumbled and churned in protest. I would break my fast first, I decided, and then let Mavis tend to my hair.

I sat down at the table and stirred my spoon in my porridge, tucking my bare feet under my legs in the chair.

"Have you heard the news, m'lady?"

"What news?" I shoveled a spoonful of steaming porridge into my mouth, admiring the morning sky outside my open window.

"They've captured a Trilarian within Acuniel's borders."

I nearly choked to death on my spoon. I coughed and sputtered, clattering the wooden spoon onto the table as I labored to get the porridge down my throat. Mavis hurried to me, patting my back hard. When I was finally able to draw a ragged breath, I gasped, "What?"

"A Trilarian man has been captured. He stole across the border illegally and has been living here for the past year. It seems there shall be an execution this day." My maid said this all matter-of-factly, as if it were of very little consequence.

I stood up and headed for the door. "I must go, Mavis."

"But, my queen, your hair... 'tis not done. And no shoes! You shall appear half-dressed!"

I ignored her and opened the door, muttering to myself. "I must stop this."

Fear for a fellow native of Trilaria spurred me onward. I was not sure what I could do to help him, but I had to try. I ran out into the courtyard, my hair flying behind me like a battle standard.

Gallows were erected at the center of the courtyard, the palace gates open to allow onlookers entrance. Rowan stood with Cassius, Favian, and all his other officials, their backs to me, watching as a man was led up and onto the platform by another man dressed in black.

"Nay! Halt! Please!" I flew across the stones and to Rowan's side. I grasped frantically at his arm and shoulder. He turned to me, frustration knotting his features. He tried to shake me off, but I would not relent.

"Arabella, what do you think you are doing? Have you gone mad? Get back inside. You look—"

"Nay, Rowan, please. You cannot kill this man just because of where he is from. 'Tis—"

"You know the law, Arabella." His tone was full of finality. "No one is exempt from it, not even you."

"But 'tis a stupid law!"

He arrowed a look at me out the corner of his eye as he turned to face forward again, his nostrils flaring. He looked over the crowd. All craned their necks to see the commotion. Even from across the courtyard I could hear their whispers; no doubt gossiping about their queen's disheveled appearance and scandalous behavior.

"Proceed!" Rowan called to the executioner.

"Nay!" I surged forward again, pushing against the arms of Rowan and Lord Cassius, extended like an iron wall to block me.

"You cannot do this!" It was wrong, unfair. All I could picture was my uncle or Frederic in this man's place, sent to the gallows simply because of where he was born.

I pushed at Rowan again. He whirled on me, grabbing my forearm in vise grip. Without even looking at me, he dragged me towards the door. "Come with me," he ground out, his teeth clenched tight. I struggled against him, trying in vain to pull my arm from his hand while my bare feet skidded along the stones behind him.

Rowan hauled me inside and behind a mammoth pillar in the entry room of the palace. He pressed my back against it and put one hand to the pillar, above my head, so that he towered over me. He leaned down, his face a mask of anger. "What do you think you are doing? You think that because I shared my pain with you that night you can suddenly do anything you wished? Change the law of the land that *I* put into place?" He jabbed his finger at me.

"You come running out there—before half the city of Caelrith—appearing like a wild creature of the forest or a street urchin, your hair draped about you like some village harlot. Completely improper!" He lifted a piece of my untamed hair.

I gasped, offended and horrified by his comparison. "How dare you liken me to such?"

"Nay. How dare *you* come *demanding* that I spare this man? He and any others like him deserve such punishment. 'Tis the law I created, and I shall abide by it."

"But why must they all be killed?" I threw out my arms, palms up. "What have they done?"

"I told you." He leaned dangerously close, until we were but inches apart. "Was it not glaringly obvious what atrocity they committed when I bared my heart to you? Something which I shall never do again!"

"*He* did not kill your father and mother. That group of men dressed in black robes were the ones! The entire country did not murder them! Why should one man give up his life for a crime committed by others? Is that not wrong to you?" Steam practically billowed from my ears. "If he is not permitted here, then send him back to across the border. But *killing* him? Is that truly necessary? 'Tis *murder!*"

Rowan stilled and a shadow crossed his face, as if he were contemplating my correctness in the matter.

It only lasted a moment before his face darkened again. "Nay! You have made me question myself enough, Arabella of Caelrith. I am the king, and I shall remain steadfast in my ideals, no matter what you do." He held my shoulders, his grip tight. "I know not what game you play, but if you believe for one second that you are changing me, then you had better think again. I will not yield!"

I stared at him, stricken. Did I truly affect him so?

He straightened, still standing very close and holding tightly to my shoulders. "And no wife of mine shall behave as you have today."

My nostrils flared and fresh rage exploded in my chest. "You do not control me. And I may be your wife, but I am not your *wife*. You do not even want me as such!"

Another emotion mixed with his look of fury. Then suddenly, before I could even draw my next breath, he seized my head in his hands and kissed me. "Who says I do not?" he growled lowly, his kiss still burning upon my lips.

I was so furious I could not control it. I did not want him to want me. *How dare he kiss me after all the things he said?*

There were few moments in my life I had ever felt so angry, and God help me, before I even knew what I was doing, I slapped him across the face.

Rowan leapt back, clutching his hand to his cheek. I covered my mouth with my hands. Had I really just slapped the king?

At first, I feared what he would do, but a moment later my boldness returned. I set my teeth and clenched my fists at my sides. My body trembled with fury. "Why do you not go ahead and hit me back? Just get it over with! I know you want to!" I stared up at him, my chest heaving as I waited, expecting one of his large hands to meet the skin of my already burning cheeks.

But he did nothing. He just stood there, staring at me with his hand against his cheek.

So then I ran.

I turned and ran through the corridors and to my room. It wasn't until I slammed my door behind me and bolted it—as well as the door to mine and Rowan's sitting room—that I remembered the unfortunate man in the courtyard, realizing that at that very moment, an innocent man lost his life. And I had failed to stop it.

I avoided Rowan at all costs after that. We spoke nary a word to one another for days. And every day, the feeling of his lips pressed firmly to mine haunted me, sending conflicting emotions through my heart. I loathed that moment, that feeling, but at the same time, felt strangely drawn by it.

It aggravated me.

Why did Rowan have to be so... *confusing*?

Just when I believed I was gaining ground and working past that hard shell that encased him, he had pushed me away, destroyed all my efforts.

We were back to the place where we had begun.

And I was back where I had been during my first days in the king's palace—in that dark, lonely pit of depression.

I had thought I was doing so well at taking advantage of my situation and trying to see the good in it. But that fiery argument had reduced all my progress to ashes.

Bitterness pricked at my heart more each day until the frustration and confusion became too much to handle.

I curled up in the chair by my window, my shutters closed against the wet, gusty wind. "Why, God?" The first drops of a rainstorm pattered outside. "What is Your purpose in bringing me here? For I still am incapable of seeing it. For that matter, is there any purpose at all?" I wiped at a tear that threatened to escape. "Some days I wonder if You are even there."

My own words to Rowan shot through my memory. *He is there.*

I knew better than to believe that God was not there at all. But that did not mean He was hearing me. Indeed, it felt as if my prayers were bouncing off the ceiling.

"Lord, I am pleading for You to notice me. I know You are an Almighty, All-Powerful God. Why should you listen to one little person's cries in a sea of so many other things?"

I stood and started pacing. Confusion wrung my heart. "Why?" was the question that kept ringing through my mind, over and over, like a maddening chant.

"Please... *please*, Lord, turn to me. Hear me. Hold my heart and comfort me. Let me find my way out of the darkness and con-fusion that plagues me so." I stopped in the center of the room and put my face in my hands. "How long must I pray until I hear You? Speak to me... please, Jesus. I cannot continue any longer feeling as though You are a million leagues away."

Amidst my desperate pleas, I heard it. A still, small voice; qui-et, yet as loud and clear as thunder.

Arabella.

I lifted my head, glancing about for a moment, half-wonder-ing if someone had intruded upon my room without my notice. But then came a flood of recognition. I knew Who spoke. It was a Voice both unfamiliar and yet as near as my own.

I have not forsaken you. I have not thrown you to the wolves that you may be devoured. I have placed you in the king's court for a reason. All shall work together in the end. Ye shall see in time, but until such time, follow me. I will guide you. I control your destiny. But you must surrender yourself to me...

Trust me... I am here.

I wept then, not out of self-pity this time, but out of shame. I was ashamed of myself for doubting Him, for believing He did not care about what became of me.

He had done this, orchestrated this entire situation for a pur-pose. It was not my place to know all the answers, for all would reveal itself in time. And though I could not see at the moment, I made up my mind to follow—however blindly—God's direction. He was in control.

Sobs escaped my throat and I trembled, barely able to stay on my feet as I stood in the middle of my chamber, surrendering to the comfort of my Father. My ears, at first, did not recognize the sound I then heard—my door opening. I turned to face the person once I realized their presence, my face wet, my eyes and lips red and swollen.

Rowan.

He stood in my doorway, hand on the frame, his face a mix of concern and surprise at my state of distress. We stared at each oth-er a long moment before he wordlessly turned and left, shutting the door behind him.

Rowan

Why is she crying? Rowan stepped back into his own quarters and shut the door.

He'd heard strange noises coming from her room, sounds like wailing and someone crying out. Worried, he had gone to check on Arabella, and was surprised—not to mention, acutely concerned—to find her weeping uncontrollably. But he had not the slightest clue as to what to say to her, not after their fight the other day, so he left without so much as a word.

What could distress her so that she would weep like that? Was she homesick again? Or could it be their fight plaguing her mind?

Their fight...

His mind went back to the moment he kissed her. The feeling, the sensation, stayed with him like a branding upon his lips. He could not escape it, and it aggravated him. Seconds before the act, he'd been struggling between the mad, unexplainable urge to kiss her, and the desire to shake some sense into her head—though he knew he could never truly do such a thing. And then, when that last outburst left her lips, he had kissed her, without thinking.

His words afterward, growled against her lips, haunted him far more. *Who says I do not?* Why had he said that? Rowan was just as aggravated by his words as he was his actions.

But... in all honesty, did he not feel that way? Did he not prefer Arabella as his wife over all others?

Rowan stopped to look at his cheek in the mirror. His fingers gingerly brushed where Arabella had slapped him. He felt the pain afresh in his mind as he examined the almost healed bruise. Yes, she had *bruised* him. Now the mark was nothing more than a slight yellowish tint to his cheek, but Rowan had received several strange, inquisitive looks from people over the past week as it healed.

He frowned and moved to sit on the edge of his bed. Rowan massaged his temples, trying to erase the look of anger on her face, the texture of her hair when he touched it. The feel of her lips.

Rowan growled, angry with himself for letting such silly sentiments slip from his mouth, and for acting in such a brash manner that now left him in a state of inner turmoil.

Arabella had become just as much of a torment to him as his parents' murder.

Chapter 17

Arabella

THE SWIFT DISPOSAL OF THE KING'S ATTEMPTED assassins, as well as the recent execution of the innocent Trilarian man, only confirmed in me the need for action. I felt deep inside that there was more than met the eye when it came to the feud with Trilaria, and I had to do something about it. Though I was unsure of how exactly to go about that.

My intrusion upon the Hall of Records had not ended well, so such sneaking around to gather information was out of the question. Questioning people who were in Dallin when the murder occurred could be helpful, but tricky. Such a thing had to be done with the utmost care.

One night, I exited from the door of the tallest tower, having spent some time there communing with God, and walked down the steps from the wall and back inside the palace. It was after supper, the darkness of night quickly closing in around the palace and surrounding capital city. Few moved about the palace and its grounds save the guards patrolling the battlements.

Warm torchlight flickered along the walls, lending the place an at once eerie and cozy atmosphere. I took my time walking to my chamber. Perhaps the more I walked, the more tired I would become, and the faster I would fall asleep. Anything to avoid the more disagreeable topics that found their way into my mind so easily at night—Rowan, our fight, his kiss, him walking into my room unannounced. Why *had* he come to my chamber that day anyway?

As I passed the doors of the library, they opened with a frightening creak. My hand flew to my chest and I breathed a sigh of relief when I recognized the person who emerged. "Oh, Lord Favian, 'tis you."

"Please, my dear, call me Favian."

"*Favian*," I amended, "you nearly scared me to death."

He laughed, a warm chuckle low in his throat. "Forgive me, my queen."

"Care to walk with me? I find the quietness of the palace at night quite relaxing."

"Oh, no. I would be intruding." He waved his hands in dismissal.

"'Twould be no bother to me at all. I spend far too much of my time alone."

"Very well, if you insist." Favian stepped forward and I linked my arm with the one he offered.

"So, is it that you cannot find sleep, or have you yet to retire?" he asked after we had taken a few steps. "'Tis late. What keeps you from retiring when all others have?"

"I could ask the same of you." I cast him a sidelong look. "The truth is… I have yet to retire because my mind is far too active."

"I believe I may take a guess… Be it the king who occupies your thoughts?"

I glanced at him again, a bit miffed by his perception. "How could you know?"

"I witnessed the display in the courtyard the other day, as well as the look on His Majesty's face when he returned outside." He paused, a teasing grin curving his lips. "Not to mention, the bright red palm print on his cheek."

My head jerked to face him.

"Fine work, my queen."

My mouth fell open.

He laughed so hard he coughed. "Yes, I noticed. As did many others. But truth be told, I am sure he deserved it. Our king needs a good slap in the head occasionally. He is too hard-headed for his own good. Being his loyal subordinate, I cannot very well hit the boy." His dark eyes twinkled as we passed a flickering torch. "But it seems you were able to, and you are still here, so…"

I threw back my head and laughed. "I feared he would order my head on a platter." Favian and I shared another laugh, then I sobered, remembering the wildfire in his eyes. The same fire that had burned within my veins.

"'Twas horrid how he yelled at me." I set my teeth and exhaled out my nose. "Truly, I have never met a man like him. He is so… *maddening.*"

"I know, my dear. Your husband has been through much, and it has made him a hard, angry man. I often think—and have told him such—that if he would just turn to God, he would find all the answers that he seeks. *He* is the only one who can change our Rowan's heart."

"Do you think…?" I looked down at the stones passing beneath my feet. "Do you think he could ever find his way back, that anything will ever change?"

Favian shook his head, his mouth grim. "I know not, my dear, but I pray every day that it may be so."

I would too. I would start praying every day that a change would happen in Rowan. *Speak to him, God. As You have to me.*

Another subject, indirectly related to the one we already spoke of, popped into my head. "Were you there the night his parents died?" I asked carefully, hoping the subject was not as sensitive to him as it was to Rowan.

Favian halted in his steps, just for half a second, before resuming our pace. "Yes. I was there that night. I found Rowan wounded and weeping over his parents' bodies, carrying on about masked assassins."

I studied Favian's face. His expression spoke of pain and sorrow. I knew he had served the previous king for many years. The two must have been great friends. When the king and queen were murdered, he no doubt was as hurt and shocked as Rowan himself. But Favian clearly handled it better.

We fell into silence for several moments, leaving me time to ponder. I wanted to test my theory that the Trilarians might not be entirely responsible for the atrocity, but trepidation nagged me. Favian may think of me as a traitor were I to suggest such a thing. But… if I was not brave, bold, if I did not ask questions, I would never know if anyone else had the same suspicions. And I would never be able to learn anything useful.

Now was as good of a time to ask as any.

"Favian… do you really think Trilaria was responsible?"

Favian stopped in his tracks, pulling me to a stop with him. His mouth opened and closed several times. "My queen—"

"What do we have here?"

Favian and I turned to face the speaker. It was Cassius, standing down the corridor from us, barely visible in the shadows. He slowly drew closer.

Favian drew back from me. "We were just conversing before Her Majesty retires to her chambers, Lord Cassius."

"Pardon my interruption, m'lord." Cassius clasped his hands behind his back. Was it in my imagination, or did I sense a bit of tension between the two? "It seemed to be a stimulating discussion. Pray tell, of what were you speaking?"

I narrowed my eyes at Cassius. "We were just discussing the late king and queen… how kind and good they were." It was stretching the truth, but I did not feel comfortable telling him what we had really been discussing.

I watched his shadowed face carefully. "Were you there the night they died—God rest their poor souls? Did you see those *cursed* Trilarians His Majesty spoke of?" I tilted my head, my eyes purposely wide and doe-like.

Cassius' normal scrutinizing gaze and blank expression told me nothing of his reaction to my question. "Yes. I was. And nay… I saw nothing." With another glance at Favian and a last look at me, Lord Cassius turned and walked away, disappearing back into the darkness.

Favian cleared his throat and turned to me again. "I believe I shall bid you goodnight, m'lady." He took my hand and kissed it. Before releasing me, he pulled me close and spoke low in my ear. "Mayhap you should not speak of that *certain* subject. For your own sake."

Then Favian turned and left me standing in the dark hall, his strange parting words echoing in my ears.

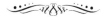

The chapel in Caelrith Palace was situated along on the western wall, allowing colorful stained-glass windows to line one side. The sun filtered through these windows like a thousand little rainbows in the daytime hours. At night, they turned dark, the moon-light lending them a silvery glow. Right now, it was somewhere in-between. The day was waxing into evening—nearly time for the evening meal, I was sure, but I could not bring myself to leave.

I knelt at the front of the chapel, not really praying, mostly thinking. I looked around the room, wondering over the previous night when Favian and I spoke, and then when Cassius approached.

Had Favian been about to say that he shared my suspicions, or that he disagreed? Then there were his strange words before he left. *Mayhap you should not speak of that certain subject. For your own sake.*

Did that mean that asking questions could put me in danger, not merely from Rowan's wrath, but also from someone else's? Whoever the killer—or *killers*—were?

Did Favian know something I did not?

Suddenly, the chapel door opened, and I turned to face the intruder.

It was Rowan.

I tried not to frown and forced my face to remain calm and placid. Polite. "Hello." I folded my hands in my lap, resisting the urge to fiddle with the pink fabric peeking through the slit in the skirt of my crimson gown.

We had yet to speak since that dreadful argument and the ensuing kiss. I doubted anything could be the same after such a thing happening between us. But exactly *how* things would be different was still a mystery.

"Your maids have been searching everywhere for you." He leaned against the front pew while I remained seated on the floor, which did nothing to aid my tension, so prevalent in the air you could almost taste it. I shifted on my knees, not liking him towering over me. It reminded me too much of those moments before our kiss.

"Do you not intend to come to supper?"

"Yes, I do. I just lost track of time."

He glanced around the chapel, taking in the expertly illustrated copy of the Holy Scriptures resting on a podium, the colored windows, the stone pillars supporting the arched, tiled ceiling. It was a pretty chapel, even if small.

"What are you doing in here?"

I forced back my sarcastic reply of, *"What do you think?"* and instead stated, "Praying. But mostly sitting in the silence."

He motioned to the pew on which he leaned, his eyebrows raised.

"Yes, of course, my king. Do sit." I did not look his way as he situated himself on the pew, but fidgeted in my own seat there on the floor. This was a most un-regal, un-queenly position, one my maids and Miss Merriweather would balk at. But I felt it would be more awkward for me to indecorously rise and take a seat beside him. So, I remained on the floor of the chapel near the altar, my feet lying to one side beneath my silk skirts.

"My mother loved this little chapel. She commissioned those windows." He gestured to them.

"'Tis indeed a very nice sanctuary, well suited for private worship."

He studied me, which made me want to squirm, but I carefully abstained from that. I looked at the pattern of the stones on the floor as if they were the most interesting thing in the world.

"You pray often, my queen?" Somehow, his use of *my queen* sounded more like an endearment today than just a title, and I blushed. Every time a word left his lips, all I could imagine was those same lips kissing mine.

"Yes, I try." Though I already knew the answer, I asked, "Do you?"

He looked away from me, shaking his head, his elbows resting on his knees and his fingers laced. "Nay. I find very little use in it." From the look in his eyes, the expression of bitterness he clearly was trying to hide, I got a sense of what his heart was saying: *If God cared about what I said to Him, my parents would still be here. I would not be married to you, a woman whom I do not love. Everything would be different.*

That look broke my heart. He was a man who was wealthy, powerful, a *king* with everything one could desire. He should be happy, yet he was not. He was broken, bitter, and angry, finding no solace in the riches around him.

Rowan needed more. Something that neither money nor power could attain for him.

"Well, I find very good use in it, sire. Joy, peace, comfort." I finally rose, feeling a small measure of boldness returning to me. I sat beside him on the pew—though careful not to sit too close. He watched me with that perpetual scowl of his.

I wondered for a moment how it must feel to frown all day. Surely it was exhausting. My fingers itched to smooth the lines from his brow and turn his lips up into a smile. I'd never seen him truly smile.

"Let me guess. You believe *I* could find use in it, as well?"

My eyes studied his face for a long moment. Carefully, I reached out and put my hand over his. "God can heal whatever it is you hold deep inside, Rowan." Again, I used his Christian name. It felt strange, yet at home on my lips. But I feared his reaction to both it and my touch.

He stared at me as though I were the most irritating creature on God's earth. But to my surprise, his blue eyes began to soften.

My cheeks burned as red as my gown under that steady gaze. I wanted to move my hand.

But I didn't.

Then the door opened.

We both turned to look, and I immediately removed my hand from his. Cassius stood at the entrance, one palm holding open the heavy wooden door. "There you are, Your Majesties. We have been searching for you both. Supper is now served in the Banquet Hall."

Rowan rose before I did, hastening to and out the door. I stayed seated for a moment longer, staring eye to eye with Cassius as he waited for me at the chapel door. Eventually, I rose and followed my husband to supper.

Rowan

There was blood.

Everywhere.

His mother's eyes stared at the ceiling, cold and distant, long gone from this world. That gruesome redness covered the front of her exquisite gown, changing its emerald green into a murky brown.

A flash of moonlight on metal.

A silver crest on a chain, against a backdrop of pitch black.

Firelight. Fighting. Pushing, shoving.

A cut, deep across his chest.

Pain, like searing fire.

A scream ripping from his throat.

Rowan's eyes flew open and he sat up, his covers damp with perspiration. He ran a hand through his hair and breathed deep, fighting against that now so common feeling of fear and anger seeping with unbearable grief.

He rose and went to his window, pushing open the shutters. The night breeze washed over his face, refreshing and soothing. Rowan closed his eyes and drew deep breaths.

Then the image of Arabella flashed through his mind.

His eyes immediately opened.

His father's voice floated through his memory, loud and clear, as if Rowan heard it there in the flesh.

"God tells us to love our wives as Christ loved the church. A man should want to love and protect his wife with everything in him. He should be willing to sacrifice his own life for hers."

Young Rowan had stared up at his father, disgusted by such mushy talk.

"So, Rowan," his father had continued, *"when you see me kiss your mother and show my love for her, when you see me protect her, care for her, you should know that is what all good husbands ought to do. And that is what* you *should do when you marry someday."*

"But I shan't ever marry, Father."

"Oh yes, you shall, son," his father had returned with a chuckle. *"One day, you shall meet a girl who will change your look on life. She will change many things. You will see."*

His father had been right about one thing. He *would* marry. He *had*. And he supposed he'd been correct about another thing, too.

Arabella was changing him, indeed.

It was what irritated him the most about her, often drawing him away from her, but also drawing him *to* her. She was the only person he had ever met who dared question him, who made him question himself about everything—his outlook on Trilaria, his own kingdom, love and marriage, God.

God. That particular *Person* had escaped his thoughts for years now, but more and more Rowan found himself thinking of Him.

Did He really care about Rowan? Why would a God who was supposedly so kind and just, the protector of His servants, allow good, innocent people to die? What had his parents ever done to deserve such a fate?

Rowan stared up at the stars, balling his fists atop the windowsill. "Why? Why is all I ask?" Rowan's jaw twitched from the tension under which he clenched it.

For a moment, he wondered if Arabella ever had the same thoughts. After all, she was the one torn from her home to marry a man she did not love. *Does she ever experience this wretched forsaken feeling?*

No. Surely his strong, stubborn, and steadfast wife did not. She was set in her beliefs. Her faith could not waver as his had.

I have never forsaken you.

A quiet voice whispered in his mind. Rowan knew straightaway that it was *the* Voice.

He growled and turned away like an angry child. He did not want to hear it, no matter his questions.

"I am not listening."

You are not now... But you shall.

Rowan strode across his room and shoved his limbs into some clothes. Then he opened his door, stalking angrily to the defensive wall of the palace and all but running up the spiraling stairs of his favorite tower, as if he could run away from that Voice. But deep inside, he knew he could not. He could never run away from the Voice, no matter how hard he tried. And he *had* tried

Rowan reached the highest keep in the tower, flinging open the door to find the very *last* thing he'd wanted to see: Arabella curled up on the stone bench just below the small window.

Suppressing a growl, he strode over to her, in such a foul mood that he planned to demand she leave at once. But then he noticed the slow and steady rise of her chest, her long, black lashes resting like feathery fans against her soft cheeks. She was asleep, still fully dressed in her red silk gown.

Blast Favian and his meddling. In his frustration, Rowan had forgotten his advisor had showed Arabella the tower.

Rowan sighed and crossed his arms, studying his wife. She lay with her head tilted at a most endearing angle against the stone, looking innocent and rather... perfect. Her hands lay curled against her chest, her knees drawn up. Her full, red lips twitched as she stirred and gave a little moan. For a moment, he feared her waking, and realized then that he did not wish to disturb her peaceful slumber—a thing he sorely lacked.

Rowan edged closer, irritatingly unable to make himself leave, or tear his gaze away. It occurred to him that sleeping on and against hard, cold stone could not be a very comfortable way to spend the night.

He could not leave her there.

Questioning the wisdom of his own notion, Rowan bent and lifted her into his arms, one beneath the bend of her legs, the other around her shoulders. She felt so light and small in his arms.

Arabella groaned and curled into him, raising her left arm to wrap it around his neck. She nuzzled her face into his chest like a kitten, her breath tickling the skin along his neckline. Rowan's heart jumped and beat an odd rhythm, pounding painfully against his ribs.

It was best to get her safely to her bed as soon as possible, for as much he hated to admit it, Rowan enjoyed the feeling of her in his arms.

He carried her all the way down the spiral staircase of the tower, finally emerging back into the night. A guard approached them and pulled up short, alarmed to see his king carrying his queen in his arms—in the dead of night no less. The knight bowed low. "Oh, Your Majesty—"

"Shhh," Rowan whispered, unable to lift a finger to his lips due to the weight in his arms. "Her Majesty sleeps."

The guard smiled and nodded, allowing Rowan to exit the wall before he resumed his dutiful trek around the allure.

Short of breath, he entered Arabella's room. The room was dark save for the pale moonlight coming through an open window.

Rowan paused beside the bed to look down at her face. She was so terribly peaceful and beautiful with her cheek nestled against him. Her eyelids twitched slightly. Was she dreaming? He sucked in a breath as she moved the hand she held at his neck, her fingers brushing through the bottom of his hair.

Rowan pulled back the bedclothes, which was quite an effort, considering he still held a person in his arms. He laid her down, dress and all, then covered her up. Her hair was styled at the nape of her neck. He knew next to nothing about women and their hair, but he figured such a style could not be comfortable for sleeping.

Though Rowan knew it was a bad idea, he reached down and carefully slid the carved bone pins from her hair, his fingers loosening the tight coil and sliding through her silken tresses. Now her dark hair fell over the bed like a waterfall, one thick piece covering part of her face. Why did the sight of her have him so transfixed? As if it had a will of its own, his hand gently smoothed the hair from her face.

His heart quickened once again, flooding with a deep longing he dared not acknowledge.

Rowan drew back as though she burned him, scowling down at the sleeping figure. She wielded control over him even when asleep!

Despising all women in general, he turned and stalked from the room. But when Rowan fell back into bed, he found that all he could do was stare in frustration at the door and wonder after his bride's dreams.

Chapter 18

Arabella

COME MORNING, I HAD VAGUE MEMORIES OF BE-
ing held. Warmth, strong arms around me, and a hard, steady beat,
like a drum, close in my ear. I thought I dreamed of Rowan sometime during the night, but I was unsure. Were those faint recollec-
tions of a dream? Or could they have been real?

I could not remember going to bed. I was sure that I had gone
to the tower. And why was I still dressed?

Surely… My cheeks blushed crimson at the thought. *Surely,
Rowan had not…*

Nay, I told myself, *you must have dreamed going to the tower. You
must have been so tired that you fell asleep in your room, fully dressed.
Rowan would not carry you to bed.*

But I remained unconvinced.

That day, the first of September, brought with it a cool front
that tamed the heat of summer. And, I soon realized, it also
brought about the departure of the king.

The sounds of men shouting and horses neighing drew me to
the courtyard. I picked up my skirts and stepped out the palace's
front door. The veil I wore over my netted hair blew in the breeze
as my eyes searched the scene before me. A company of twelve
knights prepared to ride out. They wore chainmail and armor, their
horses saddled and waiting, their reins held by baby-faced squires.
Every man either already had a weapon—or *weapons*—on him or
was busy acquiring them.

My eyes spotted Rowan mounted atop his brown gelding. His

squire sheathed the king's sword alongside his saddle while Rowan watched.

My heart leapt. Were they leaving for battle?

I made my way across the courtyard, careful not to hasten so as not to appear unladylike. I had already made myself enough of an object of ridicule with my scandalous display over the Trilarian captive. The knights stepped aside, allowing me passage with respectful bows. I briefly nodded my thanks but did not pause until I reached my husband's side. "Do you ride to battle, m'lord? Or is this simply another trip to the training grounds?" My heart thrummed with anticipation of his answer.

He glanced at me and quickly looked away. "I journey to the border, but not for battle—though I do have plans for that in the future." My stomach sank. "For now, I go to ensure the border is well secured. I do not wish for any more Trilarians to steal across."

I licked my lips, my heart fluttering. How far away was "the future" he spoke? Six months from now, three, one?

"I see." My eyes sought his face, but it remained turned from me. Why did he avoid my eye? One got the impression he was nervous, embarrassed even.

Could my suspicions this morning have been correct?

I studied him as he busied himself with his horse's reins, adjusted himself in the saddle, patted the horse's neck. "I shall return by the week's end, in time for court."

Court. My stomach churned at the reminder.

"Fret not, Arabella, for our safety, if that is why you look so distressed. It should not be a dangerous mission."

I jerked my head up. That was not the reason for my distress at all. But in all honesty, for all his faults and rough edges, I *did* wish him safe travels. I did not wish to see him dead. If I did, I would have allowed that cupbearer to give him the poisoned drink.

I smiled lightly and stepped forward to put a hand on the horse's smooth neck. "Then go with God, my king."

Rowan's brows knit together at my statement, and he offered me a single nod. Then, without another word, he turned his horse around, gave a shout to the men, and they thundered out the gate.

Rowan

His horse's hooves clomped over the dirt road as they exited Caelrith's protective walls. Cassius rode beside Rowan, his dark hair curling over his collar. His closest advisor was a serious man, grave and perceptive, and Cassius had served Rowan well, as he had his father. Rowan trusted him even more than Favian at times. When it came to major decisions concerning the kingdom, Cassius was the one Rowan turned to. In fact, he was the one who had advised Rowan to deal strongly with the Trilarians all those years ago.

Now Rowan had been warring with Trilaria for the past eight years, but neither side had ever gained much ground. It was an unending cycle of one side pulling, getting ahead, then the other pulling and gaining ground. Back and forth, but no one ever achieving victory.

Things had died down recently, since that day he'd been shot with an arrow. They had been at a tenuous standstill, with no battles and few skirmishes since Rowan had the troops pull back a month ago—all thanks to his wife's questions that gnawed his conscience. However, Rowan and Cassius had plans in the works. Plans that would reignite the war, and just possibly carry them through to victory. Finally.

Yet, as much as he wanted to see his enemies sent to meet their Maker, he did not feel the release to implement his plans at present. Not with the questions still swirling in his brain.

Was there really a difference between fighting to defend one's country and people, and fighting for his own revenge? And if so, which was he doing? Was he thinking of his country, or only himself?

Rowan ground his teeth and searched the countryside, looking for a distraction of some sort to occupy his mind.

"You seem distressed, sire," Cassius spoke up. "Tell me, what troubles your mind?"

Rowan's jaw ticked. "'Tis nothing Cassius. I am well."

Cassius eyed him, clearly not convinced. "Do you and the queen get along well? Is she an agreeable wife?"

"Yes, Queen Arabella and I get along well enough. And she is agreeable enough." Rowan avoided Cassius' black-eyed gaze, not happy with this subject. "I do not believe there is much more to be had in a marriage."

Cassius nodded. "Quite so, my king. Marriage, I believe, is merely a contract. For the peasants, a means of survival; for us of higher stature, a means to advance and gain, secure heirs for our lineage."

"And why have you not married, Cassius?"

The man shook his head and shrugged. "I have found no use for it thus far. I have a nephew whom I am close to that I have named my heir. He shall inherit my title and holdings." Cassius gave Rowan a long, questioning look. "Does such an heir seem imminent for you, sire?"

Rowan pursed his lips. "Nay, Cassius, such a one does not." He shouted for the men to speed up the pace, his captain echoed the reply, and Rowan spurred his horse onward, leaving Cassius in the dust.

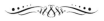

Arabella

For the week Rowan and his men were gone, the palace felt empty. Too empty.

How could it be that I *missed* Rowan? We saw each other regularly but spoke little throughout the day. However, apparently the time we did spend with one another was enough to make me miss his presence.

I was not sure whether to be disgusted or encouraged by the thought.

With the king away, I was in control of the palace and all of my time. I took advantage of that freedom by choosing to take every meal in my room, and three days after the king's departure, I invited Uncle Matthew to join me.

He arrived all smiles and good cheer, giving me a warm hug and a kiss on both cheeks as one of my attendants carefully shut the door on her way out. He held my face in his large, warm hands and grinned. "Being queen suits you well, my dear."

I smiled as he released me and motioned for him to take his

seat at my small table "Have you been well, Uncle? It feels an age since I've seen you." I took my place across from him.

"Yes, I have been very well, thank you." We paused conversation to join hands and pray over our meal, as had always been our custom. The familiar twinge of homesickness made me mourn anew my old life in that little house with my uncle, having real friends: dear Gloriana and Frederic. But as we finished our prayer, I lifted my chin and set my teeth, determined not to feel sorry for myself again. Mavis had been right all those months ago. I needed to embrace what I had been given. I needed to keep a bright outlook and not allow my sorrow to keep me from making the most of this new life.

"Who would have known that I would one day sup with the queen? My, I have advanced in this world." My uncle winked. "And who would have known that the she would be my own *niece*?" He sobered, putting his hand out to touch mine. "Your parents would be so proud of you."

My heart pricked at the mention of them, my mind drifting back to the moments when I bid each of them farewell.

I wiped at a tear and cleared my throat, pushing such depressing thoughts to the back of my mind.

"And how are you, Arabella? Does he treat you well?"

I considered that for a moment. My mind recalled all the times Rowan and I had argued, the times he had yelled at me, the time I was so angry I slapped him... But, when I really thought about it, Rowan had been good to me, in his own way. He had never harmed me physically, we had shared several pleasant discussions, and he never pressed me into doing anything I did not wish to do. He had never overstepped his boundaries, never asked me for anything other than companionship—albeit a tentative and shaky companionship—even if his advisors wished otherwise.

The only exception was when he had kissed me.

"I know of the king's harsh temper, and there is gossip around the palace saying that you *hit* him?"

I blanched at those words. *The whole palace knows of that?*

"He is good to me, uncle," I hurried to assure. "In truth, he is not as bad as I once believed. That isn't to that say he is not an ill-tempered lout who vexes me exceedingly." I shook my head and scoffed a laugh. "But we get along well enough, and I... I do not fear him as I did before. I honestly believe he would never inflict hurt upon me, no matter who else he hurts."

I looked up to find a sly grin curling my uncle's lips.

"What?"

"Nothing." He shook his head with a shrug, that annoyingly knowing smile on his lips. "Nothing at all."

Chapter 19

Rowan

ROWAN STARED AT THE CEILING OF HIS TENT, HIS hands folded behind his head. His squire sat just past the open flap, polishing and sharpening the king's sword. The boy was tall for his age, with brown hair growing past his ears and bright, young eyes. He was an apt learner, and his work pleased Rowan. Since becoming king, he had already gone through five squires, none of them ever able to do an adequate job, at least by his high standards. But this young lad—Leo, by name—if he did not get it in his head to do something incredibly stupid, was likely to stay on as Rowan's squire until he took the test of knighthood.

The boy's head lifted from his work to peer across the small camp. "Your Majesty?"

"Yes?" Rowan studied the intricate red and gold weave of his tent, unconcerned with whatever had caught the youth's attention.

"Something appears to be amiss. Captain Amaury is coming this way."

Rowan sat up and swung his legs off the cot, resting his fists on the edge. His best military captain stopped at the entrance of the tent, while Leo scurried away, taking the sword with him to resume his work elsewhere. Rowan waved the captain forward and the man entered, bowing deeply in respect.

"What is it, Amaury?"

"It appears a renegade band of Trilarians has crossed our borders. The village of Averill, west of here, is afire."

Rowan clenched his teeth and shoved off the cot, moving out

of the tent, his captain following. Arabella claimed he fought for his own interests, for vengeance, and her words had swayed him to doubt. But did this not justify his motives? Now he had assurance that the Trilarians had made an aggressive move, not against his soldiers, but his civilians, plundering the innocent. And he was going to do something about it.

See, Arabella, he silently shouted to her across the miles, *I do fight for the safety of my country! 'Tis not only for my desire for revenge.*

"We must ride there at once." Rowan gestured for Leo, who sat propped up against a tree, to bring him his sword and his horse. Soon Rowan was swinging himself into the saddle, accepting the sword from the boy. Amaury pulled up beside him atop his own warhorse, and the rest of his knights from Caelrith gathered.

"Move out!" The horses surged into motion, heading towards the smoke billowing on the horizon.

Rowan leaned forward, digging his heels into the poor beast's sides. Though he'd never admit it, Rowan had never really cared about the number of civilians harmed by the ravages of war. They were only peasants, after all. But so was Arabella. And her presence and careful inquiries were convicting him. He would ride to these people's aid, if only to quiet the voices in his head and appease his conscience.

He would prove Arabella wrong.

They bounded up to the village, stopping a short distance away to take in the scene. The small thatched roofed houses were aflame, fire consuming them with an unwieldy vengeance as a few soot-covered villagers attempted to put out the inferno. Their efforts were to no avail.

Knights bearing the crest of Trilaria emblazoned upon their tunics fought some of the braver villagers while the rest frantically searched for safety. A woman screamed somewhere, a blood-curdling cry of fright that rent the smoke-filled air. Rowan clenched his fists around his horse's reins, anger warming his veins.

He and his men charged forward with fierce battle cries, the Acunielian flag flapping in the wind as they thundered down the hill. The Trilarians whirled in surprise. They stopped what they were doing to rally into a tight line, waiting for the Acunielians and their irate king.

Rowan leapt from his horse before the beast could come to a full stop, swinging his sword to meet that of an enemy knight. He blocked the man's next swing, striking back only to have his blow deflected. Shoving against the man until he stumbled back, Rowan jabbed his sword forward. This time the blade met its mark perfectly. The Trilarian fell with a cry, clutching his pierced abdomen.

As Rowan turned to meet his next opponent, he spotted one of his men circling a Trilarian who used a village woman as a human shield. The young woman's eyes were wide with fear, her face ghostly pale.

A heavy blow from behind knocked Rowan off his feet and he collapsed with a thud. The enemy's sword angled down at Rowan's chest. He rolled to the right, the blade slicing into the dirt instead.

Collecting his sword, Roman jumped to his feet and charged. He drove the man back, back, back, towards a house raging with flames. Rowan swung his body in a circle, his sword arcing over his head. The Trilarian deflected the blow, but the force of the swing drove the man into the side of the burning building. His clothes instantly caught flame.

The man screamed and stumbled away. He fell to the ground, rolling around to put out the flames. As soon as he snuffed them out, Rowan was on him. He jumped atop the knight, putting his blade dangerously close to the man's burnt, blistering neck. Rowan leaned forward to stare into his eyes. A few months ago, he would have slit the man's throat without so much as a thought, but now, something held him back.

"Mercy, m'lord! Mercy!"

"Why should I let a low-life whelp like you live?"

The man gave no answer, but his eyes pleaded. For the first time in his life, Rowan felt compassion for a Trilarian, felt the need to extend mercy to another living soul. He panted hard, his nostrils flaring as he dealt with his conflicting emotions.

Finally, Rowan shoved himself upright, jerking his sword away. Before the man could rise, Rowan placed the tip of his sword beneath the knight's chin. "Go back to your superior and inform him that the King of Acuniel shall soon return—a day you all shall rue. And may you always remember the day *the Lord* spared you," he bit out, for truly, that was who had saved the man's life this day, not Rowan.

When they returned to the military camp, Rowan informed Cassius that they would further develop their plans for their greatest attack on Trilaria as soon as they returned to Caelrith. Before the year's end, Rowan would be back to this border. He would put the Trilarians in their place. Once and for all.

Chapter 20

Arabella

MY LEGS ACHED, KEEPING SLEEP FAR FROM MY grasp. I tried walking around my bedchamber, I tried praying, I even tried running in place in an effort to stretch the stiff muscles, but nothing helped. No matter how I laid, I could not get comfortable. It was enough to drive me mad.

Finally, I gave up and slipped out of bed. I donned the first pair of slippers I found, shrugged into my dressing gown, and took up the candle from my bedside table. I stuck the wick into the fire the chambermaid had lit for me, waiting for the small wax pillar to ignite before sticking it back in its brass holder.

Though it neared the end of the week, Rowan and his men had yet to return. There would be no one to impede my nighttime wandering—unlike last time, when I emerged to find Rowan sitting by the fire.

Exiting, I wandered through the darkness with no clear destination in mind. My candle was like one lone star in a pitch black, moonless sky. It revealed next to nothing, but thanks to a few torches that still blazed along the shadowed corridors, I was able to find my way.

I reached the walkway with the view of the courtyard and city beyond. Its tall, arched windows formed by narrow pillars along one side allowed moonlight to filter through in long, silvery slants across the floor. The spaces between lay in heavy shadow, the light blocked by the stone pillars. I went to one arched window and rested my hands, and my candleholder, atop the sill. I lifted my face to admire the twinkling stars, their celestial bodies forming pictures that had guided many a traveler through the night.

My eyes moved down to the city, past the palace's tall walls. *I wonder where Row—*

"It appears we both suffer the same ailment again."

I squealed and jumped to face the speaker.

Rowan.

"Oh, 'tis you." I realized then that I had clutched the front of my nightdress in my fright, and quickly released it to pull my robe tighter about me.

"Insomnia," he finished, ignoring my terror and my words. He sat in the sill of one arched window—how had I not noticed him there?—one leg drawn up inside it, the other hanging down. He looked so at peace, so casual sitting there with his head relaxed against the pillar, languidly scuffing his boot against the ground. The position and the moonlight only heightened his good looks, making me all the more unsettled by his sudden presence.

"When did you return? I knew not of it."

"Two hours ago. You had already retired for the night."

Had he inquired after me? If he had not thought me already asleep, would he have come to greet me?

I nodded and edged closer. Rowan looked out at Caelrith, apparently lost in thought, so I did not speak further, even though many questions circled my mind. What had transpired during his trip? What was this plan he had alluded to before he left? Had he missed me as I had missed him? Instead, I enjoyed the cool breeze against my cheeks and the almost companionable silence that had settled over us.

That silence stretched until Rowan abruptly turned to me. "What is it like, out there," he nodded with his chin towards Caelrith, "for ones such as what you used to be?"

I was shocked, to say the least, at his sudden question. Still, hope lifted my spirit. Could his heart truly be softening toward his people and their needs?

"For peasants, you mean?"

"Yes." He turned back to the city, and I desperately wished to know what he was thinking. Unfortunately, I was not blessed with such mind reading capabilities.

I settled back into my previous position, considering how to respond. The images of my mother and father, my uncle, Gloriana,

Frederic, Ellyn, Farah, all washed through my mind, bringing with them the stabbing pain of loss. However, I discovered that pain was becoming less sharp with each passing day.

"It is hard," I said at last. "For the common folk, every day is a battle for survival. From the moment we—*they* are born, they must struggle for everything. For food, for shelter, for clothing. It all must be worked hard for, earned through toil. At times, even that is not enough."

My voice fell quiet, dark memories coming to mind. "I have known many a person to die from starvation or a lack of proper shelter. While I cannot condone theft, it is no wonder why many turn to crime to survive."

I sighed, shaking off my melancholy. "The life of a peasant is challenging, that 'tis certain, but it is not without joys. I have many fond memories from my childhood."

"Did you have friends… before?" Meaning *before* I became his wife.

"Yes, I did. Gloriana was my best friend." *Frederic, too, but 'tis best if I do not mention him.* After the Trilarian man's execution, I did not wish to draw attention to my friend.

"The blonde from church that day, whom you asked to speak to?"

"Yes, that was her."

"You never told me of your parents," he said suddenly, his change in topic jarring. "I shared with you the story of how my parents died. Now I wish to know of yours."

My parents… He wanted me to speak of those terrible days I wished I could erase. Those memories haunted me enough already without having to share them with him. But, I reasoned, I *had* asked him of his parents' deaths, made him relive his own aching memories. Did I not owe him this much?

I took a deep breath of the cool night air before recalling every painful detail. "When I was fourteen, my father was conscripted into your army." My mind conjured the image of my father bidding farewell to my mother and I, his dark eyes, so like my own, filled with tears. I had hugged him around the waist, begging him not to leave me. And he had promised he would return.

"He was killed not a month after he left." A tear found its way down my cheek and I blinked back the others that wished to follow. "My mother could not handle the loss, so it was little wonder that she took sick soon after."

I glanced over to find Rowan focusing on me with attentive eyes, so I continued. "Do you remember that winter? It was one of the coldest in decades. With most of the food going to the troops at the front, the people were left with insufficient supplies to weather the bitter winter season. My mother did not admit it to me, but... I was smart and I knew. She was giving most of her food to me, often going without entirely." Another tear slipped down my cheek, running all the way to the neckline of my nightgown. My mother's beautiful face appeared in my mind. I could almost feel her cold hand gripping my own.

"She lost her strength and took ill. I stayed by her side for days until she finally left me. She told me not to cry, that she would be with Father—" My voice cracked, and I pressed a palm to my mouth, turning away. He could not see me like this. He could not! Rowan had caught me crying once already; there was no need for him to see my tears a second time.

I sensed him moving to touch me, and I put out an impeding hand. "Nay. I am well." My tears slipped silently down my face. I would not allow myself to make any sound, keeping my lips clamped tight, my teeth clenched. After a few moments, I reigned in my tears and turned around, finding that he had slid down from his seat on the window ledge and now stood before me. I offered him a weak smile, hoping to convince him I was as well as I claimed.

My husband's face looked genuinely concerned, sad. This expression of empathy was so different for him that it startled me. His eyes caught some of the silvery moonlight and glinted like a calm, crystal sea, though they were as serious and grave as a violent storm. "Arabella... I knew not. Your father... Are you saying that 'tis *my* fault?"

"Nay." I shook my head. "Though I did once blame you."

"Now I understand your reluctance to be here. You must hate me."

"Nay, Rowan, I do not."

"So, you forgive me?"

I smiled slyly and shrugged. "I suppose."

His brow shot up. "*Suppose*, my queen?"

I laughed, shaking my head and realizing that the word had

become a sort of silly, private joke between us. *Strange to think we even have such a thing.*

I met his eye again, all teasing replaced by sincerity. "Truly, Rowan. I forgave you long ago."

He kept my gaze for a long moment, saying nothing, while that statement—my confession of forgiveness—settled between us.

It was then that I realized our shocking similarities. I had once thought we were so completely different, but now I realized we were more alike than anyone would think.

We both had lost our parents at young ages due to tragedy.

We both held resentment and hatred in our hearts because of it.

We both blamed God for the bad things we believed He had allowed to happen to us.

And we had both unexpectedly been crowned monarchs of Acuniel.

I felt more connected to Rowan in that moment than I ever had before. For the first time, I was able to look at him without any prejudice and see what he felt, what he thought, why he did what he did.

Suddenly, I did not see the strong, powerful king that many feared. I saw a man broken, confused, and searching for answers.

My heart ached. How could I have had him so wrong, when I had known, firsthand, the same pain that bound his soul?

In that moment, it was as if I were one with him, of his own flesh. For I suddenly *knew* him, understood him like no other earthly being could.

And it frightened me.

I shivered under the weight of all that realization hitting me at once.

"Are you cold?" Before I could protest, Rowan's fingers had unfastened his cape and he was settling the dark velvet around my shoulders. As he finished, his broad hands ran across and down the edge of my shoulders. His scent filled my nose, pleasant and warm, distinctly male. His breath washed over my ear, his head dangerously close to mine.

My heart jolted against my ribs. I could not move... And, it seemed, neither could he. We stood there feeling the warmth of the other, breathing the same air, relishing in our closeness. That inconceivable connection I had felt with him just moments before was only heightened by his nearness. Part of me wanted the wild, spine-tingling sensation of being close to him to continue. But the rest of me wanted it to end right away.

Then I became aware of his lips brushing against my ear.

Suddenly, I feared those lips coming down to kiss mine and I knew I had to break this maddening trance.

It had to end. Now.

I pulled away enough to see his face. His eyes were clenched shut. "I… I believe I may sleep now."

The trance ended, like a piece of glass shattering.

Rowan opened his eyes. They were dark with a look that sent further chills up my spine. "Yes. Of course, go."

I turned and hurried into the dark, forgetting my candle and its holder entirely, the flame long since snuffed by the wind.

Something had just shifted between us, and nothing could ever be the same. That connection I had felt was too powerful to undo. That moment—sharing each other's warmth, standing so close we could practically hear one another's heartbeat—was too deep to forget. And though we had not kissed… from the feeling I got when his lips barely touched me… Rowan may as well have kissed me breathless.

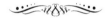

Dressed in my gold gown, my gold and ruby crown resting on my brow, my maids and I walked through the halls of the palace. The rulers of each province had arrived that morning for court, and it was once again my turn to sit quietly and listen to the long list of topics that would be debated and discussed amongst the men.

We stopped by the back door of the Great Hall where King Rowan waited and bowed low curtsies. I looked up at him as I rose, uncertain of how things would be between us. After that moment on the walkway, we'd avoided one another. Again. We saw each other at meals, but never spoke. Every time I saw him, I relived that moment. Was he doing the same?

"My queen." He bowed to me.

"My king." Must my voice tremble so?

He offered his arm and I took it as my maids dispersed, leaving us to wait for our entrance to be announced. My heart raced, my flipping stomach causing such nausea I was sure I would retch at any second. My free hand fluttered to my belly.

Rowan leaned to whisper in my ear, his breath tickling. "Fret not, Arabella. You shall win them all over, I am sure." He straightened and gave a nonchalant shrug. "And if you do not, we can always have their heads."

I gasped in horror.

He laughed. He actually *laughed*. I had never dreamed I would hear such a sound coming from this man's mouth. "I was only teasing."

I blinked and faced the door again. *Wonders never cease.*

The doors opened, held by two liveried servants. "All rise, in honor of Their Majesties, King Rowan and Queen Arabella." The nobles stood as a unified wave of bodies, bowing low as moved to take our thrones.

I settled into mine with all the queenly dignity I could muster. It was imperative I make a good impression this week. My reputation was already damaged enough thanks to my early departure on my first day in court, and then my scandalous display over the Trilarian captive. Rumors ran rampant, some suggesting me to be a Trilarian sympathizer. Though it was true, I could not allow it to be common knowledge or the kingdom would label me a traitor and I would be deposed. Such a scenario would not end prettily for me at all.

As Lord Cassius stood and read off the first item of business—taxes, again—I tried to sit and take stock of what was being said so that I would have full knowledge of it, even if my opinions were supposed to go unstated. Unfortunately, I glazed over after a few minutes. Such talk was hard to focus on.

I looked over the crowd, already knowing that the noblewomen cast surreptitious glances in my direction any chance they found. When Lord James of Azmar stood to add something to what Rowan had just said, my eyes found his wife, Lady Azmar, and their daughter, Lady Katherine. Both women stared at me without shame, their mouths drawn into identical frowns. Clearly Katherine inherited more than just her facial features from her mother.

I boldly met their stares for several seconds before casually moving on. A while later, my ears perked at the sound of a far more interesting topic, bringing my attention back to the dais.

"We must speak of this recent offense by the Trilarians," Lord Cassius said, rising from his seat beside the king. The room erupted in shouts of agreement from several of the nobles.

"Yes." Rowan punctuated the word with a rap of his fist on the arm of his throne. "That renegade group's attack on the village of Averill shall not go unanswered."

"The king himself very narrowly escaped with his life!"

Alarm rang through my heart. Why had Rowan not mentioned this the other night? He glanced at me, sensing my distress, before returning his attention to Lord Cassius.

"The king and I have been plotting a battle that could end this feud once and for all, with us finally receiving justice for our dearly departed king and his wife—may God rest their souls."

Many of the noblemen cheered, but a few hung back, uncertain. One stood up. "Your Majesty," he called, his hands put out in a pleading gesture, "are you certain this is the way to proceed? The people are weary. Has the war not done all it could do these last eight years? What shall more bloodshed and strife do at this point? Is it not possible that we may now reach a treaty?"

Rowan rose to his feet, pointing a finger at the man. "Nay, Lord Manfred, you are out of bounds. I believe I know what is best for our people." He looked to me meaningfully. "Those men killed innocent people, set the entire village ablaze, accosted the vulnerable. This shall not stand! We will reignite this war and finish it once and for all."

Cheers erupted again from those who agreed. Another lord stood up. "What would you have us do, sire?"

Rowan surveyed the room of nobles waiting with patient ears. "All knights at your disposal must be called upon, leaving only the very minimum to protect your estates. Serfs from each of your domains shall be required. We will even hire mercenaries if needed. But… we shall speak more of this later." Rowan cast me a pointed glance. "On the morrow, when the women are not present."

Unease fluttered inside me as I turned my eyes to my lap. My window of time to learn the truth about the royal murders had just shrunk. If I was to help end this war, it would have to be soon… Or not at all.

Chapter 21

WHILE THE KING AND HIS NOBLES FURTHER planned the dreaded attack the following day, I hosted a banquet for the ladies of court. I briefed the cook and her staff on the menu well beforehand, and as it drew close to time, servants laid out the meal in an elegant display in the Banquet Hall. The smell of the food drifted to my nostrils, making my stomach churn in hunger on top of the anxiety already twisting it into knots.

Soon the noblewomen would file in, their judgements at the ready.

It was a terrifying prospect.

Rowan's words of encouragement came back to me, providing courage to steady my heart. *Fret not, Arabella. You shall win them all over, I am sure.*

I smiled to myself, taking a deep, calming breath.

A servant, his face stoic and posture perfectly erect, opened the doors to my guests. "Lady Hadwisa of Ellswick."

A young woman a few years older than I entered and curtseyed low. "Your Majesty, 'tis an honor to meet you."

I nodded with all the grace I could muster. "'Tis an honor to make your acquaintance as well, Lady Hadwisa."

The noblewoman moved on, and another approached. She had a bulbous nose, sharp, disapproving eyes, and a mole on her jutting chin. "Lady Maynild of Glasborough," the servant announced.

"My queen." Lady Maynild offered a stiff curtsy.

"You honor me with your presence, Lady Maynild."

She nodded curtly, not offering any hint of a smile, and walked away.

"Lady Allis of Dallin."

My heart jumped. *Dallin? That was where the king and queen were killed.*

The lady curtsied the most elegant, graceful curtsy I had ever seen and gave a friendly smile. "Your Majesty, 'tis an honor to meet you."

"'Tis an honor to meet you as well, Lady Allis."

She rose and clasped her delicate hands at her waist. "If you will permit me to say so, my queen, I can see why His Majesty wished to wed you." Her pretty brown eyes sparkled beneath long, thick lashes and perfectly arched brows.

I blushed at her flatteries. "You are too kind." She bobbed another curtsy and started to turn, but I reached to stop her. "Lady Allis. I was wondering if you would do me the honor of sitting at my right hand?" I leaned forward and smiled. "I think you and I could be good company—and 'tis not just because you complimented me." *Or because you may have information I seek...*

She laughed softly, in a way that made her eyes crinkle at the corners. "Of course, Your Majesty. I would be honored."

Lady Allis moved on and I turned to meet the next guest. My stomach dropped to see Lady Katherine and her mother floating toward me. "My *queen.*" Katherine emphasized the word with a slight curl of her lip as she and her mother curtsied.

I lifted my chin, gathering every drop of queenly confidence I possessed. "My ladies. So good of you to come."

They smiled sugary smiles, the sort that men would say were friendly, but we women know to be the cover for intense dislike. I smiled back as genuinely as I could. *Kill them with kindness—remember, Arabella?*

"Are you enjoying your new role as queen?" Katherine took in my deep blue and gold gown, and the royal wedding ring adorning my left hand.

"Yes, I am, thank you." And I actually meant it. *Imagine that...*

"How fortunate for you." With that, she and her mother swiveled away and crossed to the other side of the room.

I repeated the process, nodding and smiling then nodding and smiling again, more times than I could count. Before long, my neck ached, and my cheeks were sore from so many smiles. Eventually, I was able to make my way to the high-backed chair at the head of the main table. Lady Allis waited behind the chair at my right.

Once I had taken my seat, I motioned for my guests to do the same. The ladies flounced into their chairs in near perfect unison. I envied their composure. Mavis said I possessed natural grace and poise, but I doubted it was anything like what these noblewomen possessed.

After I took my first bite, they followed, lapsing into the quiet conversation of highborn women and eating their food in mincing bites. Miss Merriweather had educated me in etiquette, of course, and usually it came easy. But today I felt as awkward as a bow-legged horse.

My eyes moved over the crowd of fifty or so women, observing their fluid movements and polite conversations. Lady Katherine kept glancing my way, her eyes revealing her resentment.

I turned my attention to Lady Allis and the much more important matter at hand. "So, your husband is the Lord of Dallin?"

She delicately wiped the corners of her mouth. "Yes, Geoffrey—my husband—he inherited the title after his father's death."

"From what my husband tells me, his parents died at Dallin castle."

Lady Allis' eyes widened into glassy pools of brown, and she shook her head. "Oh, yes, I am afraid they did."

"Were you there that terrible night?"

She shook her head. "Nay, m'lady. I had not yet married Geoffrey, and that was when his father was still alive. But I have heard the story from my husband." One alabaster hand fluttered to the base of her throat. "'Twas terrible, indeed. No one cares to stay in that room anymore. Not even the servants will enter to clean it. 'Tis as if the king and queen's ghosts haunt the place."

We continued talking, changing the subject to Lady Allis' family. She was a year older than I was, and completely in love with her husband. They had been married five years, six come spring.

"Have you any children?"

Her eyes lit up. "Oh, yes! A four-year-old little boy named Geoffrey, after my husband, and a two-year-old girl named Anna." Her hand rested against the bodice of her emerald gown. "And another on the way." Indeed, looking down at the young woman's abdomen, I now noticed it was rounded into the smallest of bumps. "I believe this one is another boy." That distinct motherly glow radiated from her face as she smoothed her hand over her growing child.

"That is wonderful news. Congratulations!"

As the banquet continued, my mind continually strayed, veering off to ponder another topic.

I had to find a way to question Lady Allis further. I wanted to know if her husband, or anyone else, saw anything out of the ordinary that fateful night. Was anyone seen coming or going? And if so, from or toward which direction? Rowan had mentioned, though, that the masked men vanished into the night without a trace.

Was it possible that someone *already in* Dallin Castle was responsible? I felt nauseous at the thought. Yet it made sense.

And if someone within the king's court had been behind the murders, it also made sense that the same individual, or group of individuals, was behind the attempt on Rowan's life.

Certainty settled in the pit of my stomach, chasing away my appetite. I pushed aside my food and requested water from a passing servant.

That had to be it. Whoever was behind the murders of Rowan's parents was now out to get him. Why they were only just now trying to kill him instead of doing it years ago, I did not know. But surely the two killers were one in the same.

The need for the truth was becoming more dire by the second.

After the meal, I stood with Lady Allis at the back of the room while the others mingled. Many stopped to speak to me for a moment, but Lady Allis never left my side, offering conversation that went beyond the obligatory pleasantries of everyone else. Already, her companionship was sewing shut the hole of loneliness in my heart. I silently thanked God for it.

After the latest group of women left us, Lady Katherine sauntered up. She pulled me close for a hug as though we were old friends. "My dear Arabella."

Lady Allis' eyes widened at Katherine's disrespectful use of my Christian name.

"You know, Allis, the queen and I were both candidates for queen. We became quite close." Her spiteful eyes belied her bright smile. "And how is our dear Rowan?"

I stifled a gasp. How dare she speak of him so casually?

Lady Allis blanched.

"Oh, do not look so scandalized, Allis." Lady Katherine flapped her hand. "He and I were practically betrothed." With a glance at me, she added, "Before the absurd candidate business started and he apparently changed his mind."

I snapped my mouth shut lest I say something I would regret. The woman had better watch her step. The fact was, he had *not* married her. He was *my* husband, not hers. Not to mention, her behavior was incredibly bold and disrespectful.

"Are you enjoying married life, Arabella?" Her eyes drifted to the bodice of my gown. "Could it be that we have a little prince or princess on the way?"

"Lady Katherine!" Allis cried. "Is that entirely appropriate?"

She only pinned me with her too-perceptive eyes, waiting for my answer.

"Nay… I am afraid not." My cheeks burned in embarrassment, even as my ire boiled upward, threatening to overflow.

Katherine stuck out her lower lip. "Aw, what a shame." Then she drew her chin up and flashed a grin, as if we both held some special knowledge no one else did. "Rowan is quite the romantic partner, is he not? We did have our moments." Her arrogant tone dripped with innuendo.

My mouth fell slack and a peculiar pang shot through my heart and traced down to my stomach. Lady Allis blanched further still—if that were possible—and one hand came to her mouth. Looking very pleased with herself, Katherine dipped a quick curtsy. "Your *Majesty*. Excuse me." Then she turned and strutted away, her curvaceous hips swinging sultrily.

Allis gasped, indignant. "What an awful, disagreeable woman!"

I pursed my lips, my eyes following Katherine across the room.

How dare she speak in such a way! How terribly lewd and uncouth! She spoke as if she and Rowan were *lovers* or some such terrible nonsense.

Wait.

They could not have been… Right? It could not be possible that she and Rowan were once involved. But what could she mean by, "*We did have our moments*"?

Ugh! *Involved?* Bile rose in my throat, and fury burned my chest. Picturing Lady Katherine in Rowan's arms—completely and utterly disgusting!

Nay. It was a preposterous notion. She had to be lying, or at least making something simple out to be something much more. If what she said were true, Rowan would have married her long ago. And he had not. He had married me.

Not her.

Me.

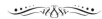

That particular subject stayed on my mind for the rest of the afternoon and evening. Surely, they could not have been… *together* as her words suggested.

I entered our sitting room, ready to go straight to bed, and found Rowan heading into his own chamber. "Oh! Hello." My stomach jumped at seeing him unexpectedly. Especially since he had been the constant object of my thoughts for so many hours.

He let go of his chamber door and faced me. "Hello. How did your luncheon fare?" He crossed his arms and studied me, his eyes kind. They were looking that way more and more often, I found.

"It went well. Thank you for asking."

He smiled softly, sending an odd jolt through my chest, and turned to enter his room.

I have to ask him. "Rowan?"

He stopped and turned to me again, head cocked in question. "Yes, *Arabella?*"

I had used his given name again. Why was I suddenly feeling at liberty to do that?

"Um, well, I was just going to say that," I stared at his feet, unexpectedly nervous, "Lady Katherine all but stated that the two of you were… *involved* at one time." I dared to look up at him.

Rowan's mouth hung open, his eyes hard as stone. "How dare

she say such a thing?" He whirled away, scraping a hand through his brown hair. "The nerve of that woman!"

"She said that the two of you were once 'practically betrothed'."

His growing anger startled me. I took a step back, starting to regret bringing up the subject.

"Her father wished that, and so did she, but *I* did not. What gave you cause to believe this? Did she say more?"

I nodded, feeling sick again at the picture of them together. "She claimed that the two of you 'had your moments'—whatever that was supposed to mean."

He scowled, confusion darkening his face. Then something seemed to dawn, and he looked away, scrubbing a hand over his jaw. "Oh...The kiss."

"You *kissed* her?"

"Nay!" He threw out a hand in defense then put it to his chest. "*She* kissed *me*! When she supped with me that night, she kissed me before I could stop her."

"Oh. I see."

"I did not enjoy it," he put in, as if it were important that I be aware of the fact.

Was it important?

"I did not insinuate that you did." I lifted my chin.

He nodded once, stiffly, and straightened his tunic. "Good." Rowan started, for the third time now, to enter his room.

I felt oddly pleased to know he did not enjoy Katherine's kiss. But I could not help but wonder if he enjoyed ours...

"Rowan." I reached out to touch his arm before I could think better of it. He stilled and slowly turned to look at me, the hair hanging over his forehead making him all the more handsome. My breath caught in my throat.

I had been intending to ask how he felt about kissing me, or say I was glad that he did not enjoy Katherine kissing him, but now... anything like that seemed embarrassingly ridiculous.

I swallowed, this sudden nearness sending my heart into a gallop. *What were you thinking, Arabella?*

"Goodnight."

He watched my hand as I removed it from his arm, a soft smile teasing at his lips. He met my eye again. "Goodnight, Arabella." Then he turned and disappeared inside his bedchamber.

Chapter 22

Rowan

ROWAN'S EYES FOLLOWED THE MANY COUPLES turning and swaying in a complicated dance across the Great Hall, following the lavish supper not an hour before. Their bodies moved in tandem to the sound of the minstrels' song filling the air. Favian and Lord Geoffrey flanked him at the edge of the dance floor, carrying on easy conversation.

"And how are your children doing, Geoffrey?" Favian asked the young Lord of Dallin.

Geoffrey beamed with pride. "They are quite well, thank you, Lord Favian. Little Geoffrey—our eldest—he thinks he is already old enough to become a knight. Though he is but four years of age, he plays in the courtyard with a wooden sword our Master of Arms made for him last Christmastide. He goes about smacking my knights in the leg, telling them to fight him." Geoffrey chuckled. "He gets very cross if they do not."

Geoffrey and Favian laughed. Rowan, arms crossed over his broad chest, grinned and laughed as well. The action was like a refreshing breath of air.

His companions' laughter stopped. They stared at him as though he'd suddenly sprouted a second head.

"What?"

Favian shook his head, astonished. "I cannot remember the last time I heard you laugh." A mischievous smile stretched across his lips. "To what do we owe this pleasure?"

He could see through his advisor's expression as easily as if the man were made of glass. Arabella. Favian was suggesting Arabella was the reason for his lightness.

"Nothing, Favian." Rowan cleared his throat and focused on the dancing couples. Was it really so odd for him to laugh or smile? Did there have to be reason for it?

Eventually, the two men left, and Rowan stood alone. He accepted a cup from a servant and sipped at the watered wine. His eyes gravitated in a certain direction, of their own accord, and found Arabella engaged in conversation with Geoffrey's wife, Allis, and another young woman whose name he could not recall. The candlelight sparkled off her crown, the gold, leafy one that suited her so well. Her dress was the color of an autumn sunset, with gold embroidery that perfectly accented her dark eyes and hair. A wisp of hair had slipped from her otherwise immaculate hairstyle, curling at her neck. Rowan's fingers suddenly itched, as if longing for the chance to brush that hair from her skin.

He took an extra-large gulp of his drink and pursed his lips as he swallowed. She glanced at Rowan as she shifted her stance, putting her back to him. He looked away, embarrassed she had noticed his staring, but his eyes only moved right back. And he could not find it in himself to look away again.

His heart warmed at the thought of their conversation the night before. She had seemed so concerned by the notion that he and Lady Katherine were once romantically involved. The look on her face when she believed he'd willingly kissed the insufferable woman was priceless.

Yet, as much as it amused him, it disturbed him. He'd been so afraid of what Arabella would think. But why did it matter so much to him?

He remembered the way she stopped him from entering his room, could still feel the warmth of her hand glowing on his upper arm. And when she told him goodnight, he'd nearly—

Rowan handed off his empty drink to a servant, accepting another immediately after. He tossed back half the goblet in a single gulp.

He did *not* like the direction of his thoughts. It was so unlike him to care like this. The last time he had cared about anyone, he had lost them, buried them in the ground. And he wasn't aiming to repeat that.

But again—Rowan groaned inwardly—*again*, his eyes sought

out Arabella. She was still where he had last seen her, chatting with a few noblewomen. He could not help but notice how the fit of her gown accentuated her slender but well-curved waist. Standing with the light from the iron chandeliers glowing down on her, making the deep hues of her gown shine, while she held herself with perfect queenly poise, admittedly stole his breath.

A man walked past, obscuring his view of his queen, and Rowan leaned to look around him.

Then someone else stepped directly in his way.

He stood straight and met Cassius' eye. His advisor turned to look over his shoulder, his gaze apparently finding Arabella and lingering there for a long moment. Too long.

"Enjoying the view, my king?"

Rowan ground his teeth. *The man should keep his words—and eyes—to himself.* "I do not believe that is any business of yours, Cassius." With one last swig of his drink, and a pointed glare, Rowan stalked away.

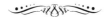

After evading Cassius and his prying, Rowan found a new place to stand, near the dais. He studied the Hall and spotted Lord James of Azmar. Which reminded him... Katherine had absolutely no right to intimate such a connection between them, and she would have to be punished for it. However, he'd decided not to make a scene. He would do something about the situation at the end of the week, after court dismissed, unless she pressed him into action sooner.

"Good evening, sire," said a sugary-sweet voice from at his left. Lady Katherine.

"Good evening." He kept his eyes the crowd. *Mayhap if I ignore her, she will go away.*

No such luck.

She moved to stand in front of him. "Are you well, sire?" Lady Katherine glanced over her shoulder, searching for someone before returning her gaze to him. "Are you happy in your recent marriage?"

Rowan finally looked down at her, irritation rising. "Yes, my lady, I am quite happy." The statement left his mouth without thought, but was it true? He was happy enough, he supposed, but *truly* happy, as he'd once been years ago? Of that, he was not entirely sure.

Her expression remained pleasant, but her eyes visibly darkened, clearly unpleased with his answer. "I see." Her pale eyes swept over him, from his waist up. "You look well, Your Majesty, if I may say."

"Ac—" An arm looped through his, cutting his words short. Arabella.

"Good evening, Lady Katherine. I trust you have had a fine day?"

The woman clamped her lips together. "Yes. Thank you, my queen." She cocked her head and flashed a grin that did not quite reach her eyes. "I trust you have had the same?"

"Yes, I have," Arabella replied brightly, "thank you for asking." The two remained locked in an unwavering stare until the tension grew so thick one could slice it with a knife. "If you will excuse me, I wish to speak with my husband," Arabella finally said.

"Of course." Katherine curtsied, her jaw clenched tight, and sauntered away.

Rowan angled his head at Arabella, who still held onto him with a vise grip. "You wished to speak with me, wife?"

She looked up at him, blinking. "Not really." She flattened her lips in displeasure. "I saw her speaking with you and thought I would aid you in ridding yourself of her." Her dark, well-shaped brows lifted. "Unless you *wished* to speak with her."

He laughed lightly. "I most certainly did not. I thank you for the rescue." Her fingers curled against his sleeve. He was enjoying her touch far more than he wanted.

Rowan arched a brow at her. "You may let go now."

Her beautiful eyes—the ones that had captured his attention that first night in the Banquet Hall—rounded as she looked down and noticed her possessive grip. Her cheeks colored prettily, and she drew away. "Oh... forgive me. I did that to... Well, I think you understand."

Why did he find her flustered state so amusing? "Yes. That I do." Her blush spread to the far-too-alluring neckline of her gown. He gave her a lopsided, teasing grin. "There is no need to be ashamed, my queen. You may hold onto me if you wish."

Arabella's mouth gaped. "I believe I will leave now." Then she gathered her skirts and hurried away, leaving Rowan staring after her, laughing for the second time that night.

Perhaps Favian was right. Perhaps Arabella *was* the reason for this lightness in his heart.

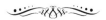

Arabella

I lingered in the Great Hall for another half hour or so, but quickly tired of the reveling. My eyelids drooped heavily over my eyes, my legs weak and sore from dancing. I needed sleep or I would soon become poor company indeed.

Thankfully, the party was nearing its end by the time I excused myself. I slipped out the back door and wearily ambled toward my room. My fingers brushed along the cold wall as I walked.

A scuffling sound froze my steps, just before I entered the stairwell that would lead to the floor on which my chamber was located. The hair on my neck stood on end. I turned at the sound of footsteps approaching from behind.

A figure appeared from among the thick shadows.

Lord Hugh.

He staggered toward me, his clothes a rumpled mess, the pungent scent of alcohol following him like a cloud. His lips curved in a catlike grin. "Hello, my pet." Lord Hugh took another halting step. Then another, and another. I matched each step, backing away. "Are you enjoying playing queen?" His words slurred together.

"Lord Hugh." Anxiety knit my stomach. I had to get away from him. Would he pursue me if I ran?

"Pardon me, m'lord, but I must be going." I lifted my skirts and turned to enter the stairwell. "Goodnight."

With a speed and sharpness that defied his current state, Lord Hugh seized my wrist. "Where are you going, Your Majesty? I have missed you." His foul breath waved over me. I gagged. His face closed in, mere inches from mine. "You know you were supposed to marry *me*. I was going to see to that—and we could have had great fun."

Fear squeezed my throat, refusing to let me scream.

"But instead, that excuse for a king stole you away from me. He has hoarded you away for himself, and I have not even had the chance to talk to you." Lord Hugh bared his teeth. His gold tooth caught the torchlight and gleamed.

"Let me go. The king would not take kindly to—"

"Silence!" He shoved me into the dark stairwell and against the wall. Pain radiated up my back from the hard impact, my breath leaving my lungs. He held my arm in a vise grip, squeezing harder and harder as his temper rose.

My terror finally took form in a scream that shredded my throat. His sweaty hands clawed at my face, pulled at my hair, and gripped my arms while I struggled against him. I screamed again as he thrust his foul face towards mine, slobbering down my cheek as he clamped me to him.

Panic raced through me, sending my heart into a wild rhythm. *God, help me.*

Suddenly, a dark form ripped my attacker away. I stayed pressed against the cool stone as the person slammed Lord Hugh into the opposite wall. "How dare you assault my wife?"

My racing heart jumped.

Rowan!

His anger, stronger than I had ever seen it, boiled over in a rage. Rowan drove his fist into the drunken man's jaw, sending the man's head cracking against the stone with a *thwack*. Rowan grabbed him and tossed him into the torchlit corridor. Lord Hugh spat curses and tried to scramble to his feet, but Rowan pounced on him. He pinned Lord Hugh to the ground, punching him until blood oozed from his lips and nostrils.

Just when I feared Rowan would kill the man, he stopped and leaned over Lord Hugh, pure fury blazing in his voice. "Do not *dare* lay a hand to the queen again, or I shall see you hanged!" He jabbed a finger in the man's chest. "You had better thank the Lord above that I am feeling lenient this day. Otherwise, you would find yourself dead this moment."

With no reply, Lord Hugh lost consciousness, his body going limp on the floor.

I trembled against the wall, my insides quavering in aftershock of my fear. I stared at Rowan with wide, terrified eyes. His broad back heaved up and down as he worked to steady his breathing.

Slowly, he turned to face me, and, seeing my trembling, hurried over as I finally peeled myself from the wall. I stumbled into his arms, falling against his hard chest, relief washing over me. Suddenly, I wanted his comfort over any others'.

My shaking hands gripped the fabric of his tunic splattered with the blood of my attacker. What would have happened to me had he not come? I shuddered to think.

"Are you well?" He gripped my arms and pulled me away from him to peer at my face. I winced at his tight grip on my sore arms.

His face twisted in fresh anger at my grimace. "Did he hurt you?"

I shook my head, eyes closed, biting my lip against the cry of pain that threatened to escape. He was squeezing my arms so hard! "Nay, not really. 'Tis just my arms…"

"Oh. Forgive me." Rowan released me and wrapped an arm about my shoulders to pull me back to his chest. I could hear his heart beating fast against my ear. My own blood fell into rhythm with his.

"Thank you for coming." Tears of gratitude pooled in my eyes. That overwhelming terror that had consumed me was blessedly gone, replaced with sheer relief. *Thank you, Lord, for sending him to me. If he had not come to my rescue…*

I lifted my face, tears poised to fall. The concerned, earnest look I found on his face surprised me. It was a concern different from any I had seen on him before.

"I… I am exhausted. I—I want to go to bed now." I pulled away, wiping at my eyes and taking a few steps back. That closeness and the feeling of his arms around me was unsettling. And I still was not sure I liked it.

"Of course." His face remained hard, though his anger was not directed toward me but the nobleman lying unconscious on the floor. "You have had quite a shock. I shall see that he is thrown in the dungeon immediately."

I nodded and stumbled up the stairs. My legs wobbled beneath me, and I prayed I would be able to make it to my chamber.

When at last I entered my room, I stripped off my gown, not bothering to summon my maids. Standing in my chemise, my hair pulled loose from its pins, I splashed water from my wash basin against my face. I shivered, scrubbing the tear stains from my cheeks.

Thank you again, Lord, for allowing Rowan to come when he did. Thank you...

Hmm... I wonder what Rowan will do to...

I felt myself falling and reached out to catch my weight on the washstand. I had fallen asleep standing up.

With a groan, I quickly changed into my nightdress and eased into bed. In a matter of minutes, I succumbed to the refuge of sleep for the rest of the night, dreaming of the moment Rowan wrapped me in his arms.

Chapter 23

MAVIS EASED INTO MY ROOM, QUIETLY CLOSING the door behind her "Good morning, my lady. How do you fare?"

I sat up in bed. Did my maid already know of my ordeal last night?

"I am well, thank you." I slipped out from under the covers, my bare feet meeting the cold floor. Chills tingled across my arms and I shuddered as an early autumn breeze blew through an open shutter.

"Let me get this, dear." Mavis hurried toward the window and closed the partially open shutter, barring it shut.

"Thank you." I moved closer to her while unlacing the front of my nightgown, preparing to pull my arms out and let the garment fall.

"I heard about what happened."

So, she *had* heard.

"How dare that brute lay a hand to you, my lady." Her face creased in anger as she put her fists on her ample hips. She clucked and shook her head. "Shame, shame."

Then Mavis' anger transformed into a teasing smile. "But I also heard the king came to save you. From what I hear, he was fiercely protective. Nearly beat the beast to a pulp, he did."

I shook my head, not wishing to speak of the incident or Rowan, especially. I let my gown fall.

Mavis gasped. She hurried to my side, her cold fingers gingerly touching the ugly bruises on my arms. "My lady!" She turned wide eyes on me. "That beast! Are you in pain?"

"Not really. My arms are a bit tender, but that is all." Memories of Lord Hugh's foul, alcohol-scented mouth moving down my cheek came to mind. I shivered, wincing at the terrifying memory.

Mavis slipped one arm around my shoulders. "He is gone now, my lady. Do not worry about that. King Rowan threw him in the dungeon. The blackguard will not be harming you again."

I nodded, resolving to push the incident from my mind as best I could. He had not succeeded in his licentious plan, and I was safe now. That was all that mattered.

"I am well, Mavis. I promise." I gave her a look that brooked no argument.

She said not another word, but moved to retrieve a gown— my lavender one with the gold embellishments across the bodice and sleeves. When she turned around, I discovered she also held a black cloak. "This is not yours, is it, Your Majesty? I do not recognize it."

It was Rowan's cape. The one he had draped around me almost a week ago now, when we stood together in the moonlight and I suddenly understood him for the first time. I had not thought to return it, and he had yet to ask. "Oh… no. 'Tisn't mine." I glanced away, embarrassment needling my cheeks. "It is the king's."

"*Ahhh.*" The woman hummed a happy tune while she helped me dress and arranged my hair. Once finished, she stepped back. "Do you require anything else, my queen?"

"Nay, Mavis. Thank you."

She bobbed a curtsey and left my chamber, her song resuming.

I sat back in my chair, staring at the cape Mavis had draped over the end of my bed. I needed to give it back to Rowan.

For some reason, I dreaded speaking with him again. After the way I grabbed hold of him during the ball, and then the rescue, I felt odd. Just remembering the way I had clung to his chest made my cheeks burn.

Why had I let that happen? I had quite literally thrown myself into him. And he had accepted me.

Rising, I picked up the cape. Moments later, I was standing outside Rowan's room, mustering my courage to knock. Finally, I did. Would he even be inside?

Reginald opened the door. The man's face revealed his surprise at seeing me. "Good morning, my queen."

"Good morning. I wish to speak with the king." I lifted the cape. "I have something of his I would like to return."

Reginald nodded and looked over his shoulder. "Her Majesty wishes to speak with you, sire."

I looked over the manservant's shoulder too. Rowan appeared behind him, dressed in black leggings, a loose white shirt, and tall boots, though he had yet to don his sleeveless tunic to finish the ensemble. He looked at me quizzically. "Good morning, Arabella." He turned to his manservant. "You may go, Reginald. I will call you back in after I speak with Her Majesty."

Reginald nodded and slipped quietly into the hall, leaving Rowan and I alone in his chamber. I realized then that I had not so much as laid eyes on this room since our wedding day.

Rowan tilted his head at me. "I hope you were able to sleep after last night's events."

"Yes, thank you, I was able to sleep—well, in fact."

"How are your arms?"

"Bruised. But they shall heal."

He stepped towards me, putting out a hand but drawing back before he could touch me. "Are you sure you are well? I was so concerned for you last night." His brows drew together. "You were quite shaken."

"Yes, I promise." I drew away and stubbornly shook my head. "Please, let us speak no more of it. He did not harm me, at least not in a way that shan't heal in a few days' time. I will be better able to forget the matter if it is not brought up."

"But Arabella—"

"Nay. Rowan." My eyes pleaded with him. "Please…"

Crickets seemed to chirp while we stared at one another for a long moment, neither of us saying a word. I fiddled with the cape folded over my arm. "Oh, this is yours." I looked from the cape to him and held it out. "From some nights past… when you gave it to me… when I was cold." My heart thudded at the memory.

He accepted the garment, looking down at it, his forehead furrowing as it so often did. I realized it was actually a rather handsome expression. Though it was nothing compared to when he smiled. "Yes. I nearly forgot."

Nearly… Had the encounter remained as fixed in his mind as in my own?

"Thank you for returning it to me," he turned to retrieve a tunic, "though I have more where it came from. You could have kept it, had you so desired." He slipped his arms into the garment and pulled it down over his head.

My eyes widened and I looked away, feeling as though I had just seen him shirtless—though he was in fact putting on his *second* shirt. "Oh... I knew not."

He adjusted the dark blue tunic, then looped a belt around his waist. "No matter." He smiled softly, his head down as he fastened his belt. "If you have need of it again, it will be here for you."

"I have my own capes."

He lifted his face, an odd gleam in his eye. "I know."

I swallowed and pursed my lips, not sure whether to feel pleasure or otherwise at his words. "Well... if that is all, Your Majesty, I will be going." I turned around, starting to open the door without even waiting for his permission.

"By all means, my queen," he said. Then the door shut behind me.

Rowan

His fingers tapped impatiently against the arm of his throne. How long would Azmar and his insufferable daughter keep him waiting?

In the morning, his nobles would depart for their own homes, so this was his last opportunity to mete out some sort of punishment for Katherine's actions. Following the night's evening meal, he had sent servants to instruct the lord and his daughter to meet him within the hour.

Rowan had now been waiting a quarter past that.

Irritation clawed at his nerves. Those two were *not* making this any easier for themselves.

At last, the doors swung open and the duo entered, gliding toward the throne, their expressions bearing a mixture of fear and excitement. When they reached him, the pompous Lord Azmar and his haughty daughter bowed low. "Your Majesty," they chimed in unison.

Rowan wasted no time cutting to the heart of the matter. "Lord Azmar, I have brought you here to address your daughter's inappropriate behavior this week."

The man opened and closed his mouth, at a total loss for words. Katherine's already pale face took on a sickly pallor. Had she really believed she could get by with such actions?

"Lady Katherine, it has been brought to my attention that you have spoken falsely, claiming to have at one time been romantically involved with myself." He stared sharply down at the young woman.

She forced a nervous laugh. "Oh, Your Majesty, I was only jesting."

"I do not see it as a jesting matter, my lady. And this is not your first offense." He glanced at Azmar before returning his gaze to the man's daughter. "You kissed me on one occasion, without my invitation. I spared you penalty then, but this time, after the way you spoke to the queen, I will spare you no longer."

Lord Azmar glared at his daughter then turned beseechingly to Rowan. "Sire, the girl meant no harm."

"Please, sire!" Katherine cried, her face twisted with fright, clearly assuming the worst of punishments. Rowan had half a mind to give her just that, but an uncharacteristic feeling of compassion pulled at his heart. "Sire, nay!"

"Enough!" Rowan stood to his feet and pointed at her. "Do not try to explain yourself to me—either of you," he said, looking from her to Azmar. Rowan took a breath, not wishing to have his anger boil over as it often did. "Lord Azmar, you and your family are suspended from my court until further notice. I will invite you back when I see fit." He met each of their gazes, from one to the next. "I will not tolerate rumors of this kind, nor such disrespect showed toward myself or my queen. Have I made myself clear?"

Lord Azmar's eyes hardened and red crept up his neck. But, to his credit, the man held his peace and bowed low. His visibly angered daughter followed suit. "Yes, sire." Then the two nobles hurried back across the expanse of the Hall, muttering and bickering amongst themselves until the door slammed shut behind them.

Arabella

A chilly north wind swept through the early morning as the noblemen and ladies prepared to depart the palace. With the recent temperatures, it seemed the coming autumn and winter would be cold indeed.

I accompanied Rowan to the courtyard where we bid our guests farewell and wished them safe travels. I watched closely for Lady Allis to appear, already dreading having to say goodbye to my new friend. We planned to correspond through letters, but it was not the same as having her company in the flesh. Also, I had yet to learn more about the night the king and queen died. Now that she and her husband were leaving, how long would it be before I had the chance to ask her about it again?

"Queen Arabella!"

I turned to see the woman in question striding towards me, letting go of her husband's arm to come greet me. She bobbed a curtsy, always so proper, even though she knew I considered her a friend.

"There you are! I was hoping to wish you farewell. I had begun to fear you had left early."

Rowan stood beside us, clasping arms with the Lord of Dallin and conversing with him in light tones.

"Oh, but 'tis just it—we are not leaving. The king has asked us to stay on for a time."

"That is wonderful news!" My heart fluttered in joy, and I was unable to resist eyeing Rowan.

He noticed and stepped close to my side. "You have yet to choose any ladies-in-waiting, and since I knew how well you and Lady Dallin have taken to one another, I thought perhaps she should stay longer. If you decide to, you can appoint her as one of your ladies."

"I thank you for thinking of me." I looked up at him, taken aback by his thoughtfulness.

His lips curved in a smile that sent warmth spiraling to my toes.

"Lady Allis?" Never breaking Rowan's gaze, I reached out a hand to her and she took it. "Would you care to walk with me? I believe the men can finish seeing off our guests."

"Yes, my queen."

We turned, linked together arm in arm. My heart swelled with happiness to know her company would continue to aid my loneliness. And that I would I have my chance to ask her about the murders at Dallin.

But…

I glanced back at Rowan.

It was my husband's desire to see that happiness that warmed my heart the most.

Chapter 24

Rowan

THE SOUND OF ROWAN'S BOOTS AGAINST THE floor echoed off the walls as he made his way to his study. All night, his mind had turned with battle plans, and now he itched to discuss them with his advisors. Favian wasn't keen on this new war campaign, but he would come around to Rowan's wishes, as he usually did. The matter of marriage was about the only thing Favian had ever refused to budge on.

Merry whistling winged toward him from further down the corridor. What servant could be whistling so close to the royal family's quarters? They normally sought to blend in, barely seen and never heard.

Rounding the corner, Rowan saw a short, heavyset man with dark hair and beard heading his way. The man's whistling stopped when he spotted Rowan. He bowed. "Your Majesty! Forgive me."

"Think nothing of it." Rowan studied the man through narrowed eyes. He seemed so familiar.

"I was just going to visit Her Majesty—she is my niece, sire."

Ahhh... Yes, Arabella's uncle. "Yes, I remember now. You are Matthew of Caelrith, the scribe."

"At your service, sire."

"I wish you well, Matthew. Carry on to your niece. I am sure Arabella is looking forward to your company."

Arabella's uncle bowed once more and moved on.

Something nagged at Rowan's brain, however, as he continued

to his study. It was no longer the man's identity he sought to re-member, but something else. Something he'd done...

Then it hit him.

Arabella's uncle was the one to reveal the plot to poison him!

Rowan had said he would do something to reward the man for his good deed, but it had somehow slipped his mind. The scribe had saved his life. Such a service *must* be honored. But how?

Favian was running late, so Rowan and Cassius waited in the study, speaking of their own things. Cassius was in the middle of saying something when Rowan interrupted. "Cassius?"

The man paused and cast him a dark look, clearly perturbed by the interruption but never one to say so. "Yes, sire?"

"There is a man who has served me very well for some time now. He has done me a great service and I wish to honor him."

Cassius raised a brow. "I see."

Rowan pursed his lips and rested his head on one fist. "I have been meaning to do this for some time, but it escaped my atten-tion. What do you think should be done?"

Cassius clasped his hands behind his back and paced away. "Well, sire... may I ask how long this man has been in your ser-vice?"

"Since before I became king."

Cassius nodded. "Then, since this man has provided you such good service, you could..." Cassius stopped and swiveled to face him, a gleam in his eye that contradicted his otherwise stoic de-meanor. "Give him one of your royal robes to wear and place a crown on his head. Have him led through the streets atop your own horse, and let it be proclaimed what service he has rendered you."

An extravagant idea, but a fitting one, he supposed. It was the least he could do for the man who had saved his life.

"Very well. It shall be so." Rowan lifted his head from off his fist and situated the papers strewn across his desk.

"And who might this fortunate subordinate be?" Cassius said with a smile, hands behind his back.

"I want you to personally see that what you have suggested is done for Matthew of Caelrith, the scribe. He is the one who uncovered the plot to poison me and informed the queen."

Cassius' expression fell. His jaw clenched and unclenched. "Matthew of Caelrith?" After a moment's pause, he gave a bow. "As you wish, sire."

The door clicked open. "Forgive my tardiness, my king." Favian stopped abruptly, his hand still upon the door, and looked from Rowan to Lord Cassius. "Did I intrude upon something?"

"Nay, Favian." Rowan gestured for the man to approach. "Come, we have much to discuss."

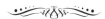

Arabella

I was pleased, and admittedly shocked, to learn of Rowan's plan to honor my uncle. It seemed so unlike him to wish to do something so generous for someone else.

My heart flooded with hope. The hope that mayhap God was working on his heart, penetrating the hard shell that encompassed it.

Or could *I* be reaching his heart?

Mayhap it was a mixture of both. But whatever it was, I was glad for it.

My uncle, of course, politely refused Rowan's generous offer. But the king would hear nothing of it. He insisted, saying that Uncle Matthew deserved such honoring for saving his life.

The day of the parade, Rowan and I walked together to the courtyard. Our horses were saddled and waiting, their reins held by Rowan's young squire, Leo, and another red-headed squire with a freckled face. Without asking, Rowan put his broad hands around my waist and lifted me to my saddle. Taken unaware, heat raced up my neck. His blue eyes met mine and his lips twitched, as if trying to form a smile. "Thank you."

That faint ghost of a smile vanished, replaced with his customary frown. "Think nothing of it." He left me and mounted his horse in one grand leap.

Uncle Matthew exited into the sunlight, a long, velvet robe trimmed in soft fur draped over his shoulders. A simple gold circlet rested atop his graying hair, lending him a noble air without making him appear above the king himself. Above it all, Uncle Matthew wore a smile so bright it made my heart soar, though the grin was mixed with an expression of humility that made him even more endearing.

He mounted Rowan's brown gelding—today, Rowan rode a sleek, black horse with a white star at his forehead—and we moved into formation. Lord Cassius led the parade, with Uncle Matthew just behind. Rowan and I followed, with Lord Favian and several knights trailing us.

As soon as we entered the streets of Caelrith, Lord Cassius shouted in his commanding voice, "Behold, citizens of Acuniel, this is the man who saved the king's life; and this day, he is honored by His Majesty the King!" On and on he repeated the announcement as we made our way through every street. People of all sorts came from their houses, shops, and alleyways to see the display.

I recognized the faces of some, the sight leaving my heart heavy with that old weight of loss. But then I forced myself to think instead of all the good I did have.

I looked over at Rowan. As much as it smarted my pride, I had to own that he was not the beast I always believed him to be. Though he still thought more of himself than others, I realized he *did* have a good heart in there somewhere. A heart only a few people were privileged enough to see.

In that moment, some days ago now, when I saw that heart, I had also glimpsed what motivated him to do the things he did. I understood the pain of loss, and it was that pain that had driven him all these years. How could I judge him, then? Had not my own pain of loss driven me to hate him, as he hated the Trilarians, and caused me to resent everything about being in the palace instead of embracing... *this?*

I looked around at the people, *my* people. I was their queen now. It was in my power to help those that starved, went without clean drink or a place to rest their head at night, or fire for warmth in winter. It was my duty to help them, I knew. The problem was Rowan knowing it, and him allowing me to aid the people in the ways I wanted.

I looked at him again, unashamedly perusing his features, not caring if he or the people around me took notice. Even if he would never admit it, he was softening, slowly but surely. I smiled to myself as another repetition of Lord Cassius' proclamation rang out.

Rowan

He felt someone watching him and turned to see it was Arabella. She did not look away when he caught her stare, but kept his gaze, a secretive smile playing at her full, pink lips. "Does something amuse you?"

"Nay. I am merely happy."

Shock sent his thoughts reeling. "You are *happy?*" Could she finally be content here? With *him?*

Her lips lifted at one corner, but she had moved her eyes to the procession in front of them. Her body swayed with the horse's slow gait. "Yes. I suppose I am."

"*Suppose?*" he teased.

She faced him then, with a merry grin. Rowan's heart thudded. "Nay. I know I am." Her dark eyes perused his face. "And you?"

He shrugged off the question, unwilling to answer.

Was he happy? He was unsure. In fact, he was not even sure he knew what happiness was anymore.

Was happiness the strange feeling that Arabella's company elicited?

The sparkle of gold caught his eye. Arabella's ruby and gold ring glinted on her left hand, reminding him of the fact that she was indeed married to him, and not just some woman sharing his home.

She intrigued him, beguiled him. With one word, she could tear him asunder; with another, lend healing to his wounds. In all his life, of all the people he had ever met, only this young woman had such an effect on him. No other person made him think, made him question himself. No one else made him want to be a better king... a better man.

Rowan clenched his jaw and straightened in the saddle, unsure how to feel about this ever-widening gap in the armor built around his tender heart. He'd been a vulnerable boy once, but he had changed in more ways than one the night his parents died. Seeing such horrors... Such things are not easily shaken off. Ever since, he had preferred to stay isolated, keeping his heart and emotions chained, bound, and bottled up, wanting no one and nothing to get through. If he cared about anyone, anything, God might just take that away too.

Why, God? Why have You left me to die in my misery? He had lost count of the times he had prayed this exact prayer.

Rowan clenched his fists about the horse's reins. Arabella was watching him again, her face full of concern. He offered her a reassuring look to say he was well—though it was a lie. She turned forward, her last soft look sending another jolt of feeling through that hole in the armor of his heart. And shifting his thoughts away from his anger with God and back to her.

Just seeing Arabella with the morning sun kissing her dark hair, the bright rays catching in her eyes, resurrected the feeling of holding her close after he saved her from Lord Hugh's assault. She had clung to him like a frightened child. And God help him, he'd felt the most overwhelming urge to protect her and ease her every fear. Nothing could dare come near and tear her from the safety of his arms.

Something stirred within him, forming a knot in his stomach.

Would they ever be together, *truly* together, as a man and wife ought to be? Would he ever find it in himself to let her near enough? Would she want that? Want *him*? Did it even matter how they felt about one another? Most marriages like theirs never amounted to anything more than fondness for one another. He *was* fond of Arabella, that much he would own, but did he love her?

The biggest question was: did he *want* to love her, and did she want to love him?

Well, no matter his feelings, something would have to happen eventually. He had to have an heir to the throne.

A growl rumbled in his throat. *I should have just insisted that the crown would fall to Cassius.*

As their trek through the streets of Caelrith continued, they passed every manner of person. Bedraggled beggars and finely dressed merchants, dirty children and beautiful young peasant women. Some watched on with fear, some with curiosity, awe, and still others... distaste.

When Rowan spotted two little children—he was sure they were the same ones Arabella had given a coin to—his heart twisted with sudden compassion. Feelings such as these were becoming more and more familiar to him.

Just how many penniless, filthy, and starving children lived in his streets? Not just in Caelrith, but in the towns and villages beyond? The sobering product of war and violence, littering the alleyways and ditches of his domain. Was anything done for them? Perhaps they received charity from the church, but that was surely all.

A war busily raged within him. As king, was it not his place to see after their welfare? Or mayhap not. He was a king, after all. Should he bother himself with the lives of mere *peasants*?

But they were not just simple peasants, were they?

His wife riding beside him was far more than that. She had a strong heart, and a mind that far exceeded the condition of her birth. She had proven herself intelligent, good, kind, and so much more. Simple was the very last word to describe her.

Could it be that more of his subjects were like her—more than he gave them credit for?

His father's voice filtered through his mind. *Your subjects will loyally serve you, in turn for your loyal serving.*

The picture of the Averill villagers, their homes ravished by the small band of overeager Trilarian soldiers, seared his memory. Seeing that village afire and its citizens running for their lives had reminded him of what happened to the innocents. And when Arabella told him how her parents died, Rowan could not help but feel guilty, like he was responsible for it.

No wonder she had despised him.

No wonder his *people* despised him.

He had neglected all of them in many ways. That was a fact Rowan could no longer deny. And, much to his surprise and a little to his annoyance, remorse burdened his heart.

Perhaps it was time to start doing more with his crown than just wage war, though he was still convinced of that mission's importance.

King Roland had always showed compassion for the poor and downtrodden. Perhaps Rowan, as his son, could start doing likewise.

It was what his father would have wanted.

Chapter 25

Arabella

WHEN THE PARADE ENDED, ROWAN ASKED IF I would care for a ride around the countryside. I, of course, did not object at the chance to escape the confines of the palace a little longer.

We thundered across the open field where I first saw Rowan, our horses' hooves crushing grass and the few wildflowers autumn's chill had yet to kill. Four knights accompanied us, riding a short distance behind. As we neared the edge of a forest, we slowed our place. The forest's dark boughs arched overhead as we ambled along its mouth. A bird chirped in the distance, its merry song echoing through the trees. A black and yellow butterfly flitted across my path and I delighted in the pretty sight.

"Beautiful day," Rowan remarked. "Though the sky is clouded."

"Indeed." I smiled, watching the butterfly fade from view. "I wish to thank you for honoring my uncle as you did. Truly, 'twas not necessary to go to such lengths."

"Nay. 'Twas only right."

I looked him over from head to waist, enjoying this kindness that was displaying in him more and more often. It was a refreshing change from the bellowing monster of rage he had become more than once.

He narrowed his eyes at me. "Are you studying me?" He frowned his usual frown and looked away. But he could not hide the fidgeting of his hands and the restless movement of his eyes.

My grin stretched wide.

Rowan was nervous.

"Forgive me. I am merely... thinking.

He raised his brows. "And what, pray tell, are you thinking of, my queen?"

I looked away, my body moving in tune with the horse as it plodded along the forest line. "My thoughts are my own, sire. At the moment."

"Ahhh, I see. Secretive, are we?"

A twisted sort of satisfaction settled in my middle. I enjoyed making him wonder after my thoughts.

Silence stretched for a time, except for the quiet conversing of the knights riding behind us, and the occasional chirp of birds or buzz of an insect. Rowan seemed contemplative, staring at the path ahead of him with a look of concentration. Something was turning in his brain, something serious, but I knew not what.

Suddenly, he spoke. "You remember those orphans to whom you gave a coin?"

I cocked my head, brow furrowing. "What about them?"

"There must be any number of children like them in Caelrith alone. I was wondering what you would think of opening... an orphanage in the city."

My heart leapt. *Lord be praised!* He really *was* changing.

I was so grateful I could have cried, and so happy that I could have flung my arms about his neck and kissed him. "Rowan, I think that is a marvelous idea!"

"We should do it then?"

"We?"

"Yes, I would want you to assist me; mayhap even run the project since... that sort of thing is so dear to your heart."

"It would be an honor." Who was this man before me? Could he even be the same man I hated for so many years?

"Thank you." My voice was thick like honey in my throat. "The people shall thank you as well."

He sniffed and looked up at the sky, the clouds drawing in for a midday shower. "Yes, well, mayhap we should be heading back. It looks like rain will soon be upon us."

We reeled our horses around and started at a fast clip for the city walls. When we drew nigh to the eastern side, Rowan abruptly pulled in his reins. His horse neighed and stomped at the ground, protesting the sudden stop.

"What is it?" The clouds had already visibly thickened over the last few minutes, and low rumbles of thunder threatened their fury.

"I thought I would show you a shorter path."

"A what?"

Rowan jerked his chin at the knights who had circled us. "You four, ride back to the palace and take our horses. The queen and I will be taking the other route."

"Yes, Your Majesty," the men replied. Before I could ask any further questions, one of the knights pulled me from my horse, Gemmula, and then led her away.

Rowan came forward and took my hand, thunder clapping as he did so. He leaned close, his voice warm beside my ear. "Come with me."

He stooped down amidst the brush that grew up against the city wall. After looking over both shoulders to check for any watching eyes, Rowan opened a door camouflaged in the earth. My mouth fell open. "A passage?"

He took my hand and led me to the black hole in the ground. "We had better get inside quick, unless we wish to be soaked through."

The first raindrops splattered on my head. I squealed, laughing and racing into the dark. "Watch your step," he cautioned. I felt stairs beneath my feet, though I could barely see them in the dim half-light of the entrance. Rain pattered on the top steps behind me, highlighting the musty, earthy scents of the passage. With Rowan's help, I descended about ten feet into the ground before my slippers met flat earth and he hurried back up to close the door.

Darkness blacker than night consumed us. For a moment, my breath froze, and I regretted my decision to follow Rowan inside this stuffy tunnel.

Soft footsteps sounded on the stairs—Rowan. He was behind me suddenly, a silent warmth at my back. Then a large hand touched me, feeling for me in the darkness, first at my lower back, then at my shoulders. "Is it safe?" I whispered, shivering at his unseen touch.

His deep voice came to me through the darkness. "Of course, it is. I often played here as a boy."

One of his hands found my right one, enveloping it in security. "You must stay very close to me so we do not lose each other in the dark." His voice was near my ear. The warmth of his breath spread across the side of my face.

I nodded, and then felt ridiculous. *He cannot see you, Arabella.* "Alright." Why could I get nothing more than a whisper from my throat?

He tugged me further into the darkness. My feet moved in quiet, tiny steps. I could feel, rather than see, Rowan's broad, muscled back ahead of me, and judging by the heat, it was only inches from my face. His smell drifted towards me—warm, manly, with a hint of cinnamon or some other delicious spice. Just as he had smelled that night on the moonlit walkway.

"Watch your head. The ceiling is very low," Rowan warned. I lifted my free hand and easily felt it above me. Wood slats had been placed over the earthen ceiling and walls at intervals to prevent cave-ins.

"So, you played here as a boy?"

"Indeed." Rowan shifted his grip on my hand.

"Did your parents know of it? I can hardly imagine them approving of your playing in a tunnel that lets out past the city walls. Is that not rather hazardous?"

Rowan shrugged—or at least it sounded that way by how his shirt rustled. "They minded not. Though my mother did not care for the creatures I would capture in here. Let us hope none of my hairy little friends still lurk."

I gasped and stopped in my tracks, pulling against his hand. "Oh nay, Rowan. Please. Why did we have to come into this cursed tunnel anyway?" I shuddered at the memory of some sort of rodent scurrying across my foot in the dungeons.

He laughed, which was no comfort at all. Infuriating man.

I pulled harder, but his grip around my hand was too strong. "Rowan…" I squeaked out his name.

"You are calling me that more and more often."

"Calling you what?"

"Rowan."

My cheeks burned. "Oh… well… Forgive me, sire. I shall stop using your Christian name if you so wish."

He stayed silent for a moment, and I wondered what his expression must look like. "I mind not." His voice was a soft echo off the tunnel walls.

I cleared my throat. "Yes, well. Back to the other subject. Why did we have to come into this place?" I complained again, looking around at the walls made invisible by the dark. "I feel as though the walls and ceiling shall cave in upon me."

Rowan chuckled and released my hand. Then his palms were at my shoulders, flooding me with warmth. "Trust me, Arabella. I would not let any harm befall you."

His talk was sounding too serious for my liking. "I do not fear the creatures will *harm* me. I just... Oh, never mind." I jerked away from him and snatched his hand, huffing out a breath. "Come along."

I could feel him smiling at me. I almost told him so but decided against it. To his credit, Rowan did not say another word, but willingly turned and resumed leading me down the passage.

We walked for I knew not how long. Just when I was sure we should be reaching the exit, we would take another step, and another, and another, with no sign of light ahead to indicate a door. It seemed we would forever wander in this pitch-blackness.

"When do you think—" Suddenly, I tripped on what I could only assume to be a rock, and fell with a thud, my hand slipping from Rowan's grasp. My chest hit the ground hard, knocking the breath from me. I moaned and gasped for air.

"Arabella!" I heard Rowan's boots shuffling in the dirt. Hands searched for me in the dark, touching my back, my head, and finally finding my arms. He helped me onto my knees. I put a hand to my chest, struggling to draw a full breath.

"Are you well?" His hands ran over my upper arms.

I nodded pointlessly for a moment, unable to find my words. At last, I choked out, "Yes."

"Are you certain? It sounded like a hard fall." One of his hands cupped my cheek.

"Yes... I am quite sure." My breath came shallow, but it was no longer from the fall.

I could not see Rowan, but oh, I could feel him. He knelt before me, one hand at my face, the other still holding my arm. Judging by the sound of his breathing, I knew his face to be close to mine.

Was he about to kiss me?

I breathed deep, unsure of what would happen next, and felt him shift, our knees touching.

Unsettled, I lifted my face. We knocked heads with an audible *thud*. I jerked back, wincing in pain, and pushed off the ground in an effort to stand. "Forgive me. We should be going."

"Here. Allow me." Rowan stood and reached for me, but I shrugged off his touch to rise on my own. I stumbled over the hem of my gown and fell forward, crashing into his chest. He let out a pained grunt, catching me in his arms as I sagged against him.

"Forgive me." I carefully extricated myself from his arms, stepping back to gather my wits. "We should hurry onward, should we not?" My heart pounded in my chest. *Quiet, stupid heart! He will hear you!*

"Certainly."

He found my hand again and I allowed him to hold it, despite the embarrassment still searing my face.

We walked a few minutes more before Rowan halted again. "Wait here." I looked up to see the faint outlining of a door. It was high above us, accessed by steep steps, just as with the other end. Rowan ascended, slow and careful with his footing. There was silence, then a thud and a scraping noise, and then more scraping as the door shuddered and moved aside. The ground seemed to shake, rattling the passage with the noise.

Wait, I know that sound.

Light flooded in from the world above. Blessed, glorious—however blinding—light. Rowan hurried back down and took my hand, leading me up the steps. When we emerged from the tunnel, my suspicions were confirmed. It was the same one I had considered entering the night before our marriage.

What would have happened had I decided to venture into the passageway that night? Would I have found my way to freedom, or been caught and brought back? And if I had escaped, would that have been any better a life than the one I had now?

I supposed I would never know for sure. But somehow, despite all the difficulty and inner turmoil of the last few months, I was glad I had stayed.

Chapter 26

OVER THE NEXT FEW WEEKS, I SPENT MANY hours at Rowan's side, helping him plan the construction of the orphanage. He patiently listened to all of my ideas and took each of them into careful consideration. Together, we chose the location for the building, lined up workers from among the city to do the construction, and discussed partnering with the church to locate suitable people to run the institution.

In about six month's time, the new Caelrith Home for Children would be ready to welcome the orphans of the city.

I had no doubt Rowan would gain favor in the eyes of the people for this move. He had already earned more favor in mine.

One day, as we sat side by side in his study, he stopped what he was doing and turned to me. "You were born for this, you know. I chose well when I selected you as my queen."

My face flushed, and pleasure swirled through my veins. "I once would have disputed that fact. But now... I believe I am where I am meant to be, as well."

His blue eyes studied my face for a long, silent moment, a smile soft on his lips. Then he cleared his throat and began shuffling through the parchments before him.

That evening, his praise of me and the sight of his smile was still at the forefront of my mind as I strolled arm in arm with Lady Allis. We walked along the promenade surrounding the inner courtyard garden. Torches flickered at intervals to light the path in the duskiness of sunset. A woolen shawl wrapped around my back and hung over my arms, keeping me in a warm embrace even as the crisp autumn air nipped at my cheeks.

Lady Allis wrapped her own shawl tighter around her thin shoulders. "I am pleased to hear of the orphanage His Majesty is opening—with your assistance as well, of course, my queen." I had tried to convince her to call me Arabella, but she had refused, saying such would be too improper. But for all her quiet, careful, and proper ways, Allis was a delight to be with, and her friendship a balm to my lonely soul.

I smiled to myself, both at the thought of my friendship with Allis and my earlier conversation with Rowan. "Yes, I am fiercely proud of him. In all honesty, I did not think it of him."

"Is that so?"

I nodded, my mind rolling back the months to my first days in the palace. "Yes, I am afraid I once thought him incapable of such kindness. I despised him when we wed, actually."

Allis cocked her head at me, eyes narrowed. "And you do not despise him now?"

Again, I thought back, seeing all that had transpired within me—and within Rowan—in the past months. No longer did I struggle to find my place here, nor did I fight to understand why God allowed me to be Rowan's wife. The questions had not completely left my mind—nay, I still thought of them often. But there was a peace, an assurance that God knew what He was doing, which had settled over me. I was comfortable. And for the moment, life was good, if not still a bit uncertain.

"Nay," I responded at last. "He is a good man... no matter what people may say."

Allis looked away, her lips pressed tight as if suppressing a smile.

"The kindness in him was covered up after his parents died," I added.

Allis nodded. "That had to have been a traumatic experience."

"Perhaps more than any of us even know..." No one, not even Favian, Cassius, or I—the three people closest to Rowan—could ever really know how deep the hurt went. Though, looking upon his face in the moonlight a few weeks ago, I had managed to glimpse his broken soul.

It was a distressing thing to behold.

The way he shut his thoughts and feelings inside himself...

"I have heard that Lord Favian found him weeping over his parents, desperately trying to wake them. He himself was wounded and bleeding, his clothes drenched…" Allis' face paled and she gulped, pressing a hand to her pregnant belly, "in blood. Both his own, and that of his parents." She shook her head and closed her eyes, wincing at the awful thought.

"I know Lord Favian found Rowan. But did others rush in as well?" I leaned closer to Allis, jumping at this opportunity to ask my much-needed questions.

"Well, naturally. A servant or two heard the noise and arrived soon after Favian did, as well as my husband—who was also sixteen at the time—and his father."

I frowned. "What about Lord Cassius? He was as close to the king as Lord Favian was. Did he not come rushing as well?"

"Oh, he did come. He and some others arrived a while after."

I furrowed my brow, turning away so she could not study my expression. If I had been so close to the king, I would have rushed to the scene straightaway. Of course, he could have just not heard the news yet. But word of such a shocking event had to have spread like wildfire throughout Dallin Castle.

"The king said masked men dressed in black attacked his parents, and he fought one of them, but they all escaped out the window. Surely someone saw something."

Allis' head tilted to one side. "Come to think of it, Geoffrey has spoken of a guard spotting the men heading to the castle wall. But when his father's knights went to pursue them, they found neither hide nor hair of the attackers, neither within nor without the castle for miles around. It was as if they were ghosts."

"I see…"

Lady Allis drew up short, narrowing her gaze at me. "May I ask why you are so interested in this subject, my queen? Why would you wish to know of such a terrible incident?"

I shrugged and took her arm, resuming our walk. Suspicion was dangerous, even if it was coming from Allis.

Perhaps you should not speak of that certain subject. For your own sake.

"If it concerns my husband, I wish to know," I said, playing the worried wife—which I was, though my concern went far deeper than just that.

Tread carefully, Arabella. I silently berated myself as we kept walking. *People shall grow suspicious of you, think you a traitor if your loyalties to Trilaria come to light. And if Trilaria isn't responsible... if the real murderers learn of your suspicions....*

Favian's words played through my head again. *...for your own sake.*

If I came too close to the truth, would someone really come after me? Or after someone that I loved? There were, after all, those servants who tried to poison Rowan. If someone had hired them—as I was becoming increasingly more convinced of—that meant someone out there still wanted Rowan dead, no doubt in order to steal the throne.

Which meant they could want me dead too. Because, with Rowan gone, I would be the only thing standing between them and the rule of all Acuniel.

Chapter 27

CRICKETS CHIRPED AND WIND WHISTLED through the bushes as I entered the garden after supper two days later. My red silk gown with the slashes of pink along the skirt dragged over the grass, the fabric making a *swish-swish* noise as I moved. My hair was restrained in an elegant style Mavis had worked so hard to fashion, topped with a filmy veil and my diamond circlet. I longed to pull it loose. I wanted... *freedom*, just for a bit. A chance to feel open, unbound, if only for a minute or two.

I looked around, checking to ensure no one watched, then tentatively removed my veil, eyeing all the while the shadowed arches surrounding the space. The other palace residents and noble guests were headed to their rooms for the night, but anyone could decide to stop by the garden for a moment's fresh air, just as I had done. If I let any of them catch me in a state of disarray, I would never hear the end of it, from either Mavis *or* Rowan.

Soon, my hair fell loose from its tight coils and tumbled over and around my shoulders. I shook it out, rubbing my fingers through it with a blissful sigh.

But that was not enough for me. My heart and body longed for more freedom, more comfort. A blessed break from the formalities of royal life.

Standing on the path, I glanced around again before sliding one foot from one uncomfortable slipper and then the other. Picking my skirts up in my fists, I stepped into the lush, green grass bordering the paving stones and sighed, relishing the feeling of cool grass between my toes.

A childish thought came to mind. *Nay, I cannot possibly. I would look so foolish...* A mischievous smile spread across my face.

Lifting my skirt again, I set off at an awkward skip across the garden, laughing to myself. I rarely received exercise, having no chores to do—a responsibility I had never gone without—so a little romp about the garden would do me good. I looked so incredibly silly, I was almost ashamed of myself, but it felt good. So good.

Eventually I broke into a run, circling through the bushes and flowers, enjoying the sensation of the chilly air stinging my lungs, and laughing at my own absurdity.

Rowan

He stood in the opening between two pillars along the promenade encompassing the garden, hidden in the shadows. A flash of red had caught his eye, halting his walk to his quarters.

It was Arabella.

Rowan caught himself smiling as she frolicked through the garden, looking very much like the playful little girl she must have been once. Her dark hair flowed behind her in the wind. She clutched the ruby fabric of her gown in her fists, while her bodice heaved with panting breath and merry laughter. It was then that he noticed her bare feet.

Rowan chuckled to himself.

When she had appeared in the courtyard in a similar state, it had angered him, and he'd likened her wild appearance to that of a disheveled harlot. Now he regretted such crass words. Though her appearance before had not been suitable for the public eye, it was *most* suitable for him. In fact, her unruly yet beautiful state made his heart pound.

Arabella stopped, her face bright with the glow of exercise, and plopped down onto the grass. The thick folds of her skirt puffed around her like a cake. She ran her fingers through her hair, twisting it over one shoulder, exposing the back of her graceful neck. Then she splayed her palms on the ground behind her and leaned back, closing her eyes, her face lifted to the sky.

Thunder rumbled in the clouds overhead and Arabella opened her eyes to look around. Quickly, Rowan ducked behind the pillar at his right, not wishing for her to catch him spying. After a moment, he looked again as the thunder rolled and lightning cracked. A smile lifted his lips to see her gazing up at the heavens, her palms out to welcome the rain to her like some sort of water nymph.

The first raindrops splattered over the garden, bouncing off the stone steps leading down into it, wetting Arabella's face, and dampening her gown. She rose once the rain became a downpour and hurried towards the stairs, lifting her skirts in order to run faster.

Rowan was planning to stay hidden and surprise her once she entered the covered promenade. But as Arabella was hastening up the steps, she slipped and went crashing to the ground.

Arabella

My knees and hands burning, I looked up through the rain that had become a torrent in the blink of an eye to see the most embarrassing sight in the world.

Rowan darted from behind a pillar and dashed through the rain to kneel before me. He grasped my upper arms and helped me sit up. *My slippers! And my veil and circlet!* I moaned under my breath, realizing I had left them in the grass.

"Are you well?"

"Yes. I am." I avoided his gaze and instead focused on my sopping wet gown. "Mavis shall have my head if this dress is ruined."

"I believe I am the only one with authority enough for that. And I shan't punish you for having a bit of fun."

I looked up at him in horror. "You were watching me?"

He gave a smirk that said, *"Mayhap; mayhap not."*

Rowan gently helped me to my feet. "Come. Let us get out of this rain before we catch our deaths."

He assisted me up the stairs and we entered the shelter of the promenade. We stood in the space between two pillars, the sound of rain splattering against stone near thunderous in my ears. I attempted to wring out my hair and dress. Rowan ran his hand through his dripping hair, the front of it plastered to his forehead and darkened to the color of mine by the rain.

"Are you well?" he asked again. Without waiting for my response, he took my hands, turning them palms up. Bright red, bloody scratches marred both, a result of catching myself on the rough stone stairs. "You are bleeding."

I shook my head, looking at my hands. "I am well. They are but scratches."

Rowan lifted one of my palms higher for closer examination. His wet fingers tickled my skin as he traced around the wound. For a moment, I thought he would kiss it.

"You were watching me?"

Again, he did not answer my question, only looked up and gave me a secretive smirk.

He lowered my hand without releasing it. His blue eyes covered my face, leaving me uncertain of what he was thinking or what he would do. Rowan took a breath and edged nearer. When he began to stare deeply into my eyes, I suddenly knew exactly what he was thinking…

Rowan's hand came to touch the curve of my waist, gently pulling me nearer to him, while his other hand still held my own, not caring that my blood coated his palm. His face was dangerously near mine, his breath washing over my cheek. I closed my eyes, feeling my pulse quicken, wanting to pull away, but at the same time not. Instinctively, I knew his lips were near to my cheek.

He was going to kiss me. I knew it. He was only waiting for my invitation.

The last time he had kissed me, I was so revolted and furious that I slapped him across the face. But this time, I was startled to realize I *wanted* him to kiss me. Suddenly, I wanted it more than I wanted my next breath.

My heart leapt into my throat.

I love him…

I love him?

I love him!

I knew I did. I knew it with such shocking clarity that it sent gooseflesh prickling along my arms and neck. For *years*, I had despised him, and when we married, wanted nothing whatsoever to do with him. But now… I knew it as certain as I knew the sun would soon set and rise again come morning… I loved him.

I loved Rowan, King of Acuniel.

How did this happen?

The weight of my realization, more powerful than any I had yet experienced, frightened me. Suddenly, I lacked air to breathe. I felt faint.

Rowan's lips brushed against my cheek with feather-light softness, and I drew my head up. When I met his eyes, our faces but an inch apart, they were so dark and intent that I shivered. "I… I have to go…"

Unable to bear the weight of what I was feeling, I pulled away from him. My side felt strangely cold without the warmth of his hand. I did not want to leave, but my mind was reeling far too much to stay.

I turned and fled down the promenade.

It was then I realized I did this a lot—running from him. I had run from him so many times; when I was angry, frightened, or after we shared a moment such as this.

Even now, I could run. I could run to the farthest reaches of Acuniel and beyond. However, no matter how far I went, I could not outrun what I felt for Rowan.

Perhaps I had loved him longer than I realized, perhaps it was just at that moment that I fell in love with him. I was not sure. But I knew that I did.

I knew it.

And there was no way I could ever deny it again.

Chapter 28

Rowan

ROWAN'S HEART AND MIND WERE SWIRLING IN A torrent of emotions just as powerful as the rain pouring outside. Once he peeled out of his wet clothes and realized he needed to talk to someone, he went to the first person he could think of, someone he felt would understand.

"My king, what is the matter?" Favian's gray brows arched high in response to Rowan's pounding on his bedchamber door for a solid minute.

Rowan pushed his way into the room, not even bothering to wait for an invitation. He found a seat in a chair by the advisor's fireplace.

Favian hurried to take the seat opposite him. "What is wrong? Has something happened?"

Rowan rested his elbows on his knees, his hands—one still smeared with her blood—clasped together and pressed to his lips. He'd nearly kissed Arabella. The desire had stunned him with its intensity. But she had pulled away before he could, breaking the spell she had managed to put him under.

However, the feelings remained. Feelings that scared, delighted, and infuriated him all at once.

"I think I love her, Favian." Rowan lifted his eyes from the fire to look into his advisor's face.

Favian's brows arched high again. "Arabella, you mean?"

"Yes! Who else?" Rowan snapped, his irritation flaring. He plopped back in his seat.

A slow smile spread Favian's lips. "I have prayed that this would happen."

"*Prayed?*" Rowan sneered.

"Yes. God knew what he was doing by bringing Arabella here."

Rowan pressed a hand, the one stained with her blood, to his face in thought. Could God have brought Arabella to him on purpose? God had not done him any good thing in the past. So why should He purposefully put a woman as wonderful as Arabella in his life?

"I nearly kissed her... just a while ago." Why had she abruptly left him? "But she pulled away."

"Mayhap she was scared." Favian gave him a questioning look. "You were not rough with her, were you?"

"Nay! Of course not. I have never been anything but a gentleman with her."

Favian sat in silence, clearly thinking it best not to press him and incite his anger any further.

Rowan exhaled in frustration. With every passing moment, he felt more and more certain of the depth of his feelings for Arabella. The way she got inside his head and twisted herself around inside his brain, driving him to the point of madness, was nothing new. She had been doing that since day one. And now he had to face the fact that she had found her way through the armor around his heart, as well, and made it her home. She had captured his heart, and he doubted he could ever take it back now.

It was exactly what he had feared would happen.

"What should I do, Favian?"

The man who had been more like a father to him leaned forward and leveled his gaze with Rowan's. "I suggest you tell her how you feel. If I know your wife at all, she shall not spurn your affections, but most likely return them. Do not try to run from this, if you know what is good for you."

Rowan rubbed his thumb over his lips. Tell her? The mere thought sent a nauseous churning through his gut. If she returned his feelings, she would not have run away!

But he longed for her... Everything inside him ached to hold her just once more, to know what it felt like to kiss her, *really* kiss her. Even merely to be the reason for her smile would thrill him.

Rowan stood and headed for the door. "Get some sleep, Favian."

"Shall you heed my advice?" the man asked, looking up at Rowan as he passed.

Rowan did not look back. "We shall see."

Arabella

I hardly slept at all that night. My mind was far too engrossed with thoughts of Rowan and how I had come to love the man I had foresworn never to. *Was this your reason for me being here, Lord? Was this Your plan all along?*

Without even hearing an answer, I knew.

It was.

And then I laughed and wept simultaneously, thinking of the incredible irony of it all.

The next morning, I wondered how it would be seeing him now. He gave me odd looks at breakfast and avoided speaking to me—at least it seemed that way by how he averted my gaze and said nothing to me all morning. I ate in silence, thinking only of the feeling of him barely kissing my cheek.

The rest of the day, I did not see him. He stayed busy with other duties of which I had no knowledge. Bored, I wandered the palace, unsure of what to do.

Voices coming from down the corridor caught my attention. I stopped at the corner and listened.

"I tire of this," came the agitated voice of Lord Favian. "I shall not—"

"Do not tell me what you tire of, old man," Cassius' voice bit back sharply.

"Nay. You are not my superior, Cassius. You cannot hinder from me from doing as I please. And I say, no more!"

I peeked around the corner. They stood in the middle of the corridor, Cassius jabbing his finger at Favian while the latter stared defiantly at the former. "Do not cross me, Favian."

Deciding to make my presence known and stop the strange argument, I casually stepped around the corner. The two lords looked over at me in surprise, ceasing their bickering at once. They bowed low. "Your Majesty."

I curtsied, eyeing them cautiously. About what had they been arguing? Never had I seen either of them so angry.

"My lords. I trust you both are having a fine day."

Favian gave me his usual friendly smile. "Yes, my queen, we are."

I smiled back, hoping they did not realize I had been eavesdropping. "I am glad." Without another word, I moved past.

My mind was whirling. Why had the two royal advisors been arguing? I remembered the tension I had sensed the time Favian and I encountered Cassius on our late-night walk. I had thought it simple, but now… it seemed there was deeper trouble between the two men.

It nagged at me all day, and I could not shake the troubled feeling that possessed me.

At the end of the evening meal, Rowan stood and headed for the door of the Banquet Hall. I stood too, starting to go after him, but Lord Favian stopped me. "My queen?"

I stopped and turned to face the man, my plans of speaking to Rowan about what transpired between us yesterday delayed. "Yes, Favian?"

"May I walk with you?"

"Of course." Did this have to do with what I overheard earlier?

Lord Favian came forward and took my arm. We walked slowly out of the Banquet Hall, entering the dim corridor. I could see Rowan's retreating figure ahead of us.

"How are you this evening, Lord Favian?"

"Well, thank you," he said. "I wish to ask you something." Favian rubbed at his chest, his eyes on the ground before him.

"Are you feeling poorly?"

"Nay, I am very well." He shook his head a bit, pausing in his next step. "I fear I am but a little dizzy. I wanted to talk to you about what you said to me once." He cast a furtive look around us. "About believing Trilaria could be innocent," he went on in a hushed whisper.

My interest piqued, I replied, "What about it?"

"I wanted to ask if you have been inquiring after that matter any further."

I tried to look innocent. "Not where Trilaria is concerned. I have asked a few questions, but—"

"Please do not ask anymore, Your Majesty. Pardon my interruption, but 'tis a dangerous matter, one that could prove dangerous to you in many ways."

"I am no traitor, Favian, if that is what you mean. I only wish to know all the facts."

Favian shook his head, looking agitated. "Nay, nay. I know your loyalties to Acuniel and to Rowan are true; I do not accuse you of treason. But others may not see it that way. And..." Favian looked around, his chest rising and falling hurriedly, "getting too much involved can have other grave consequences. I do not wish to see you harmed."

I stopped and turned to him, gripping his arms. Did he truly know something I did not? About the *real* killers? Or the attempt on Rowan's life? "What do you mean?"

He shook his head, harder this time. "Nay. We cannot speak of it here. Perhaps soon, but not now." He forced me to resume our pace. "In the meantime, *please* heed my warning."

Favian wobbled in his steps.

"Are you sure you are well, Favian?" Unease turned my stomach. He was beginning to worry me.

The man stubbornly shook his head. "Nay. I am well. As I said—only a little dizzy." He blinked slowly, his face in a strange, almost confused expression.

Eyeing him, I held his arm more firmly, trying to support his weight in case the dizziness grew worse. We walked in silence for a few moments until he spoke up again. "I also wished to ask you about His Majesty."

My heart jumped. "What of him?"

"His decision to open the orphanage speaks well of him, yes?"

I nodded slowly, unsure of where this line of conversation was leading. "Yes, I was very pleased when he told me of it."

"He really is a good man, deep down, you know."

"Yes... he is."

"Do you love him?"

The question took me completely unaware. "Wha—what?"

Suddenly, Favian clutched at his chest with a cry of pain. "Oh! My heart! It—"

"Favian!" I grabbed at his arm and shoulder as he went down. He gasped, clutching at his chest in terror. "Favian! See, I knew you were not well!"

"My—my heart!" he cried again, lying on the floor. I supported him with my arm, wrapping it around his shoulders to keep his head upright. My own heart raced in fear. *Oh God, please!*

"Rowan!" I screamed as hard I could, desperate for him to hear me from where he had just disappeared around a corner. "Rowan! Come quick! Someone! Please!" My voice was shrill with fright, panic stealing my breath.

Rowan appeared then, running towards me. "What is it?" Then he saw Favian lying on his back, in my arms. "Favian!" He went to his knees at the man's other side, opposite from me. "What is wrong?"

"He keeps complaining of his heart. And he was dizzy moments ago."

Favian's face held looks of fear, anger, and crazed desperation. "My eyes. My vision keeps going dark."

"Come now, Favian! Stay with me!" Rowan gripped the man's hand, his face a wild mask of fear. No doubt, he was recalling the night he lost his parents. That agonizing feeling of helplessness.

Favian choked, trying to catch his breath. His chest shuddered as he labored to breathe.

"Help! Someone, please! Help!" I screamed so hard my throat burned. Tears pooled in my eyes, hot and painful. When I looked at Rowan again, my heart broke in two and the tears made their way down my cheeks. For he was crying, too. Angry tears filled his eyes and he grit his teeth, squeezing Favian's hand so hard that both of their knuckles were white. Deathly white...

Hurried footsteps sounded on the floor behind us and I looked up. Two servants—one male and one female—approached us.

"My mouth is so dry," Favian said, drawing my eyes back to his pained face.

I turned to shout at the maidservant. "Fetch his lordship some water!" She stared incomprehensibly back at me, her body terrified into a state of paralysis. "*Now!* Hurry!" I barked. The girl turned and fled down the corridor, her skirts flying.

I turned back to Rowan, panic, horrible terrorizing panic—the same kind I felt when Lord Hugh attacked me—gripping my heart. "Favian, you cannot do this!" he ground out. "We shall call the physician. He will help you."

Favian shook his head, struggling to draw a breath. Bile rose in his throat and he visibly tried to force it down, nearly choking. Finally, he swallowed and looked from me to Rowan. "I fear it may be too late for a physician."

I shook my head, a sob escaping. "Nay, Favian. Nay."

Rowan growled and clutched at the man's shoulders, lifting him up off my lap. "Nay, Favian! I forbid it!"

The man let out a humorless laugh through his gritted teeth. "I… do not believe… you govern who dies… and who lives." His breath came shorter now, his words halting. He cried out, arching backward, his face contorted in agony. Favian continued to writhe and clutch at his chest as Rowan lowered him back to my lap. I held him tighter. When I put my free hand to his chest, his heartbeat thudded against my palm so hard and so fast it scared me tenfold. It felt as though his heart would burst through his shirt.

He calmed down just enough to look at my face. Tears filled his eyes, even as he continued to gasp for breath and wrestle with his raging heartbeat. One of his trembling hands came up to touch my face. "Be good to him…" I choked on a sob and nodded, tears coursing down my face. This could not be happening! It could not. It must be a dream!

Then Favian turned to Rowan and gripped his hand in both of his own. "I love you, son. Please… remember all… that I have told you. Especially… what we recently discussed." He shared a hard, intimate look with Rowan, communicating a secret between them that I was not to know. Tears ran down Favian's temples and into his gray hair. "I love you both…" He looked around at the crowd of people who had gathered around us by now: several servants, the girl with the water that was no longer needed, Lord Geoffrey and Lady Allis, and Lord Cassius. Each of them wore frightened, worried expressions, not a one sure what to do.

Then he looked back at Rowan and I, his eyes growing distant now. He held both of our hands, his grip tight and pleading. He rallied himself to lock eyes with Rowan once more. "Please, forgive me…" Another tear traced down into his hair. "There is so much I wish…" He looked between us. "People… are not always… what they seem."

Favian took a shuddering breath then let out a terrible choking sound. His head fell back and his grip on our hands loosened. He went slack in my arms… His eyes stared unseeingly into my face.

My heart sunk into the depths of my chest, ripping in two jagged pieces.

"Favian?" Rowan cradled the man's head, willing him to meet his gaze again. "Favian?"

"Rowan, he—" my voice broke off. I could not finish the words.

"Nay." He shook his head. "*Nay!*" His shout rent the air like a knife, sending my insides into a chaos of pain. He pounded his fist against the ground, hot, boiling, angry tears streaking his cheeks. Rowan never cried… And certainly not in public.

He held Favian's lifeless body in his arms. "Come now, Favian. You cannot do this! I cannot lose you, too! Not another!" A cry of fury left his throat and he closed his eyes, bowing his head over the man who had been the closest thing he had had to a father for nearly a decade.

Rowan suddenly opened his eyes and gave the small crowd a look sharper than any sword. "Go! All of you!" The anger that turned his blue eyes into swirling, dark tempests was unlike any I had seen him express before. This was different, stronger and more dangerous. He looked fit to kill.

I stood on trembling legs. "Go. Please… Leave us."

The stricken crowd, staring at the dead lord and the crying king in disbelief, slowly turned and left us alone. I locked eyes with Lord Cassius as he departed with the others and was surprised by the lack of emotion in his eyes, so opposite from the others.

Hesitantly, I moved to Rowan's side and knelt behind him, unsure if he would accept my comfort. I wrapped my arms about his trembling shoulders and clung to him. He released all the control I was accustomed to seeing, openly weeping over the loss of this man.

I wept against his back, my tears pooling on his shirt. *How could he die, God? Why did he have to die?* I let out a guttural sob, my grief starting to take full hold. Favian had been my friend, the first person to make me feel at home here. An encouragement to me in so many ways. My heart ached knowing he was gone... forever. Forever.

This cannot be true! My mind refused to believe it, while my heart felt the loss like the stabbing of a blade.

But whatever loss I felt, 'twas nothing compared to Rowan's. Favian had been his closest friend, like a father to him. And now, like his birth father, he was gone.

Just another loss for him to tally against God.

Rowan abruptly lifted his head and straightened. I slipped my arms from around his shoulders, my vision blurry through the tears. "Rowan..." I whispered. What else could be said?

Resignation weighting his movements, he carefully lowered Favian's body to the floor, closed his staring eyes with gentle fingers, and turned to me. Rowan's tear-streaked face was hardened, distant, as if he was determined to defy the emotions spilling from his eyes.

I ached to soothe his grief, but how? "Rowan... I..."

Without speaking, he rose on stiff legs and moved past the body of his friend. "You cannot just leave him here." I rose halfway, wanting to stand to go after Rowan, but also not wanting to leave Favian.

His back was to me, muscles visibly taut beneath his clothing. "You see that he is taken care of." Then he walked away, once again the hard, serious man he usually was, pulling back his tears with more control than I ever would possess.

"Rowan!"

But it was too late.

He was already gone.

Chapter 29

I SAW TO IT THAT SERVANTS TOOK FAVIAN TO HIS room to be prepared for burial. I still could not believe he was dead. Gone. Forever. Just earlier that day, he had been so *alive*. So healthy... by all appearances.

How could he have died so suddenly?

Once I knew his body was safe and comfortable—as if that made a difference now—I went to Rowan's door and knocked. For a moment, nothing happened. I heard no noise, no sign that he was inside. Then the door opened and there he stood, his face so *blank*, as if he were absent of any and all emotion. As though he were only an empty, lonely shell of himself.

I stepped inside his room and he let me past. Quietly, he shut the door and turned to face me. I fell against his chest, my arms tight about his middle, my tears returning with a vengeance. He was straight and wooden in my arms, not giving in to my embrace.

"I am so, *so* very sorry, Rowan," I whimpered, my tears wetting the front of his clothes. His heartbeat drummed in my ear, steady, strong—just as he was endeavoring to be now. He had lost hold of his emotions before everyone earlier, and now he was determined to pull those emotions back. Would he not even share his grief with me in private?

Slowly, his arms came around me, securing me in their strength. "I cannot believe it." His voice sounded numb. Dead.

I shook my head, still struggling to accept the horrible tragedy myself. It hurt. It made no sense at all that a man who should have had plenty of years ahead of him would die so abruptly. But... this had to have a purpose. Right? God had to know what He was doing by allowing Favian to leave us.

"At least he is with the Lord now. It does not make sense, but God knows what He is—"

Rowan tore away. "Do not speak to me of *God*," he spat. "If He knows what He is doing, then He knows He has stolen those that I love." He bellowed this at me in a mix of fury and incredulity. "How could a God who is supposed to love us allow us to experience such suffering and pain?" He threw out a hand, as if demanding an answer.

His words cut like a knife to my heart. How could he say such things? Then I remembered the similar thoughts I once had when I harbored resentment towards God for allowing me to marry Rowan. I could not judge him for his questions when I had asked them once myself.

I stepped close again and put my hands on his shoulders, turning him to face me. He met my eyes, his mouth clenched tight. He was reverting to his old ways. I feared all the progress he had made would be for naught, forsaken in the wake of his grief.

I touched a hand to his face, staring earnestly into his eyes. The stubble on his cheek tickled my palm. "Please... *please* do not blame God for this, Rowan. Favian would not want that. Do not turn away from Him in times of trouble, but rather turn *to* Him."

Rowan jerked his face away as if my touch pained him and stepped out of reach. "Go. Go now, Arabella." He looked at me with hard, penetrating eyes. "I do not want you here."

Rowan

The hurt expression on his wife's face before she left his room stung Rowan's heart. He should not have spoken so harshly. She did not justly deserve it. He wished he could condemn her for her talk of faith and God, but he could not. Deep inside, he knew she was right.

Still, his heart and mind screamed for an explanation. "Why, God?" he hissed, going to his window and flinging the shutters wide, letting the cool air wash over his face. "*Why?* Favian did not deserve this! He should have had years yet to live, but instead, You choose to take him!"

How could he freely love Arabella if everyone he loved was stolen from him? His parents, now Favian. Would he lose Arabella, too?

Nay. For that reason, he could not give his heart to her. He could never openly love Arabella.

This confirmation widened the gash in his heart, enflaming his pain to an unbearable degree.

Rowan beat his fist against the stone windowsill, angry tears again rising in his eyes. He hated himself for his weakness. He never cried, but now he found himself weeping like a little boy.

"You foolish, stupid man. Tears are for the weak."

He shoved away from the window, angrier than ever.

I have not forsaken you.

That Voice came to him through the torment of his mind, breaking through like sunshine on a rainy day.

But Rowan pushed it away, refusing to give in to the light. "Nay," he hissed. "I do not want Your words. They are never anything more than empty promises."

Arabella

We buried Favian two days later.

Our procession of mourners marched solemnly, silently, to the Caelrith Cathedral for the funeral service. We sang and prayed, the ache of death heavy in the air. At the service's conclusion, we proceeded to the cemetery behind the elaborate coffin Rowan had commissioned for Favian's body and laid our friend to rest.

Rowan stood by my side throughout the ordeal, but he was silent and cold as a statue, his eyes hollow.

My heart went out to him, and I wished so desperately to provide him comfort, to be there to listen or talk to him, whatever he required. But he would not welcome any such comfort that I could give. He would scarcely even meet my eye.

When we returned to the palace, Rowan disappeared into his chamber and did not emerge again for the rest of the day.

This left me to sit in worried, distraught silence in the tower. I watched smoke rising from the chimneys of houses, my mind free to wander.

Favian's strange last words kept nagging at me. *Please remember, people are not always what they seem...* What had he meant by that? Had he been referring to Rowan and even myself, trying to tell us to look past each other's outer person and see one another for whom we were deep down, hoping to bring us together? Or did he mean something else?

The royal physician said his heart was what killed him, and I supposed that made sense. Favian *was* getting advanced in years. But he had never had any health problems before that day. Because of that, and what Favian and I had been discussing just before his death, doubt haunted me. The entire situation screamed that something was wrong.

What if Favian was murdered somehow?

That thought made my stomach go cold. The man's warnings echoed through my head. *Mayhap you should not speak of that certain subject... For your own sake. 'Tis a dangerous matter... Getting too much involved can have many grave consequences.* Favian's earnest face appeared in my mind's eye. *Please, heed my warning.*

I had felt certain that Favian knew things I did not, and his apparent plan to speak to me again in private about the matter only served to prove that to me.

Had Favian gotten too close to the truth, and the men who killed Rowan's parents saw him as a threat?

Please, heed my warning.

I put a hand to my head, my mind swirling. Could it really be that Favian died because he knew the truth?

All of my talk about Trilaria... My eavesdropping... My conversation with Favian before he died. I had made myself a target. What if Favian's killer came after me next?

Please, heed my warning.

"Oh, God, I know not what to do," I whispered in prayer, feeling frantic as I stared out the tower window. "Should I forget all about this and get out while I still can? Before people accuse me of treason, or I am murdered as well?"

The only answer was another echoing of Favian's voice. *Please, heed my warning!*

This latest occurrence had struck a new fear into me. I had played with fire, and now it was clear that if I did not release it soon... I would be burned.

Perhaps the best thing really would be to back away and remove myself from the matter before I caused myself or others more harm.

Would that not be best?

And were there not other matters I needed to think of?

Rowan's acute grief worried me almost as much as Favian's strange death. It seemed all progress he had made was now lost. I laid awake late into every night, wishing and praying that he would find a way out of this. Enough grief had plagued him already, and now with Favian's death... I feared it would destroy him.

For two weeks, Rowan shut himself away from everyone, even me, which seemed to tear my heart from my chest. He stayed in his room or his study, pouring over battle plans all day. I rarely saw him—even less than when we first married—and any time our paths did cross, he said nothing to me.

One night, I opened the door of the sitting room to find Rowan propped against the wall near the fire, one leg outstretched and the other bent up at an angle. He lifted his head when I entered. His eyes were glassy, a bottle clutched firmly in his hand.

My heart ripped open further than it already had, realizing he had resorted to drinking to numb the pain.

He absently looked me over, taking another swig. "What do you want?"

I dared take a few steps forward. "Nothing. I was only headed to bed."

"Well, go on then." His speech was slurred. Rowan had never been a drinking man, but now... How much had he imbibed?

I did not move, but stayed where I stood, staring at him. I loved him—Lord, have mercy, I loved him. But he did not love me. I had thought mayhap he did, after that night in the rain, but now it seemed it was not so. And to make matters worse, he sat before me half out of his mind with drink.

God, please. I cannot bear this.

Rowan struggled to his feet, using the wall for support. His steps were wobbly, staggered, a shock of brown hair hanging haphazardly over his forehead.

"Why are you doing this?" My limbs began to tremble.

"Because I can!" He threw the empty bottle into the fire. It shattered against the back of the hearth with a loud crash. I jumped, staring at the shards as they flew and landed in the flames.

"You should not be doing this," I said as he staggered towards me. "'Tis not right. Rowan, please. I do not—"

His hand caught underneath my chin, holding my jaw. "Do not preach to me, Arabella." His eyes spat fire, covered with a bleary glaze.

I fought back tears, biting my lip to keep from shouting in agony—but not because he hurt me physically. Nay, it was my heart that was suffering. A wayward tear slipped down my temple and into my hair as I stared up at him.

"Do not... preach to me," he repeated, softer this time. Rowan let out an exasperated sigh and lowered his forehead to mine, moving his hand to the side of my face, his other arm wrapping around my waist. He closed his eyes, his brows lowered intensely. The smell of alcohol on his breath wafted over my face. His touch was hard and desperate, as if he feared to lose me, or as though I were his only way to escape death.

"You are... a torment to me... I cannot bear it."

My heart wrenched at those words, unable to determine their meaning. I sucked in a breath, catching myself before a sob escaped, and swallowed. Then I jerked out of his arms, my tears starting to fall as I tore away from him.

Flinging my door open, I hurried inside and sat by my window, releasing my tears and fervently praying that he would find a way out of this storm and discover joy again.

Because otherwise, I would lose my mind. And he, just possibly... his life.

Chapter 30

EVERY NIGHT, I PRAYED UNTIL I FELL ASLEEP. During many of these nightly vigils, I would stare at my door, wondering what Rowan was doing and hoping that he was not drinking again.

The death of Favian had affected him far more than I ever would have anticipated. It seemed this new loss, added to the ones of the past, had been his breaking point, pushing him over the edge of a metaphorical cliff.

I only hoped that it was not too late for him to climb back up onto solid ground.

Late one night, just over two weeks after Favian's tragic death, I found I could not sleep until I knew if he was well. I rose from my bed, donned my robe over my nightdress, and opened the door to our shared sitting room.

I was startled to find Rowan sitting by the fire.

He looked up when he heard me, keeping my gaze for a moment before returning his melancholy eyes to the blaze. I paused in the doorway. "I was just coming to check on you. To see if you are well."

"I am well enough."

I nodded, looking to my bare feet peeking from beneath my robe, then took a step back into my room, not wishing to press him for more.

"Stay. Please... I would like the company."

After a long moment's hesitation, I made my way to the chair beside him, my heart rising with hope at the knowledge that he wanted my company. I had a flashback to the last time I had found him sitting by the fire and he asked me to stay. Would this night end the same way?

As I took my seat, I checked his face for signs of drink, but there were none. He appeared sober, which eased my nerves a fraction.

We sat in silence for several long minutes. I wished to speak, but purposely kept my mouth closed, determined to let him make the first move.

"How are you?" he said at last, his voice low and reverberating.

His question surprised me, bringing my head over to look at him. "I am well. I thank you for asking."

His solemn blue eyes searched my face, and a battle seemed to wage inside them. What sort of battle?

"I still cannot believe he is truly gone," I said, daring to speak of the subject I knew troubled his mind.

Rowan folded his hands over his abdomen. "Neither can I." He shook his head and frowned. "I did not realize how much he meant to me until he was gone." A look of guilt crossed his face. "I should have been kinder to him, given his word more credence than I often did." His eyes turned glassy. "He was so good to me, like my own father. And I did not give him nearly enough credit."

A tear slipped down my cheek. I had not even realized any had arisen. I swiped at it as Rowan cleared his throat and sat up straighter in his seat.

He looked at me again and his blue eyes softened. With each moment, he was looking more like the Rowan I had grown to love—the one who was kind, surprisingly tender, and had a beautiful smile.

"Do not feel guilty, Rowan. Favian knew you loved him. And he loved you. He would not want for you to be unhappy."

"Forgive me for how I have been behaving of late."

My heart swelled with the intensity of my love for him, no matter how he had acted these last days. "Of course, I forgive you."

Rowan did not reply, but watched me, his gaze that covered my face bringing heat to my cheeks. I could not handle this... being so close to him, yet so very far away. There were leagues between us, though we were a mere arm's length apart. I was so weary of him shutting me out, especially now that I knew I loved him as

I had never loved anyone else. I had never dreamed that I could feel this strongly for someone, least of all him.

But he did not love me. And unreciprocated love is a terrible thing to bear.

I could not endure any more. Abruptly, I stood and turned towards my room. "If you will excuse me, I am tired and—"

"Arabella. Wait." Rowan's hand caught mine, his hold and the desperation in his voice halting me instantly. Slowly, every movement like a knife to my heart, I turned to face him.

He stood and drew me nearer, still holding my hand firmly in his. His eyes roved over my face, searching. They found their way to my lips, and my heart jumped. "I cannot go on like this," he whispered as if to himself, his eyes continuing to search my face with a pained look. "I shall not let my fear bind me any longer."

I stared at him, my hand beginning to tremble in his.

Still looking over my face, his head cocked to the side, he whispered again. "I think I love you."

My heart leapt into my throat. "You *think*?" Fragile hope fluttered to life. *Is it not too good to be true?*

His eyes focused on my lips again, then slowly came up to meet my eyes. My heart threatened to burst straight through my skin. "Nay," he said lowly, "I *know*."

Then he seized my face in his hands and covered my lips with his, kissing me deeply. I held onto his arms, welcoming his kiss and returning it freely. Finally.

Finally!

This was what I had been waiting for, praying for. Unlike the last time he kissed me, I was not angry. I was so overjoyed and caught in the overwhelming feeling of his arms moving to encircle my back that I could have laughed and cried at the same time.

He loved me. He *loved* me!

I twined my arms about Rowan's neck and kissed him deeper, pulling him closer until his chest touched mine. Abruptly, he pulled his face away, leaving me woozy, my head fuzzy from his kiss. "What is the matter?" I did not want to open my eyes for fear I would wake to find this all a dream.

"Should we be doing this?" he gasped, sounding breathless and agonized. His grip about me was tight, refusing to let go as if fearing I would disappear, just as I feared *he* would.

Finally, my eyes fluttered open to see Rowan's eyes searching my face with a conflicted look of longing. "Should we be so... *joyous*, when one has so recently lost his life? Is it proper for us to be this way so soon after Favian's death?" Unshed tears glistened in his eyes as he struggled with guilt over feeling happiness. He rubbed his hands over my arms, across my shoulders and back, his expression agony itself.

I searched those glistening eyes, joy, thankfulness, and so much else flowing from my own. *Thank you, Lord. Could it be that our love, our being together, is what shall bring him out of this darkness?*

I shook my head, playing with the hair at his ear, trailing my fingertips down the sharp and stubbled edge of his jawline. "Nay... In fact, I believe this is what he wanted all along."

Realization slowly dawned in his eyes. Suddenly, he kissed me again, pressing, searching, with such passion I could scarcely breathe. This man I had once loathed with everything in me, and now I *loved* him with the same. How it had happened and when, I was not entirely sure. I fought it for so long, but at some point, I had given in and opened my heart to him. And it appeared he had done the same.

He held me tighter—if that were possible—pressing me to him, nearly lifting my feet off the ground. His lips caressed mine without ceasing, his fingers moving through my hair that fell around my back in waves. He was releasing all his pent-up emotions into me—his joys and sufferings alike—sharing them with me, binding us as one.

I had been married to him for months now, but never had I felt *this* connected to him—not even that night in the moonlight. Never had I felt like I was *his*. Now, here we were...

I was finally his.

And he was mine.

"I love you," I managed to get out between kisses, holding his face in my hands and feeling those words in their full weight with all of my heart.

Yes... Rowan was most definitely *mine*.

And I would remain *his* forever... No matter what was to come.

Rowan

Rowan smiled to himself and sleepily opened his eyes. He rolled to his side, expecting to see his wife's beautiful face. *My wife...* He sighed, already longing for the feeling of her in his arms again.

But she was not there.

Rowan bolted upright, looking around his chamber in confusion. Where had she gone? And why had she left him? Surely, he had not dreamed last night up.

Hurriedly, Rowan dressed in the first clothes he could find and threw open the door to his room.

Somehow, he knew where to find Arabella without having to search.

He stepped onto the promenade surrounding the garden and spotted a swath of pale blue among the foliage. There she was.

He hurried down the steps and emerged into the garden. Arabella appeared from behind a bush, dressed in a pale blue gown. Her pretty eyes went wide before her lips curved in an impish grin. "I see you." He grinned wickedly. "And I do believe I shall catch you, as well." Rowan started towards her, his expression playfully cat-like. She squealed and turned to run away. Her merry laughter floated behind her as Rowan broke into a jog. He wanted to catch her, but the thrill of the chase was just as fun. He had to give her a fair chance at escape, after all.

He followed her on her weaving path through the garden, her skirt flowing out behind her heels. She glanced over her shoulder to see him getting closer, then squealed and laughed in a panic.

Rowan laughed too.

It felt so wonderfully good to laugh.

She was almost to the stairs leading down into the garden, about to disappear inside the palace, but he caught her around the waist and pulled her backward, her feet leaving the ground. Arabella's stomach muscles contracted against his arm as she laughed and squealed, pulling against him in an effort to free herself. Refusing to let her go, Rowan turned her around in his arms until she faced him. Her hands braced against his chest, she breathed heavy from her flight. Her beautiful mouth spread into a gleeful grin, and soft wisps of her dark hair framed her face.

"Why did you leave me? I was so looking forward to waking and your lovely face being the first thing I see." He lowered his forehead to touch hers, unable to remember ever being this happy in the past eight years, perhaps even his lifetime.

"I woke early and was unable to return to sleep. You looked so peaceful and I hated to wake you, but I was far too restless to wait for you to get up. So, I thought I would take a walk and let you come find me." His wife nudged him with a playful look.

"And what fun that was." Then he was covering her face in fast, lively kisses. Soon, she lifted her chin and captured his lips with hers, sending a fresh surge of longing through his heart.

Last night, he had decided he could not allow his fear of losing her to keep them apart. He loved her and could no longer hold her at arm's length, for doing so pained him more than he could say.

He would not fear losing Arabella. He would only enjoy the task of loving her.

How could he even worry when she brought him such joy?

He pulled away enough to whisper against her ear. "Let us go back upstairs, wife."

"Having a fine morning, I see?"

Rowan pulled back, looking over his wife's shoulder to see Lord Cassius standing at the top of the steps. Arabella turned in his arms, a furiously red flush staining her cheeks. He released her and she stepped behind him. "Yes, a fine morning indeed." Why could he not stop grinning like a fool? "I have the most wonderful wife in all the land."

Cassius studied him. "And that is merry news, my king." With a look at Arabella, Cassius turned to leave. "Enjoy the morning, Your Majesties."

With Cassius gone, Rowan turned back to Arabella, still unready to begin his duties for the day. He took her back into his arms, holding her close, and buried his face in her neck, savoring the sweet smell of her. "I love you." Such sentiments felt foreign on his lips, yet amazingly at home—an utter paradox.

"And I love you." With another kiss, Rowan took his wife's hand and led her back to his chamber.

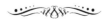

Arabella

With every moment spent with Rowan, with every kiss and embrace, fear coiled tighter in my heart. My soul wrapped desperate fingers around our love and quaked at the thought of jeopardizing this joyful place we had found together. Over and over, Favian's warning sounded like an alarm bell in my memory. *Please, heed my warning!*

After a few days, I was determined to try to put my questions and suspicions to rest. Favian's death was a firm reminder of what could happen to those who questioned the matter of the king and queen's death. And this new love between Rowan and I, this happy life we could at last share… I had ached for this contentment for too long. It was too precious to risk.

God, please, I prayed late one night, while watching Rowan sleep peacefully at my side. *Help the truth come to light without me. I cannot meddle in it any longer. I cannot.*

God had to reveal the culprit somehow. He just had to. But He had to do so without me. It was clearly too dangerous. There was too much at risk now. I would focus on Rowan and mind my own business.

Certainly, God did not need my help.

Chapter 31

THE YEARLY HARVEST FESTIVAL CAME THE FOL-
lowing week. I was accustomed to helping with the preparations,
being involved in the decorating and cooking done by many of the
peasant women of the city, but this year, that was not to be. This
time, I was the guest of honor, alongside Rowan. I did not have to
lift a finger save to inform the royal cook of what to prepare for
the feast to be held in the palace following the celebration's end.

Rowan insisted I have a new dress for the festival, which I
insisted was unnecessary. But of course, he won in the end.

He came into my room just after the fitting ended and the
seamstress had left. With a flick of wrist, he dismissed Mavis, who
stood ready to help me back into my day gown, and I turned with
a smile to face him.

He stepped towards me and gently took me into his arms. "I
spend good money on you a new gown, and this is all the woman
can produce?" Rowan teased, gesturing to my short chemise edged
with lace.

I laughed. "Nay, silly. She has a beautiful gown planned." I lifted my face up to his. "'Tis a beautiful, deep, golden red, much like
the color of a sunset. I believe you shall be quite pleased."

"Hmm." He gave a little shrug and let his eyes graze my form
from head to toe. "I know not, Arabella. The more I look at it, I
believe this dress pleases me fine."

I laughed again and playfully hit his shoulder. "I do not think
the rest of the kingdom would agree with you, my love."

He shrugged again, with a roguish smile barely suppressed,
and lowered his face to kiss me.

Rowan left a few minutes later, leaving me sighing in contentment, and Mavis stepped back in. Her face held a bold smirk of approval and I frowned at her for an instant before giving in to a smile of my own and an embarrassed laugh.

"You knew this would happen, did you not?" I wanted to ask but resisted. I already knew the answer.

My primary lady's maid had believed Rowan and I would come to love one another from the very beginning. After all, she had said, that day so long ago now, that she believed I could do Rowan a great deal of good. And by looking at the smile on his face and the gleam in his eye as he left my chamber, he had indeed been dealt a great deal of good.

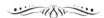

My dress was ready just in time for the harvest celebration, and it fit like a dream. Rowan looked as if his eyes would pop from their sockets when I emerged from my room, and I laughed at his response, thrilled by his obvious approval.

Down in the city square, the people were already celebrating. Men stood in clusters, laughing raucously and toasting with mugs full of frothy ale as the women chatted and busied themselves with the food. Children ran underfoot, one group of them gleefully chasing an orange tomcat who looked frightened for his life.

Trumpeters announced our arrival as Rowan and I descended from our horses and moved to the temporarily erected dais bearing a pair of wooden thrones. Everyone quieted and bowed low as we took our seats.

Rowan gestured for the crowd to stand. I noticed that he did not scowl at his subjects as he once had. This day, he gazed with interest at the people, his eyes calm and his lips relaxed.

Musicians struck up a lively tune and the citizens of Caelrith surged into motion, dancing a peasant's reel. "Oh! I always loved this one."

Beside me, Rowan winced at my offhanded comment. "Forgive me for taking away all you ever knew..."

I turned in my seat, quickly shaking my head in reassurance. "Nay, Rowan. Do not feel sorry. There is no other place I would rather be than at your side."

A small smile lifted his lips, though a shadow still darkened his eyes. I reached over and squeezed his hand, and he lifted mine to his lips.

When he released me, I folded my hands in my lap and sat back to watch the dancing. My foot involuntarily tapped with the beat.

"You may join them if you wish." Rowan's voice startled me after several moments of silence.

"Oh, nay. I should not." Then I spotted a familiar blonde head at the edge of the crowd. "However… there is one person I would speak to."

He followed my gaze and found, at the end of it, Gloriana. "I see. That is your friend, from that day at church, yes? By all means, go to her." He quickly lifted a finger at me as I was rising. "But pray, do not stay long, lest I begin to worry for you. I wish to know where you are at all times." He smiled softly. "For I do not wish to lose you, love."

I squeezed his hand tight before descending the dais stairs. The crowd parted like the waters before Moses, bringing me straight to my friend. Her back was to me, her beautiful golden hair brushed into loose waves that flowed down her back and shone in the evening sun.

I tickled her sides and she yelped. Her pretty eyes went wide when she whirled around to face me. "Arabella!" Then she paused, uncertainty crossing her face as she looked around at the people whose attention she had garnered with her shout. "Well, er… *my queen.*"

I shook my head and grabbed her in a fierce hug. "You silly goose! Nay, you are my best friend and always shall be. You may always address me normally." I playfully swatted her arm when we pulled apart.

"As you wish, *Your Majesty,*" she said, emphasizing my title for the sole sake of annoying me. Oh, how I had missed her.

"So… how have you been?"

"Well enough. I have missed you terribly." Her pink lips turned down in a pout. "As has mother—she says you were a good influence on me. But she also says not to mourn your leaving because you obtained such a high position." Gloriana rolled her eyes. "She still loses sleep wondering over what I must have done for me not to be chosen by Lord Hugh."

I laughed lightly. But then I secretly thought of what would have happened had Gloriana been chosen and Rowan married her instead, and immediately, I felt a prick of jealousy. I hated to think of him being with anyone else.

Which reminded me...

"Gloriana... do you remember when you asked me if King Rowan was a good kisser?" The girl nodded, her interest flaring before my eyes. "Well... it turns out he *is*."

My friend's hands flew to her mouth before she pulled them away to spat me on the shoulder and squealed like a little girl. "You've fallen in love with him, have you not? I can see it in your face!"

My satisfied smile was too hard to keep down, though I winced at having to eat nearly a decade's worth of my words. "Yes... I am afraid so."

She gripped my hands. "Does he love you?"

"Blessedly, he does."

Then Gloriana looked over my shoulder, her gaze sparkling with mischief. "He is watching you."

I looked back and my eyes met his. We shared a long, secretive gaze that sent warmth curling all the way to my toes before I turned back to my friend. Suddenly, I wished for the evening to pass by as soon as possible so I could be alone with him again.

"How is he? Really?" Gloriana frowned, suddenly growing uncharacteristically serious. "As much as I dreamed of having him for myself, I cannot pretend that I would not have been more than a little afraid of him. I have heard many stories of his great temper."

Rowan did indeed have a temper, that was certain, but he was... so different from when we first wed. The changes were remarkable. I trusted him now. And he was kind and gentle with me, always.

"He is most kind." I smiled to myself, thinking contentedly of our stolen kisses throughout the day whenever he found the chance to slip away from his duties. Just the thought sent my stomach flipping pleasantly. "Truly... he has changed so much in my eyes—and in everyone's, I believe—since I first came to the palace. You would scarcely believe it."

I looked up from my blissful reverie to find my friend staring at me with a look that screamed of her happiness for me. "You really *do* love him."

Before I could respond, the familiar face of a young man we both knew caught my eye. He was standing several people distant from us, watching Gloriana's every move with obvious longing. "I believe someone is looking for you."

Gloriana glanced back and spotted the man. "Ah, yes. Henry. He has been carrying a torch for me ever so long. But I do like him. We have been becoming quite friendly of late."

"Ahhh…." I nudged her with my hip. "So, you have taken up with ole Henry, I see—conveniently the son of a successful merchant."

She rolled her eyes, crossing her arms over her chest. "The money has nothing to do with it."

"Of course."

Then someone else caught my eye. A face I had not thought I would ever see again.

Frederic.

He was waving at me, calling me over to him. I returned his wave with a little shake of my head and a look that said, *I cannot possibly.* But he would not relent.

I glanced over my shoulder to see that Rowan was no longer watching me but rather observing the dancers. I turned back to Gloriana. "You go on to Henry. I believe I shall speak with Fred for a moment and find you again before I leave."

She hugged me and set off toward her potential suitor while I carefully made my way to the man that had always wished to be mine.

He grinned when I reached him, captured my hand before I could say a word, and dragged me into an alley just a few steps away. "Fred! What are you doing? If people take notice, rumors will run rampant! What would Rowan think of you pulling me into a dark corner?" I looked over my shoulder, worried someone may be watching.

Frederic waved away my protests. "I am doing nothing untoward. I only wanted to speak to you. I have not seen you in months. Not since you married *him*." He crossed his arms and gave me a once-over. "How have you been, Your Majesty?"

Why did the epithet have to sound so mocking on his lips? "Well, I thank you. How have you been?" I lifted a brow. "Staying out of trouble, I hope."

His handsome face lit with pleasure, as it always had in my

presence. "Yes, I have been a good boy. Do not worry your pretty little head."

He took a half step back and studied my eyes then, his face growing serious, his arms still crossed. I had a flashback to that day in the market when he caught me from falling. He had been so certain I would come around to the idea of marriage to him and accept his proposal one day. But that plan had gone vastly awry, and now here I was, not his wife but his *queen*. Married to the man he disliked just as much as I once had.

I had always known, though, that I could never marry Fred. We simply would not have worked well together, no matter our great friendship. I had never been sure of what my future husband would be like, but I had known he would not be Fred…

Had my heart always known it could only belong to Rowan?

"Is he good to you?" Frederic said suddenly. "Does he treat you well? Because if he is cruel to you, king or no, I shall rip him apart."

I nodded, putting a reassuring hand to his shoulder. "Yes, he is most good to me." My voice trailed off and again I felt that overwhelming sense of happiness. Contentment. "In fact… I love him, Fred."

He staggered back as if I had punched him. "*Love* him?" The shock registered across his eyes as he spit the words out like poison. "Arabella, how could you? I thought you, of all people, would despise that man until the end of your days."

"I know Fred, I thought that as well. But the more I came to know him, the more I realized he truly is a good man, deep down."

Frederic shook his head in exasperation. "I cannot understand you, Arabella. You used to profess your dislike for him, speaking against his war, his neglect of the people. You hated him."

That reminder stung. I *had* hated him. The question was not how could I love him. Rather, it was how could I have hated him so much and allowed those ill feelings to cloud my judgment? It had kept me from seeing him for who he was at heart.

"I do not hate him now, Fred. I love him," I pressed a hand to my chest, stepping forward to touch his arm, "with all of my heart." He flinched at the contact. "I know you always hoped… for something else." I glanced away to the ground. "I do not expect you to understand my change of views, but I hope you will not think ill of me for them."

"I still love you, you know." He reached a tentative hand to touch my jaw. His eyes were heavy, sad, flitting over my face before meeting my gaze. "I always will."

"I love you too, Fred." He knew my words carried a different meaning. And not the one he desired.

"I must go now," I whispered, surprised by the sudden surge of tears in my eyes. I drew away from him, my skirts lifted in my fists to keep them from the filth of the alley. "Rowan will be worried, wondering where on earth I have disappeared to. If he has been searching for me among the crowd, he shall be quite cross by now."

"*Cross*, eh? I suppose he tracks every little thing you do." Fred's voice dripped with contempt.

I cast him a sharp look over my shoulder, my heart stinging at his censure. Had I really been this harsh? Had I sounded this... *angry?*

Without another word, I emerged from the shelter of the narrow alley and moved along the border of the crowd. A knight assisted me up the wooden steps of the platform and I took my seat beside a visibly anxious Rowan. "You took longer than I thought you would. I was beginning to worry about you."

"Forgive me." Did my voice sound nonchalant enough? All I could see was Frederic's face as he declared his love for me one last time. I had a feeling Rowan would not be happy to learn of that, or about Fred's dragging of me into a dark alleyway against my will. "Catching up with an old friend can take up more time than one realizes."

"Did you and Gloriana have a pleasant talk?" His sweet smile was back.

I smiled in return, though inside I was frowning, still hearing the distaste in Frederic's voice, his resentment of Rowan and the love he and I shared. "Yes... most pleasant."

Chapter 32

THE MONTHS OF AUTUMN WERE A DREAM TO me. Every day, I woke to Rowan's handsome face, either kissing me to wakefulness or peaceful in sleep. In my heart, I feared that I would one day wake to find this was nothing but a dream... a wonderful, beautiful dream.

The only heaviness amongst this dream-like world was Rowan's continued planning for a new campaign in the war against Trilaria. He had grown distant from it, in a way, not throwing himself into the matter as much as he would have a few months before, but he did continue with the preparations. All across the kingdom, the training of new troops was well underway, and soon they would march to meet the men already at the front.

The looming battle posed many worries for me. For one, it meant more fighting with the country I still believed innocent, and death and destruction to our own weary subjects.

Secondly, it meant Rowan would soon be leaving me to lead the battle. If he did not return to me alive... I was not sure what I would do. I hated to even think of such an outcome.

And then there was something else that weighed heavily on my mind, no matter how much I had sworn off dwelling on it.

The deaths of Rowan's parents and Favian, and how the two incidents seemed horribly connected.

Several nights I woke from a fitful, nightmare-filled sleep, envying Rowan's complete ease at my side. My dreams were full of masked men chasing me with bloody knives, killing Rowan or Uncle Matthew. Or me. I would wake with cold sweats and a racing heart and be forced to pace the room or open the window for a breath of fresh air. Clasping my trembling hands, I would breathe a prayer that God would remove this anxiety and bring the killers to justice—without me. I did not want to get involved any further. I had no desire to have my throat slit like my predecessor, Queen Matilda... or to see others I loved hurt because of my curiosity.

Rowan awoke one such night, rising groggily on his elbow. "Arabella?" He blinked in the weak moonlight streaming through the window. "Are you well?"

I covered my arms with my hands, suddenly very cold. The late autumn air was chilly, piercing straight through my thin nightdress. "Yes, I am well." I closed the shutters and moved to slide back under the covers, settling in beside my husband. His arm came around my chest and he tugged me close, sighing sleepily as he nestled his chin atop my head. I inhaled. Exhaled. A breath as shaky as my hands. Not even Rowan's warming embrace could soothe me. "I merely had a bad dream..."

His only response was a gentle snore.

Rowan

He sat with his wife in the tower, which had now become their shared special place they would retreat to nearly every evening. He sat on the stone bench beneath the arched window, one leg hanging down the side, the other stretched out across it. Arabella sat before him, relaxed against his chest while he held her snug in his embrace. His fingers traced absent circles across the fabric of her bodice.

Arabella sighed and angled her face up to see him, her eyes sparkling brighter than the stars beginning to peek from the sky and swirling with a thousand thoughts he could not seem to follow. "What is it?" He held her cheek. "I can see you are thinking, but I cannot fathom what about." Rowan kissed her forehead, relishing the soft smoothness of her skin.

"Did you know we met once? Before we went on that first walk."

"Yes, I know. I saw you in the corridor when I returned home wounded."

"Nay." She shook her head. "Before that, years before that. Do you not remember that day when you and your father were out riding, and you almost ran over a group of children? That was me, Gloriana, and… a boy."

Rowan looked aside to think. Slowly, memories began to fall into place. Before long, he had an image in his mind of a young girl with flowing dark hair and beautiful dark eyes staring up at him. He had been powerless to look away, even then. "Ah. Yes, I remember."

"I was ten and you were fourteen." She smiled. How could her smile always do such odd things to his insides? "After that first encounter, I fancied you. And those feelings for you only grew when I saw you at your coronation. I thought you the most handsome boy I had ever seen."

"Do you not think so now?" He winked. It was a pleasant surprise to learn that Arabella had liked him as a young girl. Before her parents' deaths changed everything. Who would have known that ten years later she would be his wife?

"Nay." She sat up and turned to face him on her knees. Her lips found purchase on the curve of his jaw, just below his ear. "You are no boy. You are a *man* now." The way she said it indicated he took first place in this new category as well. She placed kisses down his jaw, teasing him until he could stand it no longer. He lifted her chin and kissed her full and deep. Just when he felt her melting into his kiss, he pulled away and tickled her until she was laughing and screaming for mercy.

"You insufferable cad." She wiggled out of his arms, chest still heaving from laughter, and settled back against him.

Their companionable silence resumed. Her stomach rose and fell beneath his folded hands, the steady cadence soothing. The sunset outside the tower was awash with pink, red, orange, and violet, the land beneath it black in contrast. With that spectacular view, and the most beautiful woman he knew in his arms, Rowan felt sure he was the luckiest man in the world.

And yet… he also felt as though something was missing. Like some part of him was still… unfilled. At first, Rowan thought it must be his desire for revenge that had yet to be appeased. But upon further introspection, he discovered that was not the problem. Something else kept him from feeling *complete*.

Why should he feel that way? He was the king, powerful, wealthy, about to receive his final vengeance for his parents' murder, he had Arabella for a wife—what more could a man want? What was he lacking that its absence made him feel so empty, as if a section of him were missing?

Unable to keep his wonderings to himself, Rowan sucked in a breath. "Why do I still feel... dissatisfied?" Arabella stiffened in his arms and turned her face to look up at him. "Why do I feel as though something remains missing from my life? I have you, I have everything else I can desire, but still it is not enough. Why is that?"

He did not expect her to know the answer he sought. His questions were more rhetorical than otherwise.

But she *did* answer him, sitting up and turning to face him again, her face grave and concerned, but oddly hopeful. "I know exactly what is wrong. 'Tis God that you seek to fill that void in you, my love."

Rowan grit his teeth. That was *not* the answer he wanted to hear. "I do not need God. I do not want Him."

"Oh, Rowan, please do not say such things." She put a hand to his face, but her touch no longer soothed. It burned.

He angrily batted her hand away. "You know nothing, Arabella. You cannot know how my heart aches. *God* allowed that ache to happen."

"Nay, Rowan. He loves youand He cares about your pain." She cradled his face between her hands. Her dark eyes pleaded with him to hear and accept her words.

But he would not.

Rowan pushed her arms away and gripped her shoulders, jarring her. "Nay! He does not. How can He?"

Hurt flashed in her eyes as she blinked. "Yes, He does. Listen to me, I pray thee. I understand your pain, more than anyone else in this palace does. I could very easily have blamed God for my parents' death, but I did not."

"Nay. You blamed *me*."

Regret flickered in her eyes and he almost felt sorry his words.

"I know that. But what I am trying to say is that I could have blamed God and hated Him for allowing my parents to die, but I did not. And neither should you." She earnestly searched his face. "Everything has its purpose, Rowan. Your parents' death caused you to become king and subsequently require a wife, which led you to me. God brought you to me. Is that not a good thing He has done for you?"

Rowan clenched and unclenched his jaw, unable to meet the desperate look in eyes. She did have a point. This path of pain had brought him to Arabella, and that certainly was a good thing.

"He is what you are missing, my love." Her voice was thick and trembling. "He can satisfy you and restore you in ways that I never can. Will you not allow Him?"

For a brief moment, Rowan felt his resolve fading…

But he quickly resolved himself again.

"Nay! I do not need *God* to make me happy. I need nothing and *no one* but you, Arabella. As long as I have you, I have everything. I do not need God, and I do not want Him. Do you hear me?" he roared, gripping her shoulders. "Do you hear me, woman? I *do not* want Him!"

Rowan wrapped his arms about her and pulled her to him, kissing her roughly and without relent, as if that could convince him of the truth of his words. He did not want God. He did not need Him. All he needed was Arabella. All he needed to be happy, to heal the pain he felt deep inside, was Arabella's love. That was all. That. Was. All.

I do not want You, Lord. I do not need You! You hear that? I. Do. Not. Need. You!

He gripped Arabella tighter, even as she struggled against him, her lips refusing to kiss him back. She pushed and pushed against his chest, even as Rowan held her waist and head. He was adamant, angry, refusing to release her until she finally pulled away enough to let out a pained cry.

Arabella shoved hard against his chest and finally broke free, pushing away his hands, her face crumpled in pain and despair. Tears streaked her cheeks. "Leave me alone," she cried, drawing away from him. "Leave me alone!" She buried her face in her hands, her back heaving as she sobbed.

Regret coursed through Rowan, though he was only half repentant of his actions. He regretted forcing himself on her, making her cry, but he did not regret his words. He meant them wholly.

Rowan tried to touch her back, wanting to apologize, but she shoved his arm away, her eyes spitting fire. "Do not touch me!" Her voice was vehement as she drew back from him as though he had burned her. She swiped at her tears and stood. "Please, do not touch me, Rowan." She covered her mouth to halt a sob, but it was in vain. The sob came out in an awful, guttural sound, her breath catching in her throat.

Then Arabella turned and fled from the tower keep, slamming the door behind her. Her footsteps echoed on the stairs, leaving Rowan alone to rub his hands through his hair and feel all sorts of a fool.

Arabella

I spent the next two hours fuming in my room—one I had scarcely been in for nearly two months. Not a night had gone by where Rowan and I had not been together. We were inseparable, and I had only come to my room for dressing purposes.

I wondered if that would change after this latest argument.

How could he say such things? Surely God was weeping up in Heaven when He heard Rowan's adamant rejection of Him.

My heart ached in the most painful of ways. Would he ever surrender his pride, his stubbornness, and allow God to help him? Would he ever know true peace? I had certainly made him a happier person in the last months, but God was the only one who could change him for good. God was the only one who could ever make him completely happy.

But the man was just so *stubborn!* He refused to give in.

We were unequally yoked… a situation that I knew must change for both our sakes. I spent forever, it seemed, praying that it would.

Once I had enough of my moping, I hesitantly entered Rowan's quarters, only to find he was not there.

I changed into a nightdress and climbed under the covers. The air in the room was chilly, despite the fire dancing in the hearth, and my skin pricked with goosebumps. I hugged myself, snuggled up with my knees near my chin to ward off the cold. Silent tears trickled down onto my pillow despite my effort to hold them back.

The door opened and I looked up to see Rowan standing in the doorway. His face was serious. Sad.

I looked away, back to the fire. The door closed and his footsteps sounded on the floor, drawing nearer. "I did not think you would be here."

"Shall I leave?"

"Nay," he quickly cut in. "I..." he took a heavy breath, "I want you here. I just did not think *you* would want to be here."

I shrugged, not looking at him. I heard soft noises as he undressed, then the mattress shifted, and I felt an invasion of cold as he lifted the covers. Then warmth enveloped me when he climbed in beside me.

He said nothing, though I could practically feel his desire to speak, his hesitation to touch me. Slow, sluggish minutes passed, silent save for the crackling of the flames, while we both kept to our own thoughts.

"Forgive me." Rowan's voice at last broke through the silence, "I... I should not have done that. I should not have been so harsh... or spoken so severely."

"You hurt me," I said, my voice small and weak, "in more ways than one."

"I did not mean to hurt you."

I did not respond but continued to watch the flickering flames. The crackling noise, normally soothing, only seemed to add to the strain crackling between us.

"Will you forgive me?"

Slowly, I nodded. He settled closer, tentatively, as if he feared I would jerk away—and I still was not so sure I would not.

But I did not move, deciding to silently invite him nearer. After a long moment, his hand came to touch my waist. I rolled over to face him, my eyes searching his. They were doleful and lifeless, something I could not bear. Eventually I smiled softly at him, but I knew it fell just short of reaching my eyes. He returned it, and I rolled back over, allowing him to cradle me. His steady breathing

at my back and the comfort of his gentle touch ultimately lulled me to sleep.

A knock woke us both some time in the wee hours of the morning.

I gasped and opened my eyes, instinctively drawing the covers to my chin. Rowan bolted upright, his hand touching me protectively. He rose and went to the door, opening it a crack. The fire had dwindled down to mere embers, and I was freezing, so I huddled beneath the blankets, watching my husband's back as he conversed with whoever was at the door.

I could make out a few muffled words. "Trilaria... Attack... Must come..." My heart palpitated. Had the great battle already begun? Or was it to begin this day?

Rowan shut the door and hurried to one of the trunks that stored his clothes. "Trilaria has attacked one of the towns near the border again. I must go at once."

He pulled out a simple set of clothes and began dressing. I watched, trying to memorize every line of him for fear he would not return. The jagged, pink scar running across his chest caught my eye and I shivered, reminded of the gruesome story... and of the killer still on the loose.

"Is the battle to begin?" I asked, fear tightening my throat.

"Nay, not just yet. At least not the one I have planned. A battle is raging at that town as we speak, and I am bringing reinforcements. While they see that the Trilarians are successfully stamped back, I shall meet with the heads of my military to finish laying out our plans. Not much longer, love, and we shall end this once and for all."

He belted his tunic and smoothed out his sleep-ruffled hair, then hurried to the bedside. Rowan bent over, touching my cheek, and pressed a kiss to my forehead. "Take care. I shall return to you as soon as I can."

He turned to leave, but I caught his hand, halting his departure. I drew him back to the side of the bed and sat up, staring up at him with all seriousness. "*You* take care, Rowan."

He smiled softly and held my head, kissing my forehead again. "I shall."

Then he left the room, sweeping a cape around his shoulders as he went.

Chapter 33

FOR THE SEVERAL DAYS THAT ROWAN WAS GONE, I was worried sick. During the daytime, I tried not to fret too much, endeavoring to keep busy by taking walks, spending time with Uncle Matthew whenever he was available, sewing by the fire, and venturing out to check on the construction of the Cael-rith Home for Children.

At night, however, I would lay awake in Rowan's room for hours, terrible scenarios of someone shooting him through the heart with an arrow or piercing him with a sword running through my mind, sending me into a fearful panic. I found myself shedding many a tear, having already been overly emotional of late, even without his being gone.

I shuddered to think what I would do once the *real* battle began. Surely, I would get no sleep at all for its entire duration, however long that would be.

I was sick to my stomach at night and in the morning—I supposed from the worry. The third morning, I had to rush to the chamber pot before I lost the remainder of my dinner from the night before.

What is wrong with me? I only felt more ill after retching. I clamped my hand over my mouth to keep from vomiting again. *You can survive without him. Get ahold of yourself, woman. He shall be well, and so shall you.*

Resolving to remain calm and at ease, I rose, ordered the morning meal brought to my room, and sat by my window to pray until it arrived.

"Again, my happiest wishes to you, Your Majesty." My grinning, beaming maid opened my door to exit the room and bobbed another curtsey in the doorway.

I pressed a hand to my mouth, struggling against the laughter threatening to burst from my lips. Warm tears, *happy* tears, filled my eyes. "Many thanks, Mavis. Oh, how I wish I knew if Rowan was returning home today! I can only dream of how happy he will be."

Mavis laughed, happy tears glistening in her own eyes, and disappeared out the door.

I pressed a hand to my forehead, joy and anxiety dancing in the pit of my stomach—a welcome change from the persistent nausea. How had I not connected all the obvious signs sooner? *Five days you have been gone, my love. How shall I keep this news quiet until you return?*

I had to do something, tell *someone*, or I would burst.

Uncle Matthew. If I could not tell Rowan yet, I would tell my uncle.

Deciding to find him and extend an invitation to supper, I hurried out of my chamber and down the hall, nearly colliding with the man in question when I rounded the corner. "Ah, there you are, my dear. I wanted to speak with you."

"What is it, uncle?" I flattened a hand over my stomach, willing myself into a calm, placid expression. Tonight, I would tell him properly. Not here, at the spur of the moment.

"'Tis Frederic," he leaned in to whisper

My elation floated away. "What? Has something happened?"

He shook his head. "Nay—at least, not that I know of. He wishes to speak with you. 'Tis very urgent, he says."

"Speak with me? Does he mean to request a formal audience here at the palace?"

"Nay, he refuses to cross the threshold of this place. He insists you meet him elsewhere. I tried to tell him such could not be done, but I am afraid he is most adamant."

What was so important that he wished to tell me in person rather than send the message through Uncle Matthew? And why could he not swallow his pride and hatred long enough to meet me in a proper audience at the palace?

It would not do to be seen going to a young man's house, without, or even *with*, an escort of knights. Even if having a company of guards at my side would make the visit seem more appropriate, Fred would never agree to say anything with them present. If anyone discovered his feelings toward the kingdom and Rowan... Nay, I could not be seen with him without damaging my reputation, and he could not be seen with me without bringing him unwanted and dangerous attention.

Suddenly, I got an idea.

"Tell him to go to the outside of the eastern wall. I shall meet him there."

Uncle Matthew blinked in confusion. "How exactly are you going to do that without bringing along an army of guards?"

I winked at him. "'Tis a secret."

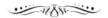

With a cape fastened around my shoulders and a torch in hand, I hurried through the tunnel. I had closed the hidden door in the wall behind me so as not to alert anyone of my departure—*hopefully*. I nearly tripped several times in my haste, but before long, I reached the opposite end of the passage and emerged into the world outside Caelrith, leaving the torch in a web-coated sconce at the bottom of the steps.

Frederic was sitting on the ground picking grass a short distance away. He startled at my sudden appearance, jumping to his feet.

"Arabella! Is that a tunnel? I had no idea—"

"Hello, Fred," I said, cutting him off. "I am afraid I cannot share the particulars. Now, what is so dreadfully important that I must come out here in the bitter cold?" I rubbed my arms in exaggeration.

He laughed. "The easy life making you soft, eh, Arabella?"

I winced at his jibe.

"Nay. Forgive me." He reached for my shoulder. "I should not have said that."

I lifted my chin and crossed my arms beneath my heavy cloak. "Of course, I forgive you. I always do. Now, what is it you must tell me?"

Fred looked down, scuffing his boot in the dirt and grass. "I am leaving, Arabella." He lifted his chin just enough to meet my eye. "I am going back to Trilaria."

My stomach sank. "What? Leaving? Why? How can you?" Sadness, anger, and confusion collided all at once. I put a hand to my head and looked back and forth between him and the dull, dying grass. "Fred, you cannot do that."

He stepped forward and took my hands. "Yes, I can. This kingdom holds no joy for me any longer…" His eyes said far more than his words ever could.

Me…

The kingdom held no more joy for him because I was officially out of his reach.

"I am sorry, Fred. Truly. But I cannot change that fact, and I shan't try."

"I know that, Arabella. Do you not think I understand that you clearly belong to another?" He shook his head, hurt flashing across his face. "You have made your heart abundantly clear and I accept it now. But still, I find no desire to remain here. I have always wanted to go back to Trilaria anyway. And…" He turned away, as if he had to in order to say what came next. "I am going to fight for them."

My mouth fell open. I drew back, pulling my hands from his. "You *what*?" I hoped, *prayed*, I had misheard. I could not believe it. I did not want to. He had no idea of the battle that was coming, a battle that would surely end his life. I shuddered to think of Fred going up against Rowan and his men. Would Rowan himself fight my dear friend? Kill him?

"Fred, you cannot!" I grabbed at his shirt. "You cannot leave like this. Do you know what you shall be called? A *traitor!*" I shook my head furiously at him. "I shall not allow it."

My childhood friend merely shook his head back at me. "You may be queen, Arabella, but you cannot control what I do. This is an action I am going to take, and you cannot stop me."

I released his shirt, so angry, so afraid, that I was shaking.

"And no one shall know of my leaving save you and my family… for you shall not speak of it, yes?" He gently raised my chin with his knuckle. His gray-green eyes searched my face, waiting for the answer he knew I could not help but give.

"I shan't speak of it…. I promise. No one shall know."

He smiled and released my chin. "Good."

Fred crossed his arms then. "I shall miss you, Arabella."

"And I, you, dear friend." My heart hung heavy with grief. He would die out there. I knew it. I *knew* it. Either in the battle or from being discovered as a traitor.

"Are you certain you know what you are doing?" I still hoped he would change his mind—no matter how ridiculous I knew that hope to be. When Fred set his mind on something, he did not change it. Just as he would not change his mind about his feelings for me…

He nodded. "I am certain."

Suddenly, I remembered my news I planned to share with Uncle Matthew later. If Fred was leaving, perhaps going to his death, I had to take this chance to share my special news with him. One last happy moment with my friend.

"Fred. I must tell you something." I let a grin chase away all my sorrow. My hands moved to cover the still flat expanse of my stomach. "I am expecting a child."

Fred's jaw dropped and he blinked, clearly taken aback by the sudden confession. "You—you—you're going to have a baby?"

I nodded, biting my lip. Would he be happy for me? Or would he only be able to think of how much he loathed my child's father?

I did not have to wonder for longer.

Fred suddenly lifted me in his arms, swinging me around with a cheer, before setting me back on my feet. "I am going to be an uncle!"

"*Uncle?*" I teased, wiping at the happy, relieved tears threatening to spill forth. "Who said you shall be its uncle?"

Fred jabbed a finger at his puffed-up chest, his chin raised proudly. "I said; that is who."

His joy was evident in every line of his face, as if it really were his niece or nephew growing within my womb. He may have still wished for me to be his wife, but he was good enough a friend to celebrate with me even so. Without warning, he grabbed my hands and kissed them, then leaned down to speak to speak to my stomach. "You be a good little one and give your mother no trouble, you hear."

I laughed and pushed him away. "Frederic of Caelrith! What if someone were to see you behaving so?"

"Oh, quit grousing, Arabella. I am only happy for you—truly I am." His eyes were earnest, begging me to believe him. "I sincerely want the best for you. If you are happy with the king—though I may not understand that—then I am happy for you and wish you all the best."

My hand flitted back to my stomach. "Yet you go to fight against my husband… perhaps even aid in his death."

He came forward again and took both my hands, squeezing them tight, shaking his head. "Nay. If I happen to face King Rowan on the battlefield, I shall let him live. I pledge that to you. No matter how I feel towards him, I want that little one to have a father just as much as you do.

"But this is what I must do, Arabella," he continued. "My duty is to my homeland. My heart has remained there even after all these years."

I nodded, finally resigning myself to this unexpected turn.

I wrapped my arms around Fred's neck and pulled him in for a tight hug. Tears pricked at my eyes and fell onto my cheeks. He and I had been best friends since we were young children. He, Gloriana, and I had been together nearly our entire lives, but now… we all found ourselves on separate paths. I had become queen, found a life and love here with Rowan. Gloriana was happy, possibly finding love in the form of Henry, the merchant's son. And then there was Frederic, who was leaving for another country to fight in a war in which he would mostly likely give his life.

Never had I dreamed such a change would occur. I had always believed we would grow up, marry, have children, and those children would play together as we once did.

But that was not to be.

Everything had changed. In some ways for the better, but in other ways, for the worse.

How has it come to this, God? This parting of the ways?

I rubbed a hand down the back of his head and sucked in a tight breath. "I love you, Fred. You take care. Please, oh please, be safe." I pulled back to look into his own tear-streaked face. "Find a life there in Trilaria and make it a good one. You shall always be in my prayers."

He nodded, kissed both my cheeks, and hugged me again,

squeezing me tight. I gave him a kiss on his cheek and stepped away, knowing it was the last time I would ever do so. "Farewell, Fred," I whispered, cherishing that last use of my nickname for him, feeling that farewell like a knife to the heart.

"Farewell, Arabella."

Then my friend turned and slowly walked away from me.

In that moment, seeing him stride away through the brittle, knee-high grass, never to return… it was as though a part of me had left as well, the last remaining piece of the little girl me. As though I were bidding my childhood farewell, for good. All of those happy days as children, all of the memories—they were officially just that… memories.

Chapter 34

Rowan

ROWAN AND CASSIUS RODE A SHORT DISTANCE ahead of the other men, looping around the eastern side of Caelrith before entering its gates.

It was along the edge of the trees, some sixty yards away from the eastern wall that Rowan first spotted Arabella with the handsome young stranger...

It felt as though a knife had plunged into his heart and exited through his back.

His wife was speaking with this young man, holding his hand, his shirt. The man swung her around in apparent delight over something she said. Then he took Arabella's hands, kissed them, and leaned down towards her stomach, doing... *something*. Was he talking to it?

Rowan's jaw clenched and his nostrils flared. What was he doing with her? Or the better question: what was *she* doing?

Surely, the man's actions did not mean...

His stomach roiled.

Such behavior implied that Arabella was involved with this man... And from the way he reacted to whatever she said, swinging her around, speaking to her stomach... Such behavior could imply that Arabella was... with child.

Could that be? Well, naturally, she could be carrying Rowan's child. But this man's obvious delight could also imply—

No. It could *not* be possible. Surely...

"Is that the queen, sire?" Cassius asked from at his side as the rest of his men slowly approached and stopped to stare. He heard the low, shocked murmurs coming from several of them, the gossip already surging to life.

Rowan's eyes never left the couple in the distance, humiliation burning up his neck. "Yes, Cassius. It is."

"Whatever could she be doing with that man?" His advisor's tone was terribly insinuating.

Rowan did not reply. His eyes stayed trained on them, his heart not wanting to believe what he was seeing, but his head jumping to its own conclusions.

A dark little voice whispered inside him. *Can you not see what she has done? She has betrayed you! You foolish man. You gave your heart away and now you have lost her, just as you always knew you would.*

Arabella wrapped her arms about the stranger and the two embraced—tightly, by the looks of it. Then she kissed his cheek, long and lovingly...

Rowan's heart sank and shattered. Disbelief, confusion, and anger made him want to yell and clang his sword into the nearest tree. How could she do this? How *could* she? How could she sneak out of the palace—obviously through the secret tunnel *he* had shown her, where he'd been so overcome by her nearness in the dark that he'd been tempted to wrap her in his arms and kiss her breathless—to meet this man, embrace him that way, kiss his cheek. He knew very well that he was not a relative of hers, for she had already told him that her uncle was her only family.

And a man did not hold a woman as that man held Arabella unless he cared very deeply for her.

Nay, Rowan. Think. He eased a calming breath in and out his nose. *There must be another logical explanation.*

"You know, sire, while I know not the young man's name, I have seen him before." Cassius gave Rowan a hesitant look. "I personally saw him and Her Majesty speaking in an alleyway, into which he most adamantly pulled her, at the harvest festival. The two looked quite... *close*, if I might say."

Rowan clenched his jaw tighter and spurred his horse toward the city gates as the man departed and Arabella disappeared back inside the tunnel. "I do not want to believe it, Cassius."

But you must! You cannot deny what is before your eyes! She has betrayed you!

"But what if it is true, my king? Have you become so enchanted by her that you cannot see what is before your very eyes?" His advisor's words echoed those in Rowan's head. "The queen is clearly having an aff—"

"Silence, Cassius!" A bird startled at his shout and dashed out of a treetop.

Betrayal! Stupid boy. Thought you could have someone as good as her? It was all nothing but an act! She does not love you!

He did not want to believe it… but the voice kept screaming at him, demanding he believe what his eyes were seeing.

His wife, the woman he had allowed into his heart and come to love, could have very well betrayed him.

How could this be? He had thought she loved him; she'd said she did. He thought they were happy.

You were not happy. It was an illusion!

There was that argument before he left… Had that created a greater rift between them than he thought? Or could she have been secretly meeting this man all along?

You see, boy? She never cared as much as she said. Never.

"Sire…" Cassius broke in cautiously, "I am afraid something must be done. This evil must be dealt with forthwith."

"Do you not think I know that, Cassius?" Rowan snapped, gnashing his teeth like a wild animal.

He kicked his horse's side and the animal leapt forward, carrying him faster and faster toward home. He did not want to believe that what Cassius and the voice in his head were saying was true, but his resolve was quickly fading.

All he could do was question her, give Arabella a chance to explain, and hope that she could put his fears to rest.

That shan't help. Everything she will say shall be lies… the dark voice whispered. Rowan could practically feel the claws wrenching around his brain and heart as it spoke knifelike words to him, drawing more blood with each syllable.

Believe it! You have lost her!

Arabella

The door to our sitting room opened, and I looked up to see the most wonderful, unexpected sight that had ever met my eyes.

I jumped up from my seat by the fire and ran to the open door. "Rowan! Oh, my darling, how I have missed you!" I threw my arms around his neck, straining up on my toes, and kissed him quickly, then laid my head against his chest. His warm, comforting smell filled my senses, making all my worries fly away.

All I could think of was the joy he would feel once I told him he was going to be a father.

Then I noticed he was not hugging me back. In fact, he stood rigid in my arms, not holding me, not touching me. Acting as though he was not happy to see me at all...

"Have you?" he asked, without an ounce of teasing, as if really doubting I missed him. He had no idea how his absence had tortured me!

I looked up, my arms still clasped about his neck. "Yes, of course. Is something wrong?"

His face was hard, almost agitated, not at all like the Rowan I had known for the last two months. More like the one I first met. *What on earth has happened?*

"I saw you with that man outside the tunnel."

My heart sunk and I stepped back, my hand flying to my chest. A sword might as well have run me through. "What?" He had seen me with Fred? Surely, he did not think something untoward had transpired between us.

Rowan stepped further into the room and I saw Cassius behind him. The advisor's black eyes bore into me, making me want to squirm.

"Who is he, Arabella? What were you doing with him?" Rowan's hurt and angry voice brought my attention back to him.

I clamped my mouth shut, my insides filling with dread. I suddenly felt terribly ill...

My worst fear had come to pass. How could I explain the situation without betraying my friend? If I explained who Fred was, Rowan would learn of his leaving to fight for Trilaria and would label him a traitor. Sentence him to a traitor's death. And his blood would be on my hands.

I could not allow that… I could not endanger him and possibly even his family still living here in Acuniel. *I shan't speak of it… I promise. No one shall know.*

I had given him my word.

My eyes slid shut. "I—I cannot tell you…"

"What? Why can you not?"

I clenched my hands in my skirts and reopened my eyes. "I—I just cannot."

"Who is he, Arabella?" Rowan's face was a mask of pain. Desperation to know the truth. "Are my worst fears to be confirmed? Have you had an affair with this man?"

"Nay!" I interjected, panicked. "Nay, Rowan, I have not! I could never."

"Then why can you not explain? Why can you not tell me who this man is, and why you were with him?"

I covered my face with my hands, turning away from him, unable to believe what I was hearing. Every word I spoke was pure agony. "I just cannot, Rowan. Please, *please*, do not make me."

He turned me around to face him. His hands came around my arms, making me lift my head to stare at him, wide-eyed. "Tell me!"

I bit my lip and shook my head. *Oh, God! How can this even be happening?* "Please. Just trust me."

"How can I, Arabella? All I can gather from what I saw is that you have been disloyal to me." His eyes spat fire. "How could you betray me?"

I shook my head furiously, my eyes clamped shut again. Nay… this was not happening. *It must all be a terrible nightmare. Soon I shall wake up and discover that all is well.*

But when I opened my eyes, all I saw was the hurt on Rowan's face. This was no dream… It was real.

Tears filled my eyes, threatening to run down my cheeks. "Please trust me, Rowan."

He roughly released me and paced away, the muscles beneath his shirt taut with stress. "If you cannot tell me, then what else can I believe?"

A sob escaped my throat. I reached out to touch his back, wanting to reassure him that he was the only one who held my heart—but how could I? How could I assure him I had not betrayed him, without instead betraying my friend?

"Nay, Arabella!" He put up a hand to stay my approach. "Do not come near me. Not right now." His fingers raked through his hair. "How could you do this to me? After everything we have been through?"

The tears were pouring from my eyes now, turning my vision into nothing but a swirl of blurry colors and shapes. I covered my face with my hands, sobbing despite my best efforts to hold myself together. The happy world I had built was crumbling to pieces. All the joy I had felt for two months was being ripped away.

"Rowan, I—"

"What shall we do with her then, sire?"

I looked up suddenly. Cassius stood near the door, his gaze hard and hateful, showing more emotion than I had ever seen from him. He clearly believed this ridiculousness just as much as Rowan.

Or... had he something to do with Rowan's staunch belief in my guilt?

Rowan turned to his advisor, fury knotting his brow into the most gruesome of expressions. He gave no answer, only stared as though he wanted to destroy everything in his path.

"This offense is treason... and adultery is a cardinal sin. Such a crime requires one to be thrown in the—"

"Nay. She shall be under house arrest until further notice."

"Sire—"

"Arabella." Rowan came towards me again, starting to reach for me but stopping as though it caused him too much pain. "You are under house arrest." His voice quavered. "If you do not cooperate, I shall be forced to publicly declare your crimes and bring you before the court to be judged."

I let out another sob. "Rowan, please!" I lunged at him and grabbed hold of his shirt, the air in the room suddenly scarce. "You have to believe me. 'Tis not as you think!"

"Oh really? Then how is it, Arabella?" His expression was hard, but in his eyes, I saw that he wanted to believe me. He just could not. Somehow, he could not find it in himself to trust me without explanation. Did it have to do with the pain and bitterness he harbored? Did those feelings from the past make him hesitant to trust me here in the present?

"You cannot do this! You cannot! What would Favian say if he saw you behaving this way?"

Now his face turned red with rage. "Do not bring him into this. That matters not!"

"But Rowan, I am with child!" I shouted, hoping against hope that the news would change his mind.

He stilled, and his gaze shifted into something softer before it hardened once again. The room fell silent. Cassius stiffened at my words. Rowan clenched his fists at his sides, his jaw twitching.

He ground out his next words, each one cutting my heart in a new place. "After what I saw... Are you sure I am the father?"

My breath left me in a whoosh.

How could he even say that?

I wailed…

And then my world went black.

Rowan

Rowan threw open his bedchamber door, banging it against the wall. Cassius tried to follow him in. "My king—"

"Do not speak to me, Cassius. Get out! Now!"

The irritated advisor obediently left the room.

Then Rowan was on a rampage.

He yelled, grabbing a pitcher and slinging it into the wall. The vessel shattered with a crash into a thousand sharp pieces. Mindless in his anger, he hurled across the room whatever else he could get his hands on.

"Why?" he growled. "How could she do this to me? I gave her everything! And how does she repay me?" he demanded of the air, whirling to pound his fist against the fireplace mantle. "By sneaking off to meet another man!"

Rowan bared his teeth, breathing heavy from his raging. "How could this happen?" He pounded his fist again, tears filling his eyes. He still loved her, and he knew he always would—which only made this worse. The woman he loved had betrayed him and that was all there was to it. If she could not explain herself, what other conclusion was there to draw than that she was involved with the man?

"I shall find that whelp and skewer him," he ground out, remembering the way the stranger had held his wife in his arms.

But what about her? She had initiated the close embrace.

An offense of this magnitude called for imprisonment, trial before the court, and, if found guilty, a traitor's death…

But he did not think he could stomach that… No matter what she did, Rowan doubted he could order her death.

Such an action would kill him too.

Yet you can cast her off this way?

Rowan growled in annoyance at his conscience. That and reason told him to trust her, but everything else kept him from listening.

What you have seen must be true, the dark voice whispered again.

It must be true.

What else can you do?

This is what I must do, he defended in his thoughts, refusing to feel further remorse "I shall not play the fool for a woman who has been unfaithful to me."

Had she ever even loved him? Had it all been a lie? Surely her feelings could not have *all* been false. But why then would she do this?

Rowan growled again and turned around, heading for his bed. But he only turned away from it again, unable to picture anything other than the night he left for battle. Arabella's tears in the moonlight, the hurt, forlorn look in her eyes, the feel of his lips against her forehead as he told her goodbye.

Then came other images. Kissing her, holding her close—so many thoughts far too precious to share aloud.

All of that was done now. Lost.

He ran his hands through his hair as he settled onto the chaise lounge in the corner of the room. Tears filled his eyes, the pain of this new loss ripping him in two. This was what he got for falling in love. Everyone he had ever cared about in the past was stolen from him, and he had known that the same would happen with Arabella. He'd just decided that his fear was not as important as being with her.

He should have listened to his head and remained distant. His worst fears had come true. He'd let himself go, and now he suffered the consequences.

Why did God punish him this way? Why did He always allow him to suffer such pain?

What was next? Would he lose his kingdom? His life? Not that any of that mattered all that much to him…

Arabella had said that she believed God brought her to him. If so, then for what? Only for Him to take her away? Show him hope and happiness, dangle it before him, let him drink deeply of it, and then rip it away again. Even now, did God sit up in Heaven mocking him, laughing at his foolishness?

"What did I ever do to deserve this?" His voice seethed bitterness. "Do You enjoy seeing me miserable?"

Rowan ran his hand down his face, hating the tears spilling from his eyes. Just when he was feeling free of the cloud of depression under which he had lived for so long, it came flying back, drenching him with its sorrowful rain.

How could he have been so foolish? How could he have let that armor around his heart fall into disrepair? Now Rowan knew why he had kept his heart locked up so tightly. He had been better off lonely, solemn, and hard-hearted. He had felt miserable even then. But what had seemed unbearable at that time was nothing when compared to what he felt now.

For now, his heart was more than wounded… it was broken.

Chapter 35

Arabella

I AWOKE IN MY ROOM SOME TWO HOURS LATER, still fully dressed and lying atop my made bed.

For a brief moment, I was puzzled, wondering how I had gotten there, thinking I had dreamed the whole morning up. But then it all came flooding back, every terrible detail of Rowan's return.

I moaned and covered my forehead with my hand. "What has happened?" My tears returned, spilling from my eyes to run down my temples and into my hair.

How could he not believe me? How could he believe that I would betray him? Never could I do so! I loved Rowan; *he* was the only man my heart continuously longed for.

And now that heart was broken and bleeding, filling every part of me with the sharpest anguish.

I rolled to my side, burying my face in the pillow at my head, grasping my stomach with one hand. My poor child. Its existence should be a cause for joy, but now everyone would despise it. The entire kingdom, the nobles, the child's own father… It was unfair that people would look upon this baby, innocent in every way, as a symbol of my undeserved disgrace. I could not bear the thought of him or her going through life not understanding why people looked at them with scorn, nor why their father would not hold them. Why he looked at them with eyes full of contempt…

I sobbed harder, weeping just as much for the child as I was for myself.

Had he ever really loved me as much as he professed? Rowan

had certainly been fervent in his affections. But had it been real, or only an act? For if he truly cared about me, would he not trust my word that nothing had transpired between Frederic and me? That was what you were supposed to do when you loved someone, right? You were supposed to trust them.

Could it all have been nothing but a ploy to achieve his own ends—to get the heir he needed?

I futilely wiped at my nose and eyes, feeling used and uncertain of everything my world had consisted of for the past two months—or, for that matter, the past six months since entering the palace.

Well, if that is the case, then he certainly got what he wanted!

I craved to scream and tear my room apart. "Why have You allowed this to happen, Lord? What can possibly come from this?"

My breath came in ragged, halting breaths. If I was not careful, I would overtax myself and faint again.

"I thought Your plan was for us to be together. But now he will not believe me and despises me. How can this be good? *How can this be good?*" My voice was shrill as it grew in rage.

I finally sat up and entwined my fingers in my hair, grasping my head. My blood pulsed there, every beat of my heart like a pounding drum. "How can you? *How can you!*"

Anger and bitterness, things I had thought were buried long ago, rose up in my chest, threatening to cut off all air to my lungs. I was angry; so *very, very* angry. More so than I had ever been before. It was consuming, like a burning hot fire running through my veins, searing me from the inside out. I wanted to shout in outrage at the sky and curse God for ever allowing me to come here when it only brought me heartache.

I leaned over, burying my face in my hands, brokenhearted tears wetting them.

Then my door opened.

Startled, I lifted my swollen, tear-stained face and found Rowan filling the doorway.

Unable to bear the sight of him, I looked down at my lap.

"I came to give you another chance to explain."

"There is nothing to explain."

"But there is," he said, his voice rising in indignation. His anger was a boiling river, ready to overflow and destroy everything in its path. "I came home to see my wife with another man, and now she will not even bother to explain to me who he is. Why is that, Arabella?"

I finally looked up at him and shook my head forlornly, feeling weak and empty from my weeping.

"For goodness sake, will you not speak to me?" He stepped forward and leaned over the bed, his fists planted firmly on the mattress.

When I did not respond, he clenched his jaw and his blue eyes grew stormy as the waves of a tempestuous sea. He pounded his fist. "Arabella, I am the king, and I demand to be answered!"

The wild, enraged feeling from just a moment before returned. My eyes flashed fire. "You are *arrogant*, that is what you are, Rowan! You know that? You are a cruel, prideful man with no thought for others!" I rose up on my knees, my eyes level with his. "You may be the king of Acuniel, but you are not the king of all! You know, there *is* Someone higher than you are. You are not above everyone!"

His face grew even more irate and he straightened. "Fine. If you see me that way, and you refuse to explain yourself, then *fine*. Be that way! But you shan't enter my presence unless permitted."

Then he turned and left, slamming the door behind him.

The entire room seemed to buzz in his wake, the air still charged with our fury at one another.

I collapsed back on the bed, my strength completely spent.

I knew I had just made a terrible mistake. I should have held my tongue and answered him calmly instead of returning fire for fire. That never did any good—it only served to make things worse.

Which was what I had just done…

Made things worse.

My fiery retort had only served to widen the gap between us.

Rumors spread like wildfire. By morning, the entire palace whispered of my disgrace. Servants chattered about our fight, having overheard the shouting. Somehow, it even became known that I had been seen with a strange man, and the story was quickly stretched to sordid extremes.

While wearily pacing my room immediately following a maidservant's exit, I overhead her and another servant speaking in the corridor. My heart stung at the words my ears registered. They spoke of terrible things, accusing me of adulterous acts that I would *never ever* do.

How could they say such things? I had once been their beloved queen, and now they spoke of me as if I were the town harlot. Their doubt of my true character stung almost as much as Rowan's did.

Of course, a few did refuse to believe the lies brought against me—such as Mavis.

She entered my room that same morning and the kind, non-judgmental look on her face caused me to fall into her embrace.

"I refuse to believe it, dear." Her voice was soft and thick with emotion as she rubbed my back soothingly. "I've seen the love in your eyes when you look at him. You love King Rowan just as sure as you live and breathe. And you are a good girl. There is a logical explanation for this whole mess—I know it. If you cannot say, then I trust that 'tis for good reason." She looked me in the eye. "I shall remain true to you, no matter what those others say."

"Thank you, Mavis." I sniffed, wiping my nose with the back of my hand. I turned red eyes to look at her, full of gratitude. "Your trust touches me more than you know."

For three days, I floundered, sinking deeper and deeper into a pit of despair so deep and dark I could scarcely breathe. As each morning dawned, the weight on my shoulders grew in heaviness, pushing me further down. I found myself sitting by my window, staring out at the world with empty eyes that were red and bleary from endless tears. Not even the thought of being a mother could bring me any joy.

I was sinking… drowning… dying from the inside out.

The only word to describe the feeling that permeated those three days is…

Blank.

I was completely and utterly… blank.

"Why, God?" I whispered almost inaudibly that third day. "I do not understand… How could you rip away my happiness and allow things to fall apart this way?"

No answer came.

"Are You even listening? Or have You forsaken me for good this time?"

Still there was nothing. Nothing but the emptiness. The despair.

I could not handle another minute of it. I had to be free.

With wooden, deliberate movements, I rose and strode to my door. I was not supposed to leave, but I cared not what my orders were. I had to get out.

My steps hastened as I gained distance from the confinements of my room. I passed two servants along the way who stopped to stare at me in shock, but I did not pay them any mind. Soon I came to the place I sought, and my hand went to touch the sconce on the wall. I tugged, and it gave way. Before long, the secret passage yawned before me.

I ran blindly into the darkness, stumbling twice along the way and having to catch myself with my arms against the ground. When I reached the stairs, I fumbled up the earthen steps and groped until I found the door latch. Finally, I was able to fling the door open and I rushed out, running to the light.

Outside, the wind howled, whipping tree branches back and forth, causing the tall grass to sway wildly. The unrelenting wind whipped my skirts about my legs as I came to a stop just beyond the tunnel entrance. My hair blew riotously in the wind, sticking to my damp cheeks.

Freedom… at last.

Unable to contain myself a moment longer, I lifted my face to the sky and screamed. I screamed so hard it hurt, stomping my foot as I did. The people beyond the city wall surely could hear me. No doubt, they thought someone was dying. Mayhap I was.

Entwining my fingers in my hair, I smoothed it from my face.

Now was my chance. I could run away if I wanted to. The road to freedom stood open before me. All I had to do was run… Run away from Rowan, from the wretched crown that had only brought me heartache, from this crumbling world I lived in. I could be free if I wanted to be…

Did I want to be free?

Hugging myself tightly against the cold December wind, I took a step forward. But immediately, I felt the separation from Rowan, and it wrenched my heart. I still loved him, deeply, despite everything. I still loved him and could not change that fact—God so help me.

Reason came rushing back in. Freedom was only an illusion. Seemingly there at my fingertips, but in reality, still leagues away. Just as with the first time I considered running from this place, I knew I could never get far without being found and brought back. And now, I also knew I could never be free of my love for Rowan.

The noise of metal and pounding feet sounded behind me, and I turned just as Lord Cassius and five knights emerged from the tunnel.

"My queen." Lord Cassius stopped before me. "You were not to leave." He looked to two of the five knights who had surrounded me in a circle. "Take her."

Strong hands seized my upper arms. I struggled against them. "Release me this instant! How dare—"

"Did you honestly believe you could run away, Arabella?" Lord Cassius sharply cut off my protests. His familiar use of my Christian name angered me.

"I did not intend to run away," I snapped, my eyes flashing fire.

"Then why are you outside the city walls?"

"'Tis no business of yours, Cassius." My anger seethed as I clenched my teeth tight. He had something to do with this situation. He had influenced Rowan not to believe me, I was sure of it. Rowan always listened to Cassius—he took the man's word for law. Cassius could easily have convinced Rowan that my innocent encounter with my friend was something more sordid.

Suddenly, I remembered Cassius' role in having the cupbearer and his accomplice executed without trial. The argument that I had overheard between the two advisors just before Favian died… The tension between them… The lack of emotion on Cassius' face when Favian breathed his last.

The air siphoned from my lungs.

I lunged at him, pulling against the men who held me in a vise grip. "This is your fault," I croaked out. "I know you had something to do with this, you—you—" I shut my mouth before I could reveal too much of what I suddenly feared was the cold, terrible truth.

Cassius glared at me and stepped closer. "How dare you accuse me of such, you lying peasant?" He turned to the knights. "Take her back inside. Now!"

The men dragged me down the steps and into the dark passage. "Let me go!" I screamed. "Release me! I am still the queen, and I say release me this instant." I kicked and fought against them, finally stepping on one man's foot. He growled and they both let go of me.

Immediately, I jerked away, snatching my skirts to the side and stepping out of their reach. "I am perfectly capable of walking on my own."

I could feel Cassius' displeasure radiating from his face, though I could not see him, hidden as he was behind the five knights.

I set my teeth and turned around, marching down the passage with my head held high. They followed closely behind me until we reached my bedchamber door. There, Cassius stepped forward, his black eyes pinning me to the floor. "Now, do not leave again, or I shall be forced to inform the king. And you do not want that, for he would then follow through with his promise to charge you before the kingdom and have you put on trial for your treason."

I narrowed my eyes at him. *You know well that I did nothing*, I wanted to say, but refrained.

Instead, I turned and entered my room, slamming the door in his face. The sound reverberated off the walls, jarring through my chest.

I strode across my room, not wanting to cry anymore. But it seemed my will was not strong enough. The tears returned and I sank to my knees, the anger dissipating and the despair returning to its place in a cloud above my head. Its rain drenched me through until I felt sure that this time, I would give up completely and die there on my floor. I had no more strength. Not another ounce left. I was done.

What is the point anymore? Who cares if I die here? I curled up on the floor. It was like ice, the fire having grown low in the hearth, but I cared not.

I covered my face with my hands, so weak, so tired of crying, tired of the depression that was overwhelming me. "Lord... if You are still there... please, I beg Thee, listen to me. I cannot go on feeling this way. I have not even the will to *live*."

But I *had* to live. I had to find the strength to carry on, if only to give my child a chance at life.

"I thought I had discovered your purpose for bringing me here. I thought that purpose was Rowan. I thought... I thought..." But that was just it—I had *thought*. And apparently, I had thought wrong. Clearly, I had gotten it all so very wrong.

"If your will is not for Rowan and me to find love, and that love be what brings him to You, what else could You have me do? What do You want from me, Lord?"

As I lay there, the question I kept returning to—or the word, rather—was, "Why?"

Why?

Why?

Why!

Over and over again, it was all I could ask. I could not understand why this terrible thing had to happen. *Why* did I have to come to the palace and become queen? *Why* did I have to fall in love with Rowan if it only caused me heartache? *Why* did Rowan not believe me?

I pounded my fist against the cold stone in anger, shouting at God, "Why have You done this? Are You even seeing the pain You are causing me?" I turned my face to the floor, my tears pooling on the ground as I lay there feeling sorry for myself.

I am still in this.

My eyes opened and I stared at the floor, shuddering at the Voice that suddenly spoke to my heart.

You believe I have forsaken you, but I have not. I am here. I shall be your comfort and your help. Trust in me and lean not on thine own understanding, for my ways are mysterious ways. You do not understand, but you shall... All shall reveal itself in due time.

Be still and know that I am God.

I sat up, covering my face as I wept, this time not in grief, but in *relief* that He had indeed heard my cries.

Rise and go to the window.

I shakily stood and obeyed, unsure why God wanted me to do this. But as I opened the shutters and looked out upon the rolling hills surrounding the city, I understood.

God had designed everything that stood out there before me: the trees, the grass, the sun, and the birds flying across the windswept sky. He had created it all and set every creation on its own course. Each one had a purpose, a time to live and a time to die. Each one was in the palm of His hand, going about its life as He ordained according to His plan. Not one thing in creation could know what God wanted to do with them, where He intended them to go in the future. They could only wait patiently and trust Him to take care of them.

God knew each bird living in the forest trees; He knew every blade of grass, every tree, every person in the world—and that included me. He had a plan for me, just as He had for all of nature, and no matter what that plan was, He was watching and taking care of me. He had not forsaken me, nor would He. I only had to trust Him and believe that His hand was still in this situation, and that, though my world seemed dark and bleak, without hope of ever seeing the light again, things would turn out for the good.

I had come to believe that once, could I not do so again?

All would be well. For even what the enemy means for evil, God can turn around and make into something beautiful, something good.

Relieved, grateful tears pooled in my eyes, blurring my view of the nature surrounding me. "I trust You, Lord Jesus. I trust You, wholly and completely. Whatever You want me to do, whatever Your will is… so be it."

Chapter 36

Rowan

A KNOCK SOUNDED ON ROWAN'S DOOR, AND REGinald went to open it, giving the king another reproving look. The man had been greatly displeased by Rowan's treatment of Arabella, and ever since—for the past four days—he'd been giving Rowan these dark looks. But Rowan paid them little mind.

A knight stood in the hall, and Reginald let him in. The man bowed. "Your Majesty, the man has been found."

Rowan's head shot up, his senses instantly alert. *The man she was with.*

After Arabella refused to explain who the man was, Rowan had provided several knights with a description from what he and Cassius could remember of the stranger, then sent the men searching for the whelp who would dare to cavort with his wife. Hold her in his arms... Kiss her cheeks...

Rowan's jealous anger stirred again, and he clenched his jaw against it. "I shall be right there."

The knight nodded, bowed, and left the room. A few moments later, Rowan followed, his fists clenched as he strode down the corridor. The man he had seen with Arabella had been found, and nothing would stop him from getting to the truth.

God have mercy upon the soul who would be on the receiving end of his wrath.

When Rowan entered the Great Hall and took to his throne, the doors at the opposite end of the room opened. Cassius entered, and two guards followed behind, dragging a young man between them. Rowan rose and hurried back down the steps of the dais to meet them halfway.

"My king, we found him on the—"

"Let him speak, Cassius." Rowan came forward and seized the man roughly by the shirt. He had green eyes and a handsome face— 'twould be no wonder for Arabella to be attracted to him.

The man glared up at him, but the depths of his eyes betrayed his true fear. "What is your name?" Rowan barked.

"Frederic of Caelrith, Your Majesty."

"And what business had you, *Frederic of Caelrith*, with *my wife?*" Rowan shoved Frederic away and punched him, knocking him out of the guards grasps and sending him sprawling onto the floor. Before he could stand, Rowan stooped over and lifted him up himself. "Why did I see my wife in your arms? Why did you swing her around as though she carried *your* child?" Rowan smashed his fist into Frederic's nose, sending blood spurting onto his tunic. "*Is it yours?*" He punched him again, and Frederic fell to the ground.

He rose up on one fist, wiping at the blood pouring from his nose with the back of his hand. Anger and hatred burned in his eyes, all traces of fear gone. "I told her she should have married me. I knew this would happen." His voice grew almost shrill with fury as he gained his feet and started towards Rowan. "I knew you would do this to her! I knew you would hurt her! I knew you were no good, you filthy blackguard!" Frederic dove at Rowan and threw a punch, which Rowan deflected.

The guards seized Frederic by the arms and held him back. Frederic yelled and jerked around, trying to free himself. "If you harm her or that baby—"

"Silence!" Rowan grabbed him by his worn and dirty tunic. "Is the child yours?"

"Nay!" Frederic spat. "'Tis yours, you fool!"

Rowan readied to punch Frederic again.

"My king!" Cassius interrupted just as Rowan was about to let his fist fly. Frederic glared at Rowan through the hair hanging in his eyes, blood dripping from his nose and firmly set mouth.

"What, Cassius?" Rowan held his fist poised in the air. His eyes never left Frederic's, their gaze electric with mutual rage and hatred.

"We found him on the road for Trilaria. He was attempting to leave the kingdom to go fight on their side."

Rowan lowered his arm and looked to Cassius. "What?" He turned back to his prisoner. "What?" he shouted again. "You would betray your country to aid my enemy?"

Frederic glared harder at him, baring his teeth. "This is not my country. I am Trilarian born, and it has always held my loyalty— not you. I despise everything about your rule. I am not ashamed to say that I would gladly fight and die for them instead of *you*, you sorry excuse for a king, *and* a man!"

Rowan bellowed and rammed his fist into the man's gut so hard he was sure he'd see his hand emerge from the other side. Frederic doubled over with a scream through his tightly clenched teeth.

"Get him out of here! I shall hear no more of this. Throw him in the dungeon!" Rowan jabbed his finger towards the door.

The guards pulled the traitorous prisoner towards the exit. He kicked his feet, shouting and hollering. Even when the doors shut, his muffled cries still reached Rowan's ears.

Rowan stumbled back towards his throne in a daze. His breath came short, his head fuzzy with shock.

The man Arabella had been with was a traitor… and Arabella had clearly known. The reason why she so stubbornly refused to tell him the truth was that she was *protecting* him.

Rowan collapsed into his throne, rubbing his hands down his face.

Cassius made his way nearer. His voice penetrated the heavy silence filling the Hall. "He professes that he is not the father, but this still does not rule out the possibility that they were involved."

Rowan shook his head. He was so unsure of everything now. He thought he was convinced of Arabella's infidelity, but now this new development—the fact that Frederic of Caelrith was born a Trilarian and was a traitor—changed everything. Arabella had clearly known about his loyalties.

Did she share them?

As if reading his thoughts, Cassius spoke, "Could it not be possible that the queen shares his loyalties, sire? I know—and I believe you know as well—that she has always been strangely interested in the subject of your parents' death, and the war. She has openly protested its continuation. Already, rumors have abounded, suggesting that she is a Trilarian sympathizer. Could it be that she has been involved with this man, not just romantically, but politically? That she is a spy, or somehow working on Trilaria's behalf unofficially?"

"I know not, Cassius. I know nothing at present." Rowan massaged his temples, trying to clear his head. "I know not what to think anymore."

His advisor moved to stand beside him. "What shall we do with the man, sire?"

"What do we normally do with traitors, Cassius?" Rowan spat sarcastically.

The man nodded. "Yes, my king. When shall it be done?"

Rowan sat and thought for a moment, then decided. Standing to his feet, he stormed toward the nearest exit. "The day we leave for battle."

Arabella

I nearly fainted when I heard the news.

Frederic had been found.

And he was to be put to death before the start of the battle… in three days.

When Mavis told me, I sunk into the nearest seat as all the air left my lungs in a *whoosh*. How could this have happened? My silence, which had caused Rowan to cast me off, had all been for naught. Fred had still been captured, he was now a known traitor, and would be put to death.

And to make matters worse, his status as a traitor put me in a similar light.

Mavis said the word around the palace was that Rowan and Cassius were considering the possibility of me sharing his sympathies; that I could possibly be involved with the Trilarians, working to bring about the downfall of the king. And from Rowan's—and everyone else's—point of view, I supposed it did look believable. After all, I had questioned Rowan and others about the war and his parents' murder on numerous occasions. Even before all this, there had been speculation amongst several of the nobles. The idea of me being a traitor had already been growing in people's minds.

And now... after this... there would be no stopping the weed of gossip.

Favian's warnings echoed through my head again, so loud and clear I trembled. *'Tis a dangerous matter, one that could prove dangerous to you in many ways... Mayhap you should not speak of that certain subject... For your own sake.*

Favian had known this would happen. He had tried to warn me.

God, help me. Help me to know how to clear my name.

"'Tis not true... correct, m'lady?" Worry creased Mavis's face.

I shook my head vigorously, trying not to panic. "Nay. 'Tis all a lie."

I had to go see Fred, right away. I had to speak with him, though I knew not what it would accomplish.

I swept past my maid and exited my room. "But, my queen, Lord Cassius said you are not to—"

"I could not care less about what Lord Cassius says!" I shouted over my shoulder.

My determined steps carried me through the palace, past the prying eyes of many servants who whispered behind my back, and all the way to the dungeon entrance. Down the dark, spiraling stair I descended, not nearly as afraid of going down there as I was the first time.

When I emerged into the dark, dank gloominess of the dungeon, the jailor stood and bowed hesitantly, clearly unsure of how he was supposed to treat me with all that was happening. "Hello... er, Your Majesty. May I help—"

"I am here to see the prisoner." I held my head high with an air of authority that no longer felt so foreign.

"Yes, my queen." The man did not question me further and hurried to do as I bid.

The jailor led me to a cell. I glimpsed a dark form between the rusty bars, lying on the filthy ground. The jailer shuffled around his key ring, the jangling noise echoing off the walls that dripped with moisture and God knows what else. Finally, he shoved a key in the lock and opened the door with a loud creak. "Wake up," he ordered sharply. "You have a visitor."

I turned to the jailor. "Please, sir, if you would give us some privacy."

He nodded and backed away with only minor hesitation.

Slowly, I entered the dark cell, my stomach roiling at the smells of human waste, stale air, and sweat. I had forgotten just how badly the place smelled, and in my current pregnant condition, the stench was nearly unbearable.

The form shifted and sat up, and the face of Frederic greeted me with the same smile he had worn the last time I saw him. But unlike last time, he was severely beaten. Even in the dim lighting I could see his right eye was swollen shut, dried blood marred the skin around his nose and mouth, and his cheeks were bruised. I could imagine who had inflicted such injuries...

"Ara—my queen."

I knelt before him, examining his face. "Frederic, are you well? Did Rowan do this to you?"

He looked at me kneeling on the filthy ground and shook his head. "You shall ruin that lovely gown. Do you not want to stay clean?"

I smiled softly and shrugged one shoulder. "A little dirt never hurt anyone."

His lips lifted slightly in return, the dried blood on his face making his skin stiff.

"Oh, Fred, I am so sorry," I whispered, not wishing for the jailor to overhear our conversation. "I kept your secret, I promise," grief welled inside me, "even at the price of my own happiness."

"Nay, do not be sorry. I should have left without telling you goodbye and kept you out of all this. Now my loyalties are condemning you as well." His good eye—the one not swollen shut—hardened. "But frankly, I take no credit for the king's rejection of you. I believe 'twas bound to happen sometime. He is a cruel man who has undoubtedly only used you, Arabella."

"*Shhh.*" I shook my head, putting a finger to my lips. "Do not make this any worse for yourself than it already is." I glanced over my shoulder at the jailor, who thankfully appeared not to have heard anything. "I know how you feel about Rowan... I cannot understand why he has done this, refused to believe me. But *I* refuse to discredit him entirely."

Fred scowled. "Can you not think it possible that he would use you? How could someone who loves you act so? How could he not believe you, think you have betrayed him, when you have been nothing but loyal—no matter how foolish I think that is."

I did not want to believe that everything Rowan and I had

shared was nothing but an illusion, a ploy. But it did look likely…
"I know not, Fred. I honestly know not what to feel or believe at present." I reached out and took his filthy hand, holding it tightly. "But I promise that I shall do all I can to stop your execution. I shall find some way to save you, my friend. I promise."

Chapter 37

Rowan

"AND WHAT SHALL YOU DO ABOUT HER MAJES-
ty?" Cassius inquired of Rowan at supper that evening.

Rowan stared into his half-empty cup, still angry and confused, unable to eat much of anything. He had thought he had the
situation figured out. Now it seemed he knew nothing for certain.
Why did she feel such loyalty to this man if he was not her kin,
nor her lover? And why had she gone to meet him if they were not
involved, whether politically or otherwise?

Scowling, Rowan tossed back the rest of his drink.

He still loved her—that much he *did* know, which was the
trouble of it. He still loved Arabella so much it hurt.

*You are a fool, Rowan. You should have kept your heart locked up
and not allowed that blasted woman in. But nay. You were beguiled by
her dark eyes and winsome smile, and now here you are, wallowing in
heartache again.*

Rowan stared hard at the food before him as the mocking,
dark voice spoke again. *How could you have believed you could have
the heart of someone like her? 'Twas all foolishness!*

"Sire?"

Rowan looked up at his advisor who waited with expectant
eyes. "Pardon?"

Cassius frowned. "I was asking you what we shall do with the
queen."

That was his dilemma. He did not *know* what to do with her.
According to the law, he should try and condemn her as a traitor,

but he could not find it in himself to condemn her to death… no matter how much his heart ached because of her.

"I know not, Cassius."

"Sire, I know how you feel about the woman, but the law is the law. We cannot simply spare one and condemn another for the same crime. If we showed such favoritism, the entire kingdom would run amuck."

"I cannot condemn her to death, Cassius. She is with child, and I cannot, in good conscience, kill such an innocent—no matter the sins of the mother."

"But if the child is not—"

"It *is* mine!" Rowan slammed his fist to the table. The servants standing nearby jumped.

His chest constricted at finally acknowledging the fact he was going to be a father. He was flooded with overwhelming joy and fear all at once. "The child my wife carries is, by right, the future prince or princess of this realm. I shan't do anything to Arabella beyond house arrest until the baby is born."

"My king, were she anyone else—"

Rowan bolted to his feet, nearly knocking his chair backwards. "I know well that even the queen is not exempt from the law! But I cannot, and will not, act any further where she is concerned until *after* the child is born!" Rowan slammed his hand on the table, knocking over Cassius' wine and sending it spilling into the man's lap. Rowan's insides trembled, his nerves rubbed raw. All this anxiety and frustration made him feel on the edge of insanity. "Do you understand me?"

Cassius' nostrils flared. "Yes, my king."

Arabella

What am I thinking? My hand rested on the latch of Lord Cassius' bedchamber door. I knew he was having supper with Rowan, leaving his room vacant.

What do you expect to find in there? You are insane, Arabella!

Completely and utterly insane! You will be caught. Someone shall come in and—

I opened the door and cautiously peeked inside. Just as I thought, no one occupied the spacious bedchamber warmed by a glowing fire crackling in the hearth.

My heart doubled its pace as I entered the room and carefully shut the door behind me. I knew it was extremely risky for me to be snooping in Lord Cassius' chamber, but I knew without a doubt that he had something—even *everything*—to do with this situation. Thinking of all that had happened involving him in the past...

A chill chased up my spine. How had I not suspected him sooner?

I moved to a trunk in the corner and rifled through its contents: tunics, leggings, spare boots, a nightshirt. Nothing.

I ran my hands under the mattress and crouched on my hands and knees to search under the bed, but still found nothing. *Does that truly surprise you, Arabella? You knew this was a foolish endeavor.*

But I had not finished looking yet. I hurried over to the desk that sat against the left wall and opened the drawers. While rifling through the second drawer, my knuckles hit against the bottom. I frowned, rapping gently against the wooden surface. A false bottom!

It took a few nerve-wracking minutes that sent sweat running down my back, but at last, I managed to pry up the piece of wood and peer into in the hollow space beneath.

My stomach grew cold.

From within the hidden compartment I withdrew a small pouch containing white flowers with jagged-edged leaves. It only took a moment for me to recognize the plant...

Jimsonweed.

Alarm bells sounded in my brain as I stared at the pouch's contents in horror. Jimsonweed was a lethal poison; its symptoms being dizziness, dry mouth, nausea, vomiting, visual problems, heart palpitations... Exactly the sort of things Favian had experienced just before he died.

I had been correct. Favian *had* been poisoned.

And Cassius *was* responsible.

My breath left my lungs in a loud gasp.

But why keep the murder weapon around if its discovery would implicate him in the crime?

Because it still serves a purpose...

I dropped the pouch back into the drawer like it was a viper.

The poison was still useful to Cassius.

And I was fairly certain I knew who he meant to use it on...

'Tis a dangerous matter, one that could prove dangerous to you in many ways...

Favian's warnings had not been the ramblings of a paranoid, old man. He had known about Cassius' involvement in the murders, and perhaps even intended to tell me about it. But he was silenced before he could.

And now, despite trying to heed Favian's warnings, it seemed Cassius had set his sights on getting rid of me as well.

"I have to get out of here."

I was just about to replace the false bottom, close the drawer, and flee, when a flash of metal caught my eye. I stilled, staring down into the drawer, the shadows cast by the fire making it difficult to see. Glancing over my shoulder, I reached in and picked up the metallic object. I raised it into the light. It fell, dangling from a black cord. The firelight glinted off the object as it twirled and twisted, finally coming to a stop.

My heart came into my throat.

The Trilarian crest.

They were going out the window.

They?

The Trilarians... They were just escaping, like phantoms in the night... dressed in long, black robes... Each of them had silver pendants bearing the Trilarian crest.... The king's specially trained assassins.

I gasped and dropped the pendant. My chest heaved as I struggled to catch my breath, shock and fear running across every nerve in my body. All the pieces were falling into place... and they made a terrible picture.

Voices echoed in the hallway. Drawing closer.

Someone was coming! I was trapped!

Heart banging against my ribs, I scrambled to pick up the pendant, cram it into the hidden compartment, and push the drawer shut. I turned in a circle, searching for a way of escape. The window was too far off the ground. And the door certainly was not an option.

There was no way out.

I ran over to the bed and wriggled beneath it, the dust stirring up and tickling my nostrils. I clamped my nose shut to keep from sneezing, pressing my other hand over my mouth to muffle my terrified breathing.

"What do you intend to do, m'lord?" an unknown voice said as the door opened.

I squeezed my eyes shut. What would happen if they found me? What if they did not leave? I would be stuck here indefinitely!

"I had hoped the king would take care of her for me, but it seems that shan't be—at least not anytime soon," Cassius' voice said, sending a chill up my spine.

"So…"

"I shall have to take care of her myself."

"When, m'lord?"

"That is for *me* to know."

Two sets of boots passed by the bed. I stiffened. *Lord, please do not let them discover me! Please, please, please…*

One man stopped directly before me, at the foot of the bed. He shifted from one foot to the other. "And what about the king? Has that plan changed now?"

I tilted my head down, just barely able to see Lord Cassius where he stood digging in his trunk.

Lord Cassius straightened and turned to the other man. He proceeded to remove his shirt. I wanted to look away, but something caught my eye and I could not remove my eyes from him.

Across Cassius' bare chest and upper left arm ran two jagged, pink scars.

My eyes flew wide. *I dealt him an equally bad blow, cutting him on his arm and chest…*

I struggled not to gasp aloud. *He* was the one Rowan had battled that terrible night in Dallin.

I tucked my head and closed my eyes while Cassius continued changing clothes and revelation upon revelation hit me in the face. Suddenly, everything—or almost everything—made sense. Cassius was the one Rowan had fought. The one who wounded him and whom Rowan, in turn, wounded. He was one of the men who killed Rowan's parents, probably the leader of the group. But why *him*, why not hire mercenaries to do the job and leave oneself out of it?

Slowly, my mind worked through the possibilities. Allis had said that when the Dallin knights tried to pursue the assassins, they could find no trace of them either without or within the castle.

Within...

By doing the deed himself, with the help of other men in the king's retinue, he and his co-conspirators were able to vanish into the shadows of the castle and reemerge as faces, *friends*, that no one within Dallin would have suspected.

Bile rose in my throat.

Cassius had successfully framed Trilaria for murder, inciting the two kingdoms to war. He had been pulling Rowan's strings this entire time, influencing him to lead the kingdom to ruin. He had been the one to hire the servants to kill Rowan. And he had killed Favian—my friend, Rowan's friend and second father. A good man who had known a just bit too much.

Just like me.

And now I knew everything.

Cassius' own words had just confirmed that he wanted me out of the picture. With me and the baby gone, only Rowan would stand between him and the throne. That was the objective, his motive for all this, was it not?

I covered my face with my hands, trembling. They were so near. Just the slightest noise and they would find me.

"You never answered my question, my lord," the unknown man said, drawing my attention. I removed my hands from my face and looked up.

There was silence for a few seconds before Cassius spoke. "That plan shall remain the same." A sinister steel coated his voice, sending fearful chills up my spine. "When the battle commences, he shan't expect his own men to turn on him." He paused, and the sick grin upon his face was tangible in the air. "His greatest battle shall be his last. King Rowan's blood shall run like a river down the Trilarian hills."

I covered my mouth again to keep from screaming. *Rowan!*

Both our lives were on the brink of ending, the kingdom on the edge of destruction... And it seemed *I* was the only one with knowledge enough to stop it.

Could I stop it?

The other man walked away, his boots leaving my view. Cassius also headed for the door—to my great relief. My sharp exhale stirred the dust, which came up into my nostrils. I sucked in a breath, about to sneeze. Panic seized me. I squeezed my nose tight, the held-in sneeze forming intense pressure in my head.

The sound of Cassius' footsteps stopped. He was pausing... searching. He had heard me.

Oh, God, please!

The steps continued out of the room, and the door shut with a low thud.

I released an enormous, pent up breath and scrambled out from under the bed, rising to my knees. Dust covered my dress, and I hurriedly swiped it away.

I had finally discovered the truth I so longed for, but now I wished I could forget it. It was deadly knowledge to harbor, knowledge that I needed to share, but was dreadfully afraid to.

Would Rowan believe me if I told him? What would Cassius do? Would he turn my words against me, use them to make me appear more of a liar than ever in Rowan's eyes?

"God, what am I to do? Oh, why could I not have left things as they were and not meddled?"

Deep in my heart, I knew God wanted me to reveal what I knew. But I was afraid. Too afraid of what might happen.

"I cannot, Lord. I cannot! No one shall even hear my words!"

I rose to my feet on trembling legs. I had to get out of this room before someone found me.

My hands jerked the door open, and I fled from the room, hastily shutting the door as I went. I ran down the corridor, anxious to get to my room and lock myself away. I could not let any food or drink come in unless Mavis oversaw its making. Nor could I allow a physician of any sort see to me, because that too would surely end with my poisoning. I had to stay isolated.

I rounded a corner and bumped straight into a hard object. When I stumbled back and looked up, my heart nearly exploded out of my chest.

Lord Cassius stood before me.

My mouth went dry.

"My queen, what are you doing out of your room again?" He took a small step forward.

I faltered a half-step back. "Nothing." My voice trembled far more than I wished it to. "Just out for a stroll."

He studied me in silence. I straightened, finding enough courage to meet his gaze. He suspected I was up to something. I could feel it. And that scared me all the more.

His black eyes bore into mine, daring me to challenge him. In them, I saw that challenge. I saw fire. Determination. Shrewdness. And most of all... death.

My spirit withered, leaving me all the more uncertain.

Did I truly have the courage to meet that challenge?

Chapter 38

I SUMMONED UNCLE MATTHEW THE FOLLOW-
ing morning, having tossed and turned all night. The information
I uncovered had haunted me without relent, keeping me awake
until the rising sun pulled me from bed.

As I sat anxiously awaiting my uncle's arrival, my stomach
roiled with a terrible bout of morning sickness. The nausea made
me weak, and I could not summon myself to rise and pace the
room as my stiff legs wished to do. My hand fluttered to my abdomen for the hundredth time that morning. Would my baby ever
know the love of its father? Would it ever live at all?

The door opened and Mavis entered, with Uncle Matthew
following just behind. "My dear girl, I have been aching to come
to you these last days but have not been able. Explain to me this
dreadful mess!" I stood to receive him, and his hands clasped my
arms at the elbows.

I looked to Mavis, who stood patiently at the door, and gave
her leave to exit the room.

Now we were free to converse.

My uncle and I sat and I proceeded to explain what had transpired. He, of course, had already heard the many sordid rumors
spread about me. I explained the situation with Fred, with Rowan,
and about my rumored treason—a thing he already knew to be
false.

"But that is not the worst of it." I bit my lip as my uncle studied my face. "I know... I know now what really happened to the
king and queen."

Uncle Matthew's brows shot high on his forehead.

"You know I have never fully believed in Trilaria's guilt. And I fear I meddled where I should have not... Lord Favian did the same, and that is why he is dead."

My uncle leaned forward, bringing his voice down. "Of what do you speak, Arabella? What have you discovered?"

I shook my head, starting to rethink my decision to share with him what I had learned. I did not want his life at stake too. I could not have that on my conscience. But I had to tell someone, and it was better him than Mavis.

"'Twas Cassius," I blurted out, careful to keep my voice low lest someone be listening at the door. "He and others—I know not whom—murdered the king and queen and framed Trilaria for it. Rowan told me he fought one of them upon catching the men as they were escaping. He said he wounded the man on his chest and arm. And Cassius has the exact scars, as well as the kind of Trilarian pendant Rowan saw."

My uncle's eyebrows arched high. "And how did you come to see these items of evidence?"

Again, I shook my head. "It matters not, uncle. What matters is that I *know*. Cassius killed the king and queen, and he hired those servants to poison Rowan. He killed Favian because he knew too much. And he has now influenced Rowan to turn against me."

I reached out and squeezed my uncle's hand, seeking the comfort he had always been able to give. "Uncle Matthew, he intends to turn the army against Rowan when they go to battle. He is going to slay Rowan and blame the war, and then ascend to the throne. But he must have me and the baby out of the way first... He intends to kill me."

My uncle's his eyes filled alarm. "What? You know this for certain?"

"Yes! I heard him speaking with one of the knights—another terrible thing. For that means some of Rowan's own knights are against us! Uncle, what am I to do?"

He opened his arms and welcomed me to his lap, cradling me as he had the day my mother passed and left me in his care. I tried in vain to hold back my tears. He rubbed my back, his touch tender as ever; but deep within that touch, I sensed a tension, a worry as deep my own.

"What am I to do?" I repeated. If I were honest, I already knew the answer, deep inside. But I feared it. I knew not whether I had the strength to take such a leap of faith and hope that God would see me through.

"You need to go before the king, explain all to him, and reveal what you have discovered." My uncle voiced the very thing I had been feeling.

I shook my head. "Nay, he said I am forbidden to come before him without invitation." A piteous sob rose in my throat. "He despises me now, Uncle. He has cast me off. I fear he loves me no longer."

"Arabella." Uncle Matthew took hold of my shoulders and gently pushed me away so he could see my tear-stained face. "No matter what the king has done, I know you love him. And even if you did not, it would still be your duty to do all you could to save his life—you did it once before already, despite your fear." His dark brown eyes, similar to my own, searched my face in earnest. "Not just his life, but the kingdom itself is at stake, as well as your life and that of your child. You have the chance to save it all. Would you not take that chance, no matter the potential cost?"

I lowered my head, knowing he was right, though I hated to acknowledge it. I had the power to put an end to all of this—a power that needed using before it was too late.

Shall the risk be worth it, Lord? Shall Rowan believe me? Cassius is his right-hand man! Already, he has taken the man's word over mine. What shall make this any different?

As if sensing my internal questions, Uncle Matthew put a hand to my face, forcing me to meet his eye. "Arabella. I know you have questioned your reason for being here. I know you must have wondered why the Lord dealt you such a fate. But mayhap it is that you have been brought to the king's palace... for such a time as this?"

It all settled within me now as I stared at him. All the pieces fell into place, finally revealing to me the answers to the questions I had long asked.

God had brought me here as queen for this express purpose. He had known that I needed to be the one to discover the truth about the king and queen's murder, that I would be the one to end the war. He brought me to this undesired place to help Rowan in many ways. By opening his eyes to the world around him. By softening his heart to God and his people. And most of all... by putting an end to the treachery that threatened to destroy him and the kingdom.

I moved off my uncle's lap and paced. *God, is this what You want me to do? Is this Your will?*

I did not have to wait for His Voice to speak. I already knew the answer.

Yes.

I had lost sight of my purpose these past months. In my fear, I had ceased searching out answers. I realized now that Rowan and I falling apart was necessary to bring about the situation in which I could discover the truth and reveal Cassius' plot. If things had continued as they were, I never would have discovered it. I would have remained completely unaware until both Rowan and I were murdered just like his parents.

If this is truly what You want me to do, Lord... You must give me strength. I know not how I can do it. It shall be the word of the king's most trusted advisor against that of a woman everyone believes to be a lying, adulterous traitor.

Now I heard Him speak loud and clear in my spirit. *Trust in the Lord with all thine heart; and lean not unto thine own under-standing. In all thy ways acknowledge Him, and He shall direct thy paths.*

I had committed to trust in the Lord multiple times before. How could I not now? He had yet to fail me, even if sometimes I felt as though He had. In the end, I always saw that He was still taking care of me and that He had not failed me in the least.

He had said that I would see, one day, why He allowed these things to happen. That all would be revealed. And this was that day.

Everything has been leading me to this: the chance to save both Rowan and Acuniel, and even Trilaria as well.

It was a daunting task, but one He had given me. And I could not let Him down.

Slowly, I turned to face my uncle. I balled my fists and raised my chin, feeling like a true queen again as determination set in. "I shall do it. And if I die trying... then so be it."

The doors to the Great Hall loomed before me and I closed my eyes against the imposing sight, breathing deeply. *Calm, Arabella. Calm.* My hand found its way to the object in my pocket and I clenched it in my sweaty palm. The Trilarian crest.

Rowan and Cassius had called for an emergency meeting of the court to prepare for the impending battle, sending out the decree two days ago to give the noblemen ample time to arrive. I'd retrieved the pendant promptly after court began, knowing I would need it to convince Rowan, and now... here I stood, working up the courage to take the next step. Into the court. Before Rowan, the man I loved. Before Cassius, the man who wanted me dead. Before... everyone else.

Morning sickness knotted my stomach tight. Already I had lost the meager breakfast I had managed to force down my throat earlier.

I put a trembling hand to my mouth. "Dear God," I whispered, "strengthen me. I cannot do this on my own."

I looked up, taking my hand away from my lips. "I will not fear. I cannot turn back now." Rowan's life, my life, and that of our child, along with the fate of both Acuniel and Trilaria depended on this moment.

I balled my hands into fists, willing courage to my limbs. "I know You are with me, and there is nothing I cannot face."

With one last breath and determination in my eyes, I threw open the doors of the Great Hall.

Gasps and shouts erupted as all eyes turned to me. Lord Cassius jumped to his feet. "My king! Will you stand for this? You know what you told this woman about coming before you uninvited!"

Rowan answered not, only stared hard at me as I slowly made my way across the expanse of the Hall. My knees felt weak. My heart drummed in my ears. A million questions flew through my mind. *What will he say? What will he do? Shall he believe me? Or will he formally charge me with treason instead?*

I could feel every scathing look sent my way, but I refused to look to the left or to the right. My eyes had to stay trained on Rowan or I would lose my courage and turn around.

Lord Cassius turned to Rowan, partially blocking my view of him. "This is an outrage! You know what you told her! This deceiver; this traitor; this—this *filthy* adulteress!"

My cheeks burned red as the din of voices swelled. It sounded as though all, or most, agreed with Cassius, and yet still Rowan did not respond. But was that good?

A wave of nausea swept over me and I closed my eyes against it, determined not to retch upon the floors of the Great Hall.

I should just give up...

Even after all this, I was tempted to turn around, run away, and hide.

You cannot, Arabella! You must do this! You mustn't stop now!

Another Voice, different from my own, sounded in my mind. *I shall be your strength. Trust in me.*

The Voice fortified my heart and limbs, making it easier to take another step, and another, and another... until at last, I reached the dais and fell to my knees.

Chapter 39

Rowan

THE NOISE OF PROTESTING VOICES PAINED ROWan's ears. Cassius shouted at him in outrage, demanding he do something about this untimely interruption. But all Rowan could think was: *Why is she here?*

His heart squeezed at seeing his wife, his love, at his feet, her head bowed and waiting for his response. Half of him wanted to rush down the steps and take her into his arms, while the other half wanted to scream in outrage at the pain her presence caused him.

Of its own accord, his hand raised, his eyes never leaving the top of her inclined head. She had worn a crown today, something she very rarely did. "Silence!" His tone demanded obedience.

The crowd hushed instantly.

Arabella slowly raised her head and met his gaze. What he saw there nearly made him crumple. Her eyes were glassy, filled with unshed tears, and mixed with more flashes of fear and uncertainty than he'd never seen in them before. And there was something else there, something he had seen in her eyes many times as he'd taken her into his arms…

Pure love.

Rowan clenched his jaw, fighting against the emotions she stirred within him.

"My king, surely you do not intend to allow—"

"Quiet, Cassius." Rowan finally tore his gaze from Arabella, turning fiery eyes on his advisor. "I shall allow what I please."

The man's face hardened, and he clamped his mouth shut.

Rowan looked back at Arabella, who was rising from her place on the dais steps. "My king." Her voice trembled. "Rowan..." she added lowly, for his ears alone. Her use of his name sent a painful tremor through his heart. How could such a simple spoken name cause such a reaction in him?

"Why are you here, Arabella?"

She gripped her hands in the sides of her long, golden cape that draped around her shoulders, covering the deep red gown that trailed across the stones behind her. "I come bearing urgent news." She lifted her chin high and squared her shoulders. Gone were the fear and uncertainty, the watery sheen of tears. Now the lines of her face bespoke confidence and finality—she was once again the Arabella he knew and loved.

"Sire, I simply must protest."

Rowan sent Cassius another pointed glare before returning to the woman before him.

"I have discovered things," she continued, "things that shall clear my name of all the lies brought against me."

Murmurings sounded among the nobles, stirring the room with hushed noises as Arabella remained steadfast in her stance, never looking away from him. Her gaze was unnerving.

"And what things must you tell me?" He leaned forward. Would she finally explain her relation to the man he intended to execute come morning?

She looked down and her jaw visibly clenched. What was she thinking? Rowan began to feel she was reconsidering her decision to come here.

Then, abruptly, she raised her head, looking more determined than ever. "The man you hold locked in your cell, Frederic of Cael-rith, is one of my dearest friends. We grew up together. His dislike of you is no secret to anyone who knows him, and 'twas only a matter of time before he decided to return to Trilaria. He asked to speak with me but refused to do so here. To prevent endangering him or inciting gossip, I requested he meet me in secret outside the city wall."

She paused to take a deep breath. "He told me he was leaving to fight with Trilaria, which I tried to discourage him of, but there is no reasoning with Frederic once he has his mind made up. After that, believing I would never see him again, I told him that I am with child, and in his excitement, he picked me up and kissed my cheek."

Rowan's jaw clenched at the memory.

"That is what you saw transpiring—not a meeting between lovers, but a farewell between old friends."

Relief washed through Rowan at knowing the truth of it, though it came begrudgingly. Other accusations still needed disproving. "But you protected him, hid the truth of his loyalties to allow his escape."

She put a defensive hand to her chest. "Before he left, he made me promise to keep his leaving a secret. And being the loyal friend that I am, I kept that promise," her eyes bore into his, giving him a knowing look filled with anguish, "even at the cost of something I held very dear.

"I committed no treason," she then declared, straightening and addressing the crowd at large, though she continued to face Rowan. "The only thing I am guilty of is being true to my word."

More murmurings came from the crowd. Cassius stepped forward again. "Shall you believe this story of hers? It could easily be false!"

"Any accusations of treason, any rumors of my conspiring with the Trilarians, are solely the result of one man." She raised her chin defiantly and arrowed a finger at his advisor. "You, Lord Cassius, have manipulated everyone into turning against me."

Rowan pulled back in shock at her bold accusation. The crowd surged with a fresh wave of outrage.

"How dare you?" Cassius bellowed, his face mottling in anger. He had never seen his advisor so distraught.

Rowan put out a hand to bar Cassius from throttling Arabella. "What reason would Lord Cassius have to intentionally discredit you?" He scowled down at her, his confusion and curiosity outweighing his anger.

Her eyes flashed as she again threw out an accusing finger at Cassius. "Because he killed your parents!"

For Rowan, the world seemed to stop, though in reality, it was turning more chaotically than ever. He stumbled back a step as the noises faded and all he heard was the pounding of his own heart and his own incredulous voice as he gasped, "*What?*"

Her eyes met his and her voice came to him through the fog

settling over his mind. "He killed your parents and framed Trilaria for it."

Cassius all but pounced on Arabella, letting out a vile curse. "How dare you speak such falsehoods? You are a lying, deceiving—"

"Arabella, you are on dangerous ground. How dare you—"

"Rowan, he was the one you fought! He has the exact scars you spoke of. When you intruded upon him and the others, you fought him and wounded him on his chest and arm. Cassius has those scars!"

"Nay." It could not be so. His advisor could not have done such a thing. "You lie, Arabella."

"Nay!" Her voice grew shrill as she took a step towards him, up the dais stairs. "I have seen them! I was hiding in his room and saw."

"My king, that proves her untrustworthiness if she has been intruding upon my private quarters!"

"*Please*, do not listen to him. I had to! I had to know the truth! Rowan, he hired those servants to poison you, and when my uncle and I foiled their plot, he had them killed to silence them. And Favian! He knew the truth, so Cassius poisoned him!"

The breath left Rowan's lungs for a moment, the atmosphere around him seeming to crush his chest. "Nay, Arabella."

She took another two steps up the dais, her eyes wide and desperate. The shouts and outraged conversations continued to swell with each passing second, fueling the impassioned look on her face and fanning the flames of his own anger. "Please, believe me! 'Tis true! He knew I was becoming a threat to him, so he manipulated you, conveniently using my meeting with Frederic to make you believe I betrayed you. Can you not see?" She reached for him.

"Nay!" he shouted, swiping a hand in a cutting gesture that forced her to her draw back.

"You cannot kill Frederic on the morrow, nor can you go to battle!" Arabella screamed, cutting him off. "Trilaria is innocent, framed by Lord Cassius! He intends to take over the throne!" Her eyes filled with fear. "He intends to turn the army against you and slay you upon the battlefield, slay me as well, and ascend the throne!"

The din of the room pierced Rowan's eardrums, making it difficult to think. This simply could not be true. He could not bring himself to believe that all these years, *eight long* years, he had fought and killed the wrong people, seeking vengeance in the wrong place, when all along the real culprit was right under his nose.

He could not believe it.

Nor would he.

The man he had trusted most besides Favian could not have deceived him for so long. It could not be possible.

"What proof do you have of this?" he gasped out, desperate to hear she had none, that all of her horrible words were untrue.

"This." She reached into the pocket of her gown. Her fist dangled an object before him, held high for all to see.

The Trilarian crest.

Rowan's heart paused its beating. He staggered back and caught himself on the arm of his throne.

The pendant was just as those he had seen the night his parents died.

Cassius cursed again, rage turning his face a brilliant shade of scarlet. He charged toward Arabella, jabbing a finger at her face. "Guards! Seize this lying woman immediately!" The men sprang to action, rushing at her as she stood holding the silver pendant aloft.

"She can only have that pendant one way, sire—by being an agent of Trilaria herself. They must have given it to her." Cassius whirled around to face him. "I tell you, she is in league with them, working with them to bring about your undoing!"

Her eyes alighted on Rowan again as the men took hold of her upper arms, forced the pendant from her hand, and started pulling her towards the exit. They jerked her back so hard that her crown toppled from her head and clattered to the ground.

"Nay! These are all falsehoods devised by *him*! But I never believed Trilaria was guilty—that much I shall own." She continued to fight against the guards tugging her towards the exit. "I am Trilarian born! That is why I have always protested against the war and your treatment of the Trilarians. I knew they could not be guilty, and I could not allow you to fight an innocent people!"

Rowan collapsed into his throne as this new revelation hit him like a slap to the face. His wife... Though she had lived most of her life in Acuniel, she was Trilarian by birth, by blood... And he had married her, fallen in love with her. The very person he had hated... he had come to love.

What cruel jest was this?

"You must listen to me!" Even from the now great distance between them, he could see the tears upon her flushed cheeks. "You must! Before 'tis too late! You must stop the battle from taking place! Please, believe me! Pl—"

The doors slammed in her face, cutting off her cries.

Arabella

The guards tossed me into my room, and I fell to my knees, weeping. I covered my face with my hands, despair vying for control again.

My worst fear had come to pass. Rowan had refused to believe that Cassius was guilty, even after I showed him the pendant.

Lord, I thought You wanted me to do this so the truth could come out, and Cassius be stopped. But it was all for naught. And now Cassius and all those involved know that I know everything.

"They shall surely come for me now," I whispered aloud, trembling in fear. "What shall I do?"

I covered my face again and leaned forward. The fear was swiftly closing in again, making the outcome of my trial look grim and hopeless, indeed. All hope started to vanish. Everything told me to give up, give in, and resign myself to death.

Nay. I shook my head, shaking off the shroud of despair. *Trust in the Lord with all thine heart. Trust!*

"I *do* trust You, Lord," I said, resolving myself to whatever came next. "No matter what is to come… I trust You."

Chapter 40

I AWOKE TO A HAND CLAMPED HARD OVER MY mouth.

My eyes flew open, adjusting to the dark to see the face of Lord Cassius leering down at me. I tried to scream, but there was no doing it with his hand held so tight across my face.

"You thought you could destroy me with that little stunt this morning, my queen?" He pressed his hand in harder, lowering his face until it was a mere breath away. "Oh, you were sadly mistaken."

He ripped me up off the bed and tossed me aside, sending me flailing to the ground. I did not even bother to worry about the modesty of my thin nightdress as I hit the cold stone with a thud. All I cared about was my life.

I pushed off the floor with my hands just as he came and wrenched me up by my arm. "Scream and I shall make you watch as I slit the throat of anyone who comes running."

A tremor of fear traced through me as I met his black eyes in the dark, highlighted only by the pale moonlight leaking into the room. My breath left me in gasps, heaving my chest up and down. I gave a silent nod, figuring it best to do as he said for the moment.

Cassius dragged me to the door and pulled me out into the corridor. Outside, the men assigned to watch my room were nowhere in sight. "Did you kill the guards?" I whispered, a shiver tracing up my spine from the cold already piercing through my gown.

"Nay," he hissed low in my ear, his breath brushing over my

skin. "Anyone can be bought with a certain price—especially if they know you shall be their king on the morrow."

"You shan't ever be king," I ground out as he led me down the corridor. "You shall be stopped." *Somehow...*

I felt the prick of metal at my back. He was holding a knife to me. "Nay. I *shall*, and there is nothing you can do to stop that, foolish girl."

He took me through the palace, still and silent in midnight sleep, and soon we emerged through a door onto the allure. Goosebumps rose all down my body at the first gust of frigid winter wind as we exited into the night. My breath fogged before my face in little clouds. His arm still clamped tight around my shoulders, and every movement sent the knife pricking into my back.

"What are you going to do to me?"

Again, his voice was right at my ear, his breath hot compared to the chill of the air around us. "I shall throw you from the palace wall. And when everyone finds your body come the morrow, they will believe it suicide, caused by your extreme guilt and despair over Rowan's rejection."

I gasped in spite of myself, earning a self-satisfied grin from my captor.

"But..." he added, the grin clear in his voice, "there is no hurt in having a little fun first." He shoved me before him. I caught myself with my hands on the stones that felt like blocks of ice beneath my palms, my knees banging against the ground. "If telltale wounds indicate foul play, no one shall accuse me, for I shall be king by then. And methinks I shan't convict myself." He sneered and rushed at me. I tried to scramble away, but my movements were clumsy, and his foot still landed against the back of my thigh.

Cassius came at me again as I rose to my feet and tried to run away. But he was much faster and shoved me from behind, then kicked me again, this time in the ribs.

All I could think of was my baby. If I could somehow manage a way out of this, my baby had to make it too. I would *not* allow him to harm my child!

Maternal instincts flaring, I jumped back up and charged at him. I swung and landed a punch across his nose. He stumbled back, cursing, but soon looked at me again with a catlike smile. "So you want to try to fight back? All the better."

I turned to run, and he chased me along the north wall. For

the first time, I realized the absence of guards. There should have been several men on patrol. But there was no one in sight...

The icy stone numbed my feet, and every inch of my skin tingled with chill bumps, but I hardly noticed. My adrenaline was pumping much too fast for me to worry about the cold or my barely clad state. All that mattered was getting away from Cassius. *Lord of all, protect me! Aid me in escaping him!*

He caught me around the waist, dragging me backwards again, clamped against his chest. My bare feet skidded as I thrashed in his embrace. I growled and tried to scream, but the fear I felt choked my cry. He caught his hand beneath my chin and pressed my head back until it was flat against his shoulder. "I said, be quiet!"

Then he tossed me back down, and when I came to my feet, pinned me between him and the notched parapets. "Why have you done this, Cassius?" My hands splayed against the short wall—the only thing keeping me from a very long fall. "Why did you kill the king and queen?"

"Why should I tell you?"

"If you are going to kill me, it shan't matter what I know, will it?"

He glared down at me, finally replying, "To get the throne— why else?" He knocked me to the side with the back of his hand. While I stayed lying on the ground, nursing my wounded cheek, Cassius snickered, apparently finding sadistic pleasure in inflicting pain. "That stupid boy was supposed to die too, but he came in at the wrong moment and disrupted the plan. He ended up being a better fighter than I thought."

My heart thudded at that admission. He had intended to kill Rowan as well all along.

"So why have you not killed him sooner?" I turned over, keeping myself upright with my hands as he towered over me, the desire to strike me again burning within his eyes.

"It has not been for want of trying," he snapped. "I had intended to kill him in battle. No one would question it if the king were killed at the front lines. But every attempt failed." He struck me again across the face, taking his anger out on my helpless form. I felt the salty pang of blood on my tongue.

"Was that what happened to him just before he decided to marry? Was he wounded after another failed attempt on his life? And then the servants with the poison, whose plot I foiled?"

He did not reply, but the fire in his eyes told me yes. I scooted back a few inches, hoping to gain some ground between us before he came after me again. "You did not want him to marry, did you?"

"I tried to discourage him of it, but Favian was too persistent." The man cursed Favian's very existence. "The man crossed me, and there was no escaping it. Then I thought the problem would be an easily solvable one." His eyes spat hatred. "I thought he would choose a silly, naïve little twit whom I could dispose of with ease. But of course, Rowan had to find the one clever one of the bunch.

"As long as there remained no heir to usurp my succession, I thought I could leave you alone for the time being. But nay. You just had to go poking your nose in places you did not belong!"

I hurried to stand and run away from him. But he was too quick. He struck me from behind, sending me reeling into the stone parapets. "Yes, and now I know everything, as well as carry the heir to the throne of Acuniel." I turned to face him and raised my chin in defiance. "My child shall sit on this kingdom's throne. Not you!"

He roared and charged at me, delivering a rattling blow to the side of my head, then in the gut. I cried out and doubled over. Cassius struck me again until I crumpled to the ground in pain. I squeezed my eyes shut, fighting against my despair. *Shall I truly die this night?*

"Why frame Trilaria?" I moaned, the pain roaring in my head leaving me unable to open my eyes

"They were perfect to blame for the murder, with disagreements between the two kings already straining their relations. It took all suspicion from me and my compatriots. And since Rowan did not die when he was supposed to, influencing him to go to war gave me the perfect opportunity and cover up for his murder."

"Compatriots. Who were the others that helped you?"

The sneer leaked into his voice. "Oh, I disposed of them long ago. Including your precious Favian."

My eyes flew open. "What?"

He laughed at me. "Yes, my queen, your saintly Lord Favian was one of those who helped me. Somewhat unwillingly of course. He helped me with my plan to kill the king and queen with the promise of a great reward, and his dear sister in Ellswick was my security. As long as I threatened her life, he would stay quiet. But with each year, his *conscience* weighed on him more and more. Then he learned that his sister took ill with a fever and died, and he no longer feared me. He dared to defy me, so I had to do away with him as I did with all the others."

I struggled for air, disbelieving my own ears. Favian an *accomplice*? He had died because he had *always* known the truth and had finally decided to reveal it. I realized that even before then Favian had begun to defy Cassius' rule over him. Favian was the one who pressed for Rowan to marry; he had been the one to push Rowan and I together. He had wanted us to fall in love, bear a child, and threaten Cassius' claim to the throne.

Forgive me… There is so much I wish… People are not always… what they seem… Now Favian's last words made so much more sense.

"You evil, lying—" I screamed and rose to my feet, lunging at him. I struck him across the face, beating at him with my fists, but it took only a moment for him to overpower me.

He slammed me to the ground with so much force that this time I stayed there, unable to rise. My body trembled with cold and anger. He had forced Favian to go along with this plot, and then when Favian stood up for himself, he murdered him!

I clenched my fists and fought to regain my strength. "And your plan for the battle on the morrow? Shall the soldiers truly turn against Rowan?"

Cassius laughed, leaning down to gruffly cup my face in his hand. "Once the people's hearts hardened against him, 'twas not difficult to quietly convince the men to revolt against the king in favor of me. Giving people empty promises of wealth and prosperity—and the occasional bribe—can get one many places."

I glared up at him, meeting him eye for eye. "You shan't *ever* be king. Your tyranny shall not prevail."

Lord Cassius tilted his head and gave me a patronizing smile, clearly relishing in the blood that dripped from my lip and nose. "Oh really? Who is this person that shall stop me?" He gripped my jaw tight, as if to crush the bone. "You are completely at my mercy and without hope of escape, for there is no one to hear or see. The guards are undoubtedly half drunk by now, counting their hefty reward for their cooperation." His nose nearly touched mine, his hot breath washing over me. "And your *precious* Rowan does not believe you. You should have known better than to challenge me, Arabella of Caelrith."

Tears rose in my eyes, unbidden, and I hated myself for them. I so wanted to be brave; but in the face of such fear and hopelessness...

"Come." He jerked me up by my arms. "I tire of this talk."

Rowan

The fire crackling in Rowan's fireplace matched that which burned within his own heart and mind. He ran his fingers over the cool metal of Arabella's crown that had fallen from her head as she was dragged away. Ever since her brave outburst that morning, he'd been haunted by her words, everything she had claimed. All of it sounded in his brain in an endless repeat.

His heart ached to believe her, to believe that she had been telling him the truth, that she had, in fact, not betrayed him in any way. But his mind refused to believe that his trusted advisor could be capable of such deception. If what she said was true, then Rowan was the most ignorant fool in the world. It meant this man had deceived him for years, influencing him to do things that had only caused others pain. It meant Rowan had fought a war over nothing these eight years, costing the lives of countless men on both sides... including Arabella's father.

He sat Arabella's crown aside and gripped his head in his hands, resting his elbows on his knees.

How could this be? How could Cassius have done something like this—killed his parents, killed Favian, torn him and Arabella apart—and Rowan have fallen for it all these years?

He was the one you fought! You wounded him on the chest and arm. He has the exact scars! Arabella's voice cried.

She is a lying traitor! screamed Cassius.

Do not listen to him! You must believe me! He killed your parents... He killed Favian... He intends to kill you, and me as well!

Then Rowan pictured the pendant bearing the Trilarian crest, the exact sort of necklace Rowan had seen when he battled the man he'd thought was one of Trilaria's legendary trained assassins.

I am Trilarian born! Arabella's final revelation echoed in his ears for the hundredth time. How was it that he had fallen in love with the very person his own law sentenced to death? No wonder she had hated him so much in the beginning and had always been so defensive of the Trilarian people.

Do not listen to her. Do not believe her again.

What if I want to? He sighed in frustration. Rowan wanted to believe her; he really, *truly* did. But his pride kept him from doing so. He hated to acknowledge he had been so wrong for all this time.

It would mean that he had caused her pain for no due reason. That he had hurt the woman he loved, possibly beyond repair... It was easier to believe she deserved his scorn than to accept that she did not and could be lost to him forever.

Then the image of her standing before him earlier that day appeared. He remembered the passion on her face, the truth that burned in her eyes, and that look of love and sincerity that had so squeezed his heart. A look that he knew he had seen on a number of occasions over the past months. A look he had seen every morning that he awakened by her side.

And then he knew... Rowan knew that she had been right. That she had been telling the truth in *everything* that she said.

Rowan jumped to his feet, grief and fear welling in his chest and constricting his lungs.

He had to find her.

And Cassius.

Before it was too late.

He rushed out of his room and threw open the door to hers without knocking, hoping—*praying*—that she would be there.

But she was not...

The room was empty.

Arabella

I tried to stand to my feet, but I was too weak, too tired. Spots of blood marred my white nightgown from the dripping of my bloody nose and mouth. My right eye was swollen—I could feel the warm pulsing of blood surrounding it. My head and every inch of me ached with pain

Cassius struck me again. I fell back on the stone, freezing, tired of trying to fight back. I had managed to land some more blows of my own, but now I was through. I could no longer fight him off. I shivered on the ground, my toes and fingers numb with cold, and the chill of the stone leaking through my nightdress.

"Enough of this." Lord Cassius leaned over and hefted me up by my arms. He grinned and looked into my eyes. "Time to die, *my queen*." He said my title mockingly, full of disdain. I spit in his face—a mixture of saliva and blood. He growled and let loose a curse, then prodded me onto the edge of the wall. I faced him, body weak and shaking as my numb feet slid backwards onto the narrow ledge.

Suddenly, he seized me around the neck, just beneath my jaw. Cold air rushed up my gown as a burst of wind whipped through the air. I wanted to scream in terror, but I could not; his grip around my throat was far too tight. I clawed and clutched at his arm, waiting for him to shove me over the edge. I could not breathe; already, my vision was tunneling. Soon I would black out, and then I would fall, and death would come.

God, please! I do not want to die! I cannot. My baby shall never get to live! And then Rowan shall die on the morrow. Please—

"Put her down, Cassius!"

My heart leapt at the familiar voice.

I opened my eyes to see Rowan standing with his sword drawn and pointed at Cassius, fury burning in his eyes. Six knights stood directly behind him.

"If you insist." Cassius' grip loosened and I teetered backward. I somehow managed to scream through my tight throat, grasping at his arm in terror.

"Nay!"

Cassius tightened his hand back around my throat, completely blocking the passage of air to my lungs. Would he really listen to Rowan?

I met Rowan's eyes, my heart constricting. Past the fury, I saw his pain and remorse.

He believes me.

Cassius turned and dropped me onto the allure. I collapsed on the stone, gasping for breath and clutching my stomach. The cold air rushed in, stinging my lungs, but I cared not. I drank it in overly fast, nearly choking.

Cassius turned to Rowan, his face hidden from me, but I knew a sneer twisted his features. "So, you have chosen to believe the wench?"

Rowan did not answer. He kept his rage-filled gaze on Cassius, his sword extended before him.

Cassius laughed and took a step forward. Two. Then three. "You fool. Love is a stupid thing."

Rowan jabbed his sword at the man, his anger seething through clenched teeth. "You *killed them*, Cassius! And all this time had me believe Trilaria was responsible!" I thought Rowan would run Cassius through then and there, but his eyes only burned with grief and rage. "Do you realize how many innocent lives your deception has caused me to take? *Do you?*" Rowan thrust his sword beneath his advisor's chin. "I trusted you, Cassius! And all this time, as I was busy plotting the destruction of the Trilarians, you, the *real* criminal, sat right beneath my nose—or rather, at my right hand!"

My heart wrenched in pain for him, my eyes never leaving his. I tried to sit up and lean against the parapets but found I had not the strength.

Tears filled Rowan's eyes. "You killed my mother and father, left them lying in their own blood! And murdered Favian!" Rowan shoved against Cassius with a ferocious growl, sending him stumbling back.

Cassius drew his sword in one swift movement. I expected him to fight back, but he merely cocked his head and laughed. "You truly are a simpleton, Rowan."

I finally found the strength to sit up, a sense of foreboding chasing along my spine.

"You should have guessed that I would have men within your ranks. As I have told your wife here, everyone can be bought with a price." Cassius jerked his chin at the knights. "Kill him."

"Nay!" I tried to stand to my feet, pulling myself up by a parapet. Rowan spun, keeping both the knights and Cassius within his vision. He was outnumbered. Seven to one.

"I shall take care of the queen." Cassius started to turn back to me to finish what he had begun, but he paused at the hesitation of the men.

Three of the knights shared an uncertain look. Then one stepped forward, pointing his sword at Cassius. "Nay."

"What?"

"Nay!" the knight repeated. "We shall not bow to your wishes anymore, Lord Cassius. King Rowan is the rightful king." The other two moved to oppose those who stood against the king.

Seizing Cassius' moment of distraction, Rowan whirled and swung his sword without warning. But Cassius recovered just in time to block the blade from slicing through his neck.

I edged back from the fight. *Dear God, help Rowan prevail!*

Cassius pulled away and swung his sword in a wild arc, the blade narrowing in on Rowan's head. I screamed as he managed to block it, his body twisting awkwardly to hold off Cassius' sword. He shoved away, sending Cassius into the parapets. The man arched backward over the wall, Rowan leaning over him with his sword pointed down at Cassius' chest. But Cassius pushed him off and Rowan fell into the opposite wall with a hard thud that made me cringe.

If Rowan died in this fight... that would be the end. That would be *my* end.

Rowan pushed himself up, gaining his feet swiftly and charging at Cassius with a ferocious battle cry.

I tore my gaze away from Rowan long enough to glance at the battling knights—just in time to see a sword pierce straight through one of those who sided with Cassius. My stomach heaved and I covered my mouth to keep from retching.

Another of Rowan's vicious yells brought my attention back to him. Rowan was battling Cassius back down the allure, coming closer to me. So close I could see the sweat sheening on both their foreheads despite the cold.

Cassius swung at Rowan, but he ducked, and then struck back, pushing the man even closer to where I huddled against the wall. "Arabella! Move!" Rowan yelled to me over the din of clanging metal and shouting men. "Get out of the way!"

Nay. I had to help him somehow. I could not sit there and do nothing while I watched him die before my eyes.

When Cassius took a few more steps back, I stuck out my foot. He tripped, letting out a curse, and fell onto his back.

It all happened so fast, like a blur. One moment, I was about to clench my eyes shut to prepare for the bloodshed Rowan would inflict; the next, Cassius had rolled to his side, grabbed me, and I found myself pinned against him. I gasped, too shocked to scream as he dragged me across the stones with him. We were both swiftly on our feet.

"Nay!" Rowan started to lunge at him.

But then I felt the cool of metal against my neck. I froze. Rowan froze too, his sword poised in the air.

Cassius' voice rumbled in his chest that pressed against my back. "Stay where you are, Rowan, or I shall slit her throat." Breath hissed through my nose, sharp and fast. I tried not to move, keeping my eyes on Rowan, his strong, powerful stance somehow providing me strength.

He glared at Cassius down the length of his blade that gleamed in the moonlight. "Let her go."

"Nay!" My captor pressed the dagger tighter to my skin. I felt the blade cut in, the slight trickle of blood running down my neck. I feared swallowing, even breathing now, certain that any movement of my throat would end my life. "I shall not let her go unless—"

Cassius' voice fell silent as a *whoosh* split the air and a dagger plunged into his chest. Directly beside my head.

My captor sagged, letting out a terrible sound. I screamed as he dropped the knife and fell backward, toppling over the side of the wall…

And taking me with him.

I heard the men's shouts, Rowan's yell, the sound of my own scream and the pound of blood in my temples. Half-alive, Cassius groped wildly at me as he fell.

I was falling, each second seeming to last an hour.

I closed my eyes, unable to breathe. I was going to die. After all this, I was going to die with Cassius.

God, I cannot die! Please! Jesus, save me!

I whispered that Name, waiting for my body to meet the ground at any second.

Then I suddenly became aware of something cold and hard beneath my fingers.

My eyes opened and I started crying the moment my vision cleared.

I had somehow managed to grab hold of a protruding stone. I was not dead. I was safe.

Thank you, Lord!

The men were shouting above me, only two or three feet up.

The relieved tears poured down my face, mixing with the blood that streaked my skin

"Arabella, hold on. I am coming." Rowan's voice came to me through the terror-induced fog that cloaked my mind. I was not sure how he did it, but before I knew, I was being pulled over the edge of the wall. Warmth enveloped me as Rowan sank to his knees with me in his arms.

I was weeping uncontrollably, my tears soaking his shirt. I gripped the fabric of his clothes, savoring the smell of him, so warm and comforting. Something came around my shoulders—a cape?—and Rowan held me tighter, cradling me like a child.

"Forgive me, Arabella. I beg you, forgive me. I should have believed you sooner and spared you from this." I felt his hand touch my face, examining my wounds. He tenderly wiped at my tears and the blood dripping from my lip. "How dare he do this? 'Tis my fault you are hurt. If it was not for—" His voice broke off, catching with emotion.

No matter what had happened between us over the last several days, no matter what he was saying to me—good or bad—I cared not. I was so *relieved* to be in his embrace. Safe…

I gripped his shirt tighter, burying my face in his chest. "You are here. Not a dream. You are real… H—here. I—I mi—" I hiccupped on a sob.

"Back away. Give Her Majesty some space," I heard him say to whichever knights survived the battle.

He shifted, making it feel as though he were letting me go. I opened my eyes wide and put my trembling hands around his neck, staring up at his dear face through my tears. "D—do not l—leave me. P—please."

"I shan't leave you." His face blurred before my eyes so I could not read his expression. Rowan pulled me closer again and rested his chin atop my head. "I promise I am not going to let you go."

The cold wind picked up, blowing through my gown even with Rowan's arms encircling me and whatever was shielding my back. I shivered violently, suddenly aware of how cold I was. I could not feel my toes or fingers.

"You must be freezing." His voice rumbled in my ear.

I nodded.

A moment later, Rowan was lifting me into his arms and standing. I felt each step he took as I sagged against his chest, my eyes closed. After some time, he opened a door and brought me into a room. When I opened my eyes, I saw that it was his—for which I was glad. I could not bear the thought of being in my own bedchamber. Not after this horrifying night.

Soon, I was lying on the bed and the covers came over me. A few moments later, someone was washing my face, cleansing the wounds from Lord Cassius' merciless beating.

One of my hands found my stomach and I suddenly grew panicked. "My baby! The baby!" I sobbed, choking on my own tears. "Is it well? It cannot be dead. It cannot be dead!"

Someone touched my head, smoothing the hair from my face. "*Shhh*, now. The baby shall be well. Fret not." It was Rowan's voice, his gentle touch attempting to soothe me.

I opened my eyes as he started to turn away from the bedside. "Nay." I reached out to grip his hand in desperation. "Please do not leave me alone. I do not want to be alone."

He shook his head. "I shan't leave."

Then Rowan laid down beside me, atop the covers. His arm came around my back and he pulled me to him, allowing me to bury my face in his chest. I gripped his shirt in my fists and trembled violently against him, still so cold that it made my spine ache.

"*Shhh*... All is well now. You are safe." My tangled nerves gradually unwound as he stroked my back. I curled into him like a frightened child, his body leaning over me like a shelter, making me feel safe and secure.

I had feared I would never feel him so near again.

There was no telling how long I wept in Rowan's protective arms, but sometime during that long, terrible night, I finally fell asleep, all the while thanking God above that I had escaped the clutches of death.

Chapter 41

WHEN I WOKE THE NEXT MORNING, I REACHED out for Rowan. But my hand found nothing save empty space.

I bolted upright, immediately regretting the action that sent pain radiating through my skull and ribs, but I could not bring myself to recline again.

Surely, I had not dreamed his presence.

The door opened and I turned hopeful eyes to it. I wanted desperately to see Rowan and have him hold me close again. And we had much to discuss…

But it was Mavis who entered, her face lighting up then growing dark with worry when she saw me. "Oh, my dear! My poor, poor dear!" She hurried to the bedside and held my face in her hands, examining my cuts and bruises. There was no telling how terrible I looked—I was afraid to see.

"That filthy blackguard did this to you?" It was more a statement of incredulity than a question. Her brow furrowed and her eyes filled with sorrow. "King Rowan told me what transpired last night. He gave me strict instructions to tend to your every need and not leave you alone."

Tears came to my eyes, unbidden. I blinked them away. "Where is he? I must go to him." I had to know… I had to know if he still loved me—if he ever truly had. If we could ever go back to how things were before all this.

I rose hastily, pushing Mavis aside. "Nay, you must rest!" My maid's protests faded in my ears as my head swam, my knees buckled, and I sagged to the floor.

"Your Majesty!" Mavis caught me in her arms.

"I am well. I need to see Rowan." My head lolled backward, my vision growing dim then righting itself.

She helped me back into bed and covered me with the bed-clothes. It was then that I realized I still wore my bloodstained nightgown.

I cringed, memories of the night before filling my pounding head.

"Where is he? Where is Rowan?" I put a hand to my head and squeezed my eyes shut. The muscles in my arm—the one that kept from me from falling to my death—screamed at the movement. "I must speak with him."

Mavis' hand smoothed my hair from my face. "He is gone, my lady."

My eyes flew open. "What?"

"He left early this morning, for Trilaria. He went to try to explain everything to King Wesley and beg they reach a treaty."

"What?" I tried to sit up, but all my previous movement had weakened me again and I collapsed back onto the mattress before Mavis could even protest my efforts. "Do you think King Wesley will listen to him after all he has done?"

I pinched the bridge of my nose, trying to breathe evenly. Worry knotted my stomach. "What if he arrests Rowan and kills him as retribution?"

My loyal maidservant smoothed my hair again. "I know not, dear. I suppose all we can do is pray that the Lord's will shall be done."

I swallowed, nodding slowly; but even then, my head ached. "Yes… I know you are right."

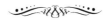

Rowan

Rowan paced before the doors to King Wesley's Great Hall. It had taken him two and a half days to ride to Trilaria and the king's castle, and he had not slept at all during that time. Just as he had not slept when he held Arabella until she fell into the blessed comfort of sleep herself, mere hours before he left.

He was bone weary, but he had to press on.

As he paced, waiting for someone to escort him inside, his stomach knotted tight. Bile rose in his throat and it was all he could do to force it back down. Throughout the grueling journey, he had questioned the wisdom of this act, though he knew it was the right thing to do. Would King Wesley believe him? Or would he soon find himself torn limb from limb by an angry mob? After all he had done, fighting and killing innocent people for nearly a decade... he would not blame them.

Rowan scrubbed a hand through his hair. *I should have listened to King Wesley when he claimed innocence all those years ago... But nay, I listened to Cassius instead.*

It seemed he had done that a lot—letting Cassius manipulate him into not believing someone when they spoke the truth.

The image of Arabella weeping against him after he pulled her to safety appeared in his mind, sending another wave of guilt slapping across his face. *How can she ever forgive me?* Yes, she allowed him to comfort her after her ordeal, but that meant nothing. Of course, Arabella desired to be held, to feel safe. She was delirious with fear and shock at having so narrowly escaped death. In a normal state of mind, she may not be nearly as welcoming.

Rowan stopped his pacing and rubbed a hand down his face, exhaling roughly. "How could I have done this to her?" Such a heavy burden of guilt—over more things than just his treatment of Arabella—weighed upon his shoulders, suffocating him. *I do not deserve her. She did nothing and I refused to believe her, even after she told me the truth. How can she love me after this?*

He shook his head, hating himself for everything done in the past eight years.

How could I have done this? Any of this?

Then the doors opened, and a guard bowed, gesturing for Rowan to follow him into the court of King Wesley of Trilaria.

Arabella

Four days after Rowan's departure, I sat by the window in his room—I still avoided own quarters as much as possible. Even after four days, my right eye remained swollen and bruised. A scabbed-over gash ran in a red line just above my eyebrow. Other cuts and bruises marred my face and arms, and my ribs ached, but I was whole. *Alive.*

And it seemed my child was too. I had feared that after the ordeal with Cassius, I would lose the baby, but by the sheer grace of God, I had yet to miscarriage.

Rowan's smiling face appeared in my mind. It seemed our baby was well, and he would be a father after all. *Thank you, God, for sparing us both.*

Yet I could find little joy or peace. Though I was so happy to be alive, other things weighed heavily on my mind…

One: I had no idea how Rowan fared in Trilaria. Was he still alive? Would I be able to feel it if his soul left this earth?

And two: if he did come home, could things ever be the same? I remembered the look in his eyes when he first told me he loved me; I knew that look was too sincere to deny. I also knew I loved him dearly in return. But we could hardly pick up where we left off. Too much had happened… The events of the past week and a half—had it only been that long?—were too devastating to simply pass over and forget.

Had the sea of lies and misunderstanding choked whatever love he had felt for me?

God, I see now what Your will for me has been. But dare I hope that it has also been for Rowan and I to find love in one another? I was certain of such before, but lately…

Could that still be part of Your plan?

I stared out the open window, unbothered by the cold breeze toying with my hair. I knew Mavis would have a fit if she knew I was allowing the cold in; she did not want my slight cough—a result of being out in the cold while clad only in my nightdress—to worsen, but I cared not. I needed something to look at other than the interior of the room, as I was on doctor's orders not to leave it for at least another day.

I rubbed my thumb over my lip, my elbow resting on the sill as I thought again of Rowan and the future's uncertainty.

What would happen when Rowan returned—*if* he returned? Would he love our child? Had he only comforted me out of guilt for allowing Cassius to harm me, or because he really wanted to?

Could I trust him after all this? How *could* I trust him if he could not trust me?

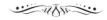

Rowan

His horse's hooves clomped across the courtyard of Dallin Castle.

The guards had let him in swiftly—upon finally recognizing who he was. Rowan had left for Trilaria in such haste, in simple clothes, with only two knights he *knew* he could trust to accompany him, so it was no wonder the guards had not recognized him.

Rowan knew Dallin Castle was a strange place for him to take refuge for the night, but it had seemed right, fitting, due to his activity over the past week.

He had been in Trilaria for five days, staying as a guest of King Wesley. The man had been understandably shocked, even angered, by Rowan's sudden appearance. But upon Rowan bowing humbly before him to explain the matter and beg for forgiveness, the king of Trilaria slowly began to soften. By the second day, Rowan had King Wesley's forgiveness and mutual agreement to reach a peace treaty.

It had taken the next three days to determine all the terms of the treaty. Both sides were to cease all combat with the other, and return any people or property stolen during the course of the war. Rowan was also to pay a hefty sum of restitution, which only smarted a little. He knew it was the least he could do to compensate the king and his people for the misplacement of judgment and the destruction caused by the war.

Throughout his time with King Wesley, the Trilarian king had treated him with hospitality. Many of the servants and nobility had sent arrowed glances Rowan's way, but their king was nothing but kind. He had even mentioned once that he felt it was God's Divine Hand that had led Rowan to this moment—a statement that still bothered him even now as he hopped from his horse and handed the reins to a stable boy.

Lord Geoffrey and his wife Allis—who had departed Caelrith three weeks before, as Lady Allis was approaching her confinement—emerged and hurried across the courtyard to meet him. Lord Geoffrey bowed, while his pregnant wife curtsied with admirable grace despite her bulbous middle. "What brings you here, Your Majesty?"

Rowan met Lord Geoffrey's curious gaze with a small, grim smile. "I have just come from Trilaria." The man and his wife looked taken aback, though he knew they were already aware of the fact that Rowan had called off the battle.

"So, you decided to believe her?" The Lord of Dallin had been one of those present when Arabella made her startling entrance into the Great Hall.

Rowan nodded, guilt hitting him again at the mention of his wife. "Yes, I am afraid she was right about everything... Cassius is dead."

Geoffrey nodded soberly.

Lady Allis looped her arm through her husband's. "I knew the rumors spreading about her could not be true. Tell me, how does the queen fare? I do miss her and have worried for her. I look forward to being able to return to her service."

"She fares well. I hope. Cassius attempted to kill her."

Lady Allis gasped and covered her mouth.

"I arrived just in time to stop him. She is now recovering under the care of a physician and her trusted maidservant." His heart squeezed, remembering Arabella's frantic grip as she begged him not to leave.

Rowan cleared his throat and swallowed. "I pray that the child is also well." *Pray?* Well, yes. He supposed he did *pray* that his child was growing healthily in Arabella's womb.

Lady Allis' hand strayed to her own pregnant belly. "Oh, dear! She *is* expecting—though I am sure the origin of it is not as people have speculated..." Her fair cheeks colored a deep red.

Rowan frowned, angered that he had allowed such talk to spread, that he himself had believed it even for a moment. "Yes, my lady."

She smiled, clearly pleased to have the rumors put to rest, then exchanged a look with her husband. "I believe I shall tell the children goodnight and retire, husband." With a squeeze of her husband's hand, she hobbled to the castle in that awkward way of pregnant women.

"My king, you are most welcome in our home." Lord Geoffrey cast Rowan a look of concern. "I only hope it causes you no discomfort."

Rowan shook his head. "Nay. In fact... I would like to see the room."

Lord Geoffrey's brows shot up, but he nodded and posed no question. "Yes, sire. Right this way. I shall have another chamber prepared for you, where you may take your rest when you are ready."

Rowan nodded as he followed his host out of the cold winter wind and into the shelter of the castle. Lord Geoffrey quietly led him through the halls and to the door of the room where Rowan's parents died. Uncertainty turned in his stomach as the dark memories arose. He had not stepped foot in Dallin since that fateful night, let alone reentered this room. He pictured himself, sixteen years old again, coming to his parents' chamber to speak with his father only to find a horrific sight awaiting him.

"Few people have entered this room since then." Geoffrey's low voice reverberated off the walls of the dark corridor.

Rowan did not reply, but entered the room while Geoffrey left to return to his wife and children.

The room was dark, illuminated only by the early moonlight. Most of the furniture had been cleared out. Only the bare, four-poster bed remained, along with a small table beside it, and a wooden chair by the fire. Dust covered everything, cobwebs hanging from the corners of the room.

An eerie feeling traced up Rowan's spine as he remembered the night that changed the course of his life forever. As clearly as if it happened yesterday, he pictured his mother lying across the mattress, her gown stained with blood, a horrid gash marring her alabaster neck. Her eyes stared vacantly at the ceiling, frozen in a look of sheer terror.

Had Cassius himself been the one to slit her throat?

Then he moved near the fireplace and pictured his father, crumpled over, lying in his own blood. Rowan had rushed to him and turned him over to see a similar gash across his father's neck, his eyes staring into Rowan's face, wide and empty of life.

Rowan sank to his knees before the dusty, barren fireplace where a dark bloodstain still marked the floor. Now more than ever, Rowan looked like his father. They both possessed the same dark brown hair and ice blue eyes, the same physique, even the same smile.

But that was where the similarities stopped.

His father had been so good and patient, while Rowan was *im*patient and short-tempered. His father had been a wise and gracious king who loved his people, while Rowan was the complete opposite of that. Rowan had been anything but wise, and, up until now, had loved himself and his own ambitions far more than the people who relied on him. Even more than that, his father had always loved his mother wholly, unconditionally, staying true to her and never failing her or betraying her trust. But Rowan...

He covered his face with his hands, kneeling in the spot stained by his father's blood. Tears welled in his eyes and Rowan did not fight them, for they had been too long coming.

He had always wanted to be like his father, but surely if he were alive, King Roland of Acuniel would be disappointed in the man and king his son had turned out to be.

Tears flowed down Rowan's face in a river. He wept in a way he never had before. These were not the angry tears he'd cried after Favian's death; these were not even the sort of tears he had shed in the first few months after his parents' passing. These were tears full of soul-crushing guilt and despair.

I do not deserve her. I do not deserve the crown. I am a failure. A sorry excuse for a king and a man, just as Frederic of Caelrith said.

His father's voice cut through his thoughts. *Rowan... you know that you can turn to God. He cares about you, son. He loves you unconditionally... I want you to know that more than anything.*

Then Favian's voice echoed: *You may not care so much about God anymore, but I do. If you will allow Him, He shall direct your path... He knows what He is doing.*

Then Arabella. *Oh, but He is there... God can heal whatever it is you hold deep inside, Rowan.*

He sobbed, feeling like an utter fool for it. "Get ahold of yourself, Rowan." He swiped angrily at his tears. "You must cease this foolishness. It shan't get you anywhere." For a brief moment, he entertained the thought of prayer, but quickly tossed it aside. *That never works. God has forsaken me.*

I have never forsaken you.

Rowan froze at hearing the Voice that spoke to his heart as clearly as though it had spoken aloud.

I have always been here. Never have I forsaken you.

Rowan started to shut off his heart to the Voice, but decided to listen, too weary and broken to resist the comfort it brought.

I said you would listen one day.

Chills raced up his spine. "God! I cannot understand why You would allow my parents and Favian to meet such ends! And now Arabella... I fear that anything once shared between us is lost forever." Rowan sobbed again, hitting the floor with his fist, such bitterness festering inside. "Why have You done this to me?"

You needed to see the truth. You needed to see that all you require may be found in me.

Realization hit him like a battering ram. Suddenly, he remembered the harsh words he'd flung at the Lord only weeks ago. *I do not want You! I do not need You!*

But he *did* need Him. Though his pride wanted to deny it, Rowan needed God more than he needed Arabella or anyone else. It had been necessary for him and Arabella to fall apart in order for him and God to fall together.

"I am so sorry, Lord. I see Your hand in this now... just as King Wesley said. Forgive me. Please. Forgive me." He gripped the front of his shirt. "I am so unworthy, Lord. I deserve nothing but Your wrath!"

He leaned over, the anger that had consumed him for the last eight years of his life crushing his spirit. He felt more lost and broken than ever. Something was pulling him, dragging him down into a pit of despair, a pit that threatened to steal his life. Rowan growled, crying out wretchedly, feeling wild with such utter torment. Claws seemed to grab at his mind, intent on ripping him to shreds and obliterating any hope of salvation from his tortured condition.

"God, help me!" he moaned in desperation.

You are beyond help. That dark voice shouted the words at him, wild and terrifying, filled with soul-destroying fire.

Nay! he replied to the fiery voice.

Give up, boy! He cannot help you! You are a lost cause! You have done too much!

Rowan leaned over until his forehead touched the cold stone. "Jesus, help me."

Immediately, the fiery voice and evil spirit oppressing him fled. Light seemed to rush in, banishing the darkness back to the pits of hell itself.

"Please forgive me. Forgive me for denying You all this time. Forgive me for casting You off. Forgive me for not listening."

Those who ask shall receive.

Those words reminded him of the burden of guilt still resting on his shoulders. "Rid me of this burden that presses upon me. Save me from the bitterness. Rid me of the anger, I pray thee! Forgive me… Please, forgive me!"

He wept harder, gut-wrenching sobs that shook his entire body, rattling his insides in such a powerful way that it scared him. He was trembling, a feeling he had never felt before overcoming his soul.

"I need You, Jesus… I cannot go another day with this weight upon my back! Deliver me!"

Instantly, what felt like arms wrapped about his middle, securing him in a tight, comforting embrace. For a moment, he thought someone had entered the room and was comforting him. But Rowan soon realized that it was the arms of the Lord, that it was the Holy Spirit which held him.

Rowan wept harder still, basking in the warmth, the comfort, the forgiveness, the love, the joy, the *freedom* that was in that unearthly embrace. Never had he felt such a sensation. It was more than he could take…

He trembled anew beneath the intensity, praise echoing from within him as every weight lifted and he felt such liberty in his spirit that he could have shouted from the rooftops.

Chapter 42

ROWAN CLIMBED SOLEMNLY UP THE TOWER stairs. As soon as he had arrived home and found Arabella absent from her room, he had known exactly where he *would* find her.

His heart was filled with joy after last night's encounter with the Lord; he could practically feel the unearthly glow upon his features. Yet his heart still bore a shroud of sorrow. Would his wife welcome his return? How could she ever forgive him for what he had done? Rowan would not blame Arabella if she tossed him out the tower window in her anger...

But nevertheless, he had to try. He would beg for her forgiveness until his voice left him, if necessary. He loved her too much to give up without a fight.

His heart hammered in his chest and his hand trembled as he opened the door to the tower keep.

Inside, Arabella sat on the bench below the window. She turned suddenly when he entered, her eyes widening. In her beautiful, dark eyes, surrounded by awful green and yellow bruises, he saw a slight spark of joy lost among fathoms of grief.

His heart broke again, and a sudden surge of guilt smote him. But Rowan quickly tossed it aside, having decided the night before to lay that at God's feet.

He slowly moved towards her as she stared up at him with a melancholy expression. "Hello..."

"Hello..."

Rowan sank to his knees before her, without warning, burying his face in her skirt and clutching the fabric in his hands. "I am *so* sorry, Arabella. I know not how you ever can forgive me, but I beg thee… Please, do." He wept against her knees, shaking with grief. "Forgive me, my love, though I am undeserving of it."

He felt her shudder and Rowan looked up to see the tears welling in her eyes. He took her hands and clasped them tightly, gripping them as though his life depended on it. *God, please… Please let me not have ruined everything with my stubbornness and stupidity. Let me not have destroyed the love this woman felt for me.*

Rowan could clearly remember the look in her eyes when he'd kissed her, *really* kissed her, for the first time that night by the fire. He wanted so desperately to see that look in her eyes again.

"You did not believe me…" Her lips quivered.

Rowan rose and sat beside her, keeping her hands in his. "I know…" He shook his head, not attempting to hold back the tears in his eyes. She must see just how much his mistake pained him.

"You claimed to love me, yet you tossed me aside." Pain shone in her eyes. "Have you any idea what you have put me through?" She hung her head and sobbed.

Rowan took her in his arms, holding her to his chest as she wept. "I longed for you, but could not see you, could not speak to you. If not for the strength of God, I would have despaired entirely. And when Cassius attacked me…" She sobbed again. "I thought I was going to die, Rowan. I feared no one would come in time, because he bribed all the guards. I—I tried to be brave… but I was so scared."

Rowan winced, closing his eyes. "I am so sorry you had to endure that. If only I had—"

"How could you not believe me, even after I told you everything at risk of my own life?" She pounded her fist against his chest. "Did you ever truly love me?"

Rowan held her away from him, her words pricking deep into his heart. "I did love you. I *do* love you, Arabella. I love you more than I can describe." The breath caught in his throat, the love he felt for her surging up in his heart until it was overwhelming.

He pulled her close again before she could say anything, cradling her, holding her head in his hand. "I love you. You are the dearest, most wonderful thing that has ever happened to me." She shook in his embrace—whether from his touch or from her emotions, he knew not. "If not for you, I would be dead. And I would never have been able to find my way back to God."

She pulled away, her eyes red and wet with tears.

Rowan smiled softly. "'Tis because of you that I was able to find my way to His feet. He has touched me, Arabella." He held her cheek and gently wiped at her tears with his thumb. A small glimmer of hope began to shine in her eyes. "Last night, the Lord healed me of everything. And 'tis all because of you."

He pulled her close again, clutching her tight. "I loved you before; I truly did. But that love only went so deep. 'Twas not nearly as deep as you deserve." He kissed her temple, her ear, burying his face in her hair, her tantalizing scent filling his senses. Then he caressed the wounds marring her face and neck, his heart aching again to think of all she had suffered because of him.

"I could not love you as I should until I learned to love the Lord... Now I know what *true* love is. 'Tis being selfless, loving without question nor condition, being constant through all, serving one another in all ways. Being willing to lay down one's life for another."

Rowan pulled away to hold her face in his hands. He wiped at her tears again with his thumbs, careful not to press upon her bruises. "That is how I love you, Arabella. I love you with everything in me, with all my soul. And I hope that you may still feel the same, for I do not doubt the intensity or sincerity of the love you showed me."

He stared into her eyes, begging her to hear his heart's earnest cry and forgive him, give him a second chance whether he deserved it or not. "Please say that 'tis not too late for us."

Arabella

Rowan held my face in his hands, his eyes filled with such longing, such love, such torment that it seemed to rend me in two.

Here he was, begging for forgiveness, as I had so wanted him to do, saying everything my ears had ached to hear. But was it enough? Could I trust him with my heart again?

I shook my head, his warm hands upon my face making my

cheeks grow hot. "How can I know that you shan't do something like this again? How can I trust you when you could not trust me?"

I tried to look down, his intense gaze too much for my still bleeding heart to handle. But his hands would not allow it. He turned my face up to meet him, one hand moving down to cup my jaw. "If I were to do such a terrible thing, if I were to break your heart twice in my lifetime, then I pray God would smite me with the wrath of His Hand. For if I were to make such a mistake twice, death would be all I deserved."

I shook my head again, more tears leaving my eyes. "But how can we make this work?" I laughed without humor. "We have done little but fight and argue. How do we know that things will not continue in the same way?"

"Every couple—even the ones most madly in love—have their arguments. I am convinced that a couple who never fought could not possibly be normal." He smiled and chuckled low in his throat, one of his hands slipping further down to hold the side of my bruised neck. "Yes, we argue, we at times say things we do not mean. But that is the beauty of it, my love." He began pulling me closer, putting one hand at my waist. "I am a pig-headed idiot with a terrible short temper. And you, my dear, are equally as stubborn in your own way, with a smart, impertinent little mouth that likes to point out the things about myself I would rather ignore."

I fought the smile that tugged at my lips even as I continued to cry, choking on my own tears.

He rested his forehead against mine, his breath washing across my face as he closed his eyes and breathed deep. Chills raced down my arms and I shuddered as he pulled me to him. "But that is one of the many things I love about you. If not for that mouth of yours, we both would be dead and the kingdom in ruin. I would never have been forced to examine my heart and see the mess I had made of everything. I never would have seen the pain I caused my kingdom, nor been able to see the truth about Cassius, or God."

He touched the side of my face again, his fingers intermingling with my hair, urging my head up ever so slightly. I closed my eyes, holding back another small sob. "You have saved me in so many ways, Arabella." His voice cracked with emotion. "I know God brought you to me for such."

Then Rowan leaned in and kissed my lips. My heart melted and butterflies flew throughout my entire being. He kissed me deeply, but with such careful tenderness that I lost my breath. I had feared I would never know such a feeling again...

He pulled away the slightest fraction, his breath short as he moved to kiss down my face, still winding his hand in my hair. I stifled a sigh. "You enchant me so—you have from the very beginning." He worked his way back to my lips and paused to whisper against them, "I love you with all of me, my queen. And I love our babe just as much. I cannot wait for the day that I may hold him or her in my arms and stare into the eyes of my own flesh and blood." Then he kissed me again, just as wonderfully as the last time, as joy and hope began to fill me. "What would I have done had you not come along? I know now that God has ordained that we should be together."

Peace slowly settled in my heart at that last statement.

The love that I felt within me for Rowan—the man I used to hate more than any other, the one who had somehow become everything to me—was a part of God's plan from the start. God had answered my prayers in so many ways. He had been with me through all the uncertainty, showing me the kind of true love Rowan had described moments before. He had showed me my purpose, answered my many, many questions of, "Why, God? Why?" Directed my path even when I felt like I was spiraling into nothingness.

And He had done more. God had placed Rowan and I together, giving us this love that, with His help, could stand the tests of time. And He even answered my greatest prayer—He had brought Rowan to the point of surrender.

We'd both had to endure much to get to this moment, but in the grand scheme of things, it was worth it.

I pulled away and touched Rowan's cheek, brushing the light stubble there and staring into his eyes for a long moment. A slow smile crept onto his lips, beautiful and joyous.

Then I wrapped my arms around his neck and kissed him. He kissed me back, encircling me in his arms, and leaning into me until my back met the wall. My love kissed me deeper, and I could feel him smiling as he did so. I was smiling too, so happy, so relieved to be back in his arms—where I belonged. Where I would always, always belong.

What God hast joined, let no man put asunder.

Rowan drew away just enough to look into my eyes. He was

aglow, from both our kiss and the freedom he felt after finally letting God back into his life. He grinned, his beautiful eyes searching my face, reminding me of that first day when I was ten and he nearly trampled me. That day that had set our entire journey into motion. "Shall you forgive me then?"

I shrugged and gave him a mischievous smirk. "I suppose…"

His eyebrows shot up. "*Suppose?*"

I laughed then—relishing in the feeling—and Rowan joined with me, before sweeping me up in another wonderful, glorious kiss.

Epilogue

Seven months later...

I GRINNED UP AT MY HUSBAND, BLINKING BACK
happy tears as we waited in the entry hall of the palace. Today was
the day we would present our child to the Kingdom of Acuniel.

Rowan's handsome face was aglow with joy and fatherly love
as he stared down at the peaceful babe held snuggly in one of his
strong arms. He cooed softly down at the angelic face and rubbed
a finger along the child's nose. My heart swelled with immense
pride, joy, love, and, oh, so very much else that words fail to describe. I thought I would surely burst with my love for this man
and the precious infant he cradled.

How could I have been so blessed?

I wrapped my hands around the bicep of his free arm and
leaned my head against him, watching my baby's face. My mira-
cle child. One that, according to physicians, should have died the
night Cassius savagely beat me.

"Are you certain you are not too disappointed about her not
being a boy?"

Rowan turned to look at me, blue eyes sparkling. "Absolutely certain." He kissed my forehead then turned to kiss the soft,
pink forehead of our week-old daughter. "Our Adelaide shall be
the most beautiful princess this realm has seen, her beauty only
matched by her mother." Rowan winked at me. "I shall be hard
pressed to keep the young fellows at bay."

Suddenly, his forehead furrowed darkly as it always used to. "God, help me… I do not want to even consider such things yet." I laughed and reached to caress little Adelaide's chubby cheek. "Nor I."

After Rowan and I smoothed things out, work to restore Acuniel and its relations with Trilaria had begun. The orphanage opened with great success, and many other new projects were being implemented to help care for our people. Already, the kingdom was prospering under Rowan's refocused reign, and the people who had once been willing to see a new king upon the throne now backed him fully.

Rowan had also released Frederic and allowed him to choose where he wished to make his home. I was not at all surprised when he still chose to return to Trilaria, and frankly, I was glad for it. My childhood friend needed a fresh start, and space to hopefully move past his continued bitterness and anger towards Rowan.

I turned my eyes to my husband and again thought of how good it was to see him so happy. The full truth behind his parents' murder and Cassius' treachery had hurt him deeply, especially where Favian was concerned. But, with God's help, he had managed to let it go… finally cast aside everything that bound him to the pain of the past and leave it behind for good.

He was a changed man, the king, brought out of his self-imposed darkness and into the light of a King even greater and higher than himself. Every day, the changes in him became more apparent. His daily prayer, the way he spoke freely of God, the way he smiled, spoke kindly to everyone, and treated me with respect and love. Every bit of it was a testimony to God's grace and power to take even the hardest of hearts and make them soft. Why, even now, the man who once would have scowled at the child in his arms grinned and spoke in a high-pitched tone to our baby, his own perfect flesh and blood.

Rowan lifted his head and moved to take my hand. He kissed my fingers and his eyes smoldered, sending a pleasant shiver up my spine. "I love you so much, Arabella of Caelrith. And I shan't ever cease telling you so."

I would have kissed him right there if not for the bundle held carefully in his arms. Instead, I settled for a private, deep look into his eyes and squeezed his fingers tightly. "I love you too, Rowan… more than I ever have."

Again, he kissed my hand, pressing deep and lingering for a moment. Something hot splashed against my skin, and when he straightened, I saw the tears he endeavored to hold back glistening in his eyes.

Then the doors to the courtyard opened and a knight stepped in. "'Tis time, Your Majesties. The people await."

Hand in hand, Rowan and I made our way out into the courtyard, where we would ascend atop the wall and present our firstborn to the celebrating people who crowded Caelrith's streets, packing them with food and dancing and an abundance of good cheer.

This was the start of a new chapter in all our lives, I knew; another step into the unknown. There was certainly no knowing what the future would bring. But looking back over the ground already covered, looking over at the man I would forever call mine, and looking up to the God that had never once failed me, I knew the journey to come, even more so than the one completed, would be a beautiful adventure worth every single step.

Acknowledgements

When I started writing my first book—not this one; it was my second!—I said that it, or whatever book of mine was published first, needed to be dedicated to my middle school English teacher because he's the one who sparked my desire to write in the first place. I kept that now eight-year-old promise. However, there are many other people I could have dedicated this book to as well, that each played an important part in my journey to becoming an author, so I cannot let this book go without taking the opportunity to thank them publicly.

To God—for putting this story in my heart to begin with, and for helping me get it on the page. All of this is *for* You, to bring honor and glory to You through this passion You've given me.

To my family—thank you for always believing in me and being my biggest fans from day one. I would have given up on this dream without your constant prayers and encouragement. Thank you, especially, to my Pawpaw for being the very first reader of this book. And to my mom for waking me up at 3 AM to let me know you stayed up late to finish reading it.

To my husband, Austin—thank you for pushing me to pursue my dream and supporting me through every step of the publishing process, telling random people about my books, and always telling me I'm going to the most famous author ever—though I *seriously* doubt that. Oh, and thanks for answering my random midnight question of, "If you stabbed someone in the heart, would they die instantly, or would they still have several seconds to live?" I'm sure it is only the first of many random, strange questions I will be asking you in regard to weapons and the wounds they cause.

To Becky Powell, now gone on to be with our Jesus—I will never forget you running up to me at TX Ladies Conference to tell me you *loved* my book—when I didn't even know my mom had sent it to you to read! Your praise, coming from a retired librarian and avid reader, has been a great encouragement to me ever since.

To author Lynne Gentry—thank you for praying with me in the middle of Lupe Tortilla that God would bless me and my writing, and for encouraging me to keep pursuing my dream. I will never forget that day!

Thank you to my favorite authors for your example. Much of what I've learned about writing has come simply from constant reading and observation of your own work.

Thank you to my first readers, outside of those already mentioned—Natalie, Catelyn, Jerrod, Laure, Karrie, and Amberly—for loving this book, offering encouragement and feedback, and helping me catch all those pesky typos! An especially big thank you goes to Natalie for helping me pick this book apart and make it better.

And thank you to *you*, dear reader, for taking the time to read Rowan and Arabella's story. I hope you have enjoyed the journey and that, like Arabella, you will learn to trust God's plan for your life, no matter your current circumstances.

"Trust in the Lord with all thine heart; and lean not unto thine own understanding. In all thy ways acknowledge him, and he shall direct thy paths."

Proverbs 3:5-6

Printed in Great Britain
by Amazon

72226860R10194